There once was a

LITTLE ENGLAND

A Story about Man's Obsession with 'Colour and Class'

ENRICO DOWNER

"On an altar of prejudice we crucify our own, yet the blood of all children is the colour of God"

~ Don Williams, Jr. (American Novelist and Poet b. 1968)

For Sarie, who came along after this journey.

This is a work of fiction. The characters and names of people and all references to establishments and organizations are fictitious. Any resemblance to actual people, living or dead, is coincidental. Some incidents were imagined and others were real but have been fictionalized.

Copyright © 2012 by Enrico Downer

Contents

1955—1956

Chapter 1	1
Introduction	1
Chapter 2	5
The Bajans of Thornville	5
Chapter 3	22
A Fallen Angel	22
Chapter 4	35
The Chronicle	35
Chapter 5	37
Opportunities Lost	37
Chapter 6	46
Janet's Wrath	46
Chapter 7	66
The Stolen Promise of Youth	66
Chapter 8	76
Aftermath of a Hurricane	76
Chapter 9	80
The Capuchin Defence	80
Chapter 10	117
The Tyranny of Grief	117
Chapter 11	131
His Brother's Keeper	131
Chapter 12	137
Blood of the Lamb	137

Chapter 13	140
The Long Wait for Justice	140
Chapter 14	146
Broad Street Encounters	146
Chapter 15	151
The Bajan Yankee	151
Chapter 16	160
From Trafalgar Square to Lower Green	160
Chapter 17	166
The Matriarch	166
Chapter 18	176
Her Majesty's Court	176
Chapter 19	191
Quest for the Truth	191
Chapter 20	215
Flight	215
Chapter 21	227
A Windstorm of Rumours	227
Chapter 22	230
De Apple don' Fall Far From de Tree	230
Chapter 23	238
A Reincarnation	238

Contents

1965—1966

Chapter 24	246
Vengeance of the Mighty	246
Chapter 25	259
Return of a Native Son	259
Chapter 26	263
A Trilogy of Tragedies	263
Chapter 27	271
Intercessions	271
Chapter 28	282
Dawn of Independence	282

Chapter 1

Introduction

HISTORICAL FICTION can be tricky. There is always more than a sprinkling of truths and the writer has to avoid portraying fiction as fact and fact as fiction while oftentimes one disguises itself as the other. I suppose it is okay to alternate between the two though I suspect that if the two are conflated the truth will always stand out in the end.

One such truth in this work of fiction is the horrific hurricane that struck Barbados in 1955. As the easternmost of the Caribbean islands, Barbados was thought by some to be the Creator's divine plan whereby the island was spared the wrath of many a hurricane that raged up and down the archipelago. Those of my contemporaries who also lived through Hurricane Janet might very well have a hundred of their own stories to tell. I have penned a few of my own told through the eyes of my book's characters. It is funny how, in the distance of time, we can talk and write about the most harrowing experiences in our pasts as though they were mere fairy tales and now conversations to entertain our friends and children. We forget that almost forty lives were lost, hundreds of homes destroyed and thousands of families left homeless in the hurricane's wake.

But there is another truth of which I write that deprived many more lives and dashed many more dreams than hurricanes ever could. I refer to an obsession with 'colour and class' and the chasm that lay deep and wide between the poor working-class and the elite ruling minority in Barbados, a divide that existed in this colonial society before the middle sixties and, to some degree, afterwards. But such truths are far from fairy tales and not so willingly recalled. So now, whom do we blame (or thank) for our obsessions? Should we not lay the seeds at the feet of those who once ruled over us with an iron fist? After all, and proudly so, Barbados has always called herself *Little England*.

The interesting thing about historical fiction is that it delights in the beautiful things we inherited (and there have been many). But it also fictionalizes the things that are not so beautiful so they cannot be so easily denied. *There Once was a Little England* was meant to do just that.

THERE ONCE WAS A LITTLE ENGLAND

The story begins innocently with children playing in the streets of Barbados, skipping and dancing in the winds. And in their naiveté they welcome the storm with open arms. In the village of Thornville they give their kites full rein. Then later, as the story goes, as the villagers brace themselves, another violent act is perpetrated right there in their midst. A twelve-year-old Bajan boy wanders onto the private property of an English landlord and he is shot and killed instantly.

The Englishman defends the action by claiming he mistook the boy for a monkey in his trees. The fury of the hurricane that wreaks havoc on the island is matched by the anger of the people as the whole island erupts. People are angered by the killing and equally angered by the dehumanizing description of the boy from the lips of a white man. The people are then further betrayed when one of their own, a brilliant Bajan barrister, steps forward to defend the Englishman.

In Barbados, a society once said by a regional politician to be "vitiated by colour and class prejudice," the lawyer is seen to be currying favour with the white upper class while turning his back on his own race. Never before in the annals of Her Majesty's Courts had a white man been escorted to the gallows for killing one of the locals, and now with the flagrancy of murder and the Englishman's degrading defence in the minds of the people, they sense the time has come to witness the dispensation of true justice.

It cannot be denied that this story was partly inspired by a true story in the 1950s. A white farmer put forward a similar defence after shooting to death a small black boy caught hiding in his bushes. He claimed that, in his mind's eye, he saw an animal. While this storyline bears no relation to that historic case, it does attempt to capture the mood that prevailed that day and further serves to remind us that in Barbados such a defence could be successfully advanced in a court of law at a time when the island's colonial past was fraught with racial inequities and the insensitivity of a ruling class.

The boy's father, Harold Prince, is caught in the storm as he wends his way home from work to learn on his arrival that his favourite son has been slain. He is later mortified to learn that his boy has been analogized to a monkey as the key to the Englishman's fabricated defence. Throughout the story we see how the people and each member of the boy's family deal with this tragic loss, a God-fearing mother, a father far less disposed to forgive and a brother severely traumatized for having witnessed firsthand the killing of his twin brother. On the other side, we see a rich white family, reluctant to surrender their illusions of supremacy on an island moving towards a future of social equality.

But the story is not only about race, murder, revenge and an addiction to social class. It is also a love story interwoven into a tapestry of tragedies. One such tragedy is a questionable rape that hangs over the head of a man in the village, a man who, many years later, comes face to face with his accuser. It is also a story of a people's conflicted love and hatred for their British rulers and a father's undying love for his dead son. These varied passions are interspersed throughout the story.

On a broader scale, the story recalls a period when Barbados was still living in the shadow of British colonialism. Caribbean Federation was then on the lips of the people though, as we now know, never on the horizon; whereas Independence was looming on the horizon but it was hardly ever on the lips—at least until later. We see the island inching away from Britain while clinging to her grand traditions and eventually attaining the goal of national statehood without a single episode of social upheaval or the spilling of blood or even the trampling of the rights of those long entrenched in power.

Still the economic reins of power would remain firmly in the hands of a few white men to be handed down only to their own children. It would be many years before wealth and political power would accrue to those who took advantage of the education afforded them and they in turn would find themselves in the same class they had previously envied. Many would now look down their noses at the less advantaged left behind. It was called "the curse of classism."

Finally, the merits and demerits of British colonialism and its class system are best left to historical writings, but even in a work of fiction, credit is due to England for her rich legacy of institutional standards: among others, a proven parliamentary system of governance, the foundations of a time-tested judicial system and an exemplary education system that elevated the people then and continues to do so today. One can always weigh this legacy against the road travelled and where we are today.

THERE ONCE WAS A LITTLE ENGLAND

In any case, while it is true that man's obsession with 'colour and class' continues to plague many a people and is the bane of many a nation today, Barbados continues to strive, however imperfectly, towards a playing field of social equity. The nation is today a beacon of democracy; it is my homeland and a place I love. It was also loved dearly at some point in their lives by three friends of mine: Harold Prince, Cissy Brathwaite and Winston Gittens.

Chapter 2

The Bajans of Thornville

THE YEAR was 1955. It was a night in September at the height of the hurricane season. Harold Prince lay in bed listening to the distant whining of a siren and the pitter-patter of rain on the metal roof of his wooden house. Sleep had deserted him as his mind drifted back fifteen years to such a night, when under his mother's roof, at the tender age of seventeen, he first discovered the joys of sex. But as is often the case that life's pitfalls are masked by the sweetest of pleasures, he also learned about the hazards of sex, for on that rapturous stormy night the sex that he had considered consensual was thereafter construed as rape and from that time forward, though he always thought himself wrongly accused, the suspicion of entrapment continued to roil his spirit on nights like this.

The news had not yet reached the tiny village of Thornville that a fearsome hurricane was stalking the horizon, threatening to crash into the southern coastline of Barbados by late morning. Even so, few would have believed it: except for the siren's mourning echoes, the air was eerily still. The sea in clear view from his window was calm, glistening, smooth as glass in the moonlight. Still he could sense a foreboding, something dark and sinister lurking in the hours ahead, rendered more pressing by the sorrowful wailing of a hurricane siren.

He had vowed never to talk about his troubled past, not even to Cissy, the woman he loved and trusted, now cuddling next to him in the dark. Sleep had abandoned her too, troubled by this aura of disquiet that pervaded the air. Without a word between them they threw their premonitions aside and made love off and on while their twin boys, David and Nathaniel, slept in the far room.

When the first rays peeped through their jalousie windows, Harold rolled over, left his woman slumbering contentedly, stretched his six-foot frame and, true to his daily routine, headed off with his bucket to the communal standpipe at the top of the gap. After a cold wash-up in the yard and breakfast of hot cornmeal porridge, he looked in at his boys. Then he grabbed his three-speed Raleigh bicycle from the shed and, in the rain, was off to work in the city. Cissy lay peacefully for a while in the afterglow of lovemaking and then began her daily cycle of chores.

She and Harold Prince lived together, unmarried and therefore in sin in the eyes of the Church and conservative Bajan folk. A dozen years had passed since their transgression was compounded: Cissy gave birth outside the bounds of holy matrimony. When they first met, one or the other had broached the subject of marriage but as the years unfolded, the idea dwindled in importance among the other exigencies of working-class living and striving to provide the best for their sons. In the ensuing years Cissy would give her soul to the Lord and afterwards secretly regret not tying the knot, but by that time her man was comfortable and calcified in his ways; marriage to him had become a mere technicality, a piece of paper for the approbation of the Church. And so, as the occasion required, she would simply answer to "Cissy" or even to "Mrs. Prince" for the benefit of the presumptuous, or more fittingly to "Miss Brathwaite" as the daughter of Maisy Brathwaite, now deceased, once the well-known and respected village seamstress, and of Gladstone Brathwaite, the father she never knew.

They lived in the midst of a row of unpretentious wooden houses. Theirs was painted a glossy pink that matched thick pink hibiscus hedges out front and around the sides. Their hand-sewn curtains, billowing day and night in the opened windows, were also pink. The front of the house was a sleepy-eyed square face: a door in the middle for a nose and a hooded window on each side for two somnolent eyes. Neighbours called it the pink house. In her thirty-two years the home had been expanded from the single gable-roofed house her mother had left her when she died to one with two pointed roofs that from a distance looked like two steep inverted saw teeth, two isosceles triangles outlined against a night sky over the village of Thornville.

In the whole of Thornville there was no woman as pleasing to the eye as Cissy Brathwaite. Women peeped through their louvers on Sunday mornings to watch her stepping out to the eleven o'clock service at Pastor Gittens's church, bedecked in dresses and hats she had fashioned, cut, sewn and finished with her own hands. First to greet the eye was her skin, coal-black and velvety, then her smile, faint at first, then broad and inviting, vaguely flirtatious as she approached friend or stranger alike.

Then as she turned and walked away, men gawked at her derrière, high, rounded and rippling under tight-fitting skirts. Her hair flowed down past her shoulders or was sometimes gathered in the back and twisted into a bun fastened with a tortoiseshell barrette. She was trim but not so slender as to invite the scorn of old Bajan women, who held that all girl children should be "fat and nice wid meat on dere bones." It could be said that any physical imperfection amounted to a slightly outward curvature in the shape of her legs, albeit lending a certain sensuousness to the way she ambled along the cart road to and from the standpipe. She was said to be the most beautiful woman within miles of Thornville; a rare compliment in an island twenty-one by fourteen.

Although she proudly claimed it was wholly African blood that flowed in her veins, something about her facial structure hinted at a sprinkling of Amerindian blood as well. Indeed she said that her mother had spoken of ancestors who started out in the backwoods of Surinam and made their way down through the Antilles, living and dying in places like British Guiana, Aruba, Curacao, Grenada, and eventually ending up in Barbados as indentured workers toiling to clothe the Europeans with precious Sea Island cotton—that was long before sugar was king in Barbados. Cissy was today a Christian woman, as had been her deceased mother and grandmother as far as she could tell, and whatever resentments had lingered towards their oppressors down through the years had now been vanquished by that Godly propensity for forgiveness that lives in the hearts of Christians.

Harold was of a different mould. His ancestral past was as traceable from the shores of Africa as was the history of all the island's black men, though at some fortuitous point in the 17th century the slave ship that ferried his father's forebears had been detoured to the island of Jamaica where his father was born; and of such a time his father had, from his son's early upbringing, planted in his head the legacy of the Jamaican Maroons defying the British slave masters, taking to the hills and waging war against the white man.

In Barbados, in the fifties, such lessons as the ancient history of black folk and of the defiance of black slaves were rarely talked about in polite conversations, or in schools handed down to the young with the same pride as was the history of the British Empire and her grand conquests. In fact the history of Africa with her kings and queens was a mythical blur and the African mainland was only mentioned in passing as one of seven continents. Children therefore deemed themselves proud adopted children of the British Commonwealth, incognizant of a fatherland, as if by some quirk of nature they had been strewn on the soil of this island paradise to multiply like the black seeds of some exotic fruit. It was only because of his Jamaican father that Harold was spared this blissful ignorance.

One could have lived in Barbados for many years and not be aware that in the parish of St. Michael there was indeed a village by the name of Thornville. It is even less likely that one remembers it was on an estate eponymously named after the wealthy English landowner. His name was Theodore Thorne. It was some time after an unlawful killing took place on the estate that the name Thornville was expunged from all official records. To this day it has been rendered a profanity on the lips of Bajans everywhere. It's as if it never was.

Thornville was a crescent-shaped row of wooden houses hugging the side of a hill. At the peak of the hill was a huge white mansion. It was the home of the English landlord. Since the killing, the village was absorbed into the neighbouring low-lying villages of Grazettes and Fairfield whose sole distinction was that they could boast of their own bus line, which for six cents transported the people to and from Bridgetown. North of Thornville was the area of Cave Hill where the University of the West Indies campus now sits, an area that was in those days a desolate landscape with neither fields nor houses, where smooth black boulders every few yards protruded from the earth like whalebacks. Cave Hill was the place for pasturing the villagers' goats and cows, or as a getaway for adolescent sex on a moonless night, or for the British Council to screen their BBC newsreels from the back of a mobile cinema, affording the Thornville children their first glimpses of life in the outside world, in the British Isles and in the vastness of the Commonwealth. Seemingly, no cinematographer had yet ventured into Africa to bring back motion pictures of little black boys and girls that looked like them, with the same noses, same lips, same hair and same shades of skin.

Thornville people were proud of the name Thornville; it connoted status and wealth of which they themselves possessed neither, whereas Grazettes and Fairfield sounded agrarian and common. The village drew the envy of people living in the lowlands because it commanded a clear and open view of the sparkling sea at Brandons Beach, whereas down below their own houses were merely reflections of themselves.

Bajan houses separated themselves along a certain hierarchy ranked by the proportionality of brick and wood. Wooden houses, reminiscent of the lowly chattel houses of the slave era, were consigned to the bottom of the scale. The shame and wretchedness of the old plantation days clung mercilessly to these wooden houses, elegant as they were, arguably more elegant than the cement houses to which they aspired. And so, masons and bricklayers were often called upon to upgrade these wooden houses with brick and cement and, in so doing, exorcise the restless ghosts of dead slaves. All around Thornville, they sat back of the narrow roadway bedecked in all the colours of the rainbow: blue, green, pink, purple, yellow, gray, orange, peaches; and in all sizes from a single gable-roofed frame and shed, to multiple adjoining frames extending back from the road like articulated boxes. Some boasted solid cinderblock foundations and cemented steps; others sat on loose limestone. If the equation of brick and wood leaned towards wood, a house still could not rise to the coveted level of a wall-house. For example, Seymour Cutting, the butcher lived in a hybrid house, a façade of brick but mainly wooden, while Winston Gittens, who pastored the Pilgrim Holiness Church, lived with his father in a veritable brick bungalow; his was the envy of the community, at the very top of the class.

But most of the houses were like that of Sister Innis, the heavyset, seventy-year-old midwife who lived alone and childless. Hers was a single, gable-roofed frame that sat on a disjointed foundation of rocks and stones with gaps like giant missing teeth, crawl spaces where her hens would lay their eggs in peace. Her thick black curtains were a challenge for inquisitive eyes and many a night intermittent moans could be heard emanating from her windows, culminating in one triumphant scream that signalled a new addition to the Thornville neighbourhood. Like this revered midwife, people never closed their windows except against high winds; the only intruders were sparrows hopping among the furniture in search of scraps. Indeed at night people lay in bed with their windows wide open to feel the caress of the trade winds fresh off the ocean and to be lulled by the soporific chirping of night crickets. Safety was never a concern; window bars and dead bolts were unheard of.

By far the lowliest house of all was the blistered and weather-beaten shack at the end of the row. It belonged to Joe Walrond, the village drunk, whose life seemed as much in ruins as was his ramshackle dwelling. The house had a rhomboidal shape: one side leaned at a precarious angle to the ground and propped itself up against a beam of greenheart lumber in the way one might lean against a cane to avoid falling. The roof was a giant sieve but in a rainstorm there would never be a danger of flooding: gaps in the floorboards like spaces between pipe organ pedals allowed safe passage through the cellar and out to the gully behind the houses. Joe, in his three-piece white suit and perennial Panama hat, staggered home in a fog from Piggott's rum shop on Friday evenings warbling one hymn after another, his favourite being *There is a green hill far away outside a city wall*. People said it was only a matter of time before his old lean-to would collapse in a rotted, termite-infested, mouldy heap. But it never did.

Next door to Joe's house lived the sometimes mortician, Ben Carson. Now in his eighties, Ben lived rent-free in a nondescript brick building that had belonged to the English landlord and which, a decade before, was the landlord's storehouse. More about Ben Carson later.

These are just a sampling of the more colourful characters of Thornville. Then there were the less notable: the Thompsons, the Thomases, the Elcocks, the Leacocks, the Maycocks, the Lords, the Kings, the Knights, the Whites, the Blackmans, the Browns—all good old English names demanding to be addressed with dignity: Sir, Mister, Mistress. And why not? Their names had once belonged to white slave owners and had been bequeathed and affixed to their forefathers like the hot branding of newly bought cattle. Yet today they were borne proudly; they were the only ones they knew; their original names had been snatched away and stomped into the dust of history.

Back in the thirties, two English spinsters who had owned the estate suddenly packed up and moved back to The Motherland and deeded the estate to their distant relatives, the Thornes. Since then,

Thorne lost his wife, allegedly to suicide. Almost immediately, he promoted his long-time mulatto cook from the kitchen to the master bedroom. She was Madame Marcella Montmartre from the island of Martinique. Also living in the mansion were Penelope, his blond-haired daughter, who in 1955 could have been in her late twenties or early thirties; and a brown-skinned, curly-haired teenager named Pierre, said to be the Martiniquen's son.

The mansion, with its dozen or so jalousie windows always propped half-open, looked down sleepy-eyed on the cluster of houses that curved around the hill. From the west side of the mansion the Thornes on a clear day could count the steamships inching towards Bridgetown, or better said, to within reach of the stevedores lining the careenage, rearing to row their barges known as "lighters" out to meet the ships to unload much-needed British, American and European goods—there was not yet a deepwater harbour.

It was said that in the old days when slavery was the scourge of the land, the mansion was known as "The Great House." Over the years, Thorne restored the old heirloom to some semblance of its original grandeur. He set about to rid the walls of the perennial honeysuckle and jasmine vines that clung all along the east side of the building harbouring green mildew along the way. The entire exterior was bathed in the glossiest white paint that glistened for miles in the sun. He erected stately Romanesque columns, installed a gigantic gate with a lion-head knocker, replaced old rotten railings with rich-red mahogany balustrades and installed a new roof of imported Italian clay tiles. Finally he had his gardeners plant an abundance of fruit trees all along the perimeter dominated by mango trees. He summarily transformed a hulking eyesore of a house into a magnificent mansion that instantly became the iconic cornerstone of Thornville. All the way from the bottom of Fairfield, through the trees and over the houses, it caught the eye: a big white promontory rising high above a clutter of wooden boxes.

Except for the servants, few had ever seen Thorne at close range, only in the distance as a shadowy figure through the tinted porthole at the rear end of his Jaguar as he rode in and out of the property once or twice a week. People knew him as the tall, eccentric, reclusive Englishman who rarely wandered outside of his house on foot. At night from their windows, they could see him and his daughter, Penelope, or sometimes the Creole and the boy, silhouetted behind thin curtains, moving back and forth like puppets or faceless actors on a cinema screen. Sometimes the girl would reach out of her window, her long hair hanging loosely, and stare down at the houses like the rich daughter of an overlord surveying their fiefdom.

Village boys, bent on demystifying the landlord, called him "de bullah man" and began to spread a rumour among themselves that "he liked boys." The younger boys were puzzled by this description but laughed anyway, not wanting to appear dumb. The knowledge that the man had been married once and now a widower with a grown daughter did nothing to invalidate the scandal in the minds of these budding rumourmongers. And so, the little ones joined the older boys to throw rock-stones at the Englishman's guard wall on the way from school as if the seeds of homophobia were already ingrained in their fertile minds.

The guard wall, six feet high and extending from one end of Thorne's private property to the other, was crudely built of brick and mortar; it was never meant to be attractive like the rest of the property. Like giant bookends at both extremes stood two columns while the wall was inlaid with shards of glass and broken upturned bottles for the same deterrent purpose that strands of razor wire might today be deployed across a fence. On the other side was a row of mango trees that were said to bear the most succulent Julie mangoes in the whole parish. During the mango season the boys would be eyeing the fruit as they turned from green to reddish yellow, then they would climb the hill, reach up and drag the branches down almost to the ground to pick the lowest-hanging fruit. They had no scruples about plundering Thorne's mango trees. Some would wait patiently for the ones bird-pecked and half-eaten by monkeys to fall. But a brazen few would brave the broken glass and climb the wall and up onto the fruit-laden trees. Thick bougainvillea vines that over time had climbed the wall entwined themselves along the rampart, concealing the pieces of broken glass until it was too late for some who would suffer the tearing of flesh and the spilling of blood; so for many years the wall was rendered virtually impassable. But over the course of time the cement cracked and became brittle with age and the wall was eventually shorn of its weapons like a disarmed minefield; the mango orchard was vulnerable once again. A wooded area of mahogany trees and useless brush sloped down to the houses and in the late months of the year when the foliage was sparse, the wall was visible to all like a long, gray giant lying supine behind the deciduous trees. To the older folk who could still remember the railway in Barbados in bygone years, it looked like an abandoned train. But the wall mattered little to the people; they needed no reminders of those two disparate worlds, the wealthy Thornes on the hill and the poor and working-class down below.

At the bottom of the hill lay a winding, rutted cart road that snaked through the village. At one end it abruptly broke off from the smooth tarred road that led to the landlord's gate and at the other it dwindled to a mere footpath that vanished into Thorne's sugarcane field. The houses lining both sides of the road were so tightly packed together that neighbours could reach out of their side windows to shake hands, borrow a cup of this or that, and without fear of being overheard, exchange some salacious gossip. In the rainy season the houses were at the mercy of water cascading down the hill from Thorne's courtyard and rushing past them in search of the ravine, and in the dry season at night, armies of centipedes slithered out of the cane fields and sneaked into cellars and up through floorboards and into bedrooms to terrorize big and small alike.

But all in all, the people were happy. Thorne got his rent money for their lots on time. Living was cheap. Food was plentiful. Every house had a piece of land out back; every garden yielded "ground food" and a cornucopia of every conceivable tropical fruit, all planted and harvested with their own hands. The rich earth gave forth all the victuals they could ever want, the fruits of their own labour: breadfruit, sweet potatoes, cassava, yams, eddoes, pumpkins, paw paws, carrots, beets, egg plants, peas, peppers ...

Everyone was poor. Some clung to poverty and cursed all those who didn't, calling them "poor great," which was even more damnable than "poor." But those who escaped their tentacles and refused to join their company of misery rejected the inevitability of their condition, engaged the struggle and rose from their lowly places to become proud, self-reliant citizens.

THERE ONCE WAS A LITTLE ENGLAND

The poorest of the poor was the one some derisively called "Coolie." He was an immigrant, a fixture in Thornville, always sitting cross-legged under a tree with his head in his hands, wearing the blank face of a castaway on some unfamiliar shore and stared at by wide-eyed natives. In some cynical way this dark-skinned stranger was always welcomed in the village, for he made the people feel relatively advantaged and therefore fortunate in their own circumstances. The Indian, they realized, was more destitute than them: he was homeless. One evening after choir practice, Cissy Brathwaite approached the Indian and asked his name. He was sitting under the clammy cherry tree on the corner staring blankly at his toes protruding from a pair of mud-caked rubber sandals. As she approached him he smelled of poverty; he was unshaven and dirty; dark sunken eyes spoke of maddening hunger, his shirt sticking to his concave chest like cellophane. With rheumy eyes he glanced up and barely mouthed the name, Mr. Babu. There was something odd and mysterious about an Indian hanging around a Bajan village, especially an Indian conspicuously down and out. The few Indians on the island usually kept to themselves; they had their own enclaves in town; they took care of their own; they crept into the island via British Guiana or Trinidad. He struck such a pathetic picture that Cissy hurried home to her larder, slapped a generous portion of corned beef in a loaf of salt bread and hurried back to the Indian. The man unwrapped the sandwich, lifted it to his nose, and promptly returned it to Cissy. Confused and feeling rebuffed, she quickly realized her indiscretion. Next morning she packed a delicious dish of sea eggs and rice for the man and ran down to the corner to make amends and to explain that the affront to his Hinduism was never intended. Mr. Babu was gone.

Thornville was far from utopian where everyone got along with everyone splendidly and harmoniously. The village had its share of confrontations, from cussing and scuffles to blows, knifing, head bashing, rock throwing, stick fighting and even all-out bloody war. Women, overcome with possessiveness, fought tooth and nail over their men, and men staked out their women as aggressively as fowl-cocks in a hen house. Still, when it came to an assault from outside on their own, the villagers rallied around one another and stood together, like on many a Sunday afternoon when the sharp whistle of a lookout would alert the men throwing dice under the mahogany tree. Constable Howard would be surveilling the area and the men would hastily gather up their dice and coppers and disappear into the bushes until all was clear. Or when the rare "out-man" would break into a house with nothing more on his mind than to cop a meal or liquor and thereafter he would find himself caught in a dragnet and served some licks worse than prison and then be chased out of the village ahead of a fusillade of rock-stones. And so, any unwelcome intrusion into their midst would foster that certain kindred spirit among the Thornville people and they would invariably come together defensively as one.

Harold Prince was born in Thornville, raised in The Ivy, schooled first at St. Stephen's and later at St. Giles. He caught a fair amount of grief from the Thornville boys; they had taken for granted that Cissy would naturally end up belonging to the luckiest one among them. That they were all St. Stephen's "old boys" while Harold had deserted their school for St. Giles only added insult to injury and rendered him less deserving of the most desirable girl in Thornville.

All the Thornville children were destined to attend St. Stephen's Boys and Girls Schools in the adjoining village of Black Rock; they lived within walking distance. Schools were segregated by gender; the Government mandated separate institutions of learning for boys and girls and their respective teachers at all levels from Head Teachers right down to First Formers. It was said that one of the progressive committee men in the Governor's administration responsible for shaping the education system had once proposed that boys and girls sit together in the classrooms, and that he was laughed out of the meeting for such an anarchic proposal, one that would at minimum be disruptive and at most be corrupting of young minds, even the minds of First Formers hardly aware of their nascent proclivity to lust. And so the two brick buildings that separately housed the St. Stephen's lads and lasses stood at the two farthest corners of an acre with the paternalistic Anglican Church at the head, and the only opportunity for the intermingling of sexes would be every third Wednesday when they would be marched into church for their monthly indoctrination. Father Elliott, the English vicar, would reach out from the pulpit for their minds and souls while their sex-starved hormones would be raging in the pews, and that rare occasion for them to sit together would not be wasted listening to vapid sermons and hieratic chantings.

Barbadian parents drilled the importance of education into their young ones. Some went on to higher education like Cissy and Harold, she to the respected St. Michael's Girls School and he to the prestigious Combermere School for Boys. From early, she always had a head for numbers, with aspirations to work in a bank in the city, perhaps at Barclays Bank on Broad Street alongside those uniformed, self-important clerks and tellers. That was until it was revealed to her that such high profile jobs were reserved for girls with much lighter complexion than hers. It was an unspoken policy. Mrs. Heather Higginbottom, the stately Headmistress, had instead suggested private lessons in typing and Pitman's shorthand, which skills she promised would guarantee her a secretarial post in town, especially with a face as handsome as hers, meaning that tucked away out of the public eye in the back office of some businessman who valued hard work and proficiency above all else, a black skin mattered not at all.

At St. Michael's Girls School, this long-standing institution of learning, second in eminence only to Queens College, she had been taught by Mrs. Higginbottom and her cadre of British-educated teachers not only the usual academic subjects but also how a young lady should carry herself in public. "Whether in school or on the street," they admonished, "whether in the bus stand, on the school bus, in your village or even in your own house, the eyes of St. Michael are upon you." Cissy had been taught the lady-like way to walk, perfected by balancing horizontally on her head two tomes of the Britannica Encyclopaedia. She was taught that laterial swaying of the hips belonged to the common folk and hems above the knee were worn by "ladies of the night." Vowels should be clipped, not wide-mouthed and harsh, and the more refined *th* should never give way to the more indolent *d* consonant. She was told that a little intellectual snobbery was not a cardinal sin in the eyes of St. Michael, but that in fact it was conducive to self-esteem, and that she should never in her life confuse her standing as a St. Michael's girl with the dross that emerged from those pretentious lower-tier secondary schools on the island. But with all this exceptionalism weighing on their shoulders, the girls still understood they were outside that supreme realm occupied by the private church-sponsored schools that catered to white girls only, and in the midst of that moral contradiction they were constantly reminded of their school's motto: *Nisi Auxilio Dei Nihil*, "Nothing without Help from God."

Boys who stopped short of secondary schooling flowered into sought-after artisans: joiners, carpenters, masons, shoemakers, tailors, blacksmiths... A few weeds languished along the wayside, like Adolphus Hinds, nicknamed "Duphus," the miscreant of the lot who spent most of his teenage years in and out of Dodds Industrial School in St. Philip, a correctional institution for wayward boys.

Along with Cissy and Harold, some who did fairly well in life were Winston Gittens, a pastor's son; Fitzroy Miller, who started his own tyre retreading business; Piggott, who became the village rum shop proprietor; and Mickey Norris, who left the island and went abroad in search of his proverbial pot of gold.

Harold Prince had always been a bright boy. Now at thirty-two, he was highly educated, a Combermerian no less. After excelling at all levels, he became a newspaperman, the senior proof-reader at *The Barbados Chronicle*. A voracious reader at school, he had distinguished himself as a student of classical literature and was complimented for his mastery of English and impeccable grammar, having studied under British professors, who were seen as curators of the English language as it were. Fresh out of Combermere, he was alerted then by his mentor, Professor Cartwright, to a job opening at *The Chronicle* newspaper. That day he donned his best shirt and tie and hurried down to the city to find himself in a queue of no less than thirteen applicants, white, black, fair-skinned and all older than he. He took his turn before the publisher for his first interview armed with a letter of recommendation from Cartwright, the one who had opened his eyes to the beauty and mystery of language.

"How much Latin you know, boy?" the publisher asked.

"Sir, here are my school records." He handed over his glowing portfolio of A-level certificates, form reports and achievements including a literal translation of the first six books of *Virgil's Aeneid* from Latin to English and back.

"Conjugate the Latin pluperfect tense of 'to be'!"

Without hesitating, he recited, "fueram, fueras, fuerat, fueramus, fueratis, fuerant."

"Define the terms: 'stet' and 'kern'! He had already memorized the arcane terminologies he knew were imperative to the job in question and was ready with the answers.

"And the derivation of 'clitoris'?"

He was caught off guard by the irrelevance of the word but managed to mumble the ancient Greek derivation for "the gatekeeper."

From all accounts, the word was near and dear to the publisher, for he abandoned the drill and hired him on the spot.

Even with his aptitude for language, Harold knew he was not indispensable to the job, less so than the white boy, Tom Ford, who sat next to him with merely an elementary education. Tom had confided to him that his father, Ossie Ford, a customs officer, had made a phone call to the publisher and the next day he was on board, no interview, few questions asked. It was all about colour and connections and lucky Tom had both, his golden keys to open any door.

The rain abated. The siren was now silent. Still the inexplicable feeling, a sensation that something dreadful was about to mar the day, rode with Harold all the way to the city. Holding steady on his Hercules pedals with the wind at his back propelling him practically all the way from Thornville to Bridgetown, he was soon pulling into the alley next to *The Barbados Chronicle*, a faceless building, partly hidden, cowering behind a store on Broad Street.

Bridgetown was alive and steaming hot as was usual this time of the year; parasols were bobbing up and down on the sidewalks. It was late September, long after the last cane stalk had been harvested and the last lorry had trundled off to any of the dozen factories around the island. Now that the grinding mills had ground to a halt and sickles and machetes had been put away until the next crop, plantation workers were swarming all over the city with bonus money, buying up everything in sight, new comforts to lighten the wearisome off-season, wandering into big-box stores like The Cotton Factory and Barnes & Company Limited, filing out with bundles underarm and atop their heads or with carts laden with precious imported goods: reams of new carpeting, rolls of linoleum, bolts of cloth, bedding, curtains, kitchenware, earthenware, furniture, larders. Then after that first flurry of shoppers, there was nothing unusual about the pulse of the city, noisy and bustling just like on any other day. Bicycles along Broad Street (a two-way thoroughfare at the time) threaded the maze of motorcars, lorries, buses, motorcycles, scooters, donkey carts, coconut carts, lumber carts, sweet drink carts—all competing for the right of way. The narrow sidewalks were choked with shoppers and loiterers; taxicab drivers were stalking a few pale-faced tourists; hawkers were squawking for notice in the alleyways; and drawing attention to himself was the indefatigable traffic policeman under his cork hat, on his pedestal at the intersection. He was happily spinning and flailing his arms like a weathervane. In other words, that morning in the city, there were no signs of concern that a monstrous hurricane was on her way, coming to disrupt lives and to raise havoc on the island. Her name was "Janet," a weatherman's joke, *"God's Gracious Gift"* in Hebrew.

Country people, hungry for excitement, longed to experience the thrills of a hurricane at least once in their barren lives, to feel the rush of the wind, to be at the centre of disarray and bedlam for just a little while, not dreaming that the storm would turn out to be as berserk as all hell. Children welcomed the day off from school. In the early morning they skipped and danced in the streets at the first impetuous winds that lifted their kites high in the heavens and flattened the long khus khus grass against the earth. How they must have wanted these early teasing winds that brushed their faces and tugged at their clothes to last forever! The air was festive. Everything around them was refreshingly alive.

The sophisticated were sceptical. They remained complacent. After all, hurricanes normally veered to the west, ruffling the waters and lashing the trees but never barging into the island full-force, at least not that anyone among them could remember.

But the older and wiser folk cautioned against their indifference. Horrific stories had been handed down through the ages about the hurricane of 1780. That one was nameless and a hundred times more violent than any other, they were told. The number of valuable slaves killed in that catastrophe was more than two thousand and was reported with equal import alongside a headcount of dead horses and cattle. The human remains of slaves were dumped in unmarked graves with the animals or fed to sharks in the Atlantic waters. Many might have survived had their owners not confined them to the plantation, to their chattel houses that collapsed or were tossed around like empty matchboxes. But today Bajans were free—or almost free—no longer living in wretched flimsy hovels but in sturdy wooden houses or in cement houses called wall-houses, and they were free to take shelter or not as they pleased.

The countdown began. Men hustled down to the Cotton Factory in Bridgetown for lumber to batten down windows and doors, returning to their villages with carts and lorries laden with plywood and two-by-fours and nails and shingles and galvanized panels. And throughout the morning, saws were screaming and hammers were clanging from rooftops; shingles and galvanized sheets were newly secured and old palings and clapboards that had been sagging all year were fastened once again. Women piled into the neighbourhood food shop and returned to stuff their larders. They lined up at the communal standpipe with extra buckets; some carried two in hand and balanced one atop their heads and made several trips to top off their water barrels. Every coal pot was stoked and ready and every lamp was replenished with kerosene, their wicks trimmed, their chimneys wiped clear of soot. They prepared themselves as best they could for Janet, this unwelcome visitor.

All along the coast of Christ Church, hotels hunkered down, girding themselves for the assault, knowing full well they would be first in line. All along the shoreline of Oistins, Maxwell, Dover, Hastings, like battalions digging trenches before the landing of an amphibious enemy, the hoteliers lined the beachfronts as far as the eye could see with coral blocks freshly reinforced with chicken wire. Frightened tourists deserted the beaches and fled to their rooms, ruing the misguided decision to set foot on the island in a hurricane season.

Still cool and unperturbed, Harold punched his time card and passed the vigilant doorman, Mr. Barrow in charge of the punch-clock. He made his way upstairs to his desk and, sure enough, he learned right away that a hurricane with the threat of island-wide devastation was heading towards Barbados. His thoughts instinctively turned to Thornville, to his two-roofed wooden house and shed, to the overarching mahogany tree at the top of the gap, which, if loosened at its roots, would crush two or three of the tightly packed houses as it crashed to the ground. But above all else, he feared for his beloved family, Cissy, David and Nathaniel, and wished he had stayed at home for the day, as dedicated as he was to this venerable newspaper.

Chapter 3

A Fallen Angel

BACK IN Thornville, Cissy, now fully awake, exhilarated by morning sex, bustled around the house before being filled with a sense of pending danger. As she made her way across the gravelled yard, out the gate and down the footpath to the outhouse toilet, she noticed that the fowls that normally rushed to her for their morning rations were cowering and scratching the earth furiously under the house. There was hardly a rustle in the breadfruit tree outside the gate where blackbirds would normally be noisily welcoming a new day and now had seemingly abandoned the branches for some secret retreat. Only the wood-doves hung around the trees cooing to one another their usual doleful song. Thick black clouds blanketed the spot where the sun would normally be rising brilliantly in the east, shooting his pyrotechnics proudly across the sky: fiery blades of red and gold and orange and all the various hues in between. Morning had suddenly turned to dusk. Between the houses and over the trees towards the west, she could see a slice of the ocean turning from blue to inky black. An aura of evil and foreboding pervaded the skies.

She looked in on her twin boys in the back room. They were fully awake and sitting quietly on the floor, their young minds not yet attuned to premonitions. They were quietly repairing last Easter's kites now torn and badly in need of fresh skins, patching them with flour paste, getting them ready. The kite season was over since Easter but these high winds that nature promised would not be wasted. They looked up. "Ma, can we go fly our kites? Catch some o' these high winds?"

Willing to please, she answered reluctantly: "Alright boys, but first make yer beds, pick up off de floor, wash yer face and hands, and come get yer cod liver oil!"

Every morning she never failed to administer the viscid tonic. Its purpose was more than bodily purification; it was a rite of passage before they were permitted to leave the house. Second to castor oil or Scott's Emulsion, it was the most feared and the most disgusting of medicines even when she rimmed the spoon with salt and lime juice. Their little faces crinkled up with scorn; they wrapped their lips around the spoon, cleaned up and then were quickly off with their kites. She lit a coal fire in the shed, filled the iron kettle and set about preparing breakfast. With Harold away at work, the boys out of the house, floors swept clean and sheets folded and put away, Cissy settled down listening to the whistling of the winds like the whistling of the tea kettle in the shed kitchen. The house still echoed with boisterous play as she began to sew and hum along with the whirring of her mother's old Singer machine. It was her time to relax and savour the morning's aftertaste of lovemaking. She shut out the world and purposely dismissed the strangeness in the air.

 That morning the hurricane was on most everyone's lips. People talked in hushed tones as if raising their voices would somehow anger the gods to unleash the storm's fury before its time. There was now a concern that this thing could indeed be real. They went from house to house huddling like sheep, wondering if they should seek shelter before the winds blocked their way out to more secure public buildings, buildings made of brick unlike their own houses, to buildings within walking distance of Thornville, like St. Stephen's Church or the government schools or The Nightingale Home for Foster Children or even Jenkins Mental Asylum, though the madhouse was not a particularly appealing option even in the worst of disasters. Some would run to the nearby Roxy movie theatre or to the St. Michael's Alms House though they knew the latter was already bursting at its seams. Some preferred to hunker down in their houses and stay put at all costs until it was over. Still, there were a few like Cissy Brathwaite who gave the rumour as much credence as she gave to the chain-dragging steel donkey that clip-clopped up and down on River Road at night and which was always heard but never seen. She remained unruffled.

 Suddenly there was a clamour of excitement at the front door. Esmay, who lived across the road, was on the front step waving her arms, panting, out of breath. She was a purveyor of all kinds of news: good news, bad news, juicy news, malicious news, baseless news; always eager to share, bursting with the latest gossip, ready to release the latest rumour on any and every ear. She barged through the door, running from one corner of the front house to the next like a wound-up toy. She was an excitable young woman with a roundish face; skin the colour of burnt coffee, about Cissy's age but plump, good-looking with nappy hair. As she hopped around the house, the searing smell of burnt hair and Vaseline wafted in the air like stale perfume. A long plastic comb was stuck in her hair like a pitchfork. Between her lips she sported a wooden toothpick which she removed only when she was about to speak, and now as she spoke, her words bunched together and poured out in quick truncated packets.

"Cissy, girl ... you get de news? You hear ... 'bout de hurricane comin'? It come over *Rediffusion* last night ... before I turn in ... they say it goin' be a big one ... Lord have mercy!"

Rediffusion was the island's sole broadcasting station staffed by full-throated British announcers. Hardly, if ever, did a Bajan melodious twang grace the airwaves. The station was hardwired to speakers that hung in pictureless frames on the walls of homes that paid the flat rental fee for its monopoly and news emanating from these speakers was gospel. Cissy had not been listening to the radio; if she had, she would have heard the hurricane warnings followed by the day's obituaries recited like admonishments from the grave. In fact the station had suspended its programming—one of a series of prosaic lectures on tropical herbs by a British botanist—to broadcast hourly five-minute alerts. Only once before had the station been called upon to render such an important public service; it was during the war when every household after sundown was ordered into protective darkness from hovering German planes and zeppelins, imagined or real. The always dependable Esmay had caught the weather report before last night's programming went off the air at eleven with "God Save The Queen."

The two women sat in Cissy's kitchen-shed over breakfast of fried eggs, fried bread, fried plantain, fried bacon, fresh lettuce and tomato, and they bantered back and forth about everything except about the impending storm. Cissy knew her neighbour had a penchant for sensationalizing the news, and even though she now knew why she had been uneasy all morning, the news was too ponderous for that early hour. They put it aside and turned to pleasant thoughts.

"Girl, you remember de day I move to Thornville?" asked Esmay, as she slurped a spoonful of Cissy's Nestle condensed milk.

"How ye mean? ... like yesterday."

"Girl, I really love dis place … so peaceful and nice," said Esmay, as if to banish the hurricane from her thoughts.

Over breakfast they reminisced about the day Esmay and her husband, a carpenter by trade, moved into Thornville. It had been almost a year. That early Sunday morning, before the sun was at its fiercest, there was a woman's voice at Cissy's front window, high-pitched and breathless with excitement.

"Miss B! Miss B!" (Until Bajans knew each other by name, every woman was Miss B.) "We movin' in 'cross de road from you."

The stranger was pointing up the road to a wooden box atop a long push-pull cart creeping in her direction with bare-backed men on both sides like pallbearers. Esmay and her husband, Egbert had brought their own house. On any other day, the same cart would have been laden with bunches of green thirst-quenching coconuts making the rounds from village to village, but that day it was serving a more noble cause. The house trembled and teetered as the cart with its big screeching wagon wheels trundled along the gravelled road and came to a stop diagonally across from Cissy's house. At first, it wasn't a welcomed sight, remembered Cissy. She had become used to the clear unobstructed view across the road, up the hill, through the serene woods with glimpses through the evergreens of the guard wall and the landlord's sprawling mansion beyond it. Somehow the view had become inspirational, a stark contrast to her drab surroundings. Would the view now be blocked by this newcomer? With four brawny shoulders at each corner of the wooden frame, the men hoisted it off the cart, panting, grunting, swearing, and plunked it down on a rectangle of rocks, neatly levelled and packed tightly together. Then with three or four limestone bricks they improvised front steps, whereupon Esmay and her husband sat and surveyed their new surroundings before entering their house as if it were their very first time. Afterwards, the men were remunerated with rum and corned beef cutters; money for their services was neither demanded nor expected. On another day, one of the other men would be moving from his own village to another, and every man would be ready to lend a hand, and another coconut cart would be co-opted for the move. Such was the collaborative spirit of the times.

THERE ONCE WAS A LITTLE ENGLAND

"We from Pie Corner in St. Lucy," she had said to Cissy somewhat abashedly that morning, meaning she was a country girl since any parish outside of St. Michael and Christ Church was rural, and since St. Lucy was the remotest of the eleven parishes it suffered the most disparagement next to St. George and St. Thomas, both derided for not having been blessed with their own beachfronts. People who lived in St. Michael took upon themselves the distinction of living near the capital city of Bridgetown, whereas people in St. James, admittedly rural and albeit a playground for the wild and decadent, could boast of their wealthy Gold Coast with its movie stars, nobles, gays, transvestites and worldly hedonists from abroad. Even the occasional visiting royalty from the Mother Country gravitated to St. James. Like nomads, Esmay and her husband had moved from parish to parish, always incrementally closer to Bridgetown and always by way of cart or lorry bringing along their house. They had paid a month's rent to the Thornes and secured a lot sufficient for their modest house. Now today, the two friends sat around the breakfast table reminiscing on innocent times while the hurricane lurked somewhere offshore, marshalling her natural forces to launch a vicious attack on the island, one that had not been seen in many a decade.

Esmay returned home and Cissy returned to her sewing. She slipped a sleeveless, half-finished dress down over her head and shoulders, pins and needles still in place, and looked at herself in the full-length looking-glass clipped to the door, turning first this way and then that way. Pondering the minor adjustments she needed to make, she slowly ran her eyes over the reflected curves of her figure and acknowledged with some vanity that in the twelve years since giving birth to twin boys her youthful shape had hardly changed. She then thought fleetingly about the coming storm and it crossed her mind that perhaps the boys should be indoors. She looked outside, up and down the gap and across to the mansion for any sign of disquiet or stirring among the servants, but all was still. She would let the boys frolic a bit longer in these early winds remembering her own childhood days flying kites with the girls.

It seemed like yesterday when the landlord would send word for the village girls to bring their Easter kites up to the mansion grounds to take advantage of the elevation. Everyone knew it was his daughter's idea since it was known that her father did not care for black people, young or old, and tolerated only a few out of necessity. Her own playmates lived far away, closer to her school, St. Winifred's, the Anglican school in Pine Hill that welcomed white girls only. The Thornes would open their gates—if not their hearts—to the little children for whom this would be their first live encounter with a white girl with blue eyes and funny blond hair hanging like dangling coils. And this would be Penelope's opportunity to rub elbows innocently with black children she had been seeing from afar. The girls would arrive in their Easter pink and yellow dresses and shiny patent leather shoes with the dainty buttoned straps, their skins scrubbed and oiled and their hair hot-combed to a stiff texture, jostling to be first in line even before the big wooden gate swung open. Back then, Penelope's parents secluded themselves in the house. They peeped warily from their blinds as if the village children were alien beings visiting for the day, and while the children played they kept their daughter in view, perhaps praying that the intermingling would not lead to some undesirable transmutation in their little darling.

But the village children were less curious of white people than they were in awe of the enormous brick house with its gazebo, marble statues, ceramic fountain, birdbaths, a birdhouse with real shingled roof, patio chairs and tables all around. They were charmed by all this grandeur, this utterly different world from their own; it was their yearly trip to a faraway wonderland. Sadly, one year, the servants broke the news; the order was given: no more tromping up the hill to the mansion grounds with their kites on Easter mornings. The reason learned was that three village boys, uninvited, had joined the girls and, whereas the intermingling of little girls of whatever colour could be tolerated, the integration of genders could not; that was too dangerous an environment for their little girl.

But Cissy alone returned again and again. Penelope, a year younger, was drawn to her and she to Penelope. There were times she would send word via the servants for her friend to come up and play with her pink porcelain dolls with the fat-cheeks and blue marble eyes. Their young minds innocent of their pasts and giddy with the present, the two girls would cavort for hours around the courtyard, both of them indifferent to the colour of their skin and oblivious to how they were viewed in the world around them.

As they grew older, the separate destinies that awaited them became pressing and real but still they never questioned whether it was by some cosmic plan that they had come to a fork in the road that would lead to those preordained worlds. Between them there was neither envy nor guilt, it was the way things were supposed to be, as natural as the alignment of the moon and the stars. Their friendship continued for a while and then like swimmers caught in conflicting currents they were swept apart and to their own separate spheres. St. Winifred's, the Anglican school for white girls, opened its arms to Penelope while Cissy went off predictably to St. Stephen's, the government school. That was many years ago but Cissy never forgot those fun years though, from all indications, neither one had pined for the other's friendship.

David and Nathaniel now flew in for a drink of whatever they could find, and soon they were off again to capture the next gale. "Be careful!" their mother called to them as they disappeared up the gap. With the winds wild and furious and gaining strength, their kites again came to life, the marlins unwinding all the way to the end of their tethers. David knew everything about flying; his kite was the bigger and the more rambunctious of the two. But with feet firmly planted, he knew how to make it wiggle, fade, somersault and cartwheel. He would manoeuvre it into a steep dive and then just before it crashed to earth, command it to soar again, the tail wriggling like a belly dancer, the bull growling in the wind. He mastered every trick in the book and invented a few of his own.

"Jeez! You see dat?" he yelled with each tug of the twine. "Man, we really should go far up de hill. Ent no trees up in Cave Hill to snag these twines if they come down."

He was the more fearless of the two, always daring to live on the edge of what was permissible in the Brathwaite household; or even to cross the threshold once in a while, risking a whipping if his brother told. He was more like his Dad, both in looks and temperament, tar-black and handsome, bold and always ready for a challenge.

"No, we goin' stay right here close to home in case Ma call," said Nathaniel. "If de wind die down we can always haul them in fast before they drop."

With that, Nathaniel lowered his own kite and wound it in. Nathaniel had the demure disposition of his mother. He was fine-featured like her, a trifle fairer of complexion than his twin brother and not nearly as physical as he. While David was willing to throw caution to the wind, Nathaniel was always measured and restrained.

Just then the winds picked up, swirled and swept David's kite away from the lowlands and in the direction of the landlord's property. Then there was a lull, the winds died, the kite leaned to a side, plummeted and vanished. The boys followed the cord up the hill through the woods to the landlord's guard wall where the kite lay despairingly captive on the highest branch of a mango tree. They stood there looking up in dismay. It was David's best kite ever, the one he built from scratch. He had spent hours carving the soft poplar wood, sandpapering the dowels thin, cutting and gluing the triangular paper skins with flour paste, designing the best sounding bull and the most colourful tail from discarded scraps of cloth from his mother's dressmaking. He loved this kite. He tried to tug it loose but the branch held on to it stubbornly.

"Gimme a hand!" he said, reaching out to his brother. His palm bore a raw stripe where the marlin had dug into the skin. "I going up."

"No, David, don' climb up on these white people wall! Ma would catch a fit if she know you climb de people tree fer a stupid kite. You can always build another kite."

"No way, man! I can't make another kite like that one! You foolish?" he insisted.

He looked up again at the kite begging to be freed, then with his eyes he measured the height of the wall and again turned pleadingly to his brother. Nathaniel gave in, cupped his hands into a stirrup from which David climbed up onto his shoulders, and from there onto the wall and lithely up the tree. Reaching almost to the highest bough, he grabbed the tail. "I got it!" he hollered. Just then Nathaniel heard two blasts like the "pax pax" of firecrackers, the crackling of a branch, and then the thud of David's body crashing onto the wall, bouncing like a rag doll, and rolling onto the soggy earth. Nathaniel reached down to his brother fully expected him to spring to his feet and run. Run from what, he had no idea. That was before he saw the blood gushing from his brother's head.

THERE ONCE WAS A LITTLE ENGLAND

The echo of gunfire reached Cissy's ears and was assumed to be fireworks, another hurricane alert. It was as much of a concern as the chimes of the Westminster clock on her shelf striking ten; or a siren wailing mournfully in the distance; or from afar the church bells of St. Stephen's tolling; or a neighbour's voice in the wind calling out to another to bring her clothes in from the line before the rain. She thought to yell out the door for the boys to haul in their kites as well; it was time for them to come home. Just then a sudden gust lifted her window curtains high. It blew her miniature crystal angel off the shelf. The angel crashed to the floor and broke in half. She picked up the angel, now wingless, set her back on the shelf and turned to close the window. Suddenly there was one loud bang as the front door was flung open. In barged Nathaniel, horror in his eyes, his chest heaving, his lips moving perceptibly but without sound, wide-eyed and panting, too fearful to cry, flinging himself into Cissy's arms. Instinctively, she looked behind Nathaniel for David; the boys were inseparable. No words needed to be spoken; his face alone told a story of something horrible, dreadful and unspeakable. In one motion, she flung her patchwork aside and flew out the door, and in an instant she was running, stumbling, clambering up the hill as fast as she could with Nathaniel pointing the way. Then the most gut-wrenching screams tore the air, a mother's wailing like a clarion echoed from one end of Thornville to the other, summoning the spirits of all the living and all the dead, calling on all the saints and all the angels in heaven to heap vengeance on the one that had so mercilessly ripped from her bosom her beloved son. David lay lifeless on the ground next to the guard wall, shot twice, his blood streaming onto a bed of wet leaves.

As if synchronized, windows and doors were flung open and people flooded out onto the road, bracing against the wind, calling out to one another, questioning and converging up the hill from all directions to the sound of a mother's cries. Egbert was the first to reach the wall with the whole village now in tow. It was he who knelt and brushed away with his fingers the bloodstained leaves and mud from the fresh wounds. The twine still dangled in the wind, strung from the treetop; the kite tail was still clutched in the boy's hand. Egbert pressed an ear to his mouth for a second and then heaved the lifeless body onto his broad shoulders, blood trickling down his shirt as he hurried down the hill with the urgency of a warrior removing his fallen comrade from the line of fire before the next mortar round. Cissy followed, her face twisted with horror. Reaching the house, she quickly lifted him, pressed him to her bosom and held him there tightly, her arms crisscrossing his back snugly as if to once again transfuse her own life's blood to her dead son.

Meanwhile up the hill a phalanx of young men gathered at the wall, their faces at first numb, then confused, staring at one another in bewilderment, then riveted with rage, eyes squinting for the slightest movement on the other side, yelling, cursing, fingers pointing to some imagined hideout—a tree, a bush, a window, a roof. Rocks flew high in the air, men attempted to scale the wall, cursing the two barking foaming Alsatians daring them to climb down on the other side. But the winds were gaining strength now, blunting their assault, pushing them away from the property as if the winds were on the side of the assassin, protecting the property from marauders. There was no one in sight; the mansion windows were all shut; except for the dogs all was still on the other side. One man with a burst of sanity braved the storm and ran all the way to Eagle Hall to the nearest police sub-station.

Half an hour passed when a whistle pierced the air. Two stone-faced constables approached, seemingly from nowhere, waving the men away from the wall, with cork hats in hand for fear of losing them in the wind, brandishing their billy clubs, confident that their uniformed authority would force the men to retreat, which they did. They chased the men away and back down the hill, chiding them for taking matters into their own hands; they would now take charge and get to the bottom of whatever was the cause of the uproar.

All of Thornville, old and young, men and women, the caring, the curious, the prayerful, the vengeful, they all defied the winds and surrounded the pink house as if to stand between it and some phantasmic evil yet to show its face. One of the officers, Constable Howard, his billy club, handcuffs and searchlight strapped to his waist, entered the house with his notepad in hand. He stared at the dead and then called for anyone with thoughts sufficiently collected to come forward and give an account of what happened. Egbert stepped forward. Not only had he been among the first on the scene but visibly the least traumatized. He described in every detail the scene as he had found it, from the entangled kite to the dangling twine to the bloody leaves to the two crater-like holes, one in the head, the other in the torso. The constables jotted copious notes on their pads but remained emotionless and phlegmatic as palace guards.

Afterwards, they walked out into the storm and, pushing against the gusts, plodded dutifully up the hill alongside their bicycles to the front gate of the mansion. Before their hands could reach the iron knocker, the big wooden gate was pushed open against the force of the wind and a short gray-haired leathery-faced black man, stooped with either age or humility, greeted them with a nervous smile. His eyes were glazed either by age or conceivably by the sadness of the moment. He looked to be a veteran servant who had been allowed to stay on long after he had outlived his usefulness. He was quickly joined by a younger male servant, his eyes wide with apprehension.

"Offisah, my name is Mr. Marshall and this hey is Sampson."

Together they led the constables along a tiled terra cotta walkway at the side of the house, past the two now kennelled dogs, and around the back to the servants' quarters which featured a staircase that led to the upper rooms. Constable Howard took one look around the room at the servants' hand-me-down mismatched furnishings and decided to stand while taking a statement from the two men. Backing the side wall was a rickety settee with shredded cane back; in each of two corners sat a worn, discoloured recliner with gouged-out armrests; two frameless mattresses lay on the floor against the wall presumably for the overnighters.

"Okay man, now tell me wha' went on hey today!" demanded the officer with his pencil and pad poised. Bajan dialect was always instrumental for the relaxing of tensions between the subordinate and the authoritarian. "I understan' they wuz a shootin' comin' from dis direction."

The old servant took charge, pausing to light a cigarette between two arthritic fingers. He explained: "We wuz back hey, offisah, putting t'ings in order before de hurricane hit when we hear de commotion and went outside to see people pon top de wall."

The constable got to the point. "I know 'bout people climbin' up pon de wall but how 'bout de gunshots, man? A lil boy got kill. I asking you who did de shooting, not 'bout who climb up pon de wall."

"Offisah, I don' know who, we hey all mornin' in de back, Sampson and me," he pleaded, "I cyan say any one o' we know 'bout no shooting, All I can tell you is that …"

He was abruptly interrupted by a woman's voice coming from the top of the stairs. Her accent was clearly not a Bajan accent. "Offisah, Mr. Thorne say he will answer to de Police Chief directly tomorrow morning." There was a peremptory tone to the voice. The constables looked at each other in bemusement.

"Well, could we have a word with de master o' de house?" asked the constable who was spearheading the questioning. "And let him know that it is de Police Chief himself that send us to investigate."

The voice fell silent. Perhaps she should have been more forceful, now having to return to her boss with a message from a lowly first-rank officer of the law. She replied, this time more adamantly: "Mr. Thorne retired fer the rest o' de day. He say, tomorrow he will give a statement to de Superintendent and turn heself in." A door banged shut on the upper floor. There was no point in probing the servants; they had already pleaded ignorance.

As the officers were retrieving their bicycles to return to their sub-station, a van bearing *The Barbados Chronicle* insignia on the side pulled up the driveway. At the wheel a young white news reporter had stumbled onto the scene attracted by the crowd and the ruckus. He had heard there was a shooting of a little boy by his landlord but the grotesqueness of the rumour begged for confirmation. He had to hear both sides. He knew the story would compete in the press with the sensational coverage of the hurricane and call for outright condemnation by all fair-minded people. But he also knew the publisher would need to walk a thin equivocal line between the highly inflamed Bajan readership and the sensibilities of his own familial and political connections. In addition, the reporter was mindful of the upcoming General Elections. It was a year of political wrangling, a season of raucous and radical oratory that pitted black against white and white against black, the lowly against the mighty and the powerful merchant/planter/landholder sector against the working-class. The story would undoubtedly stoke more coals under the already steamy political cauldron; it would be a tinderbox when the news hit the streets the next morning. When the reporter knocked on the gate, it had already been chained and locked and the landlord had likely retired to his bed or to his study to ponder his fate and to chart his next move. The storm was growing more and more intense; the reporter needed to find the boy's family; for now, he could at least get one side of the story. He knew of the landlord, Mr. Thorne, a household name in elite society, known for his land holdings and his commercial and political ties. But who was the boy and what unthinkable provocation and criminal mischief could have led to his being shot? The timing was compounded further by a hurricane in the making that commanded everyone's fears. Perhaps the storm had intensified concern with protecting property, more the concern of those who had much to protect. But to the extent of killing? There were so many questions to be answered before he could build a coherent story for the press. He drove down the hill and followed his nose to a crowd milling about a little pink house in the village. The men's voices were loud, frantic, and warlike. Women and children were buzzing around the house, each face a picture of horror and disgust. As he approached, he was struck by their defiance, by their indifference to the storm, to the winds lashing them as they held onto each other, rocking from side to side. He slowed and reached for his notepad. Someone in the crowd was sure to come forward to vent his or her version of the shooting to *The Chronicle*, the widely respected newspaper. The reporter looked up just in time to see a glutinous glob of spit sliding down his side window, then a beer bottle hurtling towards his face, smashing into the window of the news van while a flying cinder block shattered the windshield and another landed on the roof. He was sent speeding on his way. The message was clear: a white face would not be welcome in the village any time soon.

Chapter 4

The Chronicle

JOHN JOHNSON, also a Combermerian, was Harold's best friend at *The Chronicle*. A junior reporter, he was affectionately known as Jay-Jay. He was a white boy, or half-white as some would say. It was more or less derogatory to call a man half-black though that description made equal sense, or equal nonsense, since the percentage could never be ascertained. While in some other countries, half-black or coloured or even black might have been the official classification for Jay-Jay, in Barbados he was simply a white-Bajan and that was that. He and Harold laughed and skylarked between assignments, and every day they ate lunch together at Roslyn's meatball luncheonette in the alley. Harold was always the comedian with an inexhaustible repertoire of Bajan jokes and Jay-Jay was his willing foil. But at the end of the day these workmates always went their separate ways: society in Barbados had consigned them to separate social planes.

No man was more dedicated than a Chronicle man, not even a worker in the cane field or a grave digger; and at a time when jobs were hard to come by, men toiled tremulously day and night six days a week. *The Chronicle*, which narrated the daily lives of the common man, was, in Harold's eyes, its own bizarre narrative: men strutting into work wearing bowties and French cuffs, hugging empty portfolios and executive briefcases and being instantly transformed, as it were, by the magic of a punch-clock into aproned artisans: pressmen, ink mixers, loaders, line casters, lead assemblers, engravers; all with ink-stained fingers and smelling of molten lead, all proficient craftsmen superb at what they did, yet pretending to be men they were not. But Harold, who never owned or wore a suit in his life, considered himself equal to all the others, even to co-workers who, once promoted, became the tyrants they had formerly despised. Always an outsider, he looked upon the charade as a symptom of the colonialist mindset and he saw these workers as much more important than the ones they were pretending to be, for if one day they decided to fold their arms, they could bring powerful men to their knees. *The Chronicle* was only a reflection of the colonial society in which it thrived and this time-honoured newspaper never missed a day.

As senior proof-reader, he loved his role He considered his work, perhaps with some overblown vanity, as cerebral and as crucial as any other on the production line. He always made sure that all I's were dotted and T's were crossed before the presses ran, mindful of Bajan readership said to be the most literate in all the Caribbean and quick to challenge questionable spelling, grammar, syntax, placement of fact and above all, the objectivity of the press. There were other newspapers on the island but none could claim greater veracity than *The Chronicle*.

Earlier that day, the morning of the hurricane, his friend Jay-Jay was out in the field. As junior on the staff, he had been given the assignment no one else wanted. It was to scout around and report back to Mr. Benskin, the news editor, on the island's hurricane disaster preparedness, or lack thereof. Harold looked across the floor and saw little concern about the incipient hurricane on the faces of Mr. Benskin and his assistants now hunched over in their cubicles with their private thoughts. He sat at his desk and pored over raw galley space for the next day's broadsheet where three whole columns of blank newsprint had been set aside to cover the hurricane's swath. In the event she turned out to be a wimp, the space would likely be filled with syndicated pap from the archives.

At that moment, in rushed Jay-Jay and back to his desk. He hurriedly hung his jacket on his chair, pulled up his Underwood and, without a word, began to type his headline for the day. As would be the case, this young reporter had stumbled onto a story that had no relation to his assignment. It was a story that could later be described as serendipitous only because of the credit it would earn him in his ongoing career. Unbeknownst to those around him, the headline would soon quicken the pulse of the most dispirited reader, galvanize a whole village and in fact set a whole island on fire. But first, before the words reached the printing press, they would shake every fibre of Harold's body as they came across his desk: *White Landlord allegedly shoots Bajan Boy in Thornville*. The alleged shooter was unnamed but the reporter's mention of the man's colour would become a smouldering fuse.

Chapter 5

Opportunities Lost

FIVE OR six miles from *The Chronicle*, on the south-eastern coast of the island, was a cove they called Graves End. Within walking distance of its shoreline and facing Upper Bay Street was the Mission Hall of the Pilgrim Holiness Church. Pastor Winston Gittens, a Thornville resident and a St. Stephen's "old boy," whom his Bajan friends affectionately called Gitts, was half-asleep there. He was drowsily contemplating, as the hurricane neared, whether he should stay put or head back home. Away from his home in Thornville or away from his church, this is where the good pastor could be found, preparing next Sunday's sermon alone or performing the mundane duties of a deacon, assembling the liturgical appurtenances: candles, wine, manna, incense, prayer books, hymnals. At other times it was his retreat, a quiet place to meditate—no radio, no music, no worldly pleasures. His only companion was a telephone next to his armchair.

He was fairly young for the head of a church, just past thirty—average build, five-foot-eight, and with a hairline that had begun to recede before its time. He seemed overly conscious of his unlikely youth as pastor and attempted to compensate with a modest goatee that lent a certain priestly look to an otherwise unremarkable face. In his own words, "he had fallen into the ministry" not because of any particular calling from on High but because he had been born into a dynasty of pastorships and had been handed down a village church with a committed flock. The ministry was therefore the path of least resistance.

The Mission Hall was a two-story solid stone building built purportedly to withstand any hurricane that made her landfall on the southern side of the island. Legend has it that in the late 18th century it was where British troops kept their reserved rum barrels under lock and key and that at night between patrols it was used as their rum fest and whore house. Nevertheless, the building had been blessed and sanitized many times over by waves of missionaries from overseas.

With all the news about this leviathan of a hurricane that was supposed to rise up from the Caribbean Sea, Gittens was mentally prepared. He decided he would stay indoors for the day and, if necessary, unfold the canvas cot and bed down for the night. In one corner was a table stacked with Lighthouse tracts and Gideon bibles and, in another on the floor, cartons of California wines that the missionaries imported partly for communions and partly for their own imbibing. There was an abundance of fresh communion bread not yet sanctified in the missionary larder just in case hunger got the best of him. He was sure The Lord would understand. What better reasons to stay put and wait out this whale of a storm! After all, there were no little ones back home in Thornville, none other than his God-fearing father who would likely be on his knees praying for divine intervention.

The Mission Hall of the Pilgrim Holiness Church was funded by three middle-aged American missionaries, one portly, blond, long-haired evangelist and his two female disciples who together looked to have stepped straight out of a Norman Rockwell painting and onto the platform of Pastor Gittens's church with their rank folksy way of preaching and their down-home American Negro spirituals. They had come to Barbados the year before ideally for sun and surf but ostensibly to save the souls of the wicked. The place was dear to the pastor for reasons both spiritual and financial: it afforded him a quiet place to pray and, more importantly, the Americans would draw more Bajan worshippers to his church in one Sunday morning than he could ever entice in a whole month of Sundays. When attendance was down and the church funds depleted, he would walk the streets like a common hustler, tracts in hand, knocking on doors around Thornville and Fairfield and Grazettes, even as far as Black Rock where the wild boys hung out, inviting the occasional churchgoers and infidels to come to his church next Sunday for a special blessing, and they would invariably promise, "Yes, Pastor, we comin' next Sunday fer true," and next Sunday he would have to coax the few devout souls spread out among the pews to draw closer to the pulpit so he wouldn't have to lift his voice; and the few coppers the usher collected would hardly cover the felt bottom of the collection plate.

But when word was passed around that the gravel-voiced, kerchief-waving, guitar-playing Reverend Flexon from Atlanta, Georgia in America was coming to preach on Sunday morning, Bajans would flock to his church and squeeze into every pew long before eleven, fanning eagerly, their tambourines jingling with excitement, hungry souls waiting anxiously for the evangelist to appear and to deliver the sermon that he, Pastor Gittens, could never deliver so stylishly, so sweetly, with that lyrical, drawn-out, American southern drawl that mesmerized them in the seats, gushing non-stop with amens and hallelujahs and "Preach, brother!" and salivating for more, more, more. To show their appreciation and admiration for this white preacher, they would dig deep into pockets and purses for paper currency from which a percentage would afterwards be subtracted for the pastor's physical sustenance. And that would make the pastor happy and not at all envious of the exoticism and star quality of these American missionaries. So yes, the Mission Hall was indeed a God-send.

From where he sat, comfortably with his feet flung across his desk, he could see, through the back window, the ocean churning. The sea had already turned from turquoise blue to almost black with waves and waves of curling foam like frills of white lace as far as the eye could see. The surf had conquered the long reef of coral bricks that lined the shore and now the water was ploughing through the palm trees and at intervals crashing against the wooden deck in the back of the building with a resounding *"Bashow!"* He could hear waves roaring out in Graves End, the sound of the hurricane beginning to flex her might, sending forth her vanguard before launching her full brute force against the island. She had already begun to pelt her fury against the brick house, thrashing and rattling the panes, pounding on the galvanized roof like a thundering herd. In no time the water overcame the roof gutters and was cascading down the side of the building, past the windowsill, digging trenches that traced the roofline, feeding into muddy puddles all around the building.

He looked out the front window. It was late morning and the wet street was shimmering in the faint glow of the gooseneck gas lamp still burning from the night before. The road was deserted, it was a ghostly sight. On another morning there would be the steady whoosh of traffic heading to Bridgetown. Thick rain like slanted sheets of glass obliterated everything from sight beyond the glow of the gas lamp. The sidewalks were now two bustling streams. He could see the majestic palm trees at the side of the building battling the winds, their trunks bowing and straining, their fronds swaying and bucking but never breaking. He knew then for certain that Janet had come ashore.

    He resolved now to remain indoors. He reached up to the shelf where he kept the chalice and the circular collection trays and the rectangular trays with rows of half-gill communion glasses, and the thick crystal decanter filled with crimson-red wine that was not yet consecrated. Next to the decanter he kept a miniature metal-framed photo of a girl, so young in appearance that to a stranger she could easily be his daughter. He fetched them both from the shelf, decanter and picture, grabbed himself a glass and poured a drink, all the while staring at the picture as if he had never seen her before. It was an old faded black-and-white of a girl he once loved long before he entered the ministry. And how he loved her, even now! The picture had stayed with him through the years like a good-luck charm, first on the bureau in his bedroom, then tucked in his book bag at Harrison College, then pinned to the wall in his dorm at The Theological College. There was no better place to keep her away from prying eyes than here in the Mission Hall, a place where only he and the missionaries frequented. Here he kept her securely hidden among the church things like a priceless and irreplaceable masterpiece.

    He remembered the year: 1941. She was fifteen or sixteen then, he wasn't sure and she wouldn't tell. Hers was the first photograph he had taken with his state-of-the-art Kodak Brownie, a gift from his father. It was on Christmas morning in Queens Park, after church service, when the boys and girls would steal away from their parents and head to Queens Park to strut around the bandstand like peacocks in their new Christmas finery, throwing peanuts to the monkeys in the zoo and listening to carols and Sousa marches by the Police Band under the spasmodic baton of the British maestro, Captain Raison. He had saved twenty cents of his lunch money to pay for two on the traditional Christmas bus ride; it was always to Top Rock and back. That Christmas, she wrote in his autograph book a silly "Roses are red" poem, while in hers he poured out his heart in two whole pages of rambling endearments.

THERE ONCE WAS A LITTLE ENGLAND

But he was getting ahead of himself. Actually, he had known her from around the age of ten, seated every Sunday morning in his father's church as he craned over wide-brim hats and peered around shoulders to get a good look at her pretty face under her pink crinoline hat, sitting primly next to her mother like a little princess, unaware of being eyed by this precocious voyeur. And at the very first stirring of his hormones he had vowed he would marry that girl, whatever her name was. It could very well be that his propensity for lust had blossomed much too soon and then crested before falling away prematurely, for now here he was, a minister, trying to disavow all temptations of the flesh and well into his thirties, alone and unattached.

He remembered that years later, like a teenaged predator lying in wait, he lurked on the corner for her to walk by after Sunday school and would step off the pavement lightly and approach her as if their meeting had been purely coincidental, but knowing well that Aphrodite, Greek Goddess of Love herself, had chosen that moment and that juncture for the two of them to meet. And he would mumble some incoherent greeting and she would not even slow her pace, just keep on walking, head straight, offering him just the polite acknowledgement of a faint smile, perhaps mindful of her mother's admonishment that "these lil boys is nuttin' but trouble." He remembered how he would quicken his pace like a lapdog so he could be in lockstep with hers and how he would go on and on with platitudes about school or about her beautiful dress and patent leather pocketbook; or how he would try to ingratiate himself mouthing flattering words all the way from church to the gap that led to her house but stopping short of where he could be seen by her vigilant mother; and the time when they were about to part ways, in the middle of his monologue she turned to him and looked him in the eyes and asked in a voice that was pure and sweet and guileless, "So you would like to be my boyfriend, right?" He had been so stunned by the bluntness and impulsiveness of the question, as welcome as it was, that it had caught him off guard, momentarily crippling his tongue. She turned and ran down the gap to her house leaving him standing there, tongue-tied, his face transfixed in an insipid smile. It was an opportunity lost.

And then came the unsheltered independency of elementary schooldays when she would let him hold her hand from Thornville down through the lonesome cane piece and along Seclusion Road, all the way until they parted at the crossroads to their two separate schools at St. Stephen's, and not once was he forward with her, not even to let her know that they were destined to spend their lives together.

At school she was the centre of attraction. The Sixth Form boys would fight for the first dance at the Social Hall in Deacons Road when she showed up in a short, bewitching, hip-hugging skirt; and although none would admit it, she must have been the one girl in Thornville who tormented them in their beds at night until their sexual fantasies could no longer be contained and exploded into wet dreams.

Then later on in college years, standing, waiting with her at the bus stop for the Yonkers school bus that would take her to St. Michael's and him to Harrison College, if only he had thrown caution to the wind and declared his love for her right there and then; or even when she would voluntarily sit on his lap so the conductor could cram one more passenger onto the bench for the extra fare, when his generative organ would stiffen with excitement, not even then did he have the gumption to risk rejection and snuggle his arms declaratively around her waist so she could feel the thrust of his longing.

Like the tidal waves now bashing against the back wall of the Mission Hall, these tides of nostalgia came flooding back to the young pastor while the missionary wine seeped into his brain, releasing into focus memory after memory of his one-sided courtship with the girl in the picture. As time went by, his chances diminished when she became eighteen, a full woman. Vainly aware of her stock in beauty, she was committing to no one; her heart had hardened against the relentless and lascivious attention of the rude boys around Thornville and Black Rock while his own wholesome intentions went undeclared and therefore unnoticed.

But one memory as no other sets his heart pounding even today. It was the time the stage was set for their very first night of sex. There were signs she had warmed to his affections and was likely still chaste and virtuous. It suffices to say he had read the coded signs that she was ready and willing, ripe and juice-laden as sugarcane, flush and green and ready for the harvesting. He too was ready, his body hard, horny and aching with anticipation. It was in June at the height of the sugarcane season when the hot sweltering Bajan sun would sting like a raw blister all day, giving way to windless suffocating nights; and it was on such a night with just a sliver of moon above that they strolled hand-in-hand up the narrow pebbly hill that took them away from the eyes of the village, past the landlord's mansion, past the defunct lime kiln on the other side of Cave Hill, past piles of ripe green-yellow canes already cut and waiting for tomorrow's lorries, before they turned down a thin cart road that led deep into Thorne's cane fields, and then parting the canes to find a matted patch to make their bed, to make love for the very first time. There was deathly silence in the cane piece; just the faintest rustle of a zephyr through the stalks; so eerily peaceful was that night, they could hear their own heartbeats. They made themselves comfortable, side-by-side, on a soft mound of dry bagasse, looking up into the sky, not a word between them, savouring the thrill of anticipation for as long as they could, before the dikes of their carnal passions would snap, plunging them into an ocean of wild unbridled sex for the very first time.

Then suddenly she turned, clutched his arm with one hand and cupped his mouth with the other.

"Shhh! I hear something ... somebody coming."
"Where?"
"Listen!"
"Maybe a mongoose."
"Shhh! No, listen!"
"Girl, I can't hear a thing."
"Quiet!"
"You imaginin' or what?"

They clung together, staring into the dark. There was a faint rustle, a stir coming from the far end of the cart road. Then a tromping of feet over the dry cane sheaths that lay on the ground. Then closer, a loud swishing of canes parting. And soon before them in the dark a human form took shape. First the feet, then the hands, then looking down at them the face of a boy they knew as Duphus Hinds. He was the village hooligan. There was terror in his eyes at the sight of them and in his right hand was a half-opened box of Three Palms matchsticks, enough to spark a conflagration in all the cane fields in all the parishes of Barbados, much less in Thorne's modest nine acres. He was barefoot and shirtless, his peak cap was turned front to back and his black trousers were rolled up at the ankles. Were it not for the whites of his eyes gaping like an owl's in the black of the night, he might not have been recognized as Duphus, the wild coot. He had been arrested and locked up twice before his eighteenth birthday, once for stealing Miriam Miller's fowl cock the day before Christmas Eve and once for pelting rocks through her bedroom window in retaliation for her complaint to the police that led to the first arrest. He now stood there paralyzed in the cane row like a nocturnal creature caught in the beam of a searchlight, staring at the young pastor-to-be in a state of dishabille, his short pants unzipped and hanging at his ankles, and his lover, her skirt still in place but barebosomed, with one arm shielding her "bubbies" from his stare and the other locked in a terrified embrace. Duphus then found his wits, dropped the box of matches and scurried like a black-tailed jackrabbit back through the canes, the evidence scattered at their feet. She jumped to her feet and flung on her blouse; her spell had been broken; the thrill was gone. Still, in spite of the interruption, he was still aroused. A cane fire had been thwarted that night but in a split second their own fire had been rudely extinguished. He begged her to stay, but already she was leading the way out of the cane field and back to the village, their dream night shattered by one untimely and despicable intruder. But at least a crop had been saved. In the morning the cutters and the loaders would come upon the matches and wonder what change of heart had spared them another day's work for another dollar. From then on, there was an unspoken understanding that neither one of the three would mention that night for fear of self-incrimination, though had the story made the rounds in the village, Duphus would have been the eternal suspect of every cane fire in Thornville and beyond. Yet another opportunity for young Gittens had gone up in smoke.

 Just then in the Mission Hall, blinding lightening flashed through the windowpanes and set the whole interior ablaze. The shaded reading lamp next to the easy chair flickered, then died. Thunder crashed through the walls and the whole building shook. It jerked him out of his reverie. He got up and returned the old faded photograph of Cissy Brathwaite to her place on the mantel next to the holy crystal chalice.

THERE ONCE WAS A LITTLE ENGLAND

She was now a grown woman with children, still living in Thornville within a few steps of his home but technically on the other side of the planet with her two boys and their father. She came to his church on Sunday mornings and after service they would stand in the vestibule exchanging pleasantries, discretely disguising whatever sentiments might have lingered between them, feelings that were better left unspoken. He had loved her from that very first Sunday in his father's church but he was her pastor now, her spiritual leader in fact, the one who baptized her children and on that occasion gave his blessing to the union of both children and parents. Like a river that loses its flow to a counter-current, his love held no promise or future and was best left in the past, for to dwell on any prospect that she could ever be his would be bordering on the sin of covetousness. The words, *Thou shalt not cover thy neighbour's wife* would often resonate in his head and would not even allow him the exception that she was not legally the man's wife. But wait! Would he not be forgiven for coveting a woman who was once his and was in effect taken from him?

He downed his third glass of wine and leaned back listening to the waves thundering against the back wall, rolling up from the sea like the memories now flooding back from a past replete with lost opportunities. Perhaps, she wasn't meant for him, he told himself. But try as he might, he could not help but speculate on what might have been had he carried forward into adulthood the innocent audacity that possessed him the first time he saw her in his father's church. Would he be in his father's shoes today or would he have been too consumed with love for Cissy to follow his path? In solitary moments like these, the question sometimes haunted him. He was now alone but not lonesome, loveless except for the love of The One he now served. There was nothing to be gained, he thought, by re-mapping a past already cemented in history, and so, he leaned back in his easy chair with the communion wine coursing through his veins and fell asleep to the sound of howling winds and thrashing rain.

Chapter 6

Janet's Wrath

THE TELEPHONE rang. Gittens awoke in a daze. It seldom rang. Surprisingly, the line was intact, still surviving Janet's onslaught of wind and rain. Maybe the missionaries were tracking him down, checking on his welfare in this violent storm.

"Hello?"

But no, the voice on the other end was distinctly Bajan. The voice was loud, frantic and scared.

"Gitts! Is me, Harold Prince! Gitts, they shot a lil boy in Thornville!"

In the hypnagogic haze between sleep and wake, his mind grappled for clarity. He thought he was dreaming but then the words jarred him into full consciousness. The name he recognized but the words were too unreal to register fully in his mind.

"Who? What boy? Where?

The voice persisted, pleading in his ears: "Come get me! Please! Could be one o' my boys. I don' know. I can't make it home on my bike. Not in this storm." The voice was stricken with fear.

"Where're you?"

"At work. Meet me in front o' *The Chronicle*."

"Coming. Wait there! Hold tight!"

He took one more swig for the road, reached for his felt hat and umbrella, hurried downstairs, out the door and into the storm. Leaning into the wind, he waded out to the side of the building, to the waterlogged alley where his old Austin stood like a faithful horse, deep in the flood, almost up to the axles. He knew water was never a friend of these British engines but he would give her a try anyway. On the third crank she shuddered to life, sputtering in protest, and he was off to get Harold. He turned on his headlights for it seemed the sun had deserted the skies. All the while the words reverberated from an echo chamber deep in his brain: "A lil boy got shot. Could be mine." Over Harold's plaintive cries it was Cissy's voice pleading in his ears. He had to hurry to Thornville. When he got there it would all make sense; there had to be a misunderstanding, some twisting of words that would soon be made less sinister. A few people in Barbados had guns, but to hunt, not to shoot people, much less children. Not even the Police had guns; most had never held a gun; they all carried billy clubs and searchlights. Never was there a shooting in Thornville, as far as he could recall, and he had lived all his life in Thornville.

It was not a day for the outdoors, certainly not for travel in a little two-by-four motorcar. As he crept out between the Mission Hall and a boarded-up shop next door, the winds whistled up through the corridor and old Betsy rocked and trembled. Then she recovered and stood firm as he clenched the wheel. He crawled to the intersection, braked, scanned the fearsome highway up and down, then muttered to himself, "By the grace of God, Gittens," before swinging onto the coastline of Bay Street heading towards Bridgetown.

Passing the Esplanade on his left, he could tell from the fresh smell of ocean brine that the wind-driven surf was already climbing the breakers and rolling towards the public gazebo. Soon the sea would claim the highway and transform it into its own veritable river. With eyes riveted on the road ahead, he hunkered down behind the wheel and clutched it as firmly as he could, buffeted all the while by powerful gusts, rain half-blinding his vision while the lone windshield wiper batted furiously from side to side. Passing the police sub-station, his headlights fell on two constables cowering in the darkened alcove, out of the rain but still on guard. An old man with an inverted umbrella was attempting to cross the street, leaning into the wind, but the opposing force held him stationary as in a painting of watercolours. One or two motorcars had lost the battle in the flooding waters and sat abandoned on the side of the road, mortally wounded.

Farther along Bay Street, the popular Harry's Nitery was shuttered and silent. The nightclub, its doors now barred, was a haunting sight like a rare eclipse of the moon; in its long history it had never closed its doors, day or night. In calmer times, soft yellow lights would be casting a seductive glow across the floor and out the windows. Drunken sailors who had spilled out from the American frigates berthed in Carlisle Bay would be swaying to Fats Domino or Louis Jordan or Chuck Berry or whoever was the Rock and Roll flavour of the week blasting out across the street. But today, he thought to himself, Janet had sentenced the debauchees to a day of quiet reflection. Harry's Nitery was dead.

As he rounded the bend, the bells of St. Michael's Cathedral were pealing and he saw a steady procession of people heading to the doors. The Bishop was standing at the entrance to the nave with his arms outstretched and a few straggling souls were fleeing into the arms of the church.

He was now approaching the Chamberlain Bridge. The swing bridge marked the entrance to the city's core. Suddenly a colossal wave struck the underpinnings and climbed high in the air eclipsing his view with a jagged wall of white foam. He stopped to regain his bearings, then moved forward again. Big Ben atop the Public Buildings was just then striking twelve; the Union Jack was flapping maniacally, lashed by the winds off the Bay; the murky careenage waters were dipping and swelling; fishing boats were tugging furiously at their moorings like rabid dogs straining at their leashes. He could feel the bridge shuddering as he crossed over into the city which now cried out to him to turn around and go back across the bridge, but the winds, the rain and the flooded streets were no match for the cause—Cissy's cause—that propelled him onward to meet Harold and then onto Thornville. He kept going.

The pastor knew in his heart that his motivation was more than pastoral duty; if Cissy's boys were in trouble, hurt, shot, whatever, he had to be at her side. Harold was merely someone he knew but Cissy was his childhood sweetheart, one whom he could never now possess, but to whose side he would flee in this moment of need. He knew she was Harold's woman, totally and perhaps unwaveringly. He acknowledged and respected that fact and even blessed it in his own way. He had no thought of crossing that line but yet would not deny himself his tender feelings. Locked in that moral contortion, he heard her voice on some mysterious telepathic wing calling out to him. He pondered the words, *The Lord works in mysterious ways, his wonders to perform,* and fancied the telephone call from Harold nothing less than the hand of God.

Harold was standing in the rain. He flung himself next to the pastor, drenched and trembling with dread. Motioning to continue driving, he stuttered: "This reporter, Jay-Jay … just came in from the storm with the news … a shooting in Thornville … no name … just a lil boy is all I know ... a lil fella shot on the white man's property ... take me home, Gitts!"

"Jesus Christ!" breathed the pastor; no other words seemed to fit the moment. "But, man, it don' have to be one o' your boys, could be any o' the lil fellas in the village. Lots o' young boys like yours living in Thornville."

"Yes, but I got to know fer sure," he replied, allowing for the worst of all possibilities.

They drove on in determined silence while Gittens's mind flashed back to the day he presided over the christening of Cissy's and Harold's twin boys. He had christened a hundred babies since then and yet this one stuck in his mind. There was a bittersweet poignancy to that memory of the woman he loved, standing at the side of another man, two beautiful babies nestled in her arms as she radiated a contentment that said she would be forever out of his reach. The boys were born out of wedlock. The Church frowned on co-habitation. Nevertheless, Harold, always the nonconformist, could not care less for their prudery, and convinced that he and Cissy were "a match made in heaven," spared no opportunity to let these hypocritical puritans know that their union needed no earthly or legal sanction. Together the parents decided that rather than offend the Church they would have the boys christened at home and have their pastor friend intercede with the Creator, the One who mattered most, the One who would surely understand the invincibility of love and, as Harold had put it, "forgive the foibles of the flesh." Even today, jealousy welled up inside of Gittens as he remembered Harold at the christening party that followed, beaming like a war hero at an award ceremony, standing in the middle of Charlie Blackett's backyard reserved for the celebration, beating his chest and proclaiming to the whole village: "Today, I have given the world two wonderful gifts, the fruits of my seeds." Surely, he must have considered himself blessed with the other divine gift: a virginal garden that he, Gittens, had left him for the seeding, intact and unspoilt in all the years he was her lover. But it was Harold's seeds that had taken root and flourished, which had given forth two healthy baby boys. Cissy chose one name and he chose the other. He wanted to name one boy "Uhuru" (Freedom) as if the name was his last linkage to his African roots. Indeed, this one was the blacker of the two, leaning towards a purplish black. She preferred a biblical name, a strong, daring character like David. They agreed on David and Nathaniel; together the names had a good ring. She spoke wistfully of the future, that a good education for both boys would be foremost; at Harrison College, then onto Oxford or Cambridge, on Rhodes scholarships of course, then law, or medicine or politics, and on and on. "But really, all we wish for them is health and happiness all the days of their lives," she ended soberly.

Another streak of lightening lit the sky ablaze, jolting the pastor back from the past. As they inched their way to the edge of the city, there was not a pedestrian in sight, not a bus, not a motorcar, not even a stray dog; the road was bare. They rounded the corner and headed north. A sudden gust slapped the side of the car and slammed them to the side of the road. They paused for a lull in the wind and then proceeded up Baxters Road.

Baxters Road was the fun place in the city, now still as a graveyard, the place that fed the after-work crowd and the after-party revellers. He remembered the night he introduced sweet potato, roast-corn and steak fish to the American missionaries on this same street on a crowded Saturday night when they strolled up and down from one coal pot to the next, mingling with the local party people, one blond head and two redheads, lending a certain iridescence to the night crowd circling around them. The shops were now shuttered and dark, the cement steps bare, the coal pots extinguished and abandoned for the day; the wooden crates on which the fish women sat and fanned their coals were now sliding and rolling like dice in the wind. Not even a hardy drunk could be seen on the steps of the rum shops on Baxters Road.

The day had turned to night. It was early afternoon but the sun was barred by rain and heavy cloud cover. As if disoriented, the city street lamps were still lit as they fell away in his rear-view mirror to a mere shimmer. Then suddenly without a flicker they died. The island's electricity had at last succumbed to the storm. The faint amber of kerosene lamps began, one by one, to appear in curtained windows— Bajans always kept their kerosene lamps close at hand.

He pulled over and stopped to clear the debris conspiring to clog the wiper and felt the lash of the wind on his back. Then they were on their way again, silent, fearing what might lie ahead, squinting, swerving and dodging loosened galvanized sheets that were slicing the air like flying Frisbees. All the while, Gittens wrapped his arms around the wheel and kept going like a helmsman in rough seas.

At the bottom of Barbarees hill, the popular Plaza Theatre had been stripped of its neon marquee now dark and sitting on the side of the road. The oversized Hollywood posters pasted on the sides of the theatre proclaiming the week's fifty-cent matinees had been partly peeled away and were now fluttering like flags in the wind. And just when Betsy began to grip the slippery surface and take to the hill, a harbinger of things to come appeared ahead: a black Morris Minor had been blown like a plastic toy across the road and its front-end jammed onto a telephone pole now pitched like a listing mast towards one of the overhanging Victorian verandas. They pulled up alongside. The steel bumper was wrapped around the base of the utility pole and the horn, stuck on impact, was still wailing like a wounded animal. Gittens made the sign of the cross and peered inside. There was no one at the wheel but the door handle on the inside was smeared with blood. The sight of blood intensified their fears but also their resolve to push ahead even as the winds shifted and were now meeting them head-on, slowing them to a merciless crawl. Her cylinders roared again and the Austin strained but kept creeping up the hill.

In some peculiar way the pastor exuded a certain serenity of spirit; his presence alone, even without a word of conversation, was calming and reassuring. Harold's fears were gradually dissipating; he no longer nursed the pressing presumption that his family had been endangered and the odds that either of his boys had been hurt were growing more and more improbable. He knew that the landlord in Jay-Jay's headline was none other than Thorne the Englishman, but on reflection the description of a Bajan boy on the man's property fit neither David nor Nathaniel. And the likelihood of a white man shooting a village boy, trespasser or not, seemed implausible, more so at a time when there was a growing relaxation of tensions between whites and blacks. He reasoned that during violent storms, paranoia was more likely to grip those who had much to lose than those who had nothing, which might have led the Englishman to shoot at someone he perceived a thief.

He knew his boys were not the thieving kind. Thorne was one of the island's upper-class, one of the richest among them. He tried to recall the faces of all the boys in the village and mentally cast each one with the brazenness of a burglar, but all the boys he knew were good boys and disciplined like his own. On reflection, the story didn't ring true. He didn't know much about the landlord except that he sent for his rent money punctually at the beginning of each month and that failing to pay on time could result in certain eviction. He had often seen his face in a blur as he travelled back and forth in the back seat of his chauffeured sedan. The closest he had ever been to the man was seeing him one day when he paid a visit to *The Chronicle* after the much-publicized death of his wife and, wishing to express his condolences, he started with "Morning, Mr. Thorne." He did not reply but returned a crusty scowl.

Then it happened. They saw it, but their reflexes were too relaxed. They had been lulled into the false security one feels when close to home and now were sliding into a trough with just enough time to pull to the side. The engine sputtered, the sound of a dying cough, and died. The old Austin had been caught in a stream of water unforgiving to spark plugs and distributor wires. They were stalled. They had no choice but to allow the crankcase time to drip dry. The thought of deserting the pastor and his motorcar and chancing it the rest of the way on foot did cross Harold's mind once or twice but that was before he realized that such an attempt would be as futile and as foolhardy as wading from one bank to another of a raging river, such was the ferocity of the winds and the blinding force of the rain. Mother Nature seemed to be marshalling her forces against them on all fronts. They slumped behind the dashboard now dark and defeated, and waited.

They had passed that spot many a day, Harold on his way to work and Gittens to his Mission Hall, and neither had ever noticed a precarious dip in the road just before the last major road crossing. The spot bordered the rich, conservative Strathclyde community, a community of fortunate souls assumedly safe now in their all-brick houses, likely still on guard against the vengeful opportunistic natives who might dare to invade their properties at a time like this. In contrast, the poor in the nearby Eagle Hall neighbourhood, the less fortunate women and children with bags on their heads, were now running towards the formidable Roxy Theatre for shelter, to huddle with their bundles, whether in the upstairs balcony or in the lowly pit, to sit and stare at a blank screen all day and all night until the storm relented.

The two men turned to each other and silently contemplated their helplessness, stranded on the side of the road. Gittens glanced over at the profile of the man he barely knew but who in a time of need had called on him for help. Harold was the one at the centre of Cissy's world and therefore in some tangential way he was also in his. They were from the same village but they never fraternized, worked, played, ate, drank, nor worshipped together. Had he been a member of his church, the two would have been closer and might even have become good friends in spite of their former rivalry. He always made a point of learning everything he could about his church members and drawing close to them; it was the difference between a pastor and a mere preacher.

He had always considered Harold a handsome fellow—smooth-black as a raven, elegant sideburns, thin moustache, hair defiantly long and with a brush of Brylcreem slicked back to the nape of his neck. He had a self-assured, proud and slightly arrogant face. He conceded that his own face had never been as striking as Harold's. He was conscious of his own hairline, ebbing back more and more from his forehead, and of a visage more cherubic and less engaging than Harold's though it was capable of charm once people drew close to him and could see in his face the reflection of his soul. He had known him only briefly when they were both schoolmates at St. Stephen's before Harold and his family picked up inexplicably and moved from Thornville to The Ivy. He remembered how the St. Stephen's girls would sidle up to Harold as they walked across the pasture towards the Anglican Church every third Wednesday so they could sit in the same pew as Harold, and how he himself, feeling less sought after, would withdraw and assume the selfless role of pumping the pipe organ bellows for Father Alleyne, the organist. And how Harold always had his pick of the girls; they were always in his face; mostly pretty girls, except for the Headmaster's somewhat homely but prized daughter, Inez. But there was one girl, Cissy Brathwaite, who seemed not to know that Harold Prince even existed, so fond was she of him, Winston Gittens. Still they remained in those school years, all three, free and unattached.

THERE ONCE WAS A LITTLE ENGLAND

In the adult years that lay ahead, on a night that promised new beginnings, serendipity smiled on Harold Prince. It was on Old Year's Night at the swanky Marine Hotel where any young bachelor would likely show up in a rented or borrowed ripping-iron tuxedo and his date in a flowing gown, sweeping the glittering ballroom floor as they swirled to the mellifluous strains of the Percy Green Orchestra. Yes, the Marine Hotel on Old Years Night was the place for lovers, young and old. As it turned out, that night Harold was accompanying his sister, Molly, whose fiancé was on duty playing alto sax for Percy Green. She had begged him to come; after all, it was definitely not a night for a young lady in formal dress to stroll unaccompanied down the dark tree-lined walkway that led to the gala with gawking, lawless, catcalling boys on both sides; then to proceed through the brightly lit lobby under the derisive stares of Bajan girls who would say with their eyes: "How come she don' have a man? She mus' be don' know that um is Ole Years Night and yuh shount be comin' in here by yerself looking to steal somebody man." So for this one night, Molly made sure to enlist her only brother, who would otherwise have been down at the Social Hall in Deacons Road in shirt and short pants gallivanting with his friends.

Cissy and her date, Gitts—as was his nickname—sat at the rim of the dance floor at a small round table with a bottle of bubbly in the centre. They sat closely but distantly. She and a handsome stranger had spotted each other across the dance floor and held each other's gaze for the better part of the night as they circled like two barn swallows in the mating season of early Spring, he weighing the likelihood of rejection should he ask her to dance, and she wary of his disarming good looks and mildly curious about the aloof way he danced with his wife. Or was she his lover? The call of nature and the hands of time must have conspired to pull Gittens away to the restroom, for at the very instant he walked away, a hand reached out to her and he looked back just in time to see her and the tall handsome stranger (whom he did not at first recognize in his formal garb) meld into the swirl of faceless dancers waltzing to Percy Green's Auld Lang Syne. Molly's boyfriend had left his alto sax behind to dance a few bars with her at the stroke of midnight, freeing her brother for those irretrievable moments to go after the girl he had been eyeing all night. Harold Prince, the audacious one, had stolen

Gittens's magical moment of midnight before leading her back to her table with a revelatory squeeze of the hand, much too focused on the twinkle in her eyes to discern the disappointment in her friend's face; too swept away by her beauty to notice that her date was saddened to be abandoned at the pivotal stroke of midnight. The bridge between years was that neutral zone when young lovers absolved themselves of the past year's philandering and infidelities and sealed an oath to start afresh. Such was the case with Harold. But not being with Cissy in that mystical zone and seeing her in the arms of another man meant to Gittens that his dreams had withered and died like the old year. He sat there at the stroke of midnight, mocked by the explosion of noisemakers, poppers and cymbals while confetti rained down on his head and he never heard a word when she whispered in his ear, "Happy New Year!"

It bothered Harold for some time afterwards; it was not in his nature to be a poacher. Now sitting next to the man he thwarted, he thought it would be awkward, if not dishonest, to apologize. After all, she had been his life, his anchor all these years, had given him joys he never could have foreseen, two beloved sons and the conviction that she was meant for him and him alone. Nothing could ever atone for an unrequited love but his conscience found solace in knowing she kept in constant touch with her friend, joined his church, attended regularly, became a Christian and considered him her counsellor in matters of faith.. These two men, waiting out the storm in a decrepit car, inches apart in a claustrophobic cabin, their nostrils burning with the dank odour of their own sweat, had nothing in common except a love that was best kept out of their conversation for fear of rekindling old jealousies and old guilt. And so, they filled the time with small talk and banalities, careful not to bring up the past, waiting patiently for old Betsy to recover from her drowning.

Harold had regained a measure of composure. "Y'know Gitts, all these years I don' remember ever telling my boys that I love them. I mean, they must know that I love 'em, right? But I never say the words: 'I love you'. I don' know why, but all of a sudden I get the feeling that I wish I had said 'I love you' at least once."

"Well, say it while you can," said Gitts. "Actions count but words do too. 'In the Beginning was the Word.' " The young pastor tended to quote the Scriptures unconsciously, whether in or out of context.

"Maybe it's because my ole man never said it to me," said Harold, "though he taught me to love myself as a black man. He was a seaman, before he met Ma. He loved the sea, loved it more than land. Came home once a year at Christmas. Soon after he left, Ma would start getting fat. He gave her his last name and six children, five girls, all Libras. Pa was Nigerian by birth, Jamaican by transplantation, descended from slaves deposited on the island. Marrying Ma was his way of staking out the one place he really loved: Barbados. Yet he wanted to die at sea and so he did. It is strange but the same love for the sea is in my bones."

"Did yer mother still love him all those years that he was away at sea?" An embarrassing question leaked from the pastor.

"I can't really say. She would always refer to him as 'your father,' never 'my husband.' I guess with his six children, she would have to either love him or hate him, but she could never be indifferent."

"How about you? You loved him?"

"I loved the concept of him but I never knew him well enough to love him the way I hope my boys love me."

It was a cryptic reply but the pastor understood; all his life he too had to share his own father with the Church. The difference was that his father showered all his love on his heavenly Father. He believed now that Harold, like he, had never heard the words of love from a father, and so, in expressing love for his own children such words to Harold were awkward and unmanly.

He said he loved both of his twin boys. But not equally, he confessed. He was closer to David in whom he saw his own reflection. David was the extrovert, fearless, confident, and never willing to accept anything less than what he knew was rightfully his. Nathaniel was like his mother, punctilious, accommodating, walking the straight and narrow, always living by the rules.

"Y'know, I'm ashamed to admit it, Gitts," he said, "but David I love more than anyone or anything else in this world." He saw himself in David.

THERE ONCE WAS A LITTLE ENGLAND

It was well over an hour since the pastor rushed out of the Mission Hall with the conviction that God in his omniscient wisdom had roused him out of his easy chair, out of a wine-induced slumber and out into this dreadful hurricane so that He could bring him and Harold—and eventually Cissy—together in this hour of need; that the obstacles strewn in their path were tests of his own faith. Harold, on the other hand, sitting in his cubicle at work, thought he heard in his ear the whispers of Satan himself driving him on a course that in all practical terms was impossible, trying to get to Thornville on his bicycle in a raging hurricane. The pure and simple fact is that he enquired for the telephone number of the Mission Hall because Gittens was the only one he knew living in Thornville who possessed a motorcar. City buses were out of service and travel by foot or two-wheeler was out of the question. Was it divine Providence that willed the pastor to be at the other end of the line? All had been well until the moment the shocking headline crossed Harold's desk and shook every fibre of his being. In any case, now here they were, two men sitting side-by-side, shipwrecked in a sea of angry winds and brutal rains while their craft slept by the side of the road and rocked like a drunken sailor.

Harold decided to try coaxing the old Austin back to life, stepped out into the puddle and gave the crank a mighty whirl, and then another, but the engine only shook, sputtered and died again. And so, they resigned themselves to continue whiling away the time with small talk. They both had gradually dismissed the likelihood that either of the boys was the subject of the reporter's story and in their now relaxed mental state and sensing that silence between them only invited tension, they opened up to each other with the freedom of two friends sitting on a bench in a park.

"Y'know, is only because o' Cissy that I moved back to Thornville."

"So, tell me, man, why you moved out in the first place to live in The Ivy?" Gittens asked.

"Rape!" answered Harold.

Gittens at first stiffened, then thought his ears had deceived him; it was as if his companion had thrown a stink bomb in the air.

"I was accused of raping a girl in the village. That was a long time before me and Cissy."

"Well, did you?"

"Not sure," replied Harold.

"Well, you either did or you didn't, man. Ent no in between."

"Maybe I didn't or maybe I did. I don' know."

"Anybody I know?"

"I can't say."

"Well, why are you telling me about it?"

"Because you are a minister and you share stuff with God. But it just wouldn't be fair to say who, plus your God already knows who."

Gittens sifted through his mind all the likely girls he knew from one end of the village to the other and paraded their names one by one before his friend to elicit either a shake or a nod of the head, but each name was met with neither confirmation nor denial. Harold was determined not to confide the name of the girl even to a man of the cloth so well practised in the art of exhortation. There had been a long-held pledge in the Prince family never to admit anyone into that circle of secrecy, but it was a secret that had weighed on Harold's conscience for many years. Now, stuck in the storm, going nowhere, with only conversation to fill the space between the two of them, he weakened and decided to talk about that dubious rape that had hovered in his mind for fifteen long years. But in good conscience he drew a line at the mention of the girl's name.

"Alright, here's my deep, dark secret," Harold began. "Cross yer heart and hope to die?"

"Between you, me and God," said the pastor.

"But no names. Now where should I begin? I was almost seventeen. It was a night unlike any other, with rain pelting down outside my mother's two-roof house and shed. Earlier that night we could smell the rain coming, that familiar earthy dank smell of rain about to fall that we Bajans learn to tell from small. First, a little tap dance on the galvanized roof. Then some galloping feet. Then before long, a whole herd o' stampeding stallions breaking down the roof. A tropical depression was passing through. It was in May in the rainy season.

Lightening, thunder, rain beating down on the roof so loud you could not even hear yerself talk."

Harold was deliberately and devilishly building suspense in Gittens's mind by dramatizing his story, dragging it out with hyperbole and minutiae. The sound of rain, more like the sound of gravel pounding on the roof of the car and streaking down the windows and along the windshield replicated a certain reality to his version of that night like the soundtrack of a haunted movie.

He went on. "About nine, time to sleep, Ma out the light and we all turn in fer the night. My five sisters had one bedroom and one big bed. The three biggest always slept perpendicular like the Roman III to the other two at the bottom. Ma had her own bedroom, the only one with a real door. The other rooms had no doors, but strings of glass beads pretending to be curtains, very little privacy. Ma had the biggest bed, one half of which was slept in once or twice a year. We used to call it the conjugal half. And me, I had my own room, which always made me feel important since I never had to share it, me being the only stud. Well, 'stud' is the wrong word: I was a little virgin then."

"Well, at seventeen we both had something in common," Gittens interjected.

"Well, anyway, in no time at all, we all fast asleep. Y'know, in Barbados the deepest and the sweetest sleep a man could have is when the rain falling. Later on in life I found it the best time to make love. When you see rain set up in Thornville now, and the boys at school, Cissy and I closing the front door and the windows tight, tight, tight, and we heading straight fer the bedroom. And people around there know quite well not to come calling when the house shut up. I believe that the majority of Bajans were conceived in the rainy season."

"That could be true. So what now?" Gittens moved him along, not desiring to hear about his and Cissy's sexual appetites.

"So as I recall, it was a little after midnight when I heard a banging on the side of the house, which I thought was one of the sidings that loosened up and was slapping in the wind. The banging continued faster and louder. And then a voice, a thin voice, like a cat meowing or a baby crying. I thought it was my imagination because, as you know, you tend to always hear voices crying in the rain. But as it turns out, it wasn't my imagination at all. Ma, always a light sleeper, heard the banging, woke up, went to the window and I could see between the beads Ma opening the front door and letting in a little girl, no bigger than me, soaked, dripping wet, drenched from the top of her head to her bare feet, standing there in the glow of the kerosene lamp that Ma was holding up to her face. She was standing on the doormat like a wet rat. I couldn't see her face but from the voice I knew she was crying. I heard Ma say, handing her a towel, something like 'what you doin', lil girl, out here in de rain on a night like tonight? You looking to catch consumption or what? Your family know you out here in de rain?' The voice was so feeble, I couldn't hear what she said back to Ma and Ma's back was to me, so I couldn't get a good look at her face. All I could see was Ma at the door helping her to dry off and handing her one o' Molly's dresses, then she ushered her by the elbow into my sisters' bedroom saying something like, 'When de rain stop, girlie chile, back home you go. Whatever it is you have with your parents is between you and dem, is none of my business, but I cyant leave you out in dis rain and I cyant keep you here til mornin' either. I already have five girl thrildren and five is more than enough.' The conversation went something like that. And then the house was still again except fer the rain on the roof, and the thunder. And I fell off to sleep again with the impossible picture in my head of six girls like dominos in one bed."

    Gittens was now all ears, mentally prodding Harold to get to the meat of his story, to the part he described as his deep, dark secret. But Harold broke off at the sight across the road of a capsized cylindrical trashcan rolling menacingly towards them, spilling its garbage along the way and crashing with a loud metallic clang into his side of the car. Then it bounced away and continued down the hill.

    "That was the hand o' Lucifer," said Harold with a chuckle, "warning me to stop talking 'bout that night."

    But Gittens was unfazed. "Go on," he said.

    "Now, where was I?" resumed Harold. "It was two in the morning. I know it was two because the ole grandfather clock that my ole man brought from Southampton and which was standing in a corner of the front house never missed an opportunity to blast out whatever time it was, day or night whether you asleep or awake. So anyway, I am under the covers because it was a cold night, cold by Bajan standards, which it always is when there is a hard rain like that night in May. And next thing, right after the two chimes, I thought I heard the jingling of the stringed beads. Sometimes the wind through the cracks would ruffle them at night. But then I felt a tug on the bed sheet and reflexively I pulled it back over my head between sleep and wake and nestled down again. Next thing, the mattress sank and quick as a flash I felt a warm body slip beside my naked skin under the sheet pressing a hand to my mouth so that even as I woke up fully and sprang back hitting my head against the headboard, my voice was stifled in the back of my throat. And then to ensure complete silence, she thrust her tongue in my mouth like a wet rag, sealing my lips from any attempt to holler and wake up the rest of the house. When I was finally able to talk, I said, 'Who you?' In the dark, though, I had an idea who this person was from the contours of her face and her hair. She also gave off a faint scent of perfume that I knew was Chanel No. 5."

The scene Harold was describing to the pastor was intentionally comical in an effort to lighten the air but he also knew how to wax eloquent to pique the curiosity. He was a true newspaperman; he knew how to wield the language. Once again, Gittens could not help himself from mentally typecasting the girls he and Harold had known from early schooldays, especially the spirited outgoing type who by then might have become unbridled and wayward, bold enough to sneak into a boy's bedroom and into his bed in the middle of the night. Not a single girl from his youthful days, Gittens thought, was capable of such audacity and no Bajan girl he knew was that forward. But then, he was well aware of Harold's charisma; much to his chagrin he had seen him in action in his later years. Perhaps at seventeen he had already found the key to unlock young girls' inhibitions. Now he was portraying himself as the victim.

"Well," continued Harold, "she then whispered in my ear that there was no room fer her in the girls' bedroom, too many people in one bed, and could she sleep in my bed until the rain stopped when she would leave and go home. She then told me to keep my hands to myself and I quickly asked, why did she not keep her tongue to herself. She said the kiss was to thank me fer sharing the bed and that was all. Then she wriggled herself into a hollow in the straw mattress next to me and went fast asleep." He paused for a second or two and then said, "But Gitts, how could I sleep?"

Just then, lightening lit up the space between the two men and Gittens caught a snapshot of Harold's face, a picture of mock anguish. Gittens was on the edge of the car seat braced for the climactic details. He knew the next sentence would likely reveal the commission of sin to which Harold referred.

But Harold digressed. "Maybe I should try cranking up this jalopy again." He motioned to step out of the vehicle but the pastor grabbed him by the arm.

"Finish the story, man! So what happened next?"

"Well, to tell you the truth, the rest of the story is more or less in a fog, like in a dream. Maybe it *was* a dream, I don' know. I remember how the girl was up again a half hour later, grabbed Molly's oversized dress by the hem, pulled it up over her shoulders, tossed it on the floor and was on top of me as fast as you could throw a saddle on a horse and dangling her plum-sized breasts in my face fer good measure. Fer the very first time in my life, a girl in my bed, naked as a newborn, a bed cold as ever an hour before, now hot as the hot pot in the sea. I could feel the blood racing from every part of my body and flowing directly to my you-know-what. The blood was even deserting my brain, cause I couldn't think straight. Suddenly she rolled off and sank down in the same spot she was in before, leaving my whole body shaking like a rock engine. Then it happened."

Gittens leaned over and thrust his face within inches of Harold's ear. "What happened? What? Harold, did you force that girl?"

"No ... well, maybe ... I don' know, Gitts!"

"Well, which is it?" Gittens was shouting, demanding the truth.

"I don' know, man!" Harold shouted back. "I was a seventeen-year-old. Who took advantage o' who that night?"

"Seduction is not a license to rape." Gittens gave his conscience no relief. Was Harold in denial and manipulating the story to his advantage? He wondered.

"Now looking back, I should've thrown this nymphet out o' my bed. Instead, I remember waking up from a deep sleep and rolling over to find that I must've been dreaming. I reached across the bed and she was gone. I pulled the sheet up over my head and fell off to sleep again. Woke up just before daybreak to the sight of Ma in the doorway, standing with her hands on her hips. The backlight from the kerosene lamp was casting a halo around her. She looked like an apparition sent by God to smite the two underage fornicators. She stepped through the stringed beads. I can hear her now: 'Where dat girl went? She wuz in dis room, I know.' It was as if Ma was there the whole night and witnessed everything. All morning long I stayed awake, lying there and waiting fer the slap o' Ma's cou-cou stick on my backside."

Gittens saw the trace of a roguish smile on Harold's face and he too chuckled and then could not help himself from breaking out in a laugh that shattered every last bit of tension between them. Up to that point the story as told by Harold had been like a wildly erotic script for some hilarious movie about two virgins and their first sexual encounter. But as Harold proceeded to recap the rest of the story, the script took a fateful turn.

"About two or three months later, Ma got a visitor. The mother of the little flirt shows up at the front door. Tells Ma her little girl, sheltering from the rain, was attacked one night by her son. Had Molly's blue dress in her outstretched hand as proof that the crime was committed under Ma's roof. She said she would give Ma hell fer the rest of her life as long as she and her vagabond son lived in Thornville. I got the story from Molly; I was at school. The whole thing was kept very quiet fer the sake of protecting reputations though Ma never felt comfortable in the village since then. Up to this very day, Ma has not said another word to me concerning that night though in the wash next day she had to discover the evidence: the stain of virginal blood and the smell of Chanel No. 5 on her white cotton sheets. But I just know that one day she goin' confront me fer the truth and I myself don' even know the truth. And I never talked about it until now. Not even to Cissy. So Gitts, since you're supposed to be a man of God, I expect it to go no further on this earth. Now you know why we had to move out o' Thornville. Now you know the whole truth."

However, Gittens wondered if indeed he had heard the whole truth and the real question of seduction or rape still lingered in his mind, but man's carnal nature being what it is, he resolved to give Harold a pass. Now it was time to get going; Cissy was calling. "Now, let's get this baby on the road," Harold said, as if a load had been lifted. And with that, he pushed open the door and tramped through the ankle-deep water with the wind clawing at his shirt to crank the comatose car back to life while Gittens pumped the pedal and jiggled the choke. With a fresh surge of petrol, she sprang alive and with a thump of the clutch, lurched forward, shaking and smoking like an awakened dragon. They were at last on their way.

 A minute later, Thornville and the lofty white mansion were in sight through the misty rain. Their spirits lifted. But now there was something up ahead on the road in Fairfield; it was a roadblock. Drawing closer, they saw a monstrous frangipani tree, uprooted and lying across the road, its naked roots squirming like sinuous snakes in the wind. The trunk was wrapped in a tangle of cables and a fallen utility pole lay perilously nearby. Judging from the thickness of its trunk, it had to be more than two hundred years old. He stopped. Maybe he should try to go around it; maybe not, he might be stuck in the mud. His eyes squinting for sharper focus, he decided on a different path and cut across a neighbour's backyard startling a brood of chickens, then onto a cart road that led through Grazettes Village.

 Grazettes was aptly named long before their time for its former swards of pastureland. It was now packed tightly with wooden houses. It was even better known for Mr. Rogers's huge cavernous rock quarry and the village men who mined it, old black men with thin feet whitened with marl, squatting at the rim of the quarry with their pick hammers, breaking tiny pebbles into even tinier pebbles, pyramided by size to be carted off to building sites around the island for the construction of wall-houses they would never see and never dream of owning. Their work was more meaningless and more superfluous than they could ever imagine, but the benevolent Rogers kept them employed anyway, knowing full well that an investment in a single oil-belching rock engine could replace ten men and still sit idle for half a day. The name, Rogers, would inevitably spring to mind as it did now as they cut through the village, for he was a goodhearted black man who did well for himself and at the same time spared no effort to help his own people.

The winds had subsided. Gittens continued to negotiate Betsy down a thin ribbon of a road lined on both sides with canes left over from the crop. He pushed on half-blindly through the field while the stalks slashed at them from both sides until at last they reached a clearing. Through the rain he could see the Thorne mansion like a citadel on the hill. They were within a stone's throw of home. Harold's pink house appeared in the distance like a nugget of gold at the end of a mine shaft.

"At least, the ole house is still standing," he said, "and I see the roof is still intact."

"Praise the Lord!" said Gittens.

The asphalted surface leading up to the mansion now reached out to them and the old Austin welcomed the smoothness. Then at the edge of the village it branched off to a narrow gravelled road contrasted with the smooth black tarred road that led to the white family's residence. They were relieved to see the giant mahogany tree with its bulging tendons still standing at the corner, still absorbing all the punishment the hurricane could inflict, her roots like monstrous talons digging deep into the earth. As they veered off the tarred road and into the village they were blocked in their tracks by a towering mound of wet garbage that had been scavenged from the public bin by swirling winds and now lay in their way. It had been too harrowing a trip from Bridgetown to Thornville to waste time and energy trying to go around the pile. Abruptly Harold pushed open the car door and without warning bolted down the gap towards home shouting over his shoulder, "Thanks Gitts, I gone."

"Wait fer me, I coming," Gitts shouted back and abandoned faithful old Betsy in the middle of the cart road.

Chapter 7

The Stolen Promise of Youth

CISSY BRATHWAITE was lying on the floor, overwrought, spent, looking blankly into space, both arms outstretched in a posture of total surrender, her hair wildly tousled, her clothes dishevelled and indifferent. At the sound of Harold's voice, she struggled to her knees and flung herself into his arms. Nathaniel ran towards them and burrowed himself between the two. They stood clinging together, her sobbing muffled in his embrace. Throughout the morning's delirium, she had seemingly held back the height of her anguish for the moment of his coming. He looked around, something was wrong, something was dreadfully wrong, David was missing. He gently broke free and ran from room to room. "Where is he?" he shouted. The body had already been taken away to the city coroner. Any chance that his son could be dead never crossed his mind; if anything, hurt, sick maybe, but not dead. He remembered the reporter's headline never mentioned the word "dead." Her lips simply would not form the words to tell him what had happened to David. And so he looked around for others to come forward to explain. It was left to Egbert, the one with the stalwart mind, who steered him by the elbow to the back room and, alone in the relative quiet, delivered the tragic news as soberly and as gently as he could.

"Listen, Harold. Sit down. David is not here."

Harold with both hands grabbed his friend's collar and pulled his face towards his. His eyes were pleading. "I know he's not here. I ent blind, man!"

Egbert lowered his voice almost to a whisper. "Listen! Let me explain … just before de storm hit, de boys went outside to fly kites because o' de high winds. Both o' dem. De winds shift and David's kite got caught on de white people mango tree. So he went up de tree to get it."

"So what then? I am asking you what happened to David. Man, tell me what happened to David!" With each word from Egbert's lips, Harold's eyes grew wider and wider, glowering with anger, seething with impatience.

Egbert blurted it out. "Next t'ing, de boy falling out de tree, shot dead like a common animal."

Harold tensed, his face was a mask of horror, his fists tightened, his eyes no longer glowered but stared far into the distance, beyond Egbert, not seeing him, not hearing another word, staring into the face of evil, into the bowels of Hell. He sprang up from the side of the bed and Egbert threw his arms around him and pinned him to the partition. But he tore himself away, ran through the house, out to the kitchen-shed, grabbed a wooden-handled coconut cleaver from a shelf and bolted out the door in the rain and wind, cursing, screaming and clambering up the slope, through the trees, towards the wall, towards the house on the hill. Neighbours pursued him—they had been lingering around the house as if on guard, indifferent to the storm, warm with compassion for the people inside. One leg had already scaled the wall by the time they caught up with him. They hung onto his other leg. In fury and frustration he hurled the hatchet against the wall; it bounced off the bricks with a clang; a million sparks flew in the air. With the wind clawing at their clothes, they wrestled him back down the hill to where he could release his rage in the shelter and the companionship of his own home. They held him close as he simmered and trembled, his body doubled over in pain. Yet he shed not a single tear, too angry to cry.

Through her tears, Cissy finally acknowledged her friend, Gitts, and his good deed. She held his hands in hers, reached up and lightly touched her lips to his. She whispered softly: "Thanks, dear, I love you!" The words repeated themselves in his ears like the waxed grooves of a broken record until it was clear that at a time like this her kiss was no more symbolic than one of gratitude. After all, it was a time for tender mercies; he had brought safely to her side the man she loved, and for that she was grateful. There was nothing more to it, he told himself; how could there be at a time like this? She held onto his arm and groped her way slowly over to the back house where the boys slept. She told him how when they were much younger they always slept at the foot of their parents' bed. He figured they had grown too old, too big and too wise to what mothers and fathers did when they awoke in the middle of the night unable to restrain their urges and drowsily forgetting they had company. And so, their father, convinced it was time to reclaim parental privacy, had gone down to the Cotton Factory in town and brought back enough plywood to partition the back where the boys would later have their own room.

She leaned against the doorjamb looking in. The bedroom had the haunting look of a playground after dark on a windless, starless night: the swings and the merry-go-round motionless, the sandpit and the slides still echoing the sounds of children at play. David's comic books, Phantom, Rip Kirby, Superman, were strewn on the floor next to his bed, and above on the windowsill were his glassy-eye marbles, cap gun, Viewmaster, guttaperk, hopping ball; their animation seemingly suspended the moment she entered the room.

He had made his bed before he went out to play though the mattress was still sunken in the spot where he had laid all night. It was dressed in a white sheet, tucked back at one corner like a dog-eared leaf. An exercise book lay open, face down on the floor, next to a sheet of multiplication tables not yet committed to memory. Above his bed on the partition, his school shirt and khakis hung from a ten-penny nail. Every Saturday morning their mother would be skinning her knuckles against the ribs of her jucking board, then on Sunday nights pressing a knife-edged pleat in his trousers, rotating her four coal-heated flat irons, readying these time-worn clothes for the next week of school, these very same clothes that would now clothe him in his grave.

She was drawn to his cricket bat, lightly coated with linseed oil and leaning forlornly in a corner. Still dazed with the surrealism of it all, she murmured that he was ready for the weekend match between St. Stephen's and Wesley Hall schoolboys; how he had been looking forward to going up against the school champions. Now leafing through the bulging cricket album where David kept his private pantheon of legends clipped from the sports section of *The Chronicle* and stuck to the pages with clammy cherry juice, she spoke of his dreams of being famous one day, representing the West Indies all around the cricketing world. His father too held the same vision, a dream he once harboured for himself. Now what was left was a hand-me-down bat that would have no future: his brother had little or no interest in the game. David, of the two boys, was the cricket aficionado like his Dad. She mentioned his father's nurturing in his favourite son a passion for the game, feeding him stories of his own frustrated cricketing youth, when, too poor to afford the half-priced Schoolboy Stand at the Kensington grounds, he would stand outside all day pressing his face against the hot galvanized paling to peep through two nail holes at his hero, George Headley, mauling the English Marylebone Cricket Club. And how, at the entrance to the posh George Challenor pavilion stuffed with white spectators, he would loiter at the gate for a glimpse of the green velvety oval and to see his proud hometown boys in whites led by their famous white skipper who must have possessed some uncommon God-given quality that none of the black players had, which must have been the reason he was chosen to be their leader. How once, before the next over, he heard a voice of authority and felt the tap of a constable's wand on his head. "Boy, move from de gate and let de gentleman pass!" "Gentleman" and "Lady" were code names for white people. And how he would walk the entire perimeter of the Kensington Oval in the hot sun to find a tree, perhaps an almond tree or a tamarind tree, to climb and perch on the highest branch for a truly bird's-eye view of the rest of the innings, surrounded by birds' nests and penniless cricket fanatics like him. Hearing Cissy speak of the unique chemistry between father and son, there was no question in Gittens's mind that Harold saw himself in David.

She walked over to David's bed, unfolded the dog-ear, bent down and kissed the pillow. Kissing their foreheads was a nightly ritual when she tucked the boys in just before they drifted off. She confided to Gittens that she was now seized with crushing guilt and kept hearing accusatory voices in her head: "Cissy, why you didn't confine the boys to their room? Cissy, why you let them go out on the road to play in a storm? Why you didn't yell out the window fer them to come home? Why you didn't drill into your boys' heads that they should never, ever, on any condition, go anywhere close to the white people's property?" She wondered if the same questions hovered in Harold's mind; if they did, she knew they would never reach his lips.

Back in the front house, the room was gripped in stunned silence. Dejection and depression were everywhere. There were no bases of reason for what had happened and hence there were no rational words to adequately fill the space between them. And so they stared at one another like people in a trance, uniformly transfixed in their bewilderment like survivors of a car crash staring at the carnage, wishing it were all a ghastly dream from which they would soon awaken. In a darkened corner Nathaniel sat, curled up like an endangered earthworm, immobile, his back turned to the window. Cissy now sat with her arms folded across her bosom, rocking back and forth, her eyes riveted to the spot where she had last seen David dashing out the door, his kite tail trailing behind him. Esmay and her husband sat on the floor at opposite corners, the latter with his consoling arm around the shoulder of his best friend.

They were opposites in many ways, Egbert and Harold. Egbert was from St. Lucy and thus considered a country boy, while Harold was a town boy. Harold was everything Egbert wanted to be but wasn't, either by lack of opportunity or lack of will: educated, outgoing and high-spirited. Harold had shown him so much; it was sad to see his good friend who had always exuded a confidence and strength in which he himself was deficient now brought to his knees. He would now have to muster the little strength he had and find the right sentiments to ensure that his friend did not fall apart altogether.

Meanwhile the winds with renewed strength continued to buffet the house. The partitions, the floor and the roof creaked and groaned as if with disgust at the senselessness of the day. The pastor, his head bowed, began pacing the floor like an appraiser sizing up the immensity of a catastrophic loss. He too was lost, bereft of all reason. He had not set foot in this house since the day of the boys' christening. It was an old wooden house but one that had been patched and re-fortified from time to time in the aftermaths of various high winds. Still at the peak of the hurricane it shook like a maraca; the floorboards yielded ever so slightly under his feet. Now and then the winds thrust through the door slats and the roof rattled like a boiling pot cover while the flame of the lamp wick flickered wildly, shooting thick black soot high up to the rafters where a gauzy web already clung to the ceiling. Looking up he caught a glimpse of the sky clearly through a gash in the roof. Already they were running out of buckets and bowls to catch the raindrops trickling through the holes. At that moment a sudden thunderclap rattled the partitions and a shelf on the opposite wall trembled and tossed a few of its collectibles to the floor, among them one of Cissy's cherished containers used for retaining water refreshingly cold for days at a time. It was a bulbous hand-made pitcher formed with clay, with a snout and one large ear. It was mysteriously referred to as a "monkey," one of her grandmother's hand-me-down relics that had been an indispensable fixture in the home long before Cissy was born, going back to the era of slavery. On impact it shattered into three of four shards of clay. She glanced fleetingly at the fragments and offered not a flicker of concern; in the context of the day the loss was infinitesimal; on another day it would have brought tears to her eyes.

Gittens saw the faces of the grieving parents on every possession in this simple house. Her face was on the leather-bound bible, beside the kerosene lamp, on the round centre table. Her reading glasses were placed strategically within reach of the Morris chair where she now sat, where he imagined her reading her psalms at night, her face upturned to a picture on the wall where the glow of the lamp fell across a white auburn-haired Jesus, a crown of thorns on His head, prayerfully gazing towards the heavens. The depiction of Jesus in these moments gave forth an air of finality and betrayal.

In contrast, across the room, a row of iconoclastic works—judging by the titles on their spines—looked down impiously from Harold's bookshelf. Among them were *Notes of a Native Son* by some young author named James Baldwin, whose name was unfamiliar to Gittens; William Dubois's *The Souls of Black Folk;* Frantz Fanon's *Black Skin, White Masks;* Richard Wright's *Black Boy* and Marcus Garvey's *Preachments on Pan-Africanism*. Just as Cissy drew her spiritual strength from the writings of those sage apostles, Mark, Matthew, Luke and John, so did Harold turn to these heroic black authors and ex-slaves for his own sustenance and the strength to countenance the inequalities of life as a black man. They both had their heroes.

And then there they were: the boys, lined up at eye level, picture after picture, a chronicle of their young lives forging their way to adulthood. They covered the entire wall next to the window in view of where their mother spent her days cutting and stitching and sewing, next to the Singer sewing machine and the headless dress form; first in their blue baptism gowns, then crawling on the floor, then naked as jay birds in the wash tub, then on their way to school with their lunchboxes. The one that caught his eye and drew him closer was a black and white of a manly David dressed in long pants with zippered pee-hole, the pride of every little Bajan boy long before the presumption of puberty. Gittens was overcome. For the first time tears welled in his eyes. He asked: "What kind of monster would take the life of this boy, and for what?" He began to nauseate. He stepped outside for fresh air. There was a lull in the storm. He walked away from the house of bereavement and looked towards the house where Ben Carson lived.

At the very edge of the village where the cart road that ran through it disappeared into Thorne's cane field, was the house of Ben Carson. Now long retired, Ben had been Thorne's stable hand for twenty-four years, and though his master had no love for his servants, Ben had lived in the penumbra of Thorne's love for his horses. Because of this privileged exception, he was allowed to live rent-free in what was once a storehouse for the Thorne estate. It was a gray, oblong, brick structure overgrown with weeds, cleaned out and made somewhat habitable before Thorne gave it to Ben in recompense for years of service as his faithful stable hand. Surrounding the house were thick evergreen mile trees that insulated Ben from prying eyes and, through the trees, electric wires led all the way from the mansion on the hill to Ben's humble abode down below. Thus by some unlikely fortune his was the first house in the village with electricity. Running water came later. Ben, now in his eighties, ate, drank, smoked and slept in the front half of the house, which, after all these years, still bore a faint acidic smell of cow manure and the odour of rusted metal.

In the rear of the house was the so-called "death room." Ben was now the self-styled village mortician and embalmer. Here was where the dead were washed, drained, perfumed, powdered, dressed, coffined and otherwise prepared for viewing. The viewings were often at the Pilgrim Holiness Church of Pastor Gittens, the purveyor of most of his business. And to this death room poor families delivered their departed ones to be readied for viewing in the best possible state of dignity. It was not a profession he initially chose for himself but one that over the years had been thrust upon him by the poor and bereaved, and by trusting clergymen and funeral parlours. Even Codrington, the busiest undertaker in all of Barbados, would often call on Ben to help out with his overload.

THERE ONCE WAS A LITTLE ENGLAND

The work was priceless so he exacted no standard pay but instead relied on the generosity of the church and the bereaved, and proudly fancied himself an artist entrusted by them with the last phase of human vanity. Families relied on his nicotine-stained hands to enhance and rejuvenate the faces of their loved ones, even to perfect faces that had been imperfect from birth. He had no formal training. His only prior approximation to caring for the dead was on the days when his master returned from his hunting trips in the country with the Barbados Rifle and Gun Club. He would be called upon to carry the dead pheasants and guinea fowls out to the shed and perform the usual taxidermy so his master could boast of his marksmanship when his guests saw his feathered trophies on his walls. Tonight would be different. His greatest challenge would be within himself, to keep his icy resolve from melting and dissolving into a pool of tears. The only death that ever shattered that cold veneer was the loss of his boy forty-six years ago, drowned at sixteen off the rugged coast of St. Lucy near the Animal Flower Cave. That was the last time he shed a tear over a dead body.

Now here in Ben's death room, on a smooth mahogany slab, cold and stark naked lies the body of David Prince. The boy's eyes still stare, still frozen in frightful puzzlement at the horror of a sudden blow to the head and then the blinding loss of consciousness. His body is now bloodless, his cheeks still full as though death is reluctant to begin her ravage. His skin, coal-black and flawless, dimples with each touch of Ben's fingers. His school clothes, short khaki pants and starched white shirt now lying next to him had been delivered by the pastor, insinuating a particular interest in the boy and planting in Ben's mind that he be treated with extra care. Bending over, Ben stares deep into his eyes now dulled with the impassivity of death. He stares as if delving deep into the boy's soul, a soul already departed, searching for some dark untold story. Then with a soft touch he slowly squeezes the lids shut as if to grant him the peace of eternal darkness, entombing forever some unfathomable secret that brought the boy to this unspeakable end. He thinks, if only by some necromantic willing of the mind he could somehow see him laughing, jumping, running, loving life again, but the cold face of death stares back at him, the stolen promise of youth. He is seeing his own son again. He leans closer and whispers into the boy's ear, softly as into an acoustic microphone, "Lil boy? You's a martyr. Is goin' be ruction here in dis island tomorrah, watch my word!" Then he looks away, for his work affords no room for emotion; with a heavy heart it is always impossible to do his best work. Still, he cannot help but be struck by the incongruity of it all; to him death by violence in the case of children is an aberration of human behaviour too vile to comprehend.

"My God!" he prays to the heavens, "he cyant be nuh more dan twelve, dis here boy."

He doesn't know his name but had seen him many times in the evenings running up and down the gap, he and his brother, pushing their bicycle rims with bamboo rods. He had gotten the impression that this one was more daring than the other: one day he came to his door and asked if he could see where he kept the duppies. The village children called him the "duppy man" and kept him at a distance. Since it was a fair description, he never minded. They never needed his services anyway.

Over the years, Ben had made peace with the inevitability of death, like the certitude of the sun rising in the east, setting in the west. He invented his own macabre humour as he went about preparing the lifeless remains of people he had known all his life. He would picture himself standing at the fork in the road, at the neutral threshold of Heaven and Hell, and even as he faced the bereaved he would wager to himself on who would least likely enter the pearly gates. He had always needed that air of levity to face the dead all these years, but the dead were always old people; there would be no need for such wagering tonight. Now among the shelves of mystical oils, disinfectants, waxes, perfumes, powders, makeup, wrappings and unlabelled bottles of all sizes and smells, the air is humourless and heavy. White talc from his hands floats in the air like magic dust.

His next move is to turn the boy over. He gently rolls him to one side, then to the other, and is suddenly jolted back from the table by the sight of a tiny crater the size of a penny in his right scapula where the bullet must have entered and shattered a bone, immobilizing the boy but not killing him at that instant; but then another in the back of the head where it surely had scattered every atom of brain matter to all eternity. He had been apprised ahead of time by the coroner, but now seeing the raw ghastly holes firsthand, his face contorts in disgust. He is filled with fear, fear of man and his capacity for evil. He no longer sees a crude knotted slab of wood before him; it is an altar. He kneels beside it and weeps like a child, for although he has grown accustomed to natural death, he is not yet impervious to the gruesome reality of death by violence, and even less so when inflicted upon the young.

He needs a cigarette. He gets up, walks outside and reaches in his pocket for a Trumpeter. He jerks the pack and pops one between his lips. The hurricane has tapered off to a drizzle. Thunder now and then echoes in the distance, the sounds of a jubilant enemy withdrawing from its own plunder. The air is still; the match hardly flickers. In his bones he feels another storm coming that will shake the island to its core and once again lay bare the wounds of a past too often besmirched with innocent blood.

All morning, Ben had not been able to bring himself to believe the talk of the day, that his old boss, Mr. Thorne, had shot the boy.

"De man just don' have dat kinda heart," he had said to Gittens. "I wuz in dis white man employ fer donkey years and I just cyant see him tekking a life, drunk or sober, much less a lil chile. He wuz always kind and gen'rous wid de servants and de servants' thrildren. Look how he turn dis house over to me rent-free in compense fer my services, and I only paying fer lights and water. Yuh t'ink a man like dat is capable o' murder, Gitts? Good God, tell me de trute! Woe loss!"

Now at this very moment, fiercely loyal to his old master, Ben still agonizes over the question of guilt. He stomps out the half-smoked Trumpeter and returns to the boy. Minutes later, the storm lets loose her final gasps: a streak of lightning cuts through the jalousies electrifying the room, casting an eerie strobe across the dead. Then a long rending screech followed by a cracking explosion rattles the rafters and causes the green-shaded pendant lamp hanging over the body to sway and tremble as in an African ritualistic death dance. Ben looks to the ceiling and whispers, "Speak, Lord, thy servant heareth," and proceeds to dress the boy.

Chapter 8

Aftermath of a Hurricane

IT WAS six in the evening. The long tempestuous day had drawn to a close. The hurricane was finally moving on to unleash her fury on other undeserving shores. She had ravaged the island, had raped the village all day like a rapacious beast and was now departing with barely a whimper except for babbling waters rushing down the hillside from Thorne's courtyard, meeting up with thundering gutters racing to empty themselves in the ravine behind the houses.

The pastor was leaving; he had a funeral to prepare. He beckoned with arms outstretched for all to kneel. With a dismissive wave of his hand, Harold declined; there was no room in his heart for supplication. Gittens spread his arms like an eagle's wings across the shoulders of Egbert and the two women and searched his repertoire for the perfect prayer. Finding none, he dug deep into his soul for words sufficiently fitting. He prayed, then got up and left.

He glanced one last time at the mansion on the hill; the lights were out. He wondered if the people inside were resting peacefully, oblivious to the racing pulse of the village below girding for the inevitable waves of revenge.

Although the hurricane had subsided, sirens still wailed in the distance like wounded beasts locked in some mortal trauma. Church bells were still pealing from far away, faintly like wind chimes. Bullhorns still pleaded for people to take shelter from a storm already passed, repeating the same script over and over: "Attention! All those who need shelter, come to St. Stephen's! We have plenty water. We have plenty food." Food would be corned beef and Eclipse biscuits of which the island had a never-ending supply. Farsighted politicians would take charge of the food supply, feed the people and comfort the distressed. In the classrooms, desks, easels and benches would be pushed to the walls to make room for the dispossessed. Now homeless, or driven from their proud homes, the emblems that had fed their egos, the people would now all be equal, no one of a higher social standing than another, squatting on the school floor, arranging themselves into their own comforting family circles, feeling and looking naked without their belongings, wondering what remained of their houses, tears of anxiety and fear welling in their eyes, waiting humbly and obediently for the next instruction from the authorities. In these classrooms where there was always a state of disciplined decorum, confusion and loss would now reign. They would all be refugees.

Gittens drove slowly down the main road, a rutted tract that wound through the village. Devastation was everywhere. Women wept by the side of the road, their homes now shambles of wood and metal lying in heaps like roadside carcasses. In the mud and water, men trampled through the wreckage to salvage simple but treasured possessions. Little girls clung to their mothers, wide-eyed and terrified. The hurricane that fearless little boys had daringly wished for would now become their nightmares. Parents shooed their children out of puddles for fear of parasitic chiggers penetrating their tender soles. Dogs ran wild, sniffing and poking at piles of wet garbage. Sheets of corrugated metal had been peeled like banana skins from houses, whirled into the air and deposited in neighbouring yards. Shingled roofs, their nails uprooted, had landed awkwardly against other houses or in the bushes, while stronger ones had fought a good battle but had shifted atop their frames and now sat to one side like hats worn askew. Trees had been uprooted. Outhouse toilets were lying on their sides, malodorous and reeking. Palings had been flattened to the ground liberating all the chickens and precious livestock they had quarantined all year.

Its shame no longer obscured, the now infamous guard wall that belonged to the Thornes was now in full view. The trees that had faithfully hidden it from the curious were now naked but the mansion beyond it looked untouched. David's kite, now mangled, still hung entangled in the mango tree, looking down askance towards the mansion, waving its face in the breeze from side to side seemingly in a gesture of reprobation. Gittens wondered if the bloodied leaves had been washed down the hill in the cascading waters and whether the mud at the wall no longer bore witness to the dozens of feet that had trodden up to the site of the killing.

Janet had been relatively kind to Cissy and Harold though she had made her presence known: their paling lay flat on the ground and their backyard was now a scene of invasion. The storm had set their fowls free but they still insisted on cowering under the house unaccustomed or indifferent to freedom, or perhaps afraid of the mayhem that surrounded them and choosing to remain in the familiarity of their imprisonment. A tree behind where the paling had been standing had been denuded of its leaves and precious golden apples. The breadfruit tree still stood defiantly erect though all its fruit lay on the ground like errant bowling balls to be gratefully gathered up for pig feed tomorrow by Mr. Cutting, the pig farmer. All in all, the home of Cissy and Harold, so full of prayers throughout the storm, had been spared.

Gittens crept along to the edge of the estate and witnessed the greatest miracle of all: the old weather-beaten rhomboidal shack that belonged to Joe Walrond, the drunk, had survived, still leaning against its crutch of greenheart lumber. Its gaping clapboard sidings had given free passage to the winds and in return the storm had left his house to its own natural process of decrepitude. Like the casuarinas, deformed but still standing, Joe's old house had refused to die.

Awakened to his own interests, Gittens now thought of his church and hurried to the outskirts to find the glass-encased bulletin board that announced Sunday morning hymns had been ripped from the façade and now lay shattered on the front steps. One or two of the stained-glass windows had been blown out. But the hurricane had been less merciful to Piggott's rum shop across the street: she had ploughed into the siding and left ungainly holes in the wood. Before the winds had died, Piggott's loyal customers came to his aid and sealed the openings so that now a patchwork of tin placards promoting Ovaltine, Bovril and Pepsi Cola temporarily covered the fissures like metallic band-aids. But both the church and the rum shop were standing and remained in business, ready to service and heal their separate flocks.

He decided finally to head home to see the cards Mother Nature had dealt him. His father's wall-house had not been unscathed: stretching from the eaves to the foundation was a stair-step gash where the winds had clawed apart the cinder blocks at the cement seams. The roof had battled well but was still gaping at the eaves. All the window shutters hung loosely like lopsided picture frames and the front gate had been torn from its hinges and lay flat on the ground. No wonder his father's chocolate-brown pedigreed Labrador could be seen down the gap conjoined in heat with a mangy mongrel named Carla, dragging from one side of the road to the next, free to mate with any and all commoners as long as the opportunity lasted. Someone emerged from the shadows and doused the copulating dogs with a pail of cold water ... not even wild horses could pull them apart.

Gittens stood across the road, awestruck at the scars on his father's wall-house but even more so at the total collapse of neighbouring houses cursed by their preponderance of wood. He thought of a passage he had read somewhere; it could have been in the Book of Revelations, but it wasn't: "After a hurricane is come and gone, the land is never again the same." Thornville had been struck twice in the same day.

Chapter 9

The Capuchin Defence

NEXT MORNING, the news of the killing was a bombshell that exploded all across the island in a matter of hours. The evidence was overwhelming. There was no way to escape the charge that the shooter was indeed the Englishman, Thorne. His words to the constables via his mistress were that he would turn himself in that day and so Captain Foster, the Police Chief, held his horses, fully expecting Thorne to comply. He hadn't taken kindly to the snubbing of two of his men the day before but he thought twice about the highly irregular spectacle of arresting the white man in his own house, a policy unheard of in these colonial times. But a different spectacle was beginning to take shape: a crowd of angry Bajans were slowly gathering on Pinfold Street, their faces upturned to the second floor window of the office of the Superintendent of Police. The Captain was faced with a legal and moral choice.

Just then the telephone rang and a constable announced to Captain Foster that there was a gentleman needing to speak with him urgently. "He don' want to give his name, says he knows you from the Gun Club." The Captain knew intuitively who the caller was and the nature of his call. Closing his door and cancelling all calls, he ensconced himself in his plush leather chair and threw his feet on his desk, for he knew this was going to be a lengthy and useless exchange at the end of which he would have nothing to offer the man but the advice to place himself in the arms of the law.

In his tenure as Superintendent of Police, incidents of murder rarely came across his desk; more common were cases of fighting, petty larceny, lawless indecency and cussing in public. It was very unlikely that he would ever allow himself to be corralled into a private meeting with an accused whether in person or on the telephone. But murder was the gravest of all crimes and when the alleged perpetrator was white and the victim black, the whole matter had to be escalated to a different realm where motivations of race and colour and class had to be examined and the social impact in this small island weighed carefully. Barbados had come a long way from the days when white slave owners could snuff out the lives of their subjects with impunity or be given a mere slap on the wrist by a make-believe Establishment that feared reprisals from the ruling minority. Still today, the spectre of the brutal and indomitable slave master had not been expunged from the people's subconscious; rather it remained in the back of Bajan minds like the chalky residue that clings to an erased slate. Admittedly, Thorne in this day and age was far from a slave master but in their minds he bore the sins of his fathers.

Captain Foster was an imposing and powerfully built white Bajan, or Bajan-white, as some preferred to say. In any case, he was no less white than Thorne and almost as indigenous as any other since the Arawaks. He was born in a dirt-poor village in the craggy east coast region of Martins Bay known appropriately as Scotland District. He could likely trace his lineage all the way back to Scotland to a band of dissident forebears banished to the island in the seventeenth century and severed from their history almost as thoroughly as blacks were severed from theirs. Almost but not quite: they had not been stripped of their names, the McAllisters, the Baileys, the McLeods, the Kennedys. Years of endogamy had slowed their assimilation just as it preserved the whiteness of their skins, but in time their ways of living slowly melded into the cultural landscape. Unaccustomed to the scorching tropics, their forefathers were forced to acclimate to the blistering Bajan sun. Even today, the legs and necks of their descendants remained as reddened as ripe cherries, setting them apart from their healthily tanned and well-heeled erstwhile countrymen who spent their days lazing in air-conditioned homes and offices. These pale-faced people became objects of curiosity. Tour guides passing through St. John would point them out to tourists as the island's rare species. White people viewed them from afar as embarrassments. Blacks looked upon them as vindication: white people too could be poor and downtrodden just like them.

The Foster boy did well for himself. He started out as a first-rank constable walking the beat in rural St. John, reporting to his lowly Scotland District sub-station and then working his way up through the ranks. And now this descendant of Scottish rabble-rousers, come from a family of poor so-called "Red Legs" was today the Superintendent of Police, the protector-in-chief of civil order in Barbados. Some said his colour had catapulted him to the highest rung. He would not deny it; he was an honest man; he knew very well that in Barbados a white skin alone could steer a man right to the top.

The intercom rang. A voice rasped on the speakerphone: "Morning, Cap'n, Ted Thorne here! Sorry about yesterday, throwing yer boys out without giving 'em a statement. Well I say, better you hear from the horse's mouth if you know what I mean. Awful what happened yesterday. On top o' the bloody hurricane, I mean mistaking the boy in the tree for a friggin' capuchin."

"That is your statement?" asked the Captain.

"That is me statement. Certainly you of all people would know we could never shoot a lad in cold blood. After all, we're civilized, we're not animals. Got a boy-child of me own, adopted, but still me own. Was an accident, plain and simple. Me heart breaks for the lad." It was a staccato burst of quick phrases, perhaps rehearsed overnight, the last sentence carefully modulated to a tone of burning anguish.

"Well sir, accident or not, it is not for me to decide. You have to understand …"

"Well, whose side are you on?"

"I am on the side of the law."

"Well, does the law not say a man has a right to defend his own property?"

"You mean to shoot a boy in cold blood fer trespassing?"

The Englishman didn't answer but posed his own question: "Cap'n, remember that little talk you and I had some time ago?"

"When, where?"

"Shooting monkeys with the Gun Club in the country. I believe it was in Mount Hillaby in St. Andrew.

"No, can't say I do."

The Superintendent was at a loss. Yes, indeed, they were both members of the Barbados Rifle and Gun Club but no occasion came to mind when he had ever before spoken with the Englishman. Then the occasion flashed before him. Yes, they had spoken once. It was during a shoot in the country with the Club. In St. Joseph or was it St. Andrews, he couldn't recall. They had talked briefly but the gist of the conversation escaped him at the moment. And anyway, what did it have to do with the matter at hand?

"About the bloody monkeys on me property." he reminded the Captain. "Attacking the friggin' mango trees day and night, leaving a bloody mess, rotten fruit all over the courtyard. Keeping me up all night with their goddamn chattering in me ears."

Now the Captain vaguely remembered the Englishman sidling up to him in the woods, mentioning something about the growing number of capuchins on the island, which afterwards he understood to mean monkeys on the island; that they were encroaching on his property; that they were moving down from the country and taking up residence in his mango trees; that they were making his life miserable; that there ought to be a law to rid the island of these primates, as if he, the Police Superintendent, could enact a law all by himself and declare a year-round hunting assault on the monkey population. Yes, he now remembered such a conversation. He had empathized then with the man's aversion to monkeys; indeed the monkey population was getting out of hand; it was a common complaint.

On the phone, perhaps from his study, Thorne sounded perfectly at ease with the Captain, reaching out to a brother, a white man like himself, perhaps assuming an implicit oath of mutual understanding between the two. For the Captain, however, it was a fragile fraternity under the skin that reached back over oceans of turbulence and years of animus to a common continent. They had travelled different roads to arrive from there to this place and time. At some distant convergent point in their ancestral pasts they had drunk from the same cup, but the history of this Bajan white man had been scarred by the English, so that the Captain in his heart was no longer the Englishman's brother.

"Yes," said the Captain, "now I remember you telling me something 'bout a monkey invasion. So what then?"

"Well, I took the boy for a blinkin' monkey. That's all there is."

"That's all there is? Man, a lil boy is dead and today the poor mother and father must be heartbroken, crying their eyes out. Don't be a heartless shite!" Captain Foster was vexed by the callousness in the man's response.

"Surely, you don't think I shot the boy on purpose, do you? Mistaking the boy for a black capuchin was quite likely, won't you say?" His tone suggested he was taken aback by the Captain's unfavourable reaction, but his words had grated the Captain's ears, words weighted with bigotry and disdain. Then his voice exploded over the phone. "You of all people, a white man like me, must know it was an accident. I have deep remorse for the boy, but by God in heaven you and I know I never intended to take a human life. How in hell could I be sure that the boy was not a friggin' monkey?"

At first, the Captain did not respond. Perhaps he was hoping that, in the silence that followed, the venom of the Englishman's words would echo back to his ears and either prick or poison whatever conscience he possessed. When he did respond, his own words were just as virulent and equally scathing. "But tell me, Mr. Thorne, why defend a fruit tree from a monkey just when the hurricane is about to destroy the monkey, the tree, the entire orchard, and the whole blasted island including you in that big-arse house on the hill?"

"Accidents happen," said the Englishman.

At that moment one could well imagine Thorne shrinking in his chair, the phone held away from his ear, for the Captain had jumped to his feet and his voice was booming, resounding out the station window and thundering down to the street where the crowd, now increasing in numbers, must have wondered if the Superintendent of Police had suddenly gone mad.

"Mr. Thorne, first of all, you pick up a shotgun on the morning of a storm, in broad daylight, and shoot an innocent boy out of a tree and then refuse to cooperate with my officers, then you have the unmitigated gall to phone me next day and tell me you took the boy for a monkey. Mr. Thorne, you think I'm a blinkin' idiot?"

Thorne's voice fell silent. When he spoke again, his words were subdued. "I am an instrument of Fate, Captain Foster. This is goin' be a positive catalyst for change on this divided island. Maybe it took a white man killing a coloured boy by accident to wake up the people. Unfortunately, I happen to be *that* white man, you see."

"What about the boy?" asked the Captain. "The boy was an instrument of Fate too? The sacrificial lamb on the altar of Fate for the sake of change?"

"The boy was innocent, so am I. I am a good white man, Cap'n."

"Well, all I can say," said the Captain wearily, as if to finally bring the whole exhausting conversation to an end, "we have a legal system here in Barbados handed to us from your country, to determine the truth of what is an accident from what is not an accident. And, Mr. Thorne, I can tell you that the Law don' give one shite about Fate."

"Yes, I know," said Thorne.

"I suggest you get in touch with a lawyer, a good lawyer, the best you can find. Then turn yourself in before the Law comes knocking on your door. I'm giving you one more day. You are a well-known man around Barbados, and since you believe in Fate, Fate may well be on your side."

"The question is: Are *you* on my side?" asked the Englishman.

It was a nuanced question; there was disappointment in his voice; he had expected a more empathetic ear; the Captain had been rigid. After all, there had to be some commonality between them, some coded spirit of brotherhood. But in truth, the only thing they had in common was allegiance to their ceremonial trappings: the legacy of traditions handed down throughout their colonial histories. But beyond the cherished ties of protocol, like knighthoods, titles, honours and official decorum, there was no other bond, for between Thorne and the Captain there was a long and terrible history riddled with injustices reaching back to a time when a white man could be yoked to a black slave in the cane fields of Barbados. Although the scars of shame had healed over the centuries, the scabs remained.

The caller hung up from the Captain, picked up the telephone again and proceeded to take his advice. He needed a good lawyer, not just any lawyer but one who would defend him in Her Majesty's Court as deftly and as doggedly as if he were a friend. His defender had to be a native, a black man. The only one he knew who might fit the bill was a Bajan he had once helped. They had met over some legal matters pertaining to the estate and, strangely, he was the only black man who had earned his respect. He had sponsored this upwardly mobile and skilled Bajan lawyer for co-membership at the Barbados Water Club, a private gentlemen's club on the outskirts of town. The barrister was in his debt.

On James Street, a stone's throw from the powerhouse merchants on Broad Street and within walking distance of the courthouse on Coleridge Street was the office of Barrister Virgil Cunningham, Esquire. James Street was in relative terms a mere back alley with hardly a storefront that could fairly justify it as a city street. Tucked in between a typewriter repair shop and a shoemaker was the office of this enormously gifted Bajan lawyer. The front of the building, plain and windowless, was deceptive: enter and you would find yourself in a modern, well-furnished office, one that smelled of success.

The barrister returned from a Rotary Club luncheon, checked his appointments and saw that his aide had taken the initiative of scheduling a consultation with a potential defendant. She had pencilled in the name of one Mr. Theodore Thorne. The barrister had suspended preparing briefs for the rest of the year to devote more time to the upcoming 1956 General Elections; he had decided after a month or two of vacillation to throw his hat into the political ring. An enormously popular lawyer, mostly among the island's elite, he was now confident he could parlay his name recognition into the mainstream of Bajan politics. Most of his courtroom defendants over the years were from a cross-section of the merchant/planter/landholder community and this affiliation earned him a reputation among the working-class that he could not be trusted to protect the interests of poor people in this skewed society. He had to rid himself of this stigma if he were to garner much-needed working-class votes. Needing time to win their trust, he would unload all future cases into the hands of his junior associate before taking his first plunge into the maelstrom of big-time politics.

The name struck a chord, he knew the man well, an infrequent client of his, Teddy Thorne the Englishman. They were members of the same fraternity. Given all the hoopla on the street about the shooting, he knew the man was sitting on a powder keg and he most certainly did not relish an invitation to hold his hand in the eventual and inevitable explosion. It was not the right case for him since he was about to launch every possible effort to ingratiate himself with the working-class. Thus, he instructed his aide to pass him on to the young and upcoming associate, Bernie Thomas.

"But he said only you would do, sir," explained the aide. "Said he knows you from the Club. That you are the best and that he only wants the very best lawyer in town."

He bowed to the flattery, instructing the aide to go ahead and arrange the consultation. "But not in de office," he quickly added. "Make it at de Club over lunch on Friday. Leh de cheapskate limey buy me lunch and afterwards I will tell 'im I done taking cases fer de rest o' de year."

The Club referred to was the Barbados Water Club located on a beachfront on the outskirts of the city and close to Pastor Gittens's Mission Hall. It was a watering hole for men in high places, important men who on Fridays would climb down from their various pedestals of power for a few hours of camaraderie. They were men of influence like Charles Spofford III, General Manager of the Barclays Bank in Oistins; the Banfield brothers, who owned the luxury Coral Crest Hotel in Hastings; Tory Reilly, the real estate developer from St. James; the Goddards, powerful food merchants in Bridgetown; the Hunt boys, rich playboys in the nightclub circuit; Geoffrey Ward, who owned two or three sugarcane factories; and billionaire, Laughton Compton, whose source of wealth had been forever a mystery—all movers and shakers. They huddled together in intimate circles at round tables, clutching their noggins of Guinness and nibbling on dainty fish sandwiches, chitchatting about money or politics or women or cricket, exchanging macho stories and lewd jokes, laughing with that polite laughter that restrains itself in the back of the larynx.

The Club had its natural origin in the days of white exclusivity but the social forces of recent times had broken through the cordon, and now professional blacks, the newly arrived middle-class, could cross the threshold and become members as long as they had the sponsorship of existing members, who by default were white. As mentioned, Thorne had spoken for Cunningham. As said, they had met years before while consummating some legal matters pertaining to the Thorne estate.

THERE ONCE WAS A LITTLE ENGLAND

The place was not fancy, certainly with none of the luxury that could fairly characterize it as the island's most prestigious club. The building was deceptively ordinary, a plain rectangular brick structure. The wooden steps and railings on the side led to a plain metal-framed door that opened to a long wood-panelled room with a dais and microphone stand at one end and, at the other, a horseshoe bar with rotating stools and, in the middle, a dining area that was as cheerless as a mess hall. Hanging on the walls were huge framed reprints of George Challenor and W. B. Grace, two old white cricketers, the former a native Barbadian, the latter a bearded Englishman from the nineteenth century. On the opposite wall was King George IV in place of the reigning Queen, in deference to the Club's male motif. Young black waiters in their white jackets and white gloves floated silently among the tables like beautiful cherubs. And then there was Millington, the jolly round-faced bartender, always beaming, always at his station like a croupier prodding the patrons to have one more drink and raking in the chips while they indulged themselves into drunken stupor.

Today every table was buzzing with the latest news:

"Oh, by the way, I say, did you hear about the shooting up by the Thornes?"

"Yikes! Some lad took a bullet trespassing on ole Ted's property!"

"Blimey! You mean Horny Thorny and his spinster daughter?"

"Ho! Ho! Ho! Ho! Ho!"

It was Friday, midday. All heads turned. A hush fell over the Clubhouse as a tall bespectacled man entered, an Englishman known to every man in the house, nose in the air, shoulders back. He wore a white polo shirt and riding slacks with the air of a man without a care in the world. His aquiline nose made him appear more austere than he might have been. Wispy strands, silvery like corn silk, lay strategically across his balding head and his face was mottled and pale as if untouched by Bajan sun. The men lowered their heads, perhaps hoping he would not be drawn to their tables; in the last forty-eight hours he had become too radioactive for their company. Returning polite nods, he took his customary place alone at the far corner near the dais, leaned back, crossed his legs, lit his Sherlock Holmes pipe and opened his *Chronicle* to the page that featured the story of the shooting, a story he knew well.

Precisely at ten minutes past twelve, in strutted a medium-built black man with an air of artificial aristocracy, rocking from side to side much like a penguin. He wore a loose-fitting tweed suit with a bulging waistcoat that strained to contain his paunch. His eyes were bright and bulbous and his smile was broad and endearing as he strode between the tables waving to the men on both sides of the room. He peered over a pair of wire-rimmed spectacles that sat on his wide nose like an ornament and picked out the Englishman at the far end. Sitting across from him, he placed his briefcase on the table, ordered a Jack Daniels and before long they were clinking glasses, launching into relaxing banter, laughing and glad-handing before lunch. However, before long, their faces constricted as they dove into more serious matters.

"Damn it to hell, Ted! What the arse you wuz thinking?" began Cunningham, slamming the table with a closed fist. "You read today's *Chronicle*? You wanna start another blasted riot against wunna people like in 1937? This whole island up in arms."

"Well, as I told the Superintendent, I believe it is Fate that got me into this bloody mess actually," said the Englishman casually.

The barrister pounced from his chair, gesticulating with both hands in the Englishman's face. "Man, don' talk shite! Fate ent had nuttin to do with you shooting this David what's-his-name up a tree goin' after a kite. De laws o' Buhbaydus don' care one shite 'bout Fate." It was the very same tune the Superintendent of Police had sung to Thorne, though not half as profanely. As one of the young white-jacketed waiters wandered within earshot, Cunningham lowered his voice and leaned forward even closer so that his face was inches from the Englishman's nose. "You know dis boy?"

"I wasn't shooting at a boy."

Among his white peers Barrister Cunningham wore the Bajan dialect like a tattered suit; he used it to boast that he knew the other world more intimately and could relate to it more readily than any of the rest in his white circle because he had come from that other world. But when the occasion required, his English could be formal and impeccable, his elocution unmatched by any of his learned friends; though, depending on his surroundings, he could switch back and forth with the adaptive fluidity of a chameleon. His English had been properly structured under the tutelage of British professors during his four years at Harrison College, his pronunciation was later polished in the halls of the University of Oxford, and afterwards, honed and pitted to sound more natural, less affected, by mingling with the hard-bitten after-work crowd in English pubs in Oxford, like the Cock and Camel on George Street.

An only child, he came from humble beginnings. His mother used to take in laundry and scrub the white people's bungalow floors in White Park. His father cleaned out toilets for a living and could be seen in those early years wending his way home in the evening, hunched over at the helm of his donkey cart laden with buckets and shovels. Until young Virgil Cunningham was in his early teens, he was never quite sure of his father's line of work, though he always wondered about the earthy acidic smell that followed the old man home every evening like a miasmic curse. The searing stench filled the whole of their tiny wooden house; it permeated the partitions, the floor, the curtains, the clothes, the beds. It even followed him to school every day, infused in his nostrils and brain, revolting his teachers, at times compelling his classmates to pinch their noses in his presence. Nevertheless, his father made good money in those days; there was little competition in his line of work, and not having other children among whom to diffuse his savings, was able to put his boy through the best schools, feed him and clothe him as respectably as any father could, until his son was able to trim his own sails and go off to England and to Oxford University as a Rhodes Scholar. Before being called to the Bar, young Virgil studied British Law at the feet of the renowned legislator, criminologist and author, Sir Malcolm Foxworthy.

He returned to Barbados years later, a stipulation of the scholarship, and began his practice, becoming one of the most successful Barbadian lawyers of his day. Those early years growing up on Passage Road were purposely banished from his mind, though in the dead of night he sometimes heard the screeching of his father's donkey cartwheels as he made his way home from the shit pits around St. Michael, and the memory would surface like the sting of an ulcer. He never spoke of those years but supported his parents when they were alive, though he did so from a distance. He was never seen in their presence until the night he saw his father comatose and lying on a stretcher in a public ward of the General Hospital. The old man must have spent his last days questioning how and when did he manage to offend his only son. Perhaps his sin was to have brought Virgil into a world so vastly different, so black, so underprivileged, and so much more devoid of promise than the life he had grown to love in those nine years in England.

With his recent political ambitions Virgil Cunningham had played the game well; he had one foot planted to one extent or another in each camp of the elite and of the working-class. His third and current wife was an English lady, a real lady, the former Lady Maybrook, who had once been married to the famed Lord Maybrook, a British Member of Parliament. Virgil finagled his way into the role of legal counsel to the working-class Stevedore Union, so no one could fairly question his impartiality. He possessed one of the sharpest legal minds, unequalled anywhere on the island, and indeed throughout the Caribbean. In the courtroom he knew how to bamboozle both judge and jury: he was a master at chicanery. It was rumoured that he once shredded a pivotal document in the presence of an adversarial lawyer, evidence that would likely exculpate his own defendant, only to secretly recover it from the trash and piece it together again like a completed jigsaw. Next day in court he produced the reassembled document to an awestricken opponent as though he were a magician.

"You know I running fer de House, right?" he now asked the Englishman. It was a rhetorical question; everyone knew he was running. "Representing a white man that just kill a lil unarmed black boy, that ent goin' sit well wid Bajans in general. This could hobble my blasted campaign or destroy it altogether. I already up against that bastard radical Trotman from de Workers' Union. Damn communist as he is." (Fitzgerald Trotman, the solicitor, was his political nemesis.) "You had to be a blasted fool, Ted, a dumb arse fer a Englishman!"

There was a break in the diatribe as the waiter approached with lunch. Afterwards the Englishman bowed his head contritely, contemplating his dissected lobster as if indecisive about the propriety of eating while under interrogation, or whether he should remind the inquisitor that he was out of place. He was unaccustomed to being accosted or accused. In his world he was the one who barked the orders, who demanded the answers, who never in his life had had a black man throw incendiary language in his face. He resented it now, even though the flamethrower today was a man he knew and respected, a person he desperately needed, a man on whom his own life might depend. But there was something wrong with this picture: a black man berating a powerful denizen of this colonial society—and in public. This unlikely confrontation was drawing the attention of other patrons in the Club. It grated his pride, the pride of a white man with more money than this black barrister sitting before him could hope to earn in ten lifetimes of law practice in Barbados. It was a pride that automatically threw up a firewall to protect his ego from the insolence of this black inquisitor. He could choose from his inner circle a dozen other lawyers to defend him but none would suffice; he needed to be represented by a black man, a "good" Bajan lawyer like Virgil. But enough was enough! He removed the napkin from his lap, flung it on the table and sprang to his feet.

"Whoa, hold it right there, ole chap!" he shot back. "You think I'm bloody well capable of killing a human, much less a lad in cold blood? I'm an honourable Englishman, not one of your criminal countrymen!"

Cunningham could see the obstinacy and the indignation flaming in the Englishman's eyes. Had he been faced with different stakes, he would have risen at that moment, picked up his briefcase, walked away and left the man to stew in the mire of his own arrogance. But he needed Thorne as much as Thorne needed him. He had already cast his lot with Thorne's people, the rich and powerful. He was their advisor, the one they called on in everyday matters, albeit in mundane cases like acquisitions, deeds and divorces, but never a case of murder, one far from the killing of an innocent black youth, the consequences of which could be cataclysmic on this small island of Barbados. He was their hired hand across the negotiating table, appeasing the aggrieved and placating the powerless. In turn, they were his wealthy clientele, his bread and butter; they made him rich, paid him handsomely to protect their interests, welcomed him into their midst almost as one of their own— almost, but not quite. Though he saw himself as English as any one of them, in reality he would always be kept on the fringe of their core privileges.

"Man, sit down fer Chrissake! Let's start from the beginning." Cunningham switched to his lawyerly line of questioning and now to the Queen's English, reaching for his briefcase and Parker pen. "How did you come to have a gun in your hand on the morning in question?"

"Well alright, let me explain," said Thorne, taking his seat again. "The mango trees on the property are all along the guard wall, on me side of the wall of course, next to the goat shed and the nursery." On a paper napkin he sketched with his lawyer's pen a rough map of the guard wall and the orchard. "Sweetest Julie mangoes you could find anywhere in town. Goddard's Food Emporium pays me ten dollars a bag. You would not believe the amount of mangoes I get from one tree alone when I send the gardener up a tree with a couple o' crocus bags. Anyway, there used to be a time when the wild boys down in the village would climb the wall and raid the trees until I put an end to that with some glass spikes all along the wall that would cut into even the hardest shoe sole. Sometimes at night I would be lying in bed and I would hear a squealing like a bloody pig at the wall, and I would look out in time to see one of the rascals limping away and back down the hill, cursing and howling in pain, crying out like a friggin' fox caught in a coil-spring trap." He chuckled and took a drag on his Sherlock Holmes pipe. A thread of smoke curled up from the bowl like an evil genie. "That was bad enough til the bloody monkeys, capuchins that come across from St. George, from the country—don't tell me you don't know what a capuchin is, Virgil—anyway, they decided to invade the property. The wall didn't mean a bloody thing to them. They could swing from tree to tree and from branch to branch and drop down like a platoon o' black paratroopers. The next thing I know, the whole yard is full of half-eaten mangoes and seeds and slimy skins and just a mess. You would have to see it yourself, I can't describe it. So that is when I had to do something about it. I went down to the wine cellar where I keep me gun rack, unlocked it, took out me old Remington two-inch-bore and leaned it by the back door next to the wooden stairway facing the mango trees. If I could take out one or two of the little devils, the others would get the hint. You know wha' ah mean?"

It was the barrister's turn to get a word in. "You still didn't answer my question. How did you come to have a gun in your hand on the morning in question?"

"I'm getting there. Hold your horses, mate!" He paused to collect his thoughts. "I'm on the landing, about to go down the stairway, down to the goat shed. I like to feed the four goats meself in the morning. This way, I know what they're eating and I know what kinda milk I'm drinking. I only drink goat milk and only from me own goats, you see. Cow milk gives me the runs, if you know wha' ah mean. All of a sudden, I glance up and there is a black object halfway up the tallest mango tree inside the wall. Jesus Christ, Virgil! How was I to know he wasn't one o' them blinkin' capuchins on me property? Me and the Superintendent of Police know well about this problem with the monkeys here in Barbados. Ask him!"

Cunningham began to take notes.

"What time was it?"

"I dunno. Ten, ten-thirty."

"Was it raining?"

"No, but windy; the rain came later; there was a bloody hurricane on the way."

"Cloudy?"

"No."

"Any smoke in the air from cane fires anywhere in the area?"

"Not that I could see."

"Were you drinking?"

"Blimey! Why would I be drinking at ten in the morning?"

"Any witnesses? How about the servants?"

"Now, let me see…" He checked off the servants on his fingers. "Marcella, me housekeeper, she was in the hencoop out back feeding the pullets. The two gardeners, Mr. Marshall and Sampson, were still asleep. Coreen, the maid, was in the kitchen. Collymore, the boy that took over from Ben Carson, was in the stable securing the horses. And Cuthbert, the driver, was in town getting a tune-up on the Jag. The rest of the servants were looking after their own. So, the answer is no."

"And yer daughter?"

"Penelope was in bed sleeping. Had a late night."

"She didn't hear the shots?"

"You don't know me daughter. Strong sleeper, y'know. Especially after a few drinks." He chuckled again.

"And the servants didn't come running at the sound of the shots?"

"Not at all. They're used to me shooting blackbirds in the trees, a little practice off the range, getting me eye in for the season."

"When did you realize your mistake?"

"Right away, but I was not about to go out there and be skinned alive by a bunch o' black people, you know wha' ah mean? I ducked inside and waited for the worst."

"And the worst is?" asked the barrister. And then he proceeded to answer his own question. "De worse is that your white arse is goin' be strung up in Glendairy fer killing an innocent chile that you mistake fer a capuchin. Dat is de worse."

The Englishman showed him a flattering smile. "And that is why I'm retaining you to save my skin, Virgil. Because you, my friend, are the best. Name your fee and it's yours."

Cunningham closed his briefcase, flung his own napkin on the table and the two parted without a handshake.

As the barrister wheeled his bright-red ostentatious Studebaker with the whitewall tyres past the guardhouse of the Water Club and out the gate, he was bothered. First, he wondered what change of heart had caused him to engage the Englishman when his original intention was to have lunch with the man and then decline the case. Then something odd about the story began to gnaw at his common sense. There was something missing. The Englishman's story was flawed. He needed to put his finger on that one piece of the jigsaw in order to put this case together in any kind of plausible context that could be put before a judge and jury, without which he could not be sure that Thorne could be found innocent of murder, if indeed murder turned out to be the charge. Every conceivable path of reasoning led him back to the inescapable fact: the boy was shot in the act of recovering a kite, according to *The Chronicle* and the people on the street. That he was mistaken for a monkey stealing mangoes, on a clear sighting, by an accomplished gunman, without a single warning shot, made no sense. Compounding the absurdity was the timing of it all: in the hours leading up to the storm when the whole island was bracing for the most devastating hurricane in almost two hundred years, why would anyone be shooting at a monkey in a tree? True, the law defended every man's right to defend his property, but in what circumstances, and to what extent?

Then there was the whole notion of approximating the boy to a monkey, for such an aspersion was cast in private by many a white racist. The analogy would have been merely self-deprecating, even laughable, had it come from a black man like himself, but the insult from the lips of the Englishman cut like a knife, for the white man was relegating not only the boy but the barrister himself to a lower order of species when he, a British-educated and cultured black man, knew that beneath his black skin he was equal to any Englishman. But putting aside his own personal resentment, what other excuse—as objectionable as it was—could Thorne have had for shooting the boy?

Suddenly he felt inadequate. He had never before defended a case of murder. Surely he would not let the Englishman drag him into a groundless confrontation with the law and put his reputation on the line defending the indefensible. Then there was the reality of race in the society; everywhere he turned in Barbados he would face the scorn of the working-class whose votes he was hoping to garner for the upcoming elections. His political archenemy, Trotman, would seize on this perversity of Bajan character: "tekking up fer de white man." Was Thorne with his money and the approbation of his people worth that sacrifice? In years gone by, a lawyer could pack the jury with white faces by way of some backroom machinations but in the fifties Barbados had come too far for that kind of tinkering with jurisprudence. Still, he wasn't sure if he should take on the case.

He had sat and had lunch with Teddy Thorne on a few occasions and the man was always engaging; today he was cold, frivolous and remorseless. He himself, a lawyer, who always purposely distanced his emotions from cases, had cringed at the first news of the little boy who was shot like a bird out of a tree. But there sat the Englishman today across from him, digging into his salad, chomping on his crustacean, at peace with himself. These thoughts filled him with resentment and suspicion.

All the way from the Water Club, down Bay Street, across the swing bridge, through the city and up White Park Road to his bungalow on Strathclyde Drive where a servant ran up to open the gate, he was still perplexed. He lived with his English wife, Beatrice, and his stepson, Oliver. Their home nestled among a row of old gray conservative wall-houses which, unlike working-class houses, had no interest in outdoing one another or assuming garish colours to draw attention to themselves. These houses hid behind thick juniper hedges and glass-encrusted guard walls and the only betrayal of their vanity were plaques attached to their mailboxes, all bearing idyllic house-names that likely had no relation to the occupants. They were rarely seen outside their grand homes promenading along the Drive and being neighbourly; neither did their children play outside on the road because most of the houses boasted their own tennis courts, swimming pools, backyard playgrounds and private patios. Unlike the working-class, these Strathclyde residents had no idea of who their neighbours were, neither by name nor sight; nevertheless they were psychically united in opposition to strangers, even enlisting the help of the local constabulary or hiring private watchmen to prevent the unwanted from cutting through their community on their way to and from Bridgetown. Cyrus, the dreaded patrolman, sat on his motorcycle in the dark at the entrance to the Drive, casting a wary eye on strangers. It was said that the patrolman would arrest his own mother if she ever dared to set foot on the Drive. And so, black feet would tread with caution in Strathclyde. The exceptions were the maids marked by their livery, arriving at six in the morning, leaving at nine at night, and the gardeners who kept their front lawns and hedges exquisitely manicured.

There had been much rumbling the day the bi-racial couple moved in, though it was known that the husband was a Bajan lawyer of some acclaim and his wife was none other than the former Lady Maybrook. But that mattered little to the Strathclydians; even a single drop of black blood in this milky white suburban community would augur irreversible change and open the floodgates for "whosoever will." For some time after the family took possession of their new home, the watchmen were confused by the sight of Virgil Cunningham wheeling his

Studebaker onto Strathclyde Drive and would stand gawking incredulously as he turned down his long private driveway.

He now called out to his wife, a rather plain-featured, plump Englishwoman in a frumpy, unflattering frock. She looked four or five years his senior. Even with the wherewithal to hire any number of gardeners, here she was, knee-deep in her rose garden next to the stable that housed her two Arabian thoroughbreds. She quickly dropped her pruner, shed her hat and gloves, and hurried to join her husband on the patio, anxious to know how his meeting went with Thorne. Given her prior station in British circles as the wife of a British lord, and judging now from her inelegant appearance and down-to-earth demeanour, she looked to be one who had been surrounded all her life by snobbish aristocracy but remained unimpressed and unspoiled by it. How ironic that her husband of humble beginnings clung to the same hauteur that she now more than likely despised! Could it be that she now preferred to be closer to Caribbean people of different walks while her husband, a Bajan by birth, chose only the company of white people and of his own social standing?

They had met some years before over a legal transfer of some prized land in St. James, previously her ex-husband's. Barbados, redolent of all things English, offered her a window of escape from the suffocation of all that prior upper-class nobility without sacrificing any of the cultural niceties of English living. Certainly there was now an overabundance of honest, respectful and hardworking servants at her disposal, unmatched by the pool of unionized English servants on whom she had depended all her life. Neither would she miss the verdant rolling hills and lush landscape of the English countryside; that very same rusticity was right here in Barbados, ready-made for her enchantment in St. Andrews and St. Joseph and St. John. One could well imagine her in the quiet of late evenings, lying in bed and hearing in the distance Big Ben in Trafalgar Square mimicking the same familiar chimes that had been infused in her brain from small, and feeling her national pride swell as the local *Rediffusion* station, in this tiny corner of the Commonwealth bade goodnight every night to the Queen's faithful subjects with "God Save the Queen."

THERE ONCE WAS A LITTLE ENGLAND

Her weekends were spent at the all-white Carlton Cricket Club in Black Rock with friends from her Sorority. It was not that she minded an integrated cricket club like Wanderers or Spartan, or Pickwick with its Bajan-white skipper; but seeing all those Bajan-white cricketers on the green in their whites, down to the white water boys, would transport her to her old county cricket grounds in Lancashire with Lord Maybrook, watching a closely contested match against those prolific, coloured, colourful West Indian players who were bussed up from Brixton. And then there was always tea in the afternoons at Carlton with those neat delectable sandwiches with the crust cut away for extra daintiness; all of that went a long way in completing the home-away-from-home feeling. That is, until some raucous uncultured voice from the bleaches would burst out and break the decorum with: "Man, hit de ball, nuh!" and she would remember she was in her adopted Little England and laugh with the crowd.

Their marriage was solid. Opportunism had held them closer and much more tenaciously than all the vows that for a time had bound their previous three marriages, his and hers. She was her husband's gateway to a clientele of rich merchants and planters on the island, also his ticket to moderate wealth, money she had salvaged from the wrecks of her divorces and was now willing to share with this brilliant Barbadian barrister. He in turn was her shining badge of social enlightenment, a spiteful stick in the eyes of all those snobbish English friends and compatriots back home, all the way from Members of Parliament to bigoted narrow-minded commoners who held to their purebred standards that miscegenation would destroy all of civilization.

"So, darling, how did it go today with ole Ted?" Her voice had a mischievous lilt as if ole Ted had been the butt of many a joke. They were sitting on the back patio over an afternoon cup of tea, cucumber sandwiches and miniature fruit tarts. She had read about the shooting in *The Chronicle* and chatted on the telephone with her Sorority friends about the whole sad affair. She knew that if her husband decided to represent Thorne, she would be seen to be obliquely involved and many would surely rally around the Englishman. "Well, the boy was trespassing, wasn't he?" some would say. "This case should never come to court."

Her husband was hungry. He had barely touched his plate of fish stew and cornmeal dumplings at the Club; vexation had blunted his appetite. He told her, as he chomped on his cucumber sandwich, "I made sure de cheapskate buy me lunch."

"Well, what did he have to say?" she asked.

"De man is a madmun! Shooting off a gun in a tree in broad daylight just before de storm hit. He would have to be insane as shite."

"But why? And what about the boy's mother and father, my heart goes out to them," she said, appealing to his softer side. "Suppose it were Oliver, and he was shot by one of our racist neighbours that don't even speak to us, like the Beaumonts?"

He didn't answer; he never let raw emotions cloud his tactical thinking and never bled for victims unless they were his clients. Nor did she expect an answer; she was familiar with the lawyer's psyche; her first husband too was an English barrister.

She prodded: "Did he tell you how he managed to shoot the boy? Was he half-blind or plain drunk?"

"Somet'ing 'bout a mango tree and monkeys climbin' up de tree and mekking a mess wid mango skins and seeds all over de yard, mekking he life miserable as if he wuzn't miserable to begin wid. He say de Police Chief tell 'im he could shoot dem anytime, anyplace. Mistakin' de boy fer a kiss-me-arse monkey."

"What mango tree? What monkeys? My word, Virgil! The mango season was over in July. All the trees are bare … I tell you, bare! Barbados monkeys would never climb a mango tree unless the tree was full of mangoes." Astonishment peaked in her voice as if she thought her husband might be entering the first phase of dementia; it was common knowledge that the mango season was long over. "Are you sure he said it was a mango tree?"

So stunned was he at his own stupidity that the last sip of tea sputtered from his mouth and sprayed his shoes and the floor at his feet. He slapped his leg, enraged at the deception. "That blasted conniving liar!" he shouted and leapt to his feet. It was the missing piece that was nagging him all the way home from the Club: there were no mangoes and therefore there could not have been a single monkey in the tree. Thorne had spun a scenario that never existed and his own wife just now discounted the theory of mistaken identity on which Thorne had wanted him to base his defence. He was livid and embarrassed.

On further reflection it was not the lie itself that so angered the barrister but that he was not consulted beforehand. Moreover, he thought the lie was not sufficiently ingenious. "God knows," he said, "I base many a defence in my lifetime on a lil white lie or two, but this is de most dumb-arse lie I ever hear." Moreover, he was disappointed that Thorne had not come to him first but instead to the Police and that he had not solicited his help in the fabrication. "After all," he said to himself, "a defence strategy, whether built on truth or untruth, whether worthy or without merit, must be jointly devised between lawyer and client, rehearsed and tested for credibility and kept secret until the moment of judgment." He would no doubt have rejected out of hand the monkey story the Englishman had so carefully constructed in the privacy of his study. Now it was too late. It didn't matter that from the beginning he had no intentions of getting involved; to him it was now a matter of principle, not a principle of morals but one of competency.

Unlike her husband, Beatrice was stung by the depravity of it all; her face crinkled in disgust. Why would Thorne train the crosshairs of his rifle on an innocent boy and afterwards concoct a story about a mango tree that in truth and in fact was out of season and incapable of tempting neither human nor monkey? As much as she found the whole thing abhorrent, it was not her wish that he be hanged for the crime, for such a fate would lower the penal bar for all white citizens. And so her contempt for Thorne was superseded by concern for the good white people of Barbados now stuck in the collective craw of the working-class majority who would seek wholesale revenge on account of this one Englishman's hideous crime. She feared less for him than she feared for those good white people of whom she was one; she felt betrayed, offended and undermined by her fellow countryman, this odious creature among them who decided to rock the boat just when blacks and whites were beginning to sail on a sea of calm. She was angry and fearful.

For the rest of the afternoon as they dressed and prepared to attend a cocktail party at the Governor's residence, she and her husband fussed and fumed and argued about whether he should even think about defending this man. In the end, he decided he would not. On the way to the Governor's reception, she tried and failed to rid her mind of morbid thoughts, like of death and blood and hanging that could hover like a pall over the rest of the evening. After all, it was a night meant for jollity and reunion with old friends.

Government House, at the base of Government Hill, outside the city, hid behind a high wall encrusted with glass spikes all along the top of the wall. At the entrance to the long tree-lined driveway stood the uniformed sentry, stiff as an obelisk next to his guardhouse. His unloaded bayoneted rifle was always at his side. In the long history of Government House there had never been an intruder who attempted to scale the wall or get past the sentry, yet this illusion of alertness had to be maintained at all times. The house was far from palatial or showy, built in the mould of official colonial residences that denied any hint of imperialistic thought. Every British viceroy from Captain John Powell onwards, reaching back to the initial colonization in 1627, must have thought himself blessed to be commissioned to preside over such a peaceful, welcoming and accommodating people as Barbadians, no more fortunate than the select few to have recently found in their mailboxes the Governor's gold-rimmed invitation to one of his rare receptions.

The political landscape in Barbados was changing; there were new voices in the shifting winds; they were louder and more strident than ever before; they were calling for a new direction. Undercurrents of discontent with the colonial structure and the imbalance between the working-class and the ruling powers had given rise to a new socially conscious Party back in April that year. Their message was clear: from this day forward there would be a concerted moving away from the old colonial mindset, a scaling down of procedural power and eventually a total disengagement from the planter-mercantile stronghold that had gripped the island for hundreds of years. There was much concern. What did it all portend for the small band of the upper-class, those who now held the reins of economic and political power; those in whose hands lay the destiny of every man, woman and child; those who were now filing into the Governor's reception with little else on their minds than the shifting ground under their feet?

THERE ONCE WAS A LITTLE ENGLAND

Cunningham was along for the ride with one thing on his mind: to confront Thorne, who was sure to be present, to pull the boldfaced prevaricator aside, look him straight in the eyes and tell him in the vilest terms that he was no longer his lawyer, that the game was up, that he was wise to his invention. He and his wife made their way up the steps, into the foyer and stood in line to await their formal introduction. As the couple smiled graciously at the entrance to the parlour, the greeter emptied his lungs. "Ladies and Gentlemen, our esteemed guests, Barrister-at-Law Cunningham and Mrs. Cunningham!" They then stepped forward to mingle with the Governor's guests. They were all people they knew from the endless rounds of cocktail parties throughout the year, elitist parties held in exclusive neighbourhoods like Sandy Lane and Belleville and Hastings and Fontabelle and various neighbourhoods of the Gold Coast of St. James, in the ritzy homes of the Goddards and the Birminghams and the Fodringhams and the Cheltenhams and on occasion in the lavish mansion of the Thornes. Most were pillars of the planter and mercantile class. Some were expatriates, or the sons and daughters of expatriates born and bred in Barbados. Some were English, some Irish, some Scottish, and some who had made it into the realms of sports and politics. Some were on temporary contracts with the Government, working in the fields of their expertise: academia, agriculture, horticulture, architecture, engineering, chemistry and all the various sciences, schooling their apprentices to one day take over and become torch bearers shedding light in dark places. These latter folk had so completely melded into the Barbadian landscape that they now walked, talked, danced, cursed, swore and laughed like Bajans, betrayed only by their sunburned skins. But alas, some were impostors, hangers-on and freeloaders, some poor as church mice.

Besides Virgil Cunningham, the only black faces in the Governor's reception parlour were those of the servers. They stood in the dark against the walls, unobtrusive, silent, and nameless, and were only seen when they drifted in and out of the light like moths. Their eyes could spot an empty glass a mile away or tables running low of caviar canapés, codfish balls with tamarind sauce, crab claws with curried onion dip, spicy beef patties, flying fish melts and chicken strips. Above the din, their trained ears could detect the shattering of breaking glass and be on the spot in the blink of an eye with broom and scoop, or with a rag mop when some drunken, slobbering fool had had too many free drinks and puked in the centre of the Governor's oriental hand-knotted rug. Their faces were always expressionless, never smiling at a joke that reached the ear or wincing at an overheard racist slur. The women servers were dressed in black with contrasting white aprons and white gloves, and each head bore a maid's tiara-like cap pinned to the hair above the forehead. The men servers were less adorned: white gloves and dinner jackets.

To be in the presence of His Excellency the Governor, a heavyset bearded moustachioed man with an uncanny resemblance to King George IV, was in itself a rare treat. And so, the barrister, seeking to bask in the company of the host, found himself inching in the direction of where he stood in the middle of the room holding earnest discourse with a circle of political pundits. But when he reached within arm's length of the Governor, it became glaringly apparent that the big man would slink away as if his alleged association with Thorne had somehow tainted him with ugliness.

And now, speaking of the devil, in the corner of his eye and to the sound of his name, was the man he no longer trusted, none other than Thorne emerging from the darkened doorway and walking directly towards him, not even walking over first to greet the host. His daughter, Penelope, bespectacled, slim and tall like her father, accompanied him. She was met with smiles of familiarity and therefore needed no introduction. No one had ever seen her in the company of any other but her father, and now as she passed under the fluorescent lights of the entryway her sour face betrayed the expectation of another boring night in the company of incompatible and older men. Daringly dressed in burgundy open-toed shoes, crimson-red suede jacket and pleated blue skirt that clashed irreverently with all the surrounding formal evening wear, she was in fact the youngest and the most conspicuous of the Governor's guests.

"Virgil, I need to have a word with you," began the Englishman in a tone that was at once confrontational and fearful. "Shall we step into the antechamber?" They followed. "Me daughter earlier today reminded me that there were no mangoes in the tree that morning, you see. The tree was bare, actually, bare as a lamppost. I swear to God, in me mind's eye, believe it or not, the tree was full of mangoes that morning and there was a monkey up that tree ... but only in me imagination. I have come to the conclusion, Virgil, that it was me own subconscious. That is the result of being haunted by these bloody monkeys all season. Look here, Virgil! It was only after I pulled the trigger and I saw the body fall and bounce off the wall, that I realized ... Oh God! I made a dreadful mistake, it must be a young lad! I dropped the goddamn gun, ran to the bathroom and puked me guts out. I was sick as a dog. Ask Marcella." A pained expression creased his face as he proceeded to wring his hands.

Marcella was his cook and concubine of many years since the untimely death of Mrs. Thorne. Other than Penelope, his own blood, the one in his corner would be faithful Marcella Montmartre, the Martiniquen. She guarded his secrets well, and he in turn gave her full rein of the household. He had already told the Superintendent of Police she was nowhere in sight and now forestalled the barrister in his tracks by immediately admitting to a delusional misjudgement, cloaking the lie in hallucination, thereby denying Cunningham the sheer pleasure of exposing his wilful lying.

"I know so all along, Ted. I know all along that de tree wuz bare." Cunningham lied. It was his wife who had uncovered the plot. He asked, "So on what grounds should we base your defence? Temporary insanity, schizophrenia, or hatred of animals?"

Penelope winced at the sarcasm and stepped forward to defend her father. She was already on her second glass of champagne, which surely had accounted for her increasingly sanguine complexion and the fire in her eyes.

"Lemme make somet'ing clear," she snarled, "my father did not mean to kill David Prince. He loves children. He saw a monkey in the tree. It was real in his imagination. And on top o' dat, de lil boy wuz trespassing. Fer Chrissake, spare me yer bleeding hearts!"

It was clear that Bajan dialect habitually and wilfully crept in, corrupting her breeding of proper diction. At her alma mater, the all-white St. Winifred's Girls School, she had been taught to refrain from the way Bajans mangled the language, to stick to the Queen's English and to suppress those singsong inflections that belonged to the uncultured masses. But this was her way to connect with the people, to shed the image of the rich Englishman's daughter who had no feelings for the underclass and the dispossessed, as if the dialect itself qualified her to be on the same social plane.

Beatrice felt chafed by Penelope's lack of feeling for the boy. She lashed back at her, looking past Thorne as if he were a waxed replica of himself. "Dearie, if your father had fired a warning shot in the air, he would've scared the beJesus out o' the boy and he would've been scared off the property and today we would have more sympathy now for your father and far less for the boy."

"Beatrice, don' be daft! Warning shots don' scare monkeys," Penelope shot back scornfully, seeing that the barrister's wife was determined not to accept her father's story. Then she turned to her husband, modulating her tone to a sweet ingratiating plea. "You know my father as well as anybody, you are his friend and he thinks the world of you as a person and a legal mind." Then she again switched to the dialect of the masses. "Dat is why we axing you to tek on dis case, Mr. Cunningham. People in Inglund that don' even know my father on de phone every minute offerin' moral support fer dis case. It is only because you is one of us that we axe you to represent him, nobody else but you, Mr. Cunningham."

Before her husband could respond, Beatrice saw an opportunity to interject her own misgivings about her husband's involvement. Her hazel eyes narrowed with suspicion and her words were sopping with contempt. She sought to set forth on his behalf a premise for his defence of Thorne and to make it clear her husband would never proceed without his wife's assent.

"The only reason my husband would take this case would be to defend, not just *your* father, but all of us, because if your father is found guilty of this felony, as he damn well will be, he will be the first white person on this island ever to go to the gallows. After he is dead and gone, the same fate awaits any white person accused of such a crime. So it is not only about *your* father, it's about a precedent that will forever haunt all of us."

As the Governor's guests trickled through the antechamber, nodding and waving to the two couples but not intruding into their heated space, the men stood silent and motionless as the two women parried and prodded, both wanting to save Thorne from the ultimate penalty but with different motives and priorities, one, to simply save her father's life and the other, to preserve unbroken for her people a record that had prevailed for a hundred years in the archives of Her Majesty's Law Courts.

Penelope was less than pleased with Beatrice's demoting the sparing of her father's life to the cause of a speculative future. She swiped another glass of champagne from a passing tray and braced herself to retaliate. "Well, pardon me! At de present time it is damn well about *my* father. And what precedent you talkin' 'bout? Lemme tell you somet'ing 'bout de future o' dese colonies. Federation comin' soon to de Caribbean and when that day come and dese islands unite, Buhbaydus, Trinidad, Jamaica, and de rest, de whole slate of precedents will be erased. Justice hey in Buhbaydus ent goin' pay nuh mind to precedents, you hear? What is white justice today will become black justice and black justice will become white justice. De tables will turn and new laws will be put in place that will avenge de way that black people wuz treated down through de years. Judges and juries will take history into account. So, my dear Beatrice, today is still our day and today is our best chance to get my father off, based on whatever your husband come up with as a defence."

Cunningham nodded to both women to lend his enormous weight of approval to both arguments. Penelope's impassioned pleas had changed his mind; he would defend her father. He jutted his chin subtly in the direction of the parlour and to the sound of merriment. He was ready to join the party.

But his wife had one more thing to say, wagging a pointed finger of reproach at Thorne. "Let us not forget that whether it was an accident or not, a subconscious act or not, whether the boy was trespassing or not, whether the trees were full of mangoes or not, somewhere tonight in that village there is a father and a mother heartbroken because you, Theodore Thorne, took away their flesh and blood. And for that, a price will have to be paid. The only question is: What price?" She searched his face for a trace of remorse or shame and saw none.

They left the dimly lit antechamber and strolled into the bright lights of the parlour, ignoring the stares they drew from those who knew their story. Thorne was sheepish and subdued while Cunningham sank into his accustomed sullen disposition. The two women sat side by side with their glasses of champagne, smiling and civil again in a truce of desultory conversation. Moments before, they had traversed a bed of flaming red-hot coals from opposite ends but had walked away unscathed and holding hands. They needed each other; white women were a minority within a minority and they could sense that their own powerful and unscrupulous men were slowly and reluctantly ceding power, like the haemorrhaging of an endangered and dying species.

As was often the case at these elitist parties when the men would find themselves drifting to one side of the room pulled by the gravity of their own machismos, and their wives would be left alone to form their own mutual admiration circles, so it was that night at Government House. There was no danceable music to inspire the intermingling of the sexes or at least to lighten the air. It was a night of heavy, dreary conversation broken by an occasional ripple of laughter and the repetitive cheers of "Hear! Hear!" His Excellency the Governor and his aide, in their roles as gracious hosts, were busy shuttling from one side to the other of the capacious hall when conversations would wane to inaudible whispers as they approached each table, then rise again in their presence with a loud round of courtesies.

Thorne and Cunningham, finally rid of the two contentious women and buoyed by the company of men, were now able to talk freely among themselves about the way forward.

"Don' pay those women any mind," Cunningham said disdainfully. "I let dem lick dey mout' but they don' know nuttin' 'bout de laws." With the guests milling around them, he twisted his mouth like a ventriloquist's in the direction of Thorne and confided in his ear a rudimentary rule in criminal defence strategy. "De people want yer neck to swing from a blasted noose, you know that! You's de face o' every livin' and dead white man on dis island that ever offend a black person. Well, de Crown will appease de people and shoot fer a charge o' murder, which is a state of mind known in de profession as 'malice aforethought'. Manslaughter would get you off light, which is less culpable than murder, but de Crown goin' overstate de case and end up wid nuttin'. Why? Because dis is a case o' mistaken identity. Dis t'ing goin' mitigate to what is known in de profession as 'diminished responsibility'. We have to use de monkey and your state of mind at de time o' de shooting. You goin' have to prove to de court that you wuz sufferin' from what we call in de profession 'an abnormality of mind'. But fer Chrissake, Ted, don' be bringin' up no kiss-me-arse mangoes in de court. Monkeys hey in Buhbaydus know de fruit seasons better than Bajans. If anyt'ing, there wuz a blasted monkey in de tree, maybe dis monkey got lost, I don' know, but in your mind he wuz right there in de tree looking at you, you hear me?"

Thorne leaned over and placed his lips close to his attorney's ear. "Tell me, mate, how much time are we talking about for this what you call 'abnormality of mind?' How many months would you say?" The barrister showed him all five fingers on his right hand and one on his left and said not another word.

The men guests swooped over and suddenly the two men were swallowed up in a pack of backslapping well-wishing friends, acquaintances and even strangers. "Ted, we are all behind you, ole chap," slobbered an old man, who they recognized from his clerical collar as a vicar from St. John, and who looked surprisingly inebriated, given the early hour. "Keep calm, my friend," he said, "the Privy Council in London will never let an Englishman go to the gallows. We British have been squeamish about capital punishment ever since Henry the Second had the Archbishop of Canterbury hacked to death." They all laughed.

The barrel-chested, cigar-chomping Tom Atkinson, head of the Barbados Mercantile Association, his thumbs hooked in his suspenders, weighed in with a clichéd phrase of encouragement: "Well Ted, ole chap, as the saying goes, 'a man's home is his castle' and his property must be defended at all times." Tom's home was literally a castle in the parish of St. Philip where he leased an entire floor of the fabled Sam Lords Castle by the sea.

The potbellied Todd Larson, descendant from a long line of English planters, born and bred on the island and inheritor of vast acres of cane fields, approached the men with a Lucky Strike hanging from a corner of his mouth. He began to speak from experience in the dialect of his upbringing.

THERE ONCE WAS A LITTLE ENGLAND

"I goin' tell you that all o' last year's crop, I lost sixteen tons o' ripe juicy canes ready fer de mill, all because o' a few tiefing niggas—excuse me, Barrister Cunningham!—that would hide in de cane piece at night, tie up bundles o' canes that wuz on de ground ready fer de lorry next mornin' and carr' dem way just like that. Next mornin' when de lorry turn up, all de field bare, bare, bare. Y'all t'ink I jokin'? One mornin' broad daylight, s'help me God, I drivin' by one o' my cane piece and I see dis fella grab a nice juicy cane stalk wid both hands, raise a knee in de air, brek de cane on he knee, and start suckin' it right in my face. So I call my overseer to chase dis man outta my cane field, and you don' know de boy grab de cowskin from de overseer, pull he down off de horse and almost kill he wid blows? I had did to get back in my motorcar and take off cause I did know that dis fella wuz ignorant. Nowadays, dese young niggas in Buhbaydus—excuse me again, Barrister!—don' give a hoot 'bout nobody property."

And so, all night they encircled the embattled Englishman, unaware of the monkey fabrication, each man stepping forward to gladly support the morality of his cause and the justification of his deed. Only the Governor remained above it all, uninvolved in the conversations that swirled around the two men. It was late in the party when he casually approached Thorne and, alluding to the loss of the late Mrs. Thorne, asked, "Ted, how's life these days in that great big house on the hill?"

Without a hint of uncertainty in his voice, he replied, "Swimmingly, Your Excellency, swimmingly."

Then the Governor stepped up to the podium and called his guests to attention. It was time to address the matter at hand, the implicit reason these pillars of the society were assembled at Government House: to ponder the future of the powerful in a land of an increasingly restless and restive majority.

Cissy Brathwaite awoke to a long insistent knocking at her front door. She felt on the other side of the bed for Harold but he was gone. Lately he had been escaping to Brandons Beach for hours, sometimes for the whole day, weary of the solicitousness of well-meaning neighbours and the inquisitiveness of others. She knew the visitor had to be a stranger; only strangers knocked; people she knew never knocked; they called out her name and walked right in; the front door was rarely locked. Esmay, her ever-present guardian who had stayed the night, faced the stranger, a short muscular middle-aged man with a disproportionately large head and a build that suggested a retired boxer, a heavyweight. He seemed not at all bothered by beads of perspiration that glistened on his bald head like morning dew, the mark of a busy man on an intense mission. He wore a blue-striped African dashiki, carried a worn leather portfolio underarm and flashed a broad white toothy smile. Through her bedroom door, left ajar, Cissy could see his lips unmistakably oozing condolences; then after a while, his face hardened and his eyes glared as he proceeded to explain the reason for his visit.

He called out past Esmay, "Mornin', Miss Braffit, my condolences to you and your family. My name is Mr. Trotman. I am from de Workers Union, a defender of de people, de working-class here in Buhbaydus. Miss Braffit, I come to accompany you down to de courthouse. You have de right to witness what we call de preliminary hearing and arraignment. You and de boy's father, or you alone if he is not available, but somebody got to be present fer de hearing and to hear how de Crown intends to proceed based on de evidence. Nobody is goin' kill a boy-child of this Bajan soil and get away wid it." Then his voice, seemingly emboldened by its own sound, grew more strident and climbed several more octaves. "I am here to let that vagabond that kill your son know that this is a new day in Buhbaydus." His head pivoted away from the front door and towards the house on the hill, his voice thundering across the road and up through the woods. "Buhbaydus belong to black people, you hear? And no white man 'round hey goin' pick up a gun and shoot one o' we own people like a ornery animal and t'ink they can get away wid it. Massa day dead and gone long time!" Turning back to Cissy, his voice softened. "Keep calm, Miss Braffit! We goin' see dis trigger-happy madmun get de gallows."

His words seemed to be struggling to strike the right balance between words befitting the presence of the two women and words that would give free vent to his feelings. But there was no holding back when he referred to that certain city lawyer who would defend her son's killer. His contempt broke all boundaries of discretion as he launched an explosion of wild profanities. And then in true pugilistic posture, he clenched his fists and punched the air. He ended with the prophecy: "And dat is why he goin' get his arse cut in de elections, mark my word!"

"Mr. Trotman, come in and take a load off!" Esmay waved him in from the doorway, closed the door and motioned to a chair. She feared that his voice booming down the gap would soon summon another curious crowd, knowing well how Bajans in the village loved commotion. Cissy changed from her nightgown and joined them in the front house.

"Cuppa tea?" asked Esmay, removing the toothpick that had been dangling from her lips.

"No thanks, Miss. My doctor warns me to stay off de caffeine, not good fer de heart. But I'll take something hard if yuh have it."

"Well, de lady of de house have some Mount Gay. That will do?"

"Yes please. No ice, lil water on de side."

Mr. Trotman was a solicitor, but also a politician. In the gritty and hard-bitten arena of Barbadian politics, the ability to hold one's liquor was a valuable gift. It was not an art that could be instilled by practice like oratory or glibness. So gifted, Trotman would always grab the attention and earn the respect of hard-drinking fishermen and wharf men and cane cutters and rock-quarry miners and bricklayers and carpenters and bus conductors, and all those men who toiled all day in the sweltering sun, and in the evening sought the company of men who spoke the same language, who marched to the same drumbeat, whose muscles ached like theirs, whose backs were just as blistered and whose hearts and minds cried out for the solace of each other's company. They had similar stories to share and would share them over a bottle of liquor without regard to brand, from cheap Pretty Girl wine to rock-gut Babash to fine ten-year-old Cockspur rum, and the balm of sharing would soothe the pain, lift the spirits and bind them together as one. In rum shops in every corner of the island, from Bridgetown to Holetown to Speightstown to St. Lucy, Trotman would wander in and be greeted fraternally as "Trottie," and without hesitation they would pass him a glass and a flask of Jack Iron, and he would dare to bend his elbow with the biggest imbiber in the place who might still be capable of engaging him intellectually on matters of Bajan politics, and on how and when their beloved Barbados would be wrested completely from the clutches of the planter/mercantile plutocracy. It was the unending topic in every rum shop on the island.

THERE ONCE WAS A LITTLE ENGLAND

Trotman was born and raised in the rough and tumble community of New Orleans in St. Michael. In his teens, he spent one and a half years in Dodds reformatory for a petty crime that no one seemed to recall. In the library of that institution he was introduced to the principles of Law while thumbing through *Roger Colson's Introduction to Law and the Legal System*. A formal education was forced upon him in that disciplinary environment and he soon procured a government scholarship to study in Kingston. There he got his second glimpse into a career that spanned the next sixteen years when he finally found his niche in a society where justice was too often the province of the rich and those who could afford expensive lawyers. Between his boxing career and his law studies, he never rose to the level of a barrister but nevertheless devoted his life as a solicitor defending the working-class.

Now, in the company of the two women he tossed his head back, emptied a shot of rum into a corner of his mouth, swished it around from cheek to cheek, then chased it down his gullet with a gulp of water, all the while grimacing as if in some kind of masochistic pain. Wiping his mouth with the back of his hand, he now seemed recharged and ready to tell his story.

"Where was I? Oh yes, Miss Braffit, as I was saying, I stayed clear out in Jemmotts Lane where my office is, and heard about this tragedy and I swore, s'help me God, that I would come and see you to tell you that I am ready to offer my legal advice *pro bono* if you decide to entrust your cause to my legal office. De nature o' this crime got me burning inside, 'specially since I have two boys of my own from my ex-wife, one twelve and de other fifteen, both planning to enter law like de ole man. And I would like to see them grow to become honest, productive citizens and to help to move this island forward before I pass on. Your boy did not have that good fortune.

"Years ago in this here Buhbaydus, thrildren used to get their arms chop off wid a cutlass just fer pulling a few hard canes from de back of a lorry. Now they want to shoot you dead fer climbin' one o' their kiss-me-arse trees—excuse my language!—that happen to be growin' on their property and think that they can get away wid it because they got traitors like Cunningham in de legal profession that is willin' to stand up fer them and defend them in a court of law rather than takin' up de cause of his own people, and that is what is burning my arse—excuse my French again, Miss Braffit!" The alcohol had further loosened his tongue.

Mr. Trotman, a man of the soil, who knew every season of every fruit tree in Barbados, would have been fit to be tied had he known the story of the monkey in the mango tree in the month of September. When he came knocking at Cissy's door that morning, he had come to help her to avenge the killing of her boy. But he also needed her help. Election fever was gripping the land; her story was rippling far and wide across the island; he could ride that wave all the way to Election Day; it could burnish his name in every mind as the true defender of the people's rights. Cissy would be the feather in his political cap against his archenemy, Cunningham. Before returning to the business at hand, he reached for Miss Braffit's Mount Gay, poured another rum, tossed his head back and threw it down his throat. Then he stood up, grabbed his portfolio and with an air of chivalry he ushered her into the taxicab that had been waiting patiently and they headed towards Bridgetown, towards the halls of justice.

This was the solicitor's first of many visits to the home of Cissy and Harold to give her, in particular, legal advice and to caution she was up against a powerful and influential white man who might very well have the money and connections to escape the gallows. He told her how to make her case with the Crown; that her son might have been unwittingly a trespasser but on no account should be portrayed as a thief. And even so, the taking of his life was a gross injustice undeserving of any consideration of mitigation by the court. He vowed to never leave her side. But Cissy was still not assured of the outcome and as her supply of Mount Gay depleted so did her faith in lawyers and their application of Laws.

All morning, a cluster of Bajan women had been lounging expectantly along the green iron-spiked fence that girded the main courthouse, a coral-stone building on Coleridge Street, a house built in the style of the English Renaissance. Like a flock of birds bestirred by sound, the women leaning on the fence sprang to life and swarmed towards the taxicab, straining to get a good look at the woman whose name had been splashed across the pages of *The Chronicle*. They came to see the mother who had lost her boy-child at the hands of a gun-toting racist landlord up in Thornville. As she stepped out of the taxicab she was swept up into a hundred arms of giggling, gushing, cackling females thrilled to reach out and hug one of their own who was about to become their heroine, who would be their Standard Bearer of Justice, who would lead them into battle for their rights that had been withheld all these years, who would make history in Barbados with her clear-cut undeniable case of murder which would inevitably send a white man to his execution for killing one of their own sons. All through the years of serving the white man and in return being undervalued and underpaid and disrespected and under-appreciated and overlooked and overworked, finally they would get their symbolic pound of flesh because they could now unload their storehouse of resentments onto this despicable, loathsome creature, the face of all their woes, a man they didn't know personally but whom they did not need to know, because they saw in him a composite of every evil white man who ever lived on this island. As the guard waved her and her escort through the portal to the courthouse, their cries rang out:

"We love you, Cissy!"

"String he up!"

"Send he straight to de gallows!"

As she climbed the steps, Cissy, for one glorious moment, felt like a gladiator entering the arena with justice on her side, energized with the collective adrenaline of the women's bloodlust pumping through her veins. But on entering the bowels of the courthouse, she could no longer hear the women's voices as the door slammed behind her, and she found herself in a fishbowl where every man's eyes were on her, pressing upon her, examining her, these strange-looking, austere, emotionless, black-robed men wearing those fearsome white wigs. Nathaniel's deposition was read to the magistrate. She learned that the court had released the Englishman on his own recognizance. Cissy walked out of the den of legal manipulators and again into the welcoming crowd still loitering at the gate. But now seeing Cissy emerge listlessly from the courthouse, the women seemed less ready for battle, as if her expression of hopelessness had drained the enthusiasm from their faces. Somehow, she felt less assured. She knew that justice here on earth was not immutable but in the hands of mortals and their manipulable laws. She went home and decided to rest her case in the hands of a Higher Being.

Chapter 10

The Tyranny of Grief

HAROLD PRINCE had not yet shed a tear for his boy. The moment he was told that David was dead, his eyes had glistened and then quickly filled with flames. The fiery rage that had stifled the tears now possessed his whole being like an overwhelming affliction. He had battled insomnia all night and in the early morning while Cissy drifted off again to fitful slumber, he slipped out of bed, clammy with sweat, and walked slowly and robotically up to the wall in search of the spot where his son had likely fallen. He was sure he would find it.

In the faint light of early dawn, he trudged up and down along the base of the wall, around the trees, parting with his bare hands the thorny underbrush still dripping wet with morning dew and clawing aggressively at his sleeves. He felt David's restless spirit pointing the way and, sure enough, right there at his feet was a clump of mud that had been tamped with footsteps and next to it a layer of wet leaves, among them three or four leaves tainted with drops of dry blood. The shred of a kite tail was swinging in the breeze from a branch above his head and he knew then that the string of rags had to be the last thing that David touched as he tugged and tore it from the entangled kite. He reached down, gathered the bloody leaves, held them in the palm of his hand for a solemn moment, then sank to the ground and sat on the same spot where David fell. The anger that had boiled for so long inside of him welled up and an irrepressible upsurge of emotion now found release. The tears came at last.

He got up and placed both hands on the wall opposite the spot where David's blood had been spilled and then pressed his forehead on the cold hard brick as one would bend in supplication at a prayer-wall. He closed his eyes and pictured his son's last deliberate step before he took to the tree. Suddenly, the force of his body dislodged a brick from its adhesion. The storm had eaten away at the cement already weakened by age and the brick fell back to the ground offering him a window to the other side of the wall. And there he was, Thorne himself, no more than ten yards away, bent over a wooden trough of goat feed. He turned around at the sound of the fallen brick and their eyes met. Thorne called to the two Alsatians that had already started towards the wall, growling and baring their teeth. The Englishman straightened up, startled, but kept his ground, staring at the face on the other side. The dogs obeyed and retreated.

"Who are you?" he called out to the face.

Harold reached through the hole with the bloodstained leaves in the palm of his hand.

"Here, look! This is the blood of my son that you killed. You son-of-a-bitch, you killed my son!"

"Your son was trespassing," he shot back.

"So you killed him."

"We will let the court decide that … and at this moment you too are trespassing, young man."

"Well then, shoot me too! Shoot me like you shot my son … in cold blood! Here I am! Go ahead and shoot me!"

Harold could feel his heart pounding in his chest, blood surging to the outermost extremities of his hands and feet as they trembled, partially with fear, partially with helplessness and partially with the notion of scaling the wall with one leap and crossing the divide with a few bounding strides even if it meant his legs would be mangled by the two bloodthirsty dogs, as long as his own two hands could be clasped tightly around the jugular of this cold-blooded killer, unrelenting until the Englishman's blood was cut off from his evil brain, all the while that his own flesh was being torn to shreds, as long as the Englishman died in his stranglehold while the dogs butchered his own body and snuffed out his own life. Reason prevailed. Instead, he placed his other hand in the hole and pointed an index finger at the man. Then with his other fingers curled in the simulation of a revolver, all the while closing one eye and, with the other, peering over the barrel, he pulled the trigger. "Pshew!" The Englishman smirked, spat on the ground, turned around and walked away while his dogs, white foam dripping from their snarling teeth, stood barking at the face in the wall, waiting for their master's command to bound. Harold wondered if he indeed had the gall to shoot if by some wizardry a gun could have suddenly materialized in his hand. He decided that he could not; that killing another required much more than bitterness of spirit; it required a murderous heart. He just knew, however, that for the rest of that day and perhaps for many days after, his black face, framed in the hole in the wall, would stick in the Englishman's mind like a bad dream, a haunting reminder that somehow, somewhere, he would pay for his cowardly crime.

He pocketed the bloodstained leaves and started down the slope. He looked across the housetops and through the trees where he could see the ocean, blue, pure and peaceful. It called to him. He needed to calm his spirit, slow the pounding in his chest and climb down from that peak of consuming rage that threatened to cripple his capacity to reason. What better place to settle his mind than the sea? It was the beach to which he always escaped, to think, to set aside dark thoughts. Beyond the shore there was no evil, just innocent nature, unconquerable and all-powerful but innocent. He walked down the hill, past his house, through the village, down to Seclusion Road and across Black Rock and finally down to Brandons Beach.

The water was calm, at low-tide, not a single rolling wave as far as the eye could see. He took off his shoes and at the shoreline he sat hugging his knees, his toes dug into the soft white sand. A new pristine layer had been laid, new sand regurgitated by Janet during her onslaught. The whole stretch of beach was flawless save for the occasional deposit of flotsam and seaweed. Now and then a gentle ripple kissed his feet and then playfully rolled back to the sea, hissing and bubbling and then flirtatiously pursuing him again as he moved back an inch or two. A few long-winged seagulls took to the air at the sight of him and now were floating like hovercrafts just above the surf in search of fish disoriented by the storm's incursion and which, more than likely, had swum farther out to sea. Sand pips tweeting for attention flocked to him for food. Two lanky bare-backed boys, stable hands from the nearby Garrison Race Track, were coaxing their racehorses into the sea for their daily bath now that the early morning bathers had come and gone. A welcomed peace settled all around him; an aura of lassitude had been left in the hurricane's wake like the weary indifference that fills the mind after the last bus pulls out of the stand. A fisherman unfurled his net from a distant jetty, its rotted pilings further eroded by the hurricane. Tiny white sails like butterflies skimmed along the dark-blue edge of the horizon. Fishing boats, anchored for the day, bobbed and rolled in the shallow waters, waiting for the night shift to head out to sea for their next haul of flying fish, dolphin, red snapper, shark, king fish, pot fish, sprats, jacks, whichever luckless fish found their way into their scattered nets. In the serenity of his surroundings he felt a monstrous weight lift from his being, a mild cleansing of his soul. The crazed anger that had possessed him as he confronted the Englishman was now tamed and tempered with reason. Moments before, he had been a steaming, turbid cauldron, boiling with murderous intent. Now becalmed by nature's gifts, he was a man no longer possessed. He sat for an hour or so and then lulled by the briny breezes and the lapping of gentle waves, he lay back and fell into a deep sleep.

When he awoke, the barefoot fisherman was climbing down from the jetty, the tails of his open shirt knotted at the waist and the cuffs of his baggy trousers rolled up to his calves. The boys and their horses were gone. He was alone on the shore. He rose, brushed the moist sand from his trousers and started down the beach, head bowed and deep in thought, each step carving a trail of ever-diminishing footprints that the languid waves of low tide came and washed away as though his imprints were desecrations, blemishes on this beautiful stretch of white. The afternoon turned to dusk and Harold was still walking aimlessly for hours along the shoreline, oblivious of time and indifferent to wherever his feet might lead. Following the gentle contours of the island's south-western coast, each beach he passed turned into a new beach by name only with almost imperceptible deviations in natural landscape, all boasting their tall majestic palm trees bowing to the sea, sand dunes crawling with teeny crabs, clusters of sea grapes, litters of fishing boats bobbing like rubber ducks in the sea, miles of luscious green sprinkled with yellow-red hibiscus, and treacherous manchineels disguising themselves as apple trees, flaunting their poisonous fruit to the unwitting.

He strolled from one white sandy beach to another: Brandons, Brightons, Freshwater Bay, Paradise, Batts Rock, Pile Bay, until after some time he found himself on the border of the wealthy parish of St. James. Here was where the British, the Americans, the Canadians, and tourists from the European mainland came to revitalize their bodies and spirits, to luxuriate and bask in the sun and in the island's offerings of grateful servility; where Hollywood stars found refuge from the rabid American paparazzi; where foreigners came to buy up acres of prime land for private getaways secluded from the natives. He had no idea he had walked this far.

"Mister, whay you t'ink you goin'?" The voice was gruff, comical and threatening, all at the same time.

Harold looked straight ahead into the blinding beam of a searchlight as the tall, strapping, khaki-uniformed watchman stared back with an expression that was slightly quizzical as if he thought a Bajan like Harold should really know better.

"Boy, you know very well you cyant pass hey. You cyant see dis is a private beach? Dis is hotel property. Yuh will have to go 'round to get on de udder side."

The man was standing with his back to a mound of smooth gray boulders that sloped down like the side of a pyramid to the edge of the sea. On the other side of the barricade, there was the sound of steel band music, laughter, the happy squeals of children splashing around in a pool, glasses clinking, the shrill voices of women and the full-throated voices of their men all echoing back and forth. They were sounds of gaiety, of life, of freedom. In that instant of confronting the watchman, he once again saw the spectre of Thorne's guard wall and his blood again began to boil.

"But Mister," remonstrated Harold, "the beach belongs to you and me. No person or hotel can own the beach. In fact, the beach belongs to the sea which can reclaim it anytime she wants to."

But the watchman was in no mood to argue. "Listen, man, I just followin' orders. De people say no trespassin' on de beach so you will just have to find anudder way to get 'cross. I just tryin' to do my job. I got two lil thrildren home to feed."

Harold was tired and obedient. Wearily, he followed the adamant beam of the man's searchlight waving like a semaphore to the sidewalk of the Miramar Hotel and out towards the Paynes Bay highway. He walked to the bus stop and boarded the city-bound bus. He had no money; the kind-hearted conductress with a weakness for a handsome face paid his fare.

THERE ONCE WAS A LITTLE ENGLAND

He disembarked in Goodland and from there he walked towards Piggott's rum shop. He was not a drinking man but he needed the company of men, big men, black men who had learned the secrets of survival in a land to which they belonged but which did not yet belong to them. Long before he became a family man, he had been a regular in Piggott's rum shop, but in recent years he found little time for socializing that did not appropriately include Cissy and the boys. He and Piggott were partying friends in the old uncommitted days before his friend took to one of the Harrison Line merchant ships that serviced the island, and one year when the ship was docked in North America in a Seattle harbour, he jumped ship and made his way to New York City where he spent several years in Brooklyn camouflaged in the West Indian diaspora until the American Immigration sniffed him out and deported him back to Barbados. But that was not before he had put away enough Yankee dollars to build a two-roofed wooden house and converting the front portion into a respectable place of business. The house was divided into rum shop, food shop and living quarters.

Piggott was fair-skinned, tall and thin as a rake, a man of few words and, by his own discipline, a teetotaller. He tended the bar. Mrs. Piggott was his opposite in every respect: jet-black, heavyset, loquacious, and always ready to give an earful. She was known to hit the bottle as hard as any man. She ran the grocery end. Thus, between them they established a solid partnership with a prudent distribution of duties.

Harold knew that at this late hour the grocery would be closed and the whole business would be given over to the domino players and the boozers. It was the place where men came to unburden themselves, to unwind their tortured lives every evening. They gathered around like tired tribesmen returned from the jungles of the hinterlands, passing a one-litre over-proof bottle of rum from hand to hand in a wide circle like the sharing of a peace pipe, and when it was empty they all pitched in—save for one or two freeloaders—with enough coppers to start the next round. He could hear in the distance the sharp slamming of ebony dominoes on Piggott's cedar table and the cacophony of drunken voices assaulting the air, arguing, swearing, protesting, blowing off steam and out-shouting one another. Bajan god-blinding, god-damning profanities were pouring out onto the sidewalk like raw sewage. Then, just as he was about to cross the road and set foot on the scene of men clinched in battle, there were shouts of "Down de hatch!" and then a clinking of glasses and beer bottles and afterwards an explosion of spirited laughing. At that moment he realized he had been listening all along to the sounds of war games, men pretending to be bloodthirsty, feigning a will to kill and venting the day's pent-up tensions. It was the same bellicose back-and-forth that resonated in every rum shop in Barbados at the end of every payday. Most times these were fake passions fuelled by liquor over some innocuous topic like "Who is de best batsman in First Division?" He knew that rum was not the magnet that drew men to rum shops; it was the camaraderie, the love, the synergy that flowed among men with much in common. These things transcended the ritual of drink.

 Piggott spent his whole life servicing his flock. Behind him was a translucent display of multi-coloured glass backlit by two long fluorescent bulbs. Of all the various sized bottles lined up in threes like a platoon about to deploy, Mount Gay was the exalted one. Old men, steeped in superstition, would take their first ceremonial swig, straight up, no ice, swish it around from cheek to cheek and then with vehemence spit the rum disdainfully at their feet. Some swore it was for good luck; others said it was meant as a libation to some unnamed African deity. But the younger drinkers would revere every drop as if it were the very quintessence of holy water. They claimed it symbolized the precious, salty sweat and tears of black men and women, slaving in the cane fields under the broiling Bajan sun for pennies a day, every day of every season since the mighty Mount Gay Rum Distilleries Ltd was founded in 1703. Men who reached for a chaser took pleasure from the exquisite collision of Coca Cola and rum on the way down while those who insisted on mixed drinks would draw the scorn of seasoned drinkers. "Man, down de t'ing nuh! You's a man or a mouse?" But there were also the elite drinkers, the whiskey and bourbon men who savoured the smooth contrast of exotic blends and ascribed "class" to imported brands. In their twisted minds, rum was local and was therefore crass.

 Piggott rarely left his station, shuffling from one end of the counter to the other, knowing by heart each man's preference in drink, using a gill tot to measure each potion with medicinal precision as if each were a selective tonic for a specific ailment; all business in his demeanour with a pencil stuck behind one ear lobe, keeping a tab on each customer, making sure drinks were settled up before the debtors staggered out the door for the night.

This Friday evening, the conversation in Piggott's rum shop was full of rebuke, shame, and vitriol. It was all about a village boy named David and a black Bajan barrister defending his white assassin. No wonder they were open-mouthed when Harold walked in. Piggott looked up in astonishment and for the first time all night raised the leaf and left his place behind the counter to greet Harold in the doorway, wrapping an arm around his shoulders and looking straight into his eyes as if he were reuniting with a long-lost brother.

"God bless my eyesight!" he shouted. "All de years I know you, and you now decide to come back to Piggott rum shop?"

Harold let the remark pass and moved to the counter behind which Piggott resumed his post. Without a word he reached into his pocket where he had been saving the desiccated mango leaves that bore David's blood and placed them before him on the counter.

"Let's drink to my son!" he said.

"Here, pour yer own poison!"

Piggott set the rum bottle and glass with chipped ice before Harold and leaned forward within whispering distance. "Harold, boy, we want you to know dat your loss is our loss and your pain is our pain. De day dat bastard, Thorne, kill your boy up a tree, de fellas end up right here in dis rum shop after de hurricane and wuz drinkin' all night til foreday mornin'. Even I had a few, and you know I is a man don' drink. But y'know, there comes a time when every man in de very bottom pits o' despair, in de clutches o' de devil himself, have to turn to either Christ or to somet'ing dat will numb de mind like a liquor, whichever is de closest. I won't tell you a lie, big hard-back men in dis rum shop dat night wuz cryin' and drinkin', drinkin' and cryin', cryin' out o' frustration and drinkin' to ease de pain. Some who didn't even know David but know dat he share de same skin and dat we all livin' in a place where dese white people still have de upper-hand and can get away with anyt'ing at all, even murder. I tell you, dat mornin' after I close up de shop, I couldn't get dat blasted mango tree outta my head. I went back there in my livin' quarters and I wind up de old His Masters Voice gramophone dat I haven't played in ages, and I put on a old 78 dat I had brought back from Amurca, by Billie Holiday, "Strange Fruit," all 'bout lynchin' in de Amurcan South, which you might as well say ent much different from how they tek your boy life. And I start singin' along with Billie, with long tears streamin' down my face. I play dat record over and over again til de damn needle wear out."

Piggott started to sing. With his eyes fixed on the blood-spattered leaves, he sang the first two stanzas with perfect recall:

> *Southern trees bear strange fruit,*
> *Blood on the leaves, and blood at the root,*
> *Black bodies swinging in the southern breeze,*
> *Strange fruit hanging from the poplar trees.*
> *Pastoral scene of the gallant south,*
> *The bulging eyes and the twisted mouth,*
> *Scent of magnolias, sweet and fresh,*
> *Then the sudden smell of burning flesh.*

The men around the barroom abandoned their dominos and drew close, gathering around Harold at the counter and reaching out to embrace him, to knock glasses and beer bottles, and to say in different ways: "One love, my brother!" Those who knew the song, even vaguely, joined in with Piggott and before long the shop was filled with a drawling dissonant rendition of the old blues standard. Each man pledged his solidarity by vowing, regardless of the consequences, to take the day off from work on the day of the trial, to go down to the courthouse to see that justice for their friend was served.

Joe Walrond, in his half-drunken haze, stumbled over to Harold and mumbled: "Man, call me as a witness. I wuz passin' by de mansion when I hear de shot and I see de boy fall clear from de tree, *Buhdong!* I will tell dem down at de courthouse how he got kill. Tell dem to axe me!" But everyone knew that at that hour of the morning, Joe would have been oblivious, more likely fighting his own demons.

Hours after Piggott emptied the bar in compliance with the liquor laws, he and Harold stood across from each other, crying, laughing, drinking, venting and mentally slaying the Englishman a hundred times over. Then as dawn was breaking, Harold eventually made his way home with the haunting lyrics of *Strange Fruit* still ringing in his ears. Meanwhile a gruesome picture inspired by Billie Holiday rested on his mind and refused to be erased by that long night of drinking: it was an image of his son bloodied and swinging from the branch of a tree. As he turned into the cart road that led to his house, the thought of paying the mansion a visit crossed his mind but he was barely sober enough to stagger home, much less climb the hill to the landlord's front gate. It was the early morning of David's funeral. It would be held in the Pilgrim Holiness Church of Pastor Gittens, across the street from Piggott's rum shop.

The proximity of church and rum shop had always been a matter of contention, at least to the unflinching sanctity of the church. Sometimes the pastor's sermons competed with airwaves from across the street as Piggott kept his drunken flock even more sedated with music: Nat King Cole, Billy Eckstine, Louis Jordan, Joe Tex, Louis Armstrong's *I'll be glad when you dead, you rascal you*, all part of his sizeable collection of "plates" brought back from America. The disturbance was barely tolerable when Bing Crosby's vibratory baritone permeated the church walls and hovered over the congregation like seraphim; but when the lewd lyrics of Lord Kitchener's calypsos out-sang the choir, Brother Hall would rise from his seat and hurry over to admonish Piggott about his devil music crossing the street and defiling the House of God. But today the banja music would be silenced, the old records respectfully put away, for today was the day of the funeral. Today was David's day.

As the time approached, Pastor Gittens braced himself for the throng of mourners and for the deluge of tributes and tears; the funeral promised to be the biggest of his ministration. Hours before, he was fussing and fidgeting like a nervous groom, pacing up and down the aisle, dusting the pews, arranging the hymnals, aligning the kneelers, unfolding the extra chairs that had been put away for the momentous Christmas and Easter services. Then he settled down to kneel and pray beside the body lying in the shiniest hand-polished pinewood coffin he had ever seen. It was the handiwork of Egbert, the carpenter.

As he rose from his knees he was drawn to a potted plant next to the altar. It was a delicate hydrangea vine he had rescued from the railing of his veranda days before the hurricane. Already the young tendrils were beginning to weave themselves among the wooden lattices where sinners knelt to confess at altar call. In his mind's eye, the highest tentacle of the young vine was reaching up sensitively towards the casket. With David on his mind, he picked up a pitcher of water and slowly watered the vine as he pondered the zest for life common to all creation. He then donned his black cassock and walked up the aisle, pushed open the doors of the chapel and stood to one side to welcome the people.

Cissy entered the vestibule with slow, listless steps, clutching the hand of her remaining child whose face wore an expression of shock beyond grief. Through the dark veil it was seen that sleep had abandoned her; she appeared old, weak and shrunken. The allegiant Esmay and Egbert were by her side.

Next came Sister Innis, a large woman, grave and dignified. She was always the first to set eyes on the children even before their own mothers: she was the village midwife. Through the years from the moment of their birth, she doted on them with the quiet pride of a proud gardener who marvels at the first bursts from the sod and watches the saplings develop tendrils and twigs and branches and later ripen into self-sufficiency. Childless herself, she saw them as her fulfilments. She was known to emerge from the shadows to spank their backsides when she observed them misbehaving on the way from school. Afterwards, their mothers would thank her and follow with licks of their own. Pausing now at the side of the coffin, she saw David as her own flesh and blood, ripped savagely from her life's work.

Then came Teacher Farley whispering tearfully into the mother's ear, "He was my best student, my very best," which he knew was an overblown characterisation of David, but he also was aware that such an occasion called for laudation in the extreme and a generosity of posthumous praises.

Then, surprisingly, in walked Joe Walrond, now bathed, brushed and sober. He found his seat appropriately in the back row in the backsliders' section. It was his first day in church since the funeral for

Ben Carson's son. The frayed jacket he wore bulged visibly at the breast pocket, likely framing a nip bottle he had sneaked into this holy place.

Busloads of country people turned up for the funeral. They drifted into the pews, swarmed the aisle, poured out onto the front steps, gathered behind the bougainvillea hedges, peered through the stained glass windows and huddled across the road, some standing like herons in puddles from the early morning rain. A few knew David well, some barely knew him but many more only knew his story, a story that resonated around the island with its dire implications for the young, the children of colonialism. For some, it was a call to arms, to some a time for healing, and others would simply come to honour one of their own.

Pastor Gittens saved his most sweeping eloquence and his most biting metaphors for the sermon, likening Thorne's forbidden guard wall to the social walls that divided the powerful elite that ruled the land from the poor and the working-class.

"Brothers and Sisters, the day is coming when the wall will crumble like the walls of Jericho and we will all be one," he boomed his prophecy of hope from the pulpit. Then he uttered with a strange lugubrious tone: "Or God forbid, the wall will survive and we'll all exchange places like on a tennis court … but in a game of sudden death." After an hour of oration, he ended with his favourite quote: "The Lord acts in mysterious ways, his miracles to perform. Let us be grateful to the Lord." But there would be no gratitude in the hearts of the people, no recognition of a miracle, no understanding.

The service wore on for hours and through the long litany of prayers and hymns and eulogies, Cissy kept looking over her shoulder, scanning the sea of black faces and their black finery, hoping against hope that her Harold had changed his mind and come to the church. But he would not. He had given her his reasons the night before as they lay in bed, he awake and fully clothed; she pleading between murmuring sobs. Harold's faith in The Almighty, which faith had always been tenuous at best, had been bruised and battered; his mood, always light and high-spirited in the past, had now become dark and sullen. He proceeded to tell her in his most petulant passion that he now had no need for the Church and no need for the same God that Pastor Gittens shared with the pious colonial masters; no need for hymns that had for centuries served to tame the rebellious; no need for scriptures that promised to the meek the inheritance of the earth; and no need for eulogies to anesthetize his pain. He told her that the living face and spirit of David remained indelible in his heart and mind and thus he had no need to look upon his earthly remains ghoulishly displayed in death. Still she hoped he would reconsider and come to her side.

    The service over, the funeral rites continued in the churchyard in a little cemetery out back that seemed even more ancient than the church itself. Old mildew-stained headstones jutted at various angles from the earth like crooked teeth. Some were almost completely submerged, their slave names lost forever from view. Some graves bore no names, just plain wooden crosses or none at all. The ceremony came to a tearful end and people gathered around in reverential silence as the coffin rested on two wooden planks between mounds of rich, black mud. The pastor gave the last benediction and Cissy stepped forward to touch the coffin one last time. As the diggers readied their shovels, everyone turned to see a bespectacled white woman dressed stylishly in black, black hat, black dress, black high-heel shoes, running towards them, heels clacking along the cemetery walkway. She approached and laid a large green wreath at the head of the casket. She was tall, shapely and full-breasted with a sensuous waddling of the hips as she backed away from the grave. As the mourners stared at her questioningly, she then walked gingerly over to Cissy, held her hands in hers for a second or two, pressed her cheek to hers, and then deposited a crumpled piece of paper in the palm of her hand. She then watched as the coffin was lowered to the bottom before walking away.

    The woman was Penelope Thorne. They had seen each other only once since those early years, quite recently in fact when Cissy made a stop at Barclays Bank in Bridgetown to deposit some earnings. She was seated behind the counter amidst a row of uniformed lily-white tellers. She saw Cissy and with a broad smile called her to the front of the line. They chatted girlishly about the old get-togethers on Easter mornings during their innocent pubescent years; then Cissy asked her why there were no black tellers, to which she shrugged and said: "We do have many coloured employees, but they are all in the back."

The mourners all drifted away, murmuring among themselves. Cissy, with Nathaniel at her side, walked home from the churchyard. On the way, she stopped to read Penelope's handwritten note. It read:

Can Pierre come to spend the rest of the year with your son? I think that would be nice. My sympathies to you. Love, Penelope! ... PS: Stop by the bank.

She squeezed the paper into a tight ball and tossed it into the bushes along the way wondering if it had been written in the throes of her father's heavy unpardonable guilt or in a moment of cruel cynicism. She didn't know the answer but was taken aback by the presumptiveness of the note and was sure that Nathaniel would do just fine without the company of Madame Montmartre's boy.

As they rounded the corner, the sky over Thornville was gray with smoke and littered with particles of floating ash. From the distance could be heard the crackling sound of burning wood and the fearful clanging of the fire brigade. Thorne's nine-acre cane piece was going up in flames. Even Nathaniel knew why.

Chapter 11

His Brother's Keeper

WEEKS WENT by when one evening Nathaniel heard the crunching of gravel in the alley and got up to open the side door for his father, except it was Pastor Gittens, bible in hand, come to administer the nightly ritual of prayers and solace.

"Goodnight, Nathaniel. How?" Bajans always bade each other "goodnight" in the evening whether coming or going.

"Quite well, Pastor Gittens. Ma is not home, Ma went next door."

He decided to sit and wait while Nathaniel told him about his first day back at school. Summer vacation was over and the boy was relieved to escape the oppressiveness of home. He too, like his Mom and Dad, had his moments; a good chunk of his youthful spirit had been left stranded at the guard wall like David's kite. The symbiosis that had bound together the two brothers from birth had been ripped apart in the nanosecond of a bullet's hot burning flash. Only the inventiveness of imaginations that children possess would save his young mind from the abyss of depression, and so, he walked and talked with his brother all day as if he were still alive.

But nights were gloomier. His bedroom was half empty, out of balance. In bed he would lie awake and still feel the robust heftiness of his brother on his shoulders as he hoisted him onto the guard wall, and the burden would thrust him down until he would fall into a fitful sleep and later find both of them tripping and falling headlong into a dark bottomless pit. He would jump out of his sleep, sweating profusely, shrieking at the realization that his dream was half real. Many a night he was awakened by a sickly bloated glob forcing its way up to his throat from his stomach and swelling like an inflating balloon. Throwing aside the sheets, he rushed from his bed, out the door, down the slatted steps, across the yard and outside the gate to vomit up all the bilious goblins that had tormented his dreams all night. Other nights he lay in bed, sleepless, staring into the dark, hearing the haunting drone of his brother's kite, seeing his brother, the waxed marlin wrapped tightly around his fist, tugging his kite towards one side of his body then to the other, fearless and in command, yet defenceless from the fate that awaited him on the other side of a forbidden wall. The same kind of compulsion that drove his father to seek the company of men, big men, black men like himself in Piggott's rum shop, also filled Nathaniel with a yearning for young companionship, for his schoolmates, for the liveliness of school, the chatter, the contact, the mingling on the school pasture. Even the drudgery of homework would help to fill the aching void.

His brother had always been the favourite at school, ebullient and witty in company like his father; he was the one who charmed and entertained his schoolmates. At recess when they lined up in the schoolyard for their twice-daily rations of powdered milk and two biscuits each, the boys would swarm around David like bees, laughing at his bawdy jokes more heartily than they laughed at his own corny ones. David had the charisma, the presence, the physicality, the eye and reflexes for sports that won him first pick every time for the cricket match against the Old Boys. Nathaniel was the academic, the more boring brother, the one who trotted out to the middle with a cold refreshing drink for David batting at number two and already close to his half-century.

Yesterday was his first day back to school. The bright-red arched door of St. Stephen's swung open as he approached and Teacher Farley stood in the doorway with outstretched arms to greet him as if he were a wounded survivor returning from a battlefield of gunfire. He had been in the news; they would all know his story. He entered to the clamorous greetings of his friends in the front of his class: "Nat, come 'ere and gimme five, man." He could feel their warmth. Then he made his way to the back row where David sat a few weeks before, his desk now eerily vacant, left vacant in his honour by David's friends. He could tell from their silence they were not pleased to see him. He felt the sting of their stares, their eyes like tiny lasers. His knees weakened and his legs suddenly became flaccid like a puppet's. David's friends now despised him; he was supposed to be his brother's keeper and he had lost him. In the side of his vision he caught Sylvester Hollingsworth, a husky thirteen-year-old who sat next to David and was his brother's best friend. He jumped to his feet and faced Nathaniel squarely, his eyes narrowed to tiny slits. Nathaniel felt the boy's stare like razor blades hurtling deep into his skull. Then as he came closer, Sylvester muttered, "Not fer you, David would be livin' today." The words reached his ears like a dragon's flaming breath.

    Teacher Farley was facing the blackboard, his back turned but his ears tuned to the wavelength and timbre of every voice in his class. He overheard the boy. The teacher already had a soft spot for Nathaniel; long before the death of his brother he had fallen secretly in love with his mother from the very first parental meeting when she brought the bawling twins and deposited them in his First Form. It was no secret: Nathaniel had been Head Boy every year. He would be overprotective of Nathaniel during his difficult time. Without a word, he ushered Sylvester to the middle of the school where Headmaster Farnum sat at the seat of judgment on a platform two-tiers higher than the main floor whence he had an unbroken view of the entire school: every pupil, every teacher, every desk, every form. A five-foot-long tamarind rod, stripped of its bark, with one end forked like the mouth of a snake, was suspended on the pegs of an easel behind his desk. It awaited young Hollingsworth's backside like the sword of Damocles. The boy began to cry uncontrollably and the wise Headmaster perceived instantly that his tears were not of fear for the rod, but of grief. The boy had found catharsis in casting blame wherever he could within his reach for the loss of his best friend, possibly the greatest loss he had ever suffered in his young life. Intuiting this, the Headmaster, in a rare instance of mercy, merely tapped the boy's hand with his wooden ruler. The tamarind rod was spared.

    Nathaniel's first day back at school was far from what he had expected. "Man, dem fellas wuz mean ... won't speak to me all day like if I did something wrong ... like if I did kill my own brother," he said to the pastor. He had expected to be embraced, unaware that cruelty could also possess the hearts of children. But try as he might, he knew he could not be his twin brother; he could never compensate. David was the one with the magnetism and now that he was gone, the friends who were drawn to him through his brother were now falling away. He rationalized their hate: maybe they were right to feel the way they did; maybe he should have talked his brother out of climbing the wall in the first place; without his help the kite would have been unreachable; maybe now the boys were right to thrust their swords into his still bleeding wounds; maybe he deserved it.

But Time, always the appeaser, rallied the boys together again. Their capacity for prolonged and entrenched grudges was not yet fully formed as in grownups, and soon their animosity fell apart like sand. Once again they talked and laughed with Nathaniel as though their friendship had never been fractured. Sylvester Hollingsworth became his best friend.

He could now think of his brother and recall the times they spent together without being overcome with guilt and self-pity. He told the pastor how they used to climb the massive mahogany tree at the corner of the village and swing from its branches like baby possums; pitch marbles with the boys in the schoolyard after hours; jump hopscotch and play rounders with the girls; play kneel-down cricket with a tar ball; push bicycle tyre rims like unicycles up and down the gap; shoot birds with guttaperks made from forked twigs and rubber bands; build box carts from abandoned sweet-drink crates and pram wheels; stand at the edge of Mr. Rogers's rock quarry and piss long yellow-green arches down into the bottom of the hollow as they competed to see who had the longest, strongest, meanest squirt.

And then there were those hideous brown cork hats, those hard inverted bowls he and his brother had to wear to church on Sunday mornings. "Oh boy! Turn around, lemme see how grownup y'all look!" their mother exclaimed in Fogarty Department Store the day she bought them while the fair-skinned cash boys around them giggled and snickered. She meant well. How he and David complained that the hats made them look like mock-men; that Mr. Thorne's hated overseer wore a cork hat in the cane field; that the simpleton guard standing like a statue all day in the hot sun at Government Gate wore a cork hat; and that the smug-faced inspector, Mr. Culpepper, from the Board of Health, walking from house to house with his goosenecked ladle and flit gun, testing water barrels and gutters for larvae, he also wore a cork hat. Big men, important men, businessmen in suits and with briefcases in hand never wore cork hats; they wore serious felt hats with finger dimples on the sides of the crown. They would bow and remove them smartly when the ladies passed or when the dead passed on the way to Westbury Cemetery.

And so, with these resentments towards a simple hat that conjured a pride that wasn't theirs, that was seen on the heads of white men, that was copied from the British and worn by plantation overlords, a hat they perceived should have no right to be on the head of a black man, he and David sulked all the way to church until Mom gave in and let them go hatless.

The pastor was still sitting, listening to Nathaniel recap his day, reminiscing on old times, when Cissy returned and smiled approvingly at the sight of them together. Nathaniel withdrew to his room; Bajan children were taught not to linger in the company of "big people."

"Well, how is my girl?" The words escaped his lips.

She forced a smile without answering; any answer would give assent to the premise of his question. Then her mood changed. She became grave and contemplative.

"I worry about Harold, I really do. David was his favourite. He loves Nathaniel but he saw himself more in David and now that David dead and gone he's dying too and …"

Her voice broke and softened to a whisper. He reached out and wrapped his arms around her. She held onto him and he could feel her warmth, a yielding that sent his pulse racing. A flash flood of emotion welled up inside of him. His lips quivered on the brink of kissing her mouth long and sweetly. He was tempted to open his heart and let his feelings flow, to reach below the line of her bodice, down into her cleavage and caress her gorgeous breasts and twiddle her nipples between his fingers until, weak-kneed, her whole body surrendered totally in his arms, thrilled to the realization there could be no other man in her world but him. But instead, with the greatest restraint, he pressed his lips to her forehead while her body convulsed and released a stream of tears. She was Harold's woman, he reminded himself. Moreover, he could not take advantage of her weakest and most vulnerable moments.

Cissy, in the darkest days of her life, had clung to her faith, and since it could be said that her pastor was the conduit to that faith, there could be no doubt that it was he to whom she turned. After Wednesday night prayer meetings and Sunday night services, his black Austin was seen parked at the side of her house, and sometime after midnight, prying neighbours would see him emerge from her doorway with his leather-bound bible in the crook of his arm in the manner of a hunter with his Winchester tucked close to his body, returning victoriously from the foxhunt.

Chapter 12

Blood of the Lamb

UNLIKE CISSY, Harold lacked the fortitude of faith. At best he had lived his life wavering on the edge of agnosticism, but now in the disillusionment of recent times he was drifting even farther into the lonely reclusive realm of the nonbeliever. In prior years, in those first heady days of courting when lovers are wont to accede to each other's every whim, he would sit dutifully at Cissy's side in Gittens's church on Sunday mornings and endure his long-winded sermons. The sonorous words from the pulpit would soon wane in his ears to a wordless hum and his mind would wander over the past few days, recalling the week's little pleasures with Cissy and the boys; but in the end he would always give the pastor the benefit of his wisdom and silently give thanks to the pastor's God for his family, if for nothing else.

His only unnerving moment came one Sunday morning after the final amen. The choir beckoned softly with, *Just as I am, without one plea, but that thy blood was shed for me,* and the exhortation travelled like the breath of early morning mist across the heads of the congregation to where he sat, to purposely befuddle his mind so that when Cissy nudged him in the ribs he was already rising to walk zombie-like down the aisle to the altar for the ultimate surrender of his soul and, consequently, of all his free Sundays with the boys down at the cricket grounds.

"Brother Harold, did you feel your sins washed away by the blood of the Lamb?" Sister Ruth asked him as he rose from the altar, her moist palm clamped to his forehead like a bandage. At that moment he could not help but ponder the blood of the same Lamb called upon that Sunday morning in the Church of England, the Catholic Church, the Moravian Church, the Methodist Church, the Nazarene Church, the Baptist Church, the Pentecostal Church, and in all the numerous chapels and missions around the island. He imagined the same blood of the Lamb anointing the majority but also assuaging the guilt of a ruling minority.

History books had taught him about early missionaries who long ago arrived on the island with their insidious scourge of slavery duplicitously gift-wrapped along with tokens of incense and myrrh, and always ready with chapter and verse to tacitly condone the evil institution: *Slaves, obey your earthly masters with fear and trembling, with a sincere heart, as you would Christ, not by the way of eye-service, as people-pleasers, but as slaves of Christ, doing the will of God, from the heart.* His own sense of fairness wrestled with this doctrinal dichotomy: *Obey your earthly masters with fear and trembling;* for though humankind had long ago abolished slavery, nowhere in the Good Book could he find a passage equally unequivocal in its condemnation of slavery. He wanted to believe in the Word but only if it could be shown that the Word believed in him. That was only fair, he thought.

Still, he envied true believers, those Christians who had found the faith that allowed them to traverse the chasms of contradiction, as no doubt Sister Ruth had, and arrived on the other side with total conviction or blind devotion. Then and only then could a sinner unload his burden of guilt and be saved. But when Harold rose from the altar with Sister Ruth at his side, he was the same man; he felt no change; he was the same as when he entered the church and sat for an hour while the pastor extolled the incontrovertible truth and wisdom of the Scriptures.

And when the choir got up, their faces aglow, their voices steeped in devotion as they sang *Glorious Things of Thee Are Spoken* by the English hymnist, John Newton, the lyrics rang in his head, but they were hollow of all meaning, because had they not been written by a white man who had been a slave-trader himself at some point in his life, plying his ignominious trade deep in the heart of Africa.

> *Glorious things of thee are spoken,*
> *Zion, city of our God!*
> *He, whose word cannot be broken,*
> *Form'd thee for His own abode:*
> *On the Rock of ages founded,*
> *What can shake thy sure repose?*
> *With salvation's walls surrounded,*
> *Thou may'st smile at all thy foes.*

When the request went out from the pulpit for Christians to come forward and bear witness, he could see the beatific smiles and the pure afterglow of miracles on the faces of testifiers. He envied them because they believed. And oh, how he too wished to believe! If only he could reach out beyond the bounds of his own scepticism, close his eyes to the unfairness of the society that surrounded him and grab the elusive gift of faith, his greatest sin once and for all time could be washed away by the blood of the Lamb, and he could truthfully exclaim to Sister Ruth with his hands reaching towards the heavens, "Yes! Yes! Yes!" and she could welcome him into the fold, shorn of all his past iniquities, and his burden could at last be lifted, that burden of sin that had scarred him all these years.

But for now, that dubious sin of rape would hang around his neck like a millstone.

Chapter 13

The Long Wait for Justice

NOVEMBER CAME around and not a day too soon. The month marked the end of the season for hurricanes but not the end of people's fears, and their appetite for rumours gave rise to a brand new hurricane, a late bloomer, somewhere out in the Caribbean Sea. But while the island held its collective breath, the rumour was discounted by the pillars of truth, *Rediffusion* and *The Chronicle*, who both dismissed it as nothing more than paranoia that had obsessed the people since late September. And so the island slowly but surely slid back into a state of torpor and, as weeks went by, Janet receded into the distance of time and into the annals of island storms like a bad dream, a roguish bitch, a prank of Mother Nature that went disastrously awry.

Then came the 5th of November. That night, every village, every town, every parish resounded with fireworks and the sulphuric stench of gunpowder hung in the air, as it might have pervaded the skies over London's Houses of Parliament had Guy Fawkes had his way in 1605. Always faithful to British traditions, the whole island was commemorating that night. At the top of the gap in Thornville, beside the mahogany tree, a white-headed cloth mop stuck in a pyre of burning brambles and topped with a breadfruit for a head from which protruded a corn pipe, was the most infamous of all the effigies. Everyone knew it was Thorne. Grown men stood around the burning pyre all night like Sioux Indians, their faces shimmering in the watch fires of a circling camp, celebrating the end of the white devil of Thornville, an Englishman to them more despicable than Fawkes himself. As quickly as he died, another effigy replaced him all night long. It was a haunting night for Cissy. She winced at the blast of every screaming rocket. She jumped at the sound of every exploding "carboil" coffee can on the road. That night the recurring memory of real gunfire had no end.

Next morning, an Indian man on his bicycle pulled up to her front window pointing to the pillion laden with a mountain of cloth, samples of colourful cottons, fine silks, gabardines and linens, all strapped to the rear. He was clad in silken pyjama-like clothes and his exotic features and turbaned head all looked remotely familiar.

"Madam, you remember me?" he asked.

She stared intently at his face as he grinned from ear to ear. "No, I don't know you."

"Yes, madam ... is me, Mr. Babu."

No, he couldn't be, she thought. He couldn't be the one they called "Coolie" who used to hang around at the edge of the village, a lost soul, haggard and hungry. She had tried to feed him once; he remembered. Now here he was, well-attired, clean-shaven and prosperous in his bearing, beaming with a tiny gold tooth that sparkled in his smile like an ember.

"Mr. Babu selling material now. Working for my uncle Thani in town. You buy today, madam?"

"Not today."

"No, no, no, madam!" he insisted, bowing low from the waist, his hands clasped at his forehead. "No have money? No problem. I come back in two weeks. Just pick something for you."

She ordered enough gabardine to keep her busy for a month or two while she waited and waited for the court to slate a date for the trial.

"How much?"

"No problem at all, madam. No worry about pay today Next time I come back with your order, you pay, whatever you have." He fished a pencil and book from his pyjama pocket and added Cissy to his long list of customers before hopping on his bicycle and heading merrily off to the next house.

As time went by, day after day, she escaped to her sewing machine. Mr. Babu, now popular in the neighbourhood, kept her supplied with all types of fabrics, threads, needles, zippers, buttons and all the other paraphernalia of the trade. Every couple of weeks he would ride up to her door and, with his usual panache, proudly display his latest wares; and after pocketing a few coins and jotting down the newest sale, he would set off again down the road and repeat the same spiel over and over again. She knew well he would not be seen much longer in the village; that he would likely soon find himself among his own people in Bridgetown, on Swan Street, prosperous with his own clothier retail shop and haberdashery: *Mr. Babu, Importer of Fine Fabrics*. He would hire only his own, Indians like himself, and they too would start out making their rounds, cycling from house to house, collecting with disproportionate margin a few coppers at a time, inured to the coolie slurs that came their way from people with their own indignities to suffer, becoming deservedly wealthy off the meagre purchasing power of Bajans like Cissy, albeit with terms that would enable them to survive. These Indians came from the farthest corners, some via Trinidad and British Guiana, and they reached out to their own like they had reached out to Mr. Babu amongst the poorest of the poor. Meanwhile, Cissy Brathwaite and many other women in the village, foster children of an imperial power, would spend their bi-weekly Friday mornings listening for the *brrrring brrrring* of the Indian cloth vendor as he made his bicycle rounds.

What was at first a source of distraction soon turned into a business as word spread that she was following in the footsteps of her mother, the erstwhile seamstress of Thornville. Soon she would try her hand at elegant bridal gowns and formal dresses. Not for a single moment did her work dispel the memory of David but instead steadied her disposition and, along with her Christian faith, kept her sanity on an even keel waiting for the next year and the day of the trial.

"Any news yet?" The question came from Mrs. Mordecai, the nosy heavyset milk woman. She was poking her head in at Cissy's front window enquiring about the court case. The same question had been on the lips of every person in the whole village since the landlord's arraignment.

"No, nothing yet, Mrs. Mordecai, but soon," she offered. It was true that Barrister Cunningham had requested and had been granted a continuance by the court.

The milk woman was not pleased. "Well, dis t'ing tekking a mighty long time. I don' know why dey have to be a court case anyway. Everybody know he shoot and kill de boy in cold blood. Dey shoulda string he up ever since fer murder in de first degree." Her padded head jerked from side to side under the weight of a four-gallon milk bucket in a balancing act much like a head-swaying Turkish dance.

"Milk fer you today, girlie?"

"A pint, please."

The milk woman reached up, twisted a tiny silver-plated spigot and the pungent goat milk poured down past her face down to her waist and four times into her gill tot without a drop spilled.

"Miss Braffit, I don' know how you could tek dis t'ing lyin' down. If it wuz me, I woulda been up in dat mansion nex' mornin' wid my cutlass and b'Christ, all like now I would be sittin' in Her Majesty's Glendairy Prison fer choppin' off he head clean, clean, clean from ear to ear. You t'ink I mekking sport?" Between clenched teeth she drew a wicked Bajan steupse, the sucking sound of a long and dry perverted kiss.

"Yes, de trial is coming soon, Mrs. Mordecai, after de first o' de year." She said these words so the milk woman would know she was neither indifferent nor forbearing. "We just have to let de law run its course."

"Run its course up my tail!" she retorted.

Cissy knew well that Mrs. Mordecai was full of empty bluster. Deep down inside, she herself secretly wished to taste even a sweet morsel of revenge but so far the only avengers were young boys throwing stones over the wall in the cover of night and yelling for the white man to come out and show his face.

As if she read Cissy's mind, she said, "Anyway, 'revenge is mine, saith the Lord,' cause I just now pass in front o' de mansion and de worse smell you could ever imagine comin' from dem white people property. Nasty, nasty, like a breath worse dan death. I don' know where de stench comin' from but I feel Thorne dead in dat big house and de servants lookin' all 'bout and cyant find de body. Oh God, it stink!"

And with that, she pocketed the pennies and sashayed down the gap, steupsing and muttering her imprecations, her buttocks seesawing under her dress like two undulant waves.

Constable Howard was also making his rounds. Under the Government's health inspection mandate he had sampled Mrs. Mordecai's goat milk the past year and detected an unacceptable though harmless percentage of water content. The monetary fine for the offence was a week's worth of milk. She saw his cork hat and brown uniform in the distance approaching; his eyes were squinting; suspicion was painted on the constable's face. On an opportune patch of loose gravel she stumbled and fell to her knees. The milk bucket toppled from her head and the lid went rolling along the road like a loosened hubcap. The precious goat milk poured out, finding its way down through the bushes and into the gutter, denying the officer any possible evidence of adulteration.

"Mornin', offisah!" she greeted him with a perfunctory wave, as she proceeded to retrieve her utensils.

The milk woman was right. Cissy stepped outside and also smelled the strange foul odour of rotting flesh. It emanated from the direction of the mansion, through the trees and down to the road where people walked back and forth to the standpipe, to the shops, or down to the corner to catch the city bus. They held their noses and ran. In the heat of afternoons the stink would overpower the cloth swatches soaked in Limacol and wrapped around their faces. Surely, they in the mansion must have smelled it. Could it be that the Englishman in a final act of maleficence had chosen to martyr himself behind his secretive walls to chase them out of their homes in order to escape the putrid smell of his mouldering flesh? Was his dead body the repository of their collective hate that now in death he would cause to boomerang into their miserable faces? The nauseating smell persisted day and night. Sometimes a steady breeze would carry it deep into the village as if to smother the houses. It became unbearable.

Help was on the way. Thorne's senior gardener, Mr. Marshall, a man from the village, volunteered to put an end to everyone's misery. Tired of all the fuss, he showed up with exasperation etched on his face. His tolerance for such smells must have been heightened by years of feeding horse dung to Thorne's fruit trees, for in no time at all the old man braved the effluvium and traced it to a mango tree, the same tree in which David had been shot. There, high on a branch overhanging the infamous guard wall was a tightly wrapped package the size of a Christmas ham, smothered with flies and swinging in the breeze like a ripe soursop. He plucked it from the tree and with his garden shears he snipped open the crocus wrapping. Inside was a bloated decomposing dog, stinking of rotted flesh and faecal matter, its lips still snarling back from its teeth. It was one of Thorne's Alsatians.

Later that evening in Piggott's rum shop, there was much indignation and embarrassment among the men who were behind the plot, for how could a caper so meticulously planned be so ineptly executed. No thought had been given to a detail as elemental as the direction of the wind, always from the east. It was Duphus Hinds who had killed, packaged and planted the dog on Thorne's property so that in a matter of days the stench would rise up and drive the Englishman and his family out of their house. He had hung the dead animal downwind in the wrong tree, and so the caper backfired and the village was overcome by the nauseating smell. In the people's minds, the white man and Satan had once again won the day.

These childish acts of revenge gave Cissy no relief. In her mind there could be no just price for the death of her son short of his killer's own life, and for that she would wait with much impatience for the law to do what was right. When she found herself thinking of committing the ultimate revenge herself, her friend the pastor and his sermon of "revenge is mine, said the Lord" would leap before her mind's eye like a mighty cross. But divine retribution was so long in coming.

Chapter 14

Broad Street Encounters

THE DAYS wore on. With every nerve in his body on edge waiting for the trial of Theodore Thorne, Harold turned to the distraction of work and to the rhythm of the workday to steady his disposition as he teetered on the brink of insanity. Given the compassionate accountability for his absence, surely he would be welcomed back at his desk. He hopped on his saddle and headed down to the city, but as he rounded the corner onto Broad Street there was a mob outside his work building. *The Chronicle* men, overworked, underpaid and no longer passive, had walked out on strike. Every newspaperman—save for the editors and writers, who justly considered themselves the fountainhead and above the indignity of brawling for more money—had heard the Union's call and abandoned their posts. Even the sleepy-eyed crewmen of the graveyard shift had come to picket the building. They had hung up their long-sleeved shirts and ties and donned regular home clothes to pace up and down, flooding the alleyway, blocking the entrance, hurling invectives at any lowlife scab that dared to cross the line. Harold had no thoughts of venturing across. Lunch vendors in the alley, severely affected by the suspended wages of the strikers, untied their aprons and left their wooden trays of fruit, sweeties, cheese and corned beef cutters, and gleefully joined the boys in the procession. Marjorie Hinckson, the flamboyant peanut seller, beloved by all the workers, stepped out of the picket line to greet Harold as he crossed the street. She reached out and impulsively planted a wet kiss on his mouth.

"How you hol'ing up, sugar plum? I cyant wait fer de trial next year, God spare life. You feel he goin' get de gallows doh? I really don' know, cause dem Inglish people know how to wiggle out o' all kindsa situations. I wuz glad enough as a lil girl livin' in Cheapside when de Germans torpedo de Cornwallis out in Carlisle Bay when my mudda run down to de wharf and get she some good can food that wuz floating pon top de water like dead fish. We wuz rooting fer de Germans all de way and every time I see 'Kilroy wuz here' scrawl all over de place on public buildings and school walls and even on churches, we wuz prayin' to God that Hitluh wuz Kilroy and he wuz really hey in Buhbaydus fer true to sweep all dem Inglish people off de island so we could run dis place by we self or even let Hitluh take over. Hitluh wuz de only man that could outsmart de Inglish. Every time they had he cornered, de belt 'round he waist would get tight, tight, tight and he would take off again. Anyway, sweetie, you hol' tight and t'ings will work out, God willin'." Before Harold could respond, she swaggered back in line, cackling over her shoulder, "Man, I just love a bassa-bassa!"

Big Darcy Bradshaw, the union steward, was the mainspring of the insurrection; he was the only man on the island who knew how to operate the gigantic Heilderberg press that spat out ten thousand papers every night. With the press grounded to a halt, it would be an unprecedented disaster in the history of this longstanding newspaper. In this small island of Barbados with its wealth of literacy, it would be like the death of a noble patriarch. A true warrior without a shred of empathy for Harold, Darcy called to him with an invitation to join the strike. "United we stand, divided we fall!" was his cry.

But Harold was fighting his own personal wars; he had no strength left for petty skirmishes. His mind was set on a more pervasive enemy; he was revolting internally against the white man and was locked body and soul in a visceral hatred of everything British, and in everything British he thought he saw the face of his son's killer. Harold had succumbed to the demons of irrational fears. He strolled down the main thoroughfare with England on his mind, past the copycat side streets, past pompous Big Ben with her pretentious chimes, past the imperious Union Jack waving in her vainglory, past one-armed supercilious Lord Nelson spattered from head to boot-tip with the gray excrement of black birds. And appropriately so, thought Harold, for wasn't it Nelson who railed against the liberation of African slaves? So why did we continue to lionize this man, this monument in the Square? If we were compelled to honour a British hero, then why not Wilberforce, a white man, who argued in his own Parliament for the manumission of slaves? Why not a statue in the Square for our freedom fighters? Like Bussa? Or Garvey? Or Wynter Crawford? Or even Clement Payne, the rabble-rouser?—all staunch defenders of the black man and the working-class. Why not? These questions pained him; they took possession of his mind and held it in a vice grip all the way from one end of the city to the other, as he ambled along, muttering to himself. Bystanders stared at him. They shook their heads. Those who knew him were saddened; he was once an easygoing and cheerful young man, always smiling, always friendly, always well-disposed. Now they saw him as a deranged person, walking the streets of Bridgetown like a vagrant, talking to himself, a man with an unsound mind.

Broad Street, true to its name at the time, was where the powerful merchants held sway with their fashionable inherited stores: Fogarty's Department Store, Cave Shepherd & Company Limited, DaCosta & Sons, Harrison's Limited. Harold turned his attention to this epicentre of island commerce that had endured through the years and wondered how much of that concentration of wealth lay indirectly on the backs of the indentured and the enslaved, on sugar plantations, and before then, on acres and acres of coveted Sea Island cotton, and before then, in groves of the finest tobacco leaves from Havana to Virginia? He had no just reason to malign these giants of retail but his tortured mind was in no mood for fairness. Their windows dazzled with white mannequins modelling British tweeds, foppish hats, elegant dresses and exquisite pieces of East Indian jewellery. He wandered into Fogarty's and mindlessly peered into the gleaming glass cases and gazed at the racks piled high with imported merchandise, all exuding taste and quality and opulence. The rich locals mingled with the tourists, and the cash boys, not a dark skin among them, darted from clerk to register and back; the atmosphere was all so airy and worldly. Clotelle, the scantily clad bag-woman from Arthur's Seat, St. Thomas, trailed by her five little children, equally half-naked, wandered in for alms and a taste of the fancy. She shuffled up to a register; the clerk dropped a few coins in her hand and ushered her gently to the exit. He headed over to Cave Shepherd where in a corner of the doorway, Harcourt the foulmouthed street beggar, known to one and all, squatted cross-legged like a snake charmer. Harcourt owned the spot. Pretending to be crippled, he was in truth as strong and fit as any man. He held out his tin cup to Harold, who, short of cash himself, passed him by; whereupon the mendicant peppered his back with a stream of maledictions, calling on God to blind him right there on the spot. It was all too familiar to Harold, this culture of classes, this pageant of citified and country, this juxtaposition of privileged and poor, of black and white, all coexisting in this small island of walls decidedly distinct and discriminate.

He walked to the corner, turned and made his way to Swan Street, a mile-long tight-knit bazaar of multi-cultural stores owned by Jews, Indians, Syrians and other foreigners. Their merchandise spilled outside onto sidewalk displays while inside were shelves and tables laden with exotic fabrics and pickings that rivalled the Broad Street goods with lower prices and lower overhead. They manned their own registers and bargained face-to-face with anyone inclined to linger and haggle a while. There was not an indigenous Bajan storeowner among them. These proprietors, now domiciled on the island, had come from halfway around the world to rule Swan Street.

Bajan vendors owned the alleys, the narrow and barely passable straits that joined bustling Broad and Swan Streets. In Busby Alley they squatted in their allotted spots behind trays piled high with produce from their own country grounds: breadfruits, pumpkins, yams, cassavas, English potatoes, paw-paws, carrots, peas, beets, eddoes, and more. They had no need for scales, they weighed their provisions by hand; they needed no registers, they worked the numbers in their heads or on fingers like on an abacus. They made change as quickly as they could dig into their apron pockets or reach into their brassieres or untie money-kerchiefs knotted at one end like miniature sacks. Receipts were neither offered nor expected; trade was conducted in good faith and with trust.

Carmita, an old hardened tray seller approaching her eightieth year and who had owned the spot at the corner of Busby Alley for forty of those years, spied Harold in her peripheral vision as he crossed the street. "See muh hey!" she called out. He knew her well, she lived in his village, took the early bus every morning to claim her spot in the alley. She was sitting low on an empty Coca Cola crate with her legs spread wide apart, her dress and apron drooped discretely between them.

"Anyt'ing new 'bout de court case?"

"Soon," he told her.

"Well, darlin', God don' like ugly. What goes around comes around, you hear? Day does run til night catch it; time longer than twine; and, believe you me, every dog has his day."

Carmita was full of these aphorisms, old Bajan everyday incantations that magically buoyed the spirits of the poor and those at the bottom of this stratified society. Now she laid them on Harold in his time of distress. He wondered if by some good fortune Carmita would one day escape Busby Alley and find a more visible place for her wares, but he knew that life had consigned her to this cramped, dank and dirty alleyway, perhaps for the rest of her days. As he turned to walk away, Carmita imparted one last word that said much more than she intended: "Every rope has an end." He already knew he was nearing the end of his.

Chapter 15

The Bajan Yankee

FARTHER ALONG on Broad Street, a man called to him from the sidewalk. "Harold Prince, is that you, mayn?"

The voice seemed to parody an American drawl. It was tinged with uncertainty that it was Harold. He turned around and searched the man's face; it was slow to register.

"Don' remember me, brother?

The face was vaguely familiar to Harold but his clothes were distracting. On his head was a tilted fedora, a peacock's feather stuck in the band. He wore a pink open-neck shirt with fluffy sleeves, high-waisted zoot suit, the jacket hooked over his shoulder with one finger while several gold bracelets dangled extravagantly from his left wrist. He was most assuredly a foreigner, thought Harold; no Bajan would have the gall—or the wherewithal—to dress that way in the centre of Bridgetown.

"Is me, Mickey Norris."

"Mickey Norris?"

The name belonged to an old Elementary schoolmate who had dropped out in the Fifth Form and vanished from sight. He hadn't seen him in ages; they used to be the best of friends. The face returned but the voice might well have belonged to some remote ventriloquism lip-synched effortlessly with not a hint of a Bajan accent. The Mickey Norris he once knew at school was a shy, unpopular, laconic type shunned by the other fellows. It was undoubtedly through compassion in those days that he had befriended him and become perhaps his only friend. Mickey wore the same bedraggled shirt, flip-flops and short pants to St. Giles every day, and at roll call when Headmaster Martindale marched the boys outside for fingernail inspection and patrolled up and down the line like a drill sergeant, he was always one to feel the spank of the ruler on his knuckles and ordered off to the school pipe. Now here he was, the antithesis of coy, a model of exhibitionism.

"Where you been all these years, Mickey?"

"Brother, ah been living in the States, yes sirree! Working fer Mr. Charlie. Flew in last night from Idlewild. Yeah!" Mickey spat out a string of short phrases as if the English language tended to be too much of a burden.

It was rumoured that he was born in Nelson Street, the roaring red-light district of Bridgetown, to a less than virtuous woman, and had been left to his own survival instincts at a very young age. People said his mother spent most of her life in a stupor of alcohol and dope and that his father had preferred to remain in the shadows. Seeing Mickey now, a long way from the squalor of his upbringing, Harold took a while to mentally reconcile the friend he knew with the man now standing before him.

"What brings you back home, Mickey?"

"Back here to put a decent roof over the ole lady's head. Yeah! Move her out of Nelson Street. Sick ole woman she is. Find her a nice bay house to live in Silver Sands. Gotta make her comfy before she kick the bucket. Know what ah'm saying? Never did much fer me when ah was little but hell, she's still mah mother, right?"

Harold gathered that in Mickey's new language the white man was "Mr. Charlie" and that black men dressed like Mickey on the streets of America. His friend had metamorphosed into a Yankee through and through but his heart in the process remained in the right place, humane, caring for a mother who had cared much less for him.

"You hear 'bout my boy?" asked Harold. How could he not!

"You'd better believe it, Jack! That news is all over Brooklyn. It was even in one o' them Harlem newspapers, *The Renaissance*. Bajans in New Yawk and all over the States placing bets on the trial. Mr. Charlie should swing fer sure but it ain't gonna happen. No way! Time for some damn justice fer black folks. Ah'm sorry, brother, sorry to hear!"

Perhaps not wanting to dwell on a distressful story, Mickey digressed. "Brother, Bim is a beautiful place! Good to be back on the rock. The view from that Pan Am Clipper just before she banked and put down at Seawell. My! My! My! That gorgeous white coastline, that clean blue ocean, those lush fields in St. Philip looked like a beautiful quilt, a sight for sore eyes. Yes, sirree!

"Been living in Nashville. That's in Tennessee, y'know. Making some serious money. Which you can do in the States s'long as you willing to work yer arse off. Know what ah'm saying?"

THERE ONCE WAS A LITTLE ENGLAND

Harold quipped, "I can see what you mean, Mickey, looking at these clothes you wearing."

Mickey drawled on. "Got me a job driving an oil truck. Working fer a cracker by the name o' Jackson. Bob Jackson is his name. Yeah! First day on the job he says to me, 'Call me Bob, that's mah name, not Mr. Jackson!' Hell, here in Bim, you call yer boss by his first name, you might as well start walking. Damn!" Harold could attest to that last remark. Mickey's head leaned back and two gold-capped incisors sparkled, as he laughed loud and heartily in the middle of the sidewalk, indifferent to shoppers left and right stopping in their tracks to either admire or decry this flashy Bajan Yankee.

Suddenly, sobriety took over his whole demeanour. "But that damn racism is what's wrong with the States, 'specially in the South. Now dig this! Imagine me walking down a street couple o' months ago outside o' Nashville—that's in Tennessee, y'know. It was a hot, hot day, steam coming out o' mah ears. Whew! You think Bim is hot? Well, brother, you got to feel Southern heat. And believe me, that morning ah was thirsty, mah throat was dry, dry as a husk. So ah sees these two coloured guys pruning some white people's hedges and ah say, 'hey bro, where can a brother get a cool drink o' water'. So they point me to the same country house where they working at. Nice friendly ranch. Cute little white children playing on the lawn. And so ah head over to the window and knock. Ah reckon whoever's living in that there house had to be okay, 'specially since ah'm hearing the sweet soulful voice of Mahalia Jackson coming from the Victrola: *'Amazing Grace, how sweet the song that saved ah wretch like me.'* Know what ah'm saying? So ah proceed to ask fer a glass o' water and, sure enough, a lady's hand reaches out the window with a big glass o' ice-cold water. Ah say to mahself, they got some Good Samaritans here in the South, don't care what they say up North 'bout these Rednecks. So anyway, ah'm sweating like a mule, grateful fer this cold refreshment from this generous white lady. Ah down the water in three or four gulps, thank this Good Samaritan, return the glass and start off again, cool, refreshed and collected. Well, guess what!"

At this point, Mickey interrupted his own story, laughing and coughing uncontrollably, bending over and hugging his belly as if locked in an epileptic seizure right there on the sidewalk of Broad Street with people milling around, gazing curiously at the two of them as if they were two slapstick performers in a vaudeville play. Harold waited patiently for the punch line.

Mickey recovered and continued. "Before ah could reach the end of this lady's driveway, ah hear 'Plax!' and ah look back just in time to see the glass ricocheting off the porch column next to the window. B'Christ, the innocent glass ah had just held to mah black lips had been corrupted and ah didn't even know it. Shoot! Not even soap and water could redeem that poor glass. The unfortunate glass had lost its rightful place alongside all the other fine crystal in this woman's cupboard. It had to be destroyed forthwith, never ever to come in contact again with her lips or her children's lips." Mickey bent forward and roared with laughter.

"But y'know," he resumed, regaining his composure, "even then, ah really didn't feel no animosity towards this Southern woman. Only pity. She wasn't an evil person. Hell, if she was evil she woulda laced that glass with some good ole arsenic fer this son-of-a-bitch to drop dead right there in the driveway fer having the gall, me a black man, to walk boldly up to that white people's house, not even 'round the back, but to the front window, and embarrass her in front of the neighbours and the two other niggas in the hedges who sent me to that front window in the first place and now laughing their arses off."

Harold chimed in. "Well, at least the woman knew her bible alright. 'If anyone is thirsty, let him come to me and drink,' says the Good Book, don' it!" Now both he and Mickey doubled over with laughter.

Mickey then proceeded to recount story after story of colour prejudice and discrimination, witnessed or experienced in his four and a half years in the American South, and at the end of every contemptible, shameful narrative, his face shone with amusement. In a strange way, Harold envied his friend; he had developed his own effective antidote of laughter, his own carapace of comedy to inoculate him from the stings and bruises of a racist society and to nullify the hate before it could penetrate and poison his spirit. Mickey had found mirth in every racial episode, and every dishonourable act of Mr. Charlie was written into his own hilarious comedy: a wooden cross, the very symbol of the Christian Crucifix burning on the front lawn of a black homeowner who dared to move into a white "Christian" neighbourhood; cowardly eyes peering from holes in ghostly white shrouds; "Whites Only" signs at public fountains with water no more potable than water elsewhere; city buses with the most comfortable seats in the rear for the most discomfited. Mickey had deemed these racist symbols not just evil but laughable, and as such they could never diminish his Bajan pride.

"Brother, just before ah left the South," he said with a serious face, "this tired black lady refused to surrender her seat to a white woman on the bus. Was a big scene, brother. Yeah! Made the news on TV and everything. And guess what! Mr. Charlie put her off the bus and black people shut down the whole damn transit right there in Alabama. Now that's what ah'm talking about! And that is what we Bajans have to learn from our brothers and sisters in the States; we have to learn to agitate. Yeah! Agitate! Where is the outrage over your boy? Where is justice? Get our people together! Surround the house of that Englishman that killed your son! Parade 'round the courthouse in town! Block all the traffic on Broad Street! Close down the city! Call attention to your situation, to your predicament, mah friend! Demand justice! Fight back! Get arrested! Agitate! Agitate! Know what ah'm saying?" Mickey punctuated each phrase with a closed-fisted jab as if Mr. Charlie were right there in his face.

It occurred to Harold that somewhere in Mickey's outburst there had to be a kernel of truth. The people's fury that erupted the day his son was killed had crested and then fell silent. Like the hurricane's wrath, it had come and gone. Bajans today only walked by the scene of the crime, fulminating with a few explosions of home-grown cuss words and with prayers that God would rain down vengeance on the mansion and on the man who lived there, and on his mother, and on his mother's mother, and on his whole bloodline, and on every Englishman who ever set foot on the island. It was the usual empty bluster, no action, no demonstration, only from young boys, the ones with spunk, who lobbed rocks over Thorne's guard wall into his courtyard at night. He thought, maybe these boys will be the leaders of tomorrow, the ones who will lead the people into a new day.

But he also deduced that Barbadians were naturally a benign, peace-loving people: after hundreds of years the island was still living passively in the shadow of her colonial past, like a beautiful embryonic butterfly, reluctant to wriggle out of her cosy chrysalis. On the other hand, he knew colonization was not savage and brutally conquering like the hegemonies of old, but subtly overpowering with the occasional sedation of goodwill.

"Bajans don't take to the streets," he said to Mickey. "The last time we did was in 1937; I was fourteen. When the riot was over, my old lady got a three-shilling raise from the plantation after cutting canes from the time she was a teenager. We are not agitators."

"Well then, in that case, you are destined to be second class," replied Mickey.

"So why you want to live in America to be second class when you could be second class right here at home?" Harold quickly shot back.

Mickey paused with a grave look of introspection on his face. He removed his fedora and ran his fingers along the brim. For the first time Harold saw his Sammy Davis, Jr. hair, complete with a cowlick which he now tossed back smartly from his forehead. Mickey looked down pensively at his Florsheim two-toned shoes.

"Fair question, mah brother, fair question. It's not about love for America. It's about the money. *Muh-Nee*." He emphasized each syllable mockingly, deliberately, with a playful pursing of the lips as if he were teaching a toddler the proper way to enunciate the word. "Brother, think back to your Latin days to Virgil, that epic poet of Roman times. *'Amor Omnia Vincit'*. Well, brother, ah'm here to tell you that Virgil was wrong; it is *money* that conquers all, not love. Know what ah'm saying? Here, in this place of mah birth, the Englishman will smile graciously and say to me, 'Mr. Norris, come in out of the hot sun, ole chap. It's a hot one today, a real scorcher, isn't it? Would you fancy a warm cuppa tea?' 'No, Mr. Charlie, but ah would fancy a glass of cold water.' And then he would hand you a few drops o' lukewarm water in a tin cup. 'Terribly sorry, Mr. Norris, we're a bit short of water today actually.' "

Mickey was trying to speak mockingly like an Englishman but his adopted American twang was getting in the way. "Y'see, brother, here Mr. Charlie is all smiles and titles and courtesies. Know what ah mean? But in the States they pay you fer a day's work even if they hate yer stinkin' guts. They offer you a full glass o' water even if they break the friggin glass as soon as you turn yer damn back."

His words gave Harold pause. He thought of his years at *The Chronicle*, five days a week, half days on Saturdays, anxiously looking forward to the end of the week when he would hold out his hand for the cantankerous woman bookkeeper to grudgingly shell out a pittance of fourteen bills and ten coppers, hardly a decent wage for a conscientious worker with a bunch of Advanced Level certificates under his belt. He was grateful for the additional income from Cissy's dressmaking to make ends meet. With enough Yankee money he could do a lot for his family: add another roof to their two-roofed wooden house and shed, or build a nice airy veranda, or move out of Thornville altogether and live in one of those wall-houses in White Park.

But could he live in America, in Mickey's world? Harold thought not. Barbados was his rightful home, where black people were still met with white civility, where meanness wore a patina of good old British gentility; where the inevitable frictions in society were lubricated with good manners; and where those who ruled the land had learned to manipulate the people with gloved hands.

Mickey Norris, as said, had come from humble beginnings, poorer and humbler than the world in which Harold had been raised. Following is the snapshot he gave to Harold of his life since dropping out of school. From an early age he had learned the value of the American dollar from his prostitute mother in Nelson Street; had seen the Yankee sailors flash their greenbacks in her face; had witnessed firsthand their lavish spending in the bars and in the nightclubs on Bay Street and Suttle Street; on the streets of Bridgetown, Yankee money flowed like water from the fountain in Trafalgar Square. It was easy money, thought Mickey. Lacking the parental guidance and the education that fed the minds and bolstered the ambitions of his friends, he needed some of that easy money to short-circuit the long, arduous climb on which his friends had embarked. When the opportunity arose through a worker recruitment programme, he escaped to the promised land of America, endured two years of frigid winters in the North ("Mayn, some days in New Yawk was cold as a witch's tits," he had said to Harold.) and four and a half of naked racism in the South before returning with a comfortable bank account.

But alas, during his sojourn, America instilled within him new big-city ways. A culture of violence had clung to him like a new skin. He now said to Harold, "Ah ain't telling you what to do, brother, but if it was mah son that he killed, ah would take 'im out."

"He would take 'im out," repeated Harold to himself and figured that his friend meant he would shoot the Englishman dead, another of Mickey's vague Americanisms. "Well, the trial is coming up. We'll see," Harold responded with an insouciant shrug.

"Ah tell ya, Mr. Charlie is gonna walk free, mark mah word. Like ah say, nothing less than a life for a life. If you wanna settle things ah have a friend who can help. You know where ah'm coming from?"

"Who's yer friend, Mickey?" Harold's face lit up; perhaps Mickey had a lawyer friend, someone more effectual than Solicitor Trotman.

Mickey glanced over his left shoulder, then over his right, then whispered, "Stick yer hand in this here pocket." Harold reached into Mickey's breast pocket and felt the cold, hard, tubular steel of a gun muzzle. He had never touched a gun before. Reflexively, he jerked his hand free as if he had unwittingly disturbed a bag of pet snakes.

"22 Smith & Wesson," said Mickey. "You can have it, mah friend. Take care of Mr. Charlie!" The smile fell from his face.

"Can't do it, Mickey. Got to let the law run its course."

Harold turned to say goodbye. Mickey grabbed his right hand and guided it through a ritualistic sequence of pumps, grips, squeezes and twists, an esoteric handshake learned from his American brothers. "Best o' luck on that trial, brother. Ah'm saying, not a day in jail for Mr. Charlie. For your sake, brother, ah hope ah'm wrong."

Harold was even more troubled than he had been before the bizarre encounter with his friend, Mickey Norris, the *nouveau riche*. As his friend walked away, he heard him say, "Harold, come see me at mah mother's … Nelson Street and King William. Yeah mayn!" Farther along on the busy sidewalk, across from Knights Drugstore, he saw Mickey resuming his Napoleonic pose, basking in the admiration as much as ignoring the sneers of his Bajan countrymen.

THERE ONCE WAS A LITTLE ENGLAND

In his mind, Harold compared the two encounters, one with his flamboyant friend, Mickey, the other with down-to-earth Carmita, the tray seller in Busby Alley. His friend had reinvented himself in the parody of the Uncle Sam he had seen in pictures, standing above the crowd on stilts, in top hat and tails, and red, white and blue striped trousers. Mickey had overcompensated for the cards he had been dealt. But at least he could now thumb his nose at those who had condemned him to a life of destitution, as black and as undereducated as he was. Somehow Harold's encounter with Carmita had been much more uplifting.

Chapter 16

From Trafalgar Square to Lower Green

THE YEAR 1955 in Barbados was a banner year for political campaigning. A new Party had been formally established in April that year. A pivotal general election loomed large in the upcoming year for its promise of a new ministerial government with a cabinet system. New exciting political happenings were now on the edge of the horizon.

The roads in every village, every town and every parish echoed with the blaring of bullhorns. Up and down the island, from their lorries festooned with all kinds of garish banners and thumping with steel band music, politicians shouted their messages to people in their houses, on the roads, in the fields, in the shops, exhorting, cajoling and bludgeoning the voters with their grandiose promises. Their flyers littered the streets and the gutters; posters screamed from every public wall in Bridgetown displaying the faces of black men who professed to have seen a light at the end of the tunnel and had stepped forward on behalf of their various districts. Two or three lorries even ventured onto the cart road in Thornville and were pelted with rock stones.

The stages were set. The years ahead spoke of unchartered waters to be navigated, and into that maelstrom of wild uncertainties stepped the two political enemies, two proud and able black men, Barrister Virgil Cunningham and Solicitor Fitzgerald Trotman. Cissy and Harold took the bus down to the city for a close look at the two candidates in action, one on the side of their son's alleged killer and the other, on their side, the self-appointed counsellor in the search for justice. Harold had not yet met the barrister and he had deep distrust for Trotman.

Their first stop was at Cunningham's campaign meeting. He had evidently resolved to juggle the Thorne case with his political pursuit. Bajans were already converging on Trafalgar Square where, now and then, a jubilant crowd of Cunningham worshippers poured out of a city bus and made their way to the open-air theatre. Their man was the illustrious and learned lawyer. They were salivating for his eloquent speeches and already smelling triumph over Trotman. Others came by motorcar and parked tightly together in a sign of solidarity on the far side of the public fountain. Their children sat on the bonnets and older folks unfolded their metal chairs and lounged alongside their vehicles. They brought out their picnic flasks and sandwiches and prepared themselves for a night of enlightenment and entertainment. These were not the affluent set; the affluent purposely stayed away from public masses; these were the up and coming middle-class, people moderately placed in the society. They sat away in the back far from the sweaty pack bunched together closer to the stage. A scruffy bearded man known to everyone as "Clarkie," a would-have-been lawyer, who went mad in his better years studying in England for the Bar, was working the crowd, handing out pages of the Cunningham manifesto. He was barefoot, dressed in purple pyjamas and appeared to be ignorant of Cunningham's political ideas, for when someone asked what Cunningham stood for, he simply recited excerpts from Shakespeare, most notably from Macbeth: *Look like the innocent flower, but be the serpent under it.* Was he alluding to his own man?

The more fanatical stood tightly up front, some at the rim of the stage where they could shake Cunningham's hand or even touch the hem of his garment as he ascended to the dais. These were the persuaded working-class, the infatuated poor. They made no moral judgments of their candidate; they were captivated by his style, his persona and his way with words, some which to them had no meaning but were sweet sounding in their ears. They were inspired by his rise from the dire pits of poverty, pits as abysmal as the toilet pits his late father used to clean for a living. His money, his fame, his erudition, impressed them all. His road to success was vicariously theirs, notwithstanding the long trail of scruples he had trampled along the way. Cunningham needed these poor devoted souls in order to succeed in his campaign; with only the rich and the powerful on his side he could never make it to the finish line.

It was the hottest, sweatiest night of the year. Not even the puff of a breeze came off the Bay to cool impatient heads waiting for the main speaker to appear. People were fanning frantically, wiping their faces and armpits, perspiration streaming down into the creases of their necks, their faces glistening with sweat as they sucked on shaved-ice known as "travellers" and downed gallons of ice-cold mauby. Some sat on the scalloped edge of the water fountain, cooling their bare feet in the waterfall. In the dimly-lit surroundings they waited for their man to appear on stage to spin his web of delicious eloquence with big words interspersed with splashes of salty language, after which they would return to their homes, their spirits uplifted, their longings quenched like prayerful souls returning from a revival meeting. Yes, Cunningham was their man; he would protect their interests; he would save them from the creeping radicalism of Trotman and his dangerous hordes.

That night in Trafalgar Square, Harold could see the ghost of David looming behind the dais like a cinematic backdrop, and as the preliminary speakers stepped up one by one to the microphone, his spirit lurked in the shadows while Harold heard the murmuring of his name in the pauses between each sentence, drowning out the rhetoric and the jokes and the promises. How he wished that his name would also resound through the Houses of Parliament at the top of Broad Street and to the steps of Her Majesty's Courthouse on Coleridge Street and all the way up to Government Hill to Government House, where the Governor would plead for calm, fearing another riot like in 1937 when the working-class armed with rocks, stones, sticks and bottles rioted all over Bridgetown, prompting one of his predecessors to call out a police detachment with orders to kill, shooting over a dozen rebellious Bajans to death and goring dozens more with their bayoneted rifles.

Suddenly a drum roll rippled up from the back of the stage. Cunningham strode to the lectern, cool as a cucumber. A clatter of applause went up from the crowd. Those seated in the back rose from their folding chairs with their hands in the air, clapping, whistling and hooting; people in the front pressed forward towards the stage. The spotlight fell on the barrister resplendent in a white three-piece suit, light-blue shirt, red tie and pocket kerchief. With a papal wave of his hands, he acknowledged the applause and then gestured to his followers that he was ready to bless and reward them for having endured the oppressive heat of the last hour awaiting his presence. Then he reached into his waistcoat for his opening remarks. At that instant, without warning, from every corner of Trafalgar Square came a volley of stones and bottles and all kinds of projectiles like on that night of 1937, over the motorcars, over the buses in the bus stand, over the water fountain, over the seats, and onto the canvas canopy above the speakers' platform. Cunningham fled into the arms of two petrified police officers. They bundled him into the back of a police van and sped from the scene. The insurgents were yelling, "David! David! David!" as they barrelled into the crowd and stormed the stage, brandishing sticks, trampling bodies, tackling anyone in the speaker's entourage. The police waded into the crowd, blowing their whistles and waving their billy clubs in the air, but the officers were overpowered. Folding chairs were hurled onto the platform; the platform was upended and the loudspeakers toppled. It was all over. Cunningham's people scurried away from Trafalgar Square. Motorcars fled the scene in all directions like roaches.

Holding hands, running away and down Broad Street towards the Trotman camp on the opposite side of town, Harold and Cissy faced an oncoming cavalcade of policemen on horseback heading towards the fracas. In the distance, Trotman's stentorian voice grew louder and louder as they approached the Lower Green. The self-proclaimed defender of the working-class was holding forth from the platform of a cane lorry.

A more homogeneous crowd had gathered to hear the Solicitor. His people were the common folk, plain folk, unpretentious folk, people not ashamed to talk and laugh out loud and unrestrainedly or to be rowdy or even to be vulgar. They were all the same and therefore neither self-conscious nor driven to be different one from the other; men in short pants, rubber sandals, and tee shirts; women in long frumpish dresses and "walk-forwards," their heads tied, their manners unaffected. They seemed not to be put off by the prickly heat; they seemed to welcome it. They came on foot, by bicycle and by bus, from as far away as St. Philip, St. Joseph, St. Lucy and St. Andrew. They thronged to his meeting, some for no other reason than for the free entertainment, hugging their bellies with laughter, rocking back and forth with loud rip-roaring cackles, whooping it up at every jab at Trotman's opponent now fleeing Trafalgar Square. Their ears let pass the outpouring of grandiose promises from Trotman, promises they knew would not be kept and enticements of a new day they were sure they would never see. They closed their minds to his glaring hypocrisies and lies and they promised to vote for him anyway because he made them feel good and made them laugh. But the question was always whether Trotman could rely on these followers once they returned to their weary lethargic lives in the countryside and his bristling humour had left their ears and the euphoria of the campaign had faded like the dying strains of a marching band disappearing off into the sunset.

On the political stage Trotman was not half as unctuous or as smooth as Cunningham but he knew how to wrap insults and slander, sarcasm and execrations into ingenious packets of humour so that people could swallow them without tasting the bitter contents. He knew how to enter the people's heads and to be seen as a simple man, a selfless man, risen from poor seedy New Orleans, chosen to be their voice, to take their message to the ones in power, using the people's vocabulary, eschewing the lofty self-indulgent language that belonged to Cunningham, his political nemesis.

In Trotman's camp the atmosphere was festive. A carnival. Women hawkers lined the three lanes of the Lower Green bus stand, squatting on empty Ju-c crates, behind trays piled high with peanuts, ackees, fat porks, sugar apples, mammy apples, cashews, sour dunks, plums, sugar-coated tamarind balls, English toffees, red and white cock-comb peppermints, white sugar cakes, brown sugar cakes, pink sugar cakes, dark sugar cakes and black-bitch sugar cakes. They wound through the crowd, balancing their heaping trays, their heads padded with towels against the weight of the trays, calling out, "Pack o' nuts, anybody? See muh hey! You want me?" Fathers hoisted children onto their shoulders for a good look at the man who might very well be the one to pave the way forward. They surrounded the lorry and reached up to the platform to shake Trottie's hand. He was their man, the man of the people. Trottie would not disappoint them; he would tell them everything they wanted to hear.

His campaign meeting that night was no different from any other, except that Cissy and Harold were present. They wanted to observe firsthand his manner, his tenacity, his heart, his way with words when he took their case to the prosecution. As the flood lights drifted towards the periphery of the crowd, a glimpse of Cissy standing next to her man sparked a few fiery lines from Trotman as he bellowed into the megaphone while pointing in their direction.

"Hey, look Miss Braffit over they! Cunningham sellin' out he own people, defendin' de white man that pump two holes in Miss Braffit boy-child. If you don' believe it is de white man puttin' money in Cunningham pocket, go down by de all-white Water Club and see dem hangin' round him like puppy dogs. How in God's name a black man like he could have de heart to turn he back on he own people and tek de side of a limey dat snuff out de life o' dis poor mother and father boy-child?" A chorus of groans went up from the crowd as the lights momentarily shone on the two heavyhearted parents. They were assets to his campaign.

Harold was wary of Trotman. He felt that his folksy style and comedic delivery would do well in politics among the unsophisticated, but would be ineffectual in legal matters, especially in contrast with a serious legal mind like Cunningham. Moreover, he was secretly suspicious of his motives and considered them less altruistic and more opportunistic than Cissy had imagined; after all, he was a politician seeking to ingratiate himself with the working-class. Harold wished he had the ruthless Cunningham in David's corner instead but knew the barrister was beyond his reach, that he belonged to the rich, the whites, and the powerful. So while Cissy leaned on the solicitor who had knocked on her door and had come to their home to offer a hand and had accompanied her down to the courthouse to bear witness to the arraignment, Harold deemed him a loser. Moreover, a solicitor was just a solicitor, thought Harold, unqualified to either prosecute or defend.

As time went by, the acrimony that fuelled the campaigns still floated in the air like volcanic ash. Cunningham was prevailing on the shoulders of the powerful, the rich and the middle-class, but he also was helped by the gullible and infatuated poor. Trotman was sinking fast. At a time when communism was considered the scourge of all mankind, the solicitor was saddled with a stigma he could not deflect since many of his followers were indeed radicals and malcontents railing day and night against the inequities of the ruling system.

The end of the year was approaching and all the political rancour softened as the minds of the people turned to the joys of another Christmas season.

Chapter 17

The Matriarch

CHRISTMAS THAT year returned reluctantly to the pink house in Thornville, for the hearts and minds of this family were far removed. Yet Cissy needed to get her house in order to instil some semblance of the season within its walls and, as luck would have it, help arrived like a band of angels on a mission of mercy. It came in the persons of Ma Prince and her five daughters, bounding through the front door early on Christmas morning.

Bajans traditionally were so possessed with this holiest of days that the whole month of December was a long anticipatory drum-roll. But it was also a time when a spirit of goodwill reigned and it was that spirit that helped to temper the angry passions that had been churning within the hearts of many since the death of David Prince. And so it was with Ma Prince. Although neither a churchgoer nor a woman of profound religious convictions but a moral person nevertheless, she was warmed to the spirit of Christmas though not greatly imbued with its spiritual meaning. She lacked the steadfast Christian faith that Cissy possessed and having no faith to which she could cling, she had suffered alone and in silence. As she entered the house, she made no mention of David but Cissy could see that grief had taken its toll: her eyes were red and her face swollen fat from crying.

Ma Prince was a pitch-black handsome woman, tall and with an immense presence like her son. She possessed a large frame, ample bosom, broad hips and heavy arms. Born in 1890, she had been a cane cutter in her younger days and the hardened calluses on her right palm bore testimony to years of swinging a wooden-handled sickle in the cane fields that were the property of Mr. Thorne's predecessors. The curved blade, now rusted, still hung like a war trophy on a nail in the back of her house in The Ivy, just as it did in Thornville before she had been forced to move to escape the persecution of those who had accused her of encouraging illicit behaviour under her roof. That day had brought tears to her eyes, leaving behind her comfortable three-roofed wooden house, upgraded from the one-roofed chattel shack that had been the birthplace of her mother, an ex-slave. The only other relic retained from the old house was a scrolled copy of the Emancipation Act dated August 28th, 1833 with the eventual abolition throughout the British Empire the year after. Her mother kept it under the bed for fear of confiscation by the slave master, who would sometimes visit without forewarning. It had been rendered almost illegible by age, moth bites and water stains, but Ma Prince had the first few words reproduced in elegant cursive penmanship, framed and hung in the front house for all to read. She lit a shrine of two candles nightly in remembrance of her grandparents who had not lived to witness the declaration:

> *WHEREAS divers Persons are holden in Slavery within divers of His Majesty's Colonies, and it is just and expedient that all such Persons should be manumitted and set free . . .*

As a young girl, Ma Prince had been ahead of her time in manner of dress and style, wearing bright-red lipstick, eye-popping shorts, mini-dresses and stiletto heels; even in Bridgetown, where one day she caught the eye of a young handsome Jamaican sailor boy who happened to be in port that day. They married on his next stopover and immediately began, he to sow his seeds from time to time, and she to give birth in a continuum that yielded five girls, whom because of her predilection for the letter "M", she christened Molly, Margaret, Mildred, Myrtle and Marjorie. Harold was her only boy.

Now here she was, the stout-hearted matriarch of the Prince family, come to prepare this cheerless house for the holidays, the flab of her sleeveless arms jiggling merrily as she darted from one chore to the next, first opening wide each window and methodically removing its blinds for sunlight to suffuse the whole house, then rearranging the furniture to suggest a more spacious and airy surrounding, then placing a stick of burning incense on the centre table for its thread of fragrance to ward off any evil spirits that might dare to invade her space. She hung every door and window with red bunting and clothed the dining table in red. She glanced in the mirror at her corn rows like perfectly aligned trenches, and then wrapped them with a red and white polka dot scarf, before standing tall and dishing out peremptory commands to her girls with the cadence of a drill sergeant. She first dispatched the girls up the hill to the defunct limekiln where they would shovel up enough marl to blanket the backyard from corner to corner with pure white "snow." She ordered that the sorrel pods be spread out on the roof of the rabbit coop in the sun and when dried to be steeped in seasoned water which, before long, would miraculously turn into a delicious deep-red "wine." She reached down and raised the hem of her dress to the height of her knees and then, untwisting a knot in the folds of her stockings, she peeled off four coins, despatching Molly off to the ice factory in town. A brick of solid ice would be delivered later that day and quickly shrouded in a crocus bag with rock salt, and then placed in a huge oval steel tub in the shed-roof where the ice would be stabbed from time to time with a wooden-handle ice pick.

In the front house, the Danish ham, a gift from Pastor Gittens's church, had been hanging from a rafter for weeks like a convicted felon. Ma Prince climbed on a chair, snipped the noose and liberated it from its crocus and tar-coated prison. Every house at Christmas would boast of a ham from Goddards Food Emporium. She fetched from the walnut larder a yellow mound of Wisconsin cheese and sliced it into judiciously thin wedges, mindful of the multitude of lickerish mouths that would be coming to the house that day, oozing with condolences but expecting to be fed. But from those same mouths she would conceal her baked pork, fried chicken, pigeon peas and rice, macaroni pie, jug-jug, and all the other delicacies that would contribute to her family's moderate celebration of Christmas.

And so, a bitter sweet blend of joy and sadness pervaded the air on Christmas morning. Ma Prince enlivened the house in keeping with the season but discretely maintained the decor of a home still mourning its loss, and though custom ruled that every Bajan house in every village in every parish be joyous, celebrating in plenitude the birth of the Holy Child, this house was moderately reflective of the spirit of Christmas, and even with the haunting memory of a son who had been ripped from their midst, she managed to brighten the faces of the rest of her beloved family.

That morning, Pastor Gittens was standing in the vestibule to welcome all who would grace his church with their presence on this hallowed day, among them, Cissy, Nathaniel and his five aunts. Bajans of all stripes, Christians and nonbelievers alike, even those who had not been inside of a church all year and would likely not be back until the following Christmas, would be flocking to his church and to churches all across the island, filling the pews and jamming the aisles. Women would be showing off their brand new Christmas finery and men would be sporting their new three-piece suits collected just minutes before from the always tardy village tailor. Brand new tight-fitting Bata shoes would make their first strutting on Christmas morning, as Bajans wended their way to churches of their choice, decked out in their finest sartorial splendour.

The pastor had already commissioned Reverend Flexon, the corpulent American missionary with the gravelly voice, to give the Christmas sermon. He always delivered the biggest bang for the buck with his solo singing and guitar playing before launching into a passionate prayer with a Southern drawl that enthralled the congregation. When the two round mahogany collection trays were passed from pew to pew and hand to hand, the people showed their appreciation generously because this selfless white man had sacrificed being with his own people on a snowy-white mistletoe Christmas like the ones pictured on those exotic Christmas cards from Amurca.

Ma and her son stayed behind. That certain inviolable space between mother and son, distinct and separate from the bond held with the girls, welcomed this time together and alone. She plunked her weary body down on the side of the bed where her son lay fully awake and sullen. Like a lioness cuddling her wounded cub, she placed his head gently on her lap. Still, she would not bring herself to talk about David or the cascade of events since his death, but sought to steer his mind to happy thoughts.

"Guess what I got you fer Christmas?"

"A motorcar?" he asked facetiously.

"Under de breadfruit tree."

Like a child, he bounced off the bed, ran out to the yard and out the gate with Ma in pursuit, and there, leaning against the trunk, was a new shiny Raleigh bicycle. He beamed like a child and wrapped his arms around her waist. "Love you, Ma."

But this gesture of love would be a prelude to some serious heart-to-heart talk. She needed to relieve her mind of things she had kept bottled up for a long time, questions begging for answers only Harold could give. She went to the kitchen-shed, lit a fire, put the kettle on, strained two cups of boiling water through some Red Rose tea leaves and sat across from Harold at the little centre table. Before her first sip, she reached into a pocket of her proud new à la mode cotton dress that Cissy had given her for Christmas, fished out a one-inch-square metal snuffbox, tapped the lid lightly, and then delicately placed a pinch of the powdered tobacco at the tip of each nostril. Two sharp sniffs were sufficient to clear her head for what she was about to say. She closed her eyes, wriggled her nose, and with a stamp of her feet she let loose a hearty self-induced sneeze that shook the plywood partitions.

"Son, I never ask you dis question before and I swear I will never ask you again, but tell me what really happen that night between you and dat girl?"

Harold was taken aback. It had been fifteen years. It was the very first time his mother had referred to that night since she parted the beaded blinds and entered his bedroom to stand with her hands on her hips. He was not inclined to talk about an incident he had euphemistically deemed a youthful indiscretion, though it was one that had continued to rankle all through the years like a festering sore. The guilt of knowing that Ma had to move out of the village on his account would sometimes surface and ride his conscience for days. But lately, the whole matter had receded into the distance of time and forgotten in the predominance of his grief. It was not worthy of recall. He shook his head from side to side in a gesture of displeasure that his mother had resurrected a time in his youth that was ugly and distasteful.

She interpreted the gesture as confirmation of his innocence; to her it meant that nothing had happened that night.

"Praise de Lord!" she shouted, with her hands towards the heavens, "I always know you wuz innocent, son. I know my son and all my thrildren. De night she wuz ponging on my house, standing there outside my door in de rain, barefoot with hardly no clothes on she backside, begging me fer shelter, and I out o' de goodness o' my heart, open my front door and give her one o' Molly clean dry dresses so she won't catch consumption, dat is de night she tell her parents that my boy-child grab her out o' de girls' bedroom like a lil concubine and force her to lie down in his bed and do rudeness and desecrate my house when I know all along that de lil seductress wuz lying."

His mother was steaming; he had released from her a firestorm of righteous suspicions and by his silence confirmed them all. He reached over, softly kissed her brow and said, "Maybe she wasn't all that guilty and maybe your son wasn't all that innocent." But Ma would not allow him to retreat from the assumed innocence. She proceeded to tell him about the ugliness that ensued when the girl's mother showed up on her doorstep months later.

"De woman threaten to take we to court. Say she would forget de charge under one condition, that we, de Prince family, not breathe a single word 'bout what happen that night to nobody. Not to mention it to one livin' soul. Otherwise it would be hell to pay fer de shame and scandal that we brought on she family. That she would turn to de law courts and you would be up at Dodd's reformatory fer boys all like now, without a decent education, a respectable job, and a beautiful woman like Cissy. And so, I had to clap my mouth shut like if you wuz de guilty one, cause it woulda been your word against hers, and fer more reason than one, de laws in this island woulda come down on me like a ton o' bricks. And so fer de sake o' peace and quiet, I had to move out o' Thornville and find a place to live in The Ivy. Is only because o' Cissy and de grace o' God that you now back hey livin' in dis God-forsaken village."

She snorted another pinch of the mustard-coloured powder and whispered to Harold reassuringly, "Son, don' ferget I born you. So I know all along that you could never ever be capable o' rape. You just too gentle and kind. You are my Prince by name and nature."

Then she asked, "You mention dat night to anybody, son?"

"Only to Gittens."

"Well, dat is like telling it to God, ent it?" And with that, a cackling belly laugh rattled the walls in that house on Christmas morning, one that had not been heard in that house of suspended mourning for a very long time.

Christmas Day came and went but like an insatiable lover she refused to relinquish her grip on the hearts and minds of Barbadians everywhere. All week long, wistful songs of mistletoe and sleigh rides and jingling bells dominated the airwaves. *Rediffusion*, that tireless ubiquitous speaker in the shape of a trapezoid, that hung in a faceless frame in a corner of every house, piped carols all day and all evening until it was time to call it a night at eleven sharp with "God Save The Queen." Harold had already turned the volume control, the only knob on the radio, all the way down; the constant carolling only seemed to mock the air. He wanted it to end, but Christmas Day repeated itself boringly all around him every day of that week.

      Then came Old Years Night to evoke that fortuitous night many years ago when he met Cissy just before the stroke of midnight at the Marine Hotel and stole her literally from under the nose of her friend. He didn't have the heart to pop the cork from a rare bottle of Dom Perignon champagne the pastor had left them the day before. The gift was in itself a magnanimous gesture of forgiveness and was still partially gift-wrapped and put away in the liquor box until he could muster the nerve. To mark their anniversary—or perhaps it was simply out of habit—they made love. It was without passion, just full of tenderness and tears: the pain of their loss had temporarily doused the flames.

      He fell asleep in her arms minutes before twelve and in a dream that evolved into a nightmare he saw himself rising from a dark, sepulchral place where he had been lying for many days and walking unevenly down a long carpeted corridor that led to white blinding sunlight at the distant end; and when he approached the exit, shading his eyes from the rays, he saw a form silhouetted against the glare. It was David. But David's back was turned to him and he was saddened by not having seen his face, as though his son was displeased with him, or discontented, or his soul was not at peace. He called out to him but he walked away and vanished into the refulgence of the sun. He awoke, drowsily mumbling his son's name. He interpreted the corridor in his dream as the corridor of his mind forever haunted by the untimely death of his son and now tugged by guilt of not having gone to the funeral to say goodbye to his lifeless body, not wanting to see him unnaturally reposed in a bed of light-blue satin for all to see, for all to pretend by saying how well and how real he looked. For the very same reason, he had stayed away from Ben Carson's death room, preferring to remember his son only as he was the morning he walked past his bedroom on his way to work. And so, David's face had not been pressed into his memory with the same cadaverous quality with which others now remembered him.

It was just after midnight. A new year. This would be the year when Thorne would soon face the law for the killing of his son. The bedroom, through the open window, was bathed in the pale light of a full moon. He got up and impulsively walked over to look at a picture on the dresser of their two babies. Then he peeped in at Nathaniel. "I love you, son," he said softly, not imagining that his son could be still awake. On the verge of falling asleep, Nathaniel, who had been waiting up for the midnight chimes, sprang up off his bed as if his ears had been slapped by a clap of thunder. He had never heard those words uttered by his father before and at first they sounded hollow and strangely empty of meaning. He looked around with his mouth wide open and saw his father leaning on the jamb of his bedroom door, smiling and holding a picture in the palm of his hand.

On Harold's lips, the words felt awkward like the first attempt at a foreign tongue but, once said, they echoed sweetly in his ears. He said, "I love you, son" once more and this time the words purred from his mouth like the first sweet lyrics of a sonnet. He sat on the side of the bed and pointed to the two babies in the black-and-white photograph dressed in their white handcrafted baptismal gowns, one in each arm of their mother, so indistinguishable one from the other that he dared Nathaniel to guess which one was he. He could not.

"This was in Pastor Gittens church, Dad?"

"No, the baptism was in this very house."

To explain to his son that he was born outside of the law and outside of the church's favour would be too confounding and irrational an explanation for the boy's innocent powers of reasoning. But he proceeded to recapture the awesome pride he felt the moment the holy water anointed the two delicate foreheads.

"And where are you, Dad?"

"Behind the camera, son. And that drooping sleeve in the corner belongs to Pastor Gittens." Harold's Brownie Hawkeye box camera was busy that morning.

Then Harold's tone of voice became grave, his words prescient and troubling. Still pointing at the partial black sleeve of the pastor's cassock, he said, "I want you to know something very important, son. If anything should happen to me, I want Pastor Gittens to take care of you and your mother. She already knows this."

"What you mean if something ever happen to you, Dad?"

"I mean if I die before you can take care of yourself, and you and your mother should be left here alone in this house."

"Well, you planning to die anytime soon?" the boy asked half-jokingly.

"No. But your brother wasn't planning to die either. Anybody can die any time."

"Well, Dad, did you ask the pastor to take over if and when?"

"I *know* he will."

"How do you know, Dad?"

"Because he loves your mother ... and you too."

The answer was pregnant with meaning not completely lost on the boy. Nathaniel knew of the tender feelings the pastor held for his mother; all the signs were there: the smiles between whispers like little children confiding secrets; the embraces that locked increasingly longer; the after-service blessings and prayers that lingered well into the night; these were tokens of more than spiritual upliftment. He was fond of the pastor too but his father was irreplaceable. He didn't know it then, but the pastor's love for him, though tangential, was also real.

"Something else," continued his father in a tone even more solemn than before. "I need to find out why your brother was killed."

"But I already told you, Dad. He was shot because he was on the white people's property."

"I know, son, but that is only half of the truth."

"But Dad, I was there. Plus Ma said that was exactly what Mr. Thorne would tell his lawyer and that was what his lawyer would tell the court. Ma said they could even show pictures of the tree and the property line."

"Yes, son, I know, but whatever the man who shot your brother says in court will be to avoid the consequences of the real truth. Half of a truth is worse than a lie. If he told the court that he never fired a shot, nobody would believe him. A lie will always come into the light, but a half-truth is always disguised as the real truth."

Nathaniel was somewhat puzzled by his father's denial of the obvious. In his mind there could be no other truth.

His father cautioned, "Son, whatever the consequences in life, you must always speak from the heart. If you hide the truth, as ugly as it might be, it will burn inside o' your gut all your life; it will haunt you in the day and keep you awake at night."

"So, Dad, when you were a lil boy like me, did you always speak the real truth from your heart?"

His father thought about the question; it was a fair one. In the vernacular of cricket, the boy had come back with a "yorker" that had to be defended truthfully and forthwith. "No. When I was a young boy, I might have done something to someone that was wrong. I am not sure, but I might have stolen something that I could never return. Ever since then, I've been sharing only half of the story of what happened. The consequences of the whole truth were too great. But I never lied outright, just kept telling what I thought was half of the truth and the rest stayed in my gut for years like rancid fruit."

"So, Dad, what was *your* half of the truth?"

"I can't say, son. It is just not fit for your ears."

"Well, then, how about the other half?" The boy prodded.

His dad ignored the question. "And now I need to know the rest of the truth, the real truth of why he killed David. It is not only fer me, son. I need to know fer your brother's sake, so his soul can rest in peace."

"And how you plan to find out the real truth?"

"By confronting the only one who knows the real truth, Mr. Thorne himself."

The answer made perfect sense to Nathaniel but he was afraid to pursue the manner in which his father was planning to confront his brother's killer. He was afraid for his father.

Chapter 18

Her Majesty's Court

FINALLY! THE day of the trial: February 17, 1956.

When Solicitor Fitzgerald Trotman walked through the portal of Her Majesty's Court on Coleridge Street on that day, he was alone. The look that crossed the face of the officer on guard as he waved him through was one of gratitude tinged with compassion, as one who might look upon another who had fought valiantly on his behalf but was about to be crushed by overwhelming forces. The officer had already admitted a hundred vociferous, excited Bajans now pushing and surging like a rolling sea at the arched door of the courthouse, four or five abreast, waiting impatiently to enter the public gallery. The working-class had turned out in impressive numbers to witness history, to hear the only verdict that would vindicate their true sense of justice and reassure a flagging faith in the decency and fairness of the institution. For months now, they had been chomping at the bit, waiting for this day, constantly querulous about the delay but never taking the law into their own hands. Never before in Barbados had a white man paid with his life for the killing of a black man or woman, though history showed the reverse was never in doubt.

Thornville was represented. Esmay and her husband, Egbert were among the first in line, followed by Sister Innis, the midwife; Mrs. Piggott, the shopkeeper's wife and the domino players from the rum shop; Fitzroy Miller and his woman; Cutting, the butcher and Mrs. Cutting. Carmita Blackman, the tray seller, took the day off from Busby Alley to come down to the courthouse. Marjorie Hinckson and Mrs. Mordecai, the milk woman, were there. The Water Club had temporarily closed its doors; the cooks and servers had taken the day off. Also in line were most of the off-duty *Chronicle* crew. Bajans from far and near converged on the courthouse that morning. Neither Cissy nor Harold was present.

Ben Carson, the octogenarian mortician, also came. Ben still had his doubts about the guilt of a man who had been so generous to him, who had put a roof over his head, provided him with electricity, running water and everything that came with the tool shed. How could he then be capable of committing such an act against a boy almost one-seventh of Ben's age? He was the only person in all of Thornville who could not bring himself to believe that the Englishman had killed the boy. He came to court to make up his mind and to let the Law decide.

The doors swung open. In no time the crowd was swallowed up into the vast interior of the courthouse with all its ornate furnishings dominated by richly polished mahogany tables, cushiony carpeting, shiny banisters and velvet-padded benches. The court was a bold attempt to mimic in miniature Old Bailey in London, which had so often been depicted in post-war British movies. All the minutiae of British court decor were replicated as faithfully as one could expect in this tropical corner of the Commonwealth. One distinguishing feature standing in the foyer was a life-sized Blindfolded Lady Justice, armed with sword and scales, sculpted precisely to detail from a mound of local clay. It was the work of a talented Bajan artist, Carl Brody. It was said that he was practically capable of breathing life into any clump of clay that came in contact with his fingers.

The heat was intense. Despite the efforts of four noisy oscillating fans that looked down from the uppermost corners of the walls, the public gallery was a motion picture of improvised fans: kerchiefs, hats, newspapers, pieces of cardboard, anything that came to hand. Hot, heavy, sultry air lay over the courtroom like a fleece. Only the men in black robes seemed cool and at ease. The accused, flanked by two blank-faced officers, fidgeted, waiting to swear to tell the truth, the whole truth and nothing but the truth. Barrister Cunningham tugged repeatedly at the chain of his pocket watch, anxious to get on with the proceedings. Solicitor Trotman looked peeved and strangely out of his element, perhaps wishing to have had Cissy at his side to bask in the public's favour of her righteous cause. Shafts of bright morning sunlight from the upper windows fell on the white wavy wigs of black men in black robes, a picture that drew giggles of ridicule from some in the gallery. But in truth, these robes and perukes lent an air of order and continuity to the proceedings, for they could be traced to the very provenance of English Law and these men were sworn to adhere to the highest standards though they sometimes strayed and resorted to courtroom shenanigans.

Three bangs of the magistrate's gavel commanded silence. It was time. The Clerk stepped forward. He exclaimed, "All those having any business before this Criminal Court in the case of the Crown versus Thorne draw nigh and give your attention. 'God Save The Queen.'"

Penelope, brightly dressed in yellow, and her father dapper in a sombre black suit and tie, exchanged smiles as he, now sworn in, stiffened for the inevitable show of assaultive questioning from a white man like himself.

"You are Theodore Augustus Thorne?" asked the Clerk.

"Yes."

"Theodore Augustus Thorne, you are charged with the murder of David Prince on the morning of the twenty-fifth day of September, 1955. How do you plead?"

"Not guilty."

Whispers of "Shameless dog!" and "He ent got nuh shame, doh," could be heard emanating from the back of the gallery. Bang! The gavel at first failed to command silence and the mutterings continued. Then they waned to complete silence as the judge glared at the crowd. Solicitor Trotman shook his head sadly from side to side. Cunningham smiled; perhaps he considered the charge of murder more defensible than manslaughter and that the Prosecutor's aim for the ultimate conviction was overzealous.

Representing the Crown was a white Barbadian-born Cambridge-educated Counsel, Tom Husbands, chosen as much for his dogged tenacity on behalf of the Crown as for the perceived counterweight of colour and erudition between him and the defence attorney. The Counsel was tall, semi-bald, erect and elegant, with one lazy eye which sometimes had a mind of its own and which likely created confusion among some of the jurors as to whether his words were directed to the bench, the dock, or to them. At this moment, however, once the jurors were given their instructions, Counsel Husbands managed to focus both eyes on Thorne to establish that the multiple discharging of a Remington two-inch-bore shotgun, Exhibit A, on the morning of September 22nd 1955, aimed at the head of David Prince by the indicted, were simple facts that were beyond dispute. Neither could it be claimed, he asserted, given the forensic evidence, two spent cartridges, Exhibit B, and a sworn statement by the dead boy's brother and witness to the murder, Nathaniel Prince, that the accused could have been in danger or threatened by the boy in such a manner that could legally or morally justify the deployment of a lethal weapon.

"Had you known the said David Prince, Mr. Thorne?"

"Never saw him in me life."

"Did you know his family?"

"No. Never saw 'em either."

"Mr. Thorne, would you tell the Court what was your motivation for shooting in the direction of a tree in broad daylight on the morning in question when a little boy happened to be in the said tree in the process of recovering a kite that had been caught on one of its branches."

Barrister Cunningham sprang from his seat. "Objection, m'Lawd! My learned friend implies that the defendant had foreknowledge of a boy in the tree in question."

"Sustained. Rephrase the question!" barked the Magistrate.

But the Counsel abandoned the question to pursue the previous answer in which the defendant denied any knowledge of the boy's family.

"Mr. Thorne, you deny knowing the boy's family but is not his mother a friend of your daughter and was she not a frequent visitor to your home as a young girl? Then how can you say you never saw her and you have no knowledge of who she is?"

The Counsel swivelled on his heels, turned his back to the defendant and walked towards the jury rail, fixating his good eye on the jury while his other eye veered lazily. And this for the jury: "I have heard tell she is of such beauty as not likely to be missed."

"Irrelevant questioning, m'Lawd! Objection!"

"Objection sustained!"

And so the proceedings dragged on for an hour and a half with the predictable duelling between Counsel and Defence, objecting and withdrawing, directing and redirecting, attacking and counter-attacking, advancing and retreating; two learned men armed with the weaponry of words and the leveraging of laws, sparring within the latitude set by the judge to score that one irreversible checkmate. When Husbands paced around with his usual histrionics, portraying the Englishman as the antichrist incarnate with no regard for human life, notably the life of poor black people, Cunningham rose to rehabilitate the image of his client with illustration after illustration of his generosity towards the Thornville families and stories of a lavish of affection for their children, and how every year when his daughter, Penelope, was a young girl, he would invite them into his home on Easter mornings. When the Counsel's unruly eye would wander over the jury box depicting a man who would subjugate the life of another human being to his own inviolable property rights, Cunningham would rise again to redirect and restore the image of the Englishman as deftly and as painstakingly as a modern-day artist retouching a discoloured Rembrandt or reassembling a mutilated monument. Meanwhile, the Englishman and his daughter from across the courtroom held each other's gaze with a confidence as palpable as if they were holding hands.

Pastor Gittens was late to the trial, caught up in matters of the church. The court was in session, the main entrance locked. The clergy had its privileges, nevertheless, and he was sneaked in through a side door. Knowing that the parents would not be in the courtroom that day, he had wanted to be their eyes and ears. No sooner had he squeezed himself into the only remaining public space before he heard the voice of Barrister Cunningham. He was about to witness a masterstroke from the ingenious defence lawyer.

"M'Lawd, on behalf of the accused, the Defence wishes to call Superintendent of Police, Captain Foster." All eyes turned as the Captain strode into the witness box. He who had long ago taken the oath to defend the laws of Barbados from people of all races who would seek to violate them; he who had excoriated the Englishman on the telephone for his inexplicably poor judgment; he who had denied the Englishman the sympathy expected of another white man; he would now be sworn in and be asked to come to the defence of Thorne.

The barrister asked, "Captain Foster, would you tell the Court how long you have known the man before you, Mr. Theodore Thorne." The Superintendent squirmed visibly at the first question; he knew the Defence was aligning his shooting ducks in a row.

"I don' know how long but we are both members of the Barbados Rifle and Gun Club."

"And was it not on a monkey-hunting trip on June 22nd of 1954 in the parish of St. John with the said Barbados Rifle and Gun Club, that you and Mr. Thorne had a conversation about the unfortunate proliferation of capuchins on the island—a capuchin and a monkey being one and the same? And that during that exchange, Mr. Thorne mentioned that hundreds of these primates were destroying his fruit trees, creating havoc on his property, chattering loudly day and night and causing Mr. Thorne and his family much anguish, and that he expressed to you his wish that their population on the island would be decimated?"

"Yes, I do remember such a conversation."

"And did you not on that day of the monkey hunt assure Mr. Thorne that if these creatures were indeed terrorizing him and his family, even to the extent that he saw them in his subconscious, whether asleep or awake, that he was within his rights as a gun owner licensed by the Barbados Rifle and Gun Club to shoot them on sight whenever they appeared on his property? Did you not assure him that to do so was well within his rights?"

"Yes, but …"

"Thank you, Captain. That will be all."

These questions with the force of negative phrasing were flung into the lap of the Superintendent as though the captain had literally placed the rifle in the Englishman's hand that day. No further explanation from the witness would be allowed to weaken the cornerstone of the defence.

The magistrate had noted a salient point in the barrister's questioning and moved to clarify, asking, "Barrister, did you say that the accused had imagined them, the monkeys, in his subconscious, and that he had described them as such to the witness, as is the testimony of the witness today?" Even the judge seemed to buttress the defence.

"That's right, m'Lawd, that is precisely the case."

Thereafter, the Counsel's cross-examination of the Captain was timid and deferential. No one in his right mind living in a small society like Barbados would choose to shame and discredit the Superintendent of Police without taking into account the certainty of future consequences, notwithstanding the gaping holes in his answers that invited scathing rebuttal. The Crown had done its homework and had been ready to debunk any assertion that there could be live monkeys in the mango trees at that time of the year, but the Superintendent's testimony had closed that loophole with the claim that the monkeys were living in the subconscious mind of the accused. Nevertheless, whereas he would not risk challenging the integrity of the Superintendent, he would not shirk from his responsibility as the Queen's Counsel to defend the dead boy.

"Ladies and gentlemen," he began his summation, facing the jury with his fingers inches away from the Remington two-inch-bore shotgun and with his eyes severely out of alignment. "It is my duty as a servant of the people of this fair land to speak on behalf of one of our dear children who is not able to sit among us today because he was struck down by, not one, but two bullets from this awesome weapon in the hands of the defendant, an accomplished marksman. At the tender age of twelve, David Prince must have wondered what on earth was that sudden massive blow he felt to the head in the split second before he plunged into eternal darkness, while the second bullet from Mr. Thorne's shotgun bore a ghastly tunnel through his delicate body. Needlessly so, for he had already been dead. Ladies and Gentlemen, look at the size of this cartridge! The evidence is clear and cannot be contested." He held up one of the gunpowder casings and some of the jurors seemed to shiver with disgust.

"The only unwitting dispensation of mercy from this murderer was that David's death was swift, though the anguish lives on in the broken hearts of his family. The defendant has admitted—no, I say confessed—to having raised this powerful gun to his shoulder and shot twice into that tree without warning, in broad daylight. I ask you, ladies and gentlemen of the jury, is it at all reasonable to assert, as the Defence would have you believe, that Mr. Thorne would choose to defend his fruit trees at a time when his entire property was about to be assaulted by Mother Nature? And then to claim it was all a case of mistaken identity as if in truth and in fact his racist mind perceived no difference between a little black boy and a sub-human? As if today he sees a parallel between black persons and imperfectly formed creatures of evolution incapable of acquiring even the most elemental rudiments of civilization? Does he not know that to be aligned with monkeys is the damnedest insult you could hurl at the pride of a black man? Or was it the judgment of this racist sadistic killer that the trespassing by black people on his private property was an offence deserving of death?"

These words froze the public gallery; they were like a volley of sharp knives flung from the well of the court to tear into the heart of every black man and woman in the audience. Their eyes were now fixed on none other than their black brother, Barrister Cunningham. His head was bowed. Counsel Husbands concluded his summation with a series of emotional crescendos that riveted the courtroom to stony silence. The Prosecution rested and then it was the Defence's turn.

Cunningham rose and slowly walked over and closed the gap between the table for the Defence and the jury. He scanned each row and peered over his glasses into the eyes of each juror. He would now set out to demolish every shred of defamation hurled at his worthy defendant while careful not to diminish the horror and the misfortune of what he deemed an accidental shooting.

"Ladies and gentlemen," he began, "my heart bleeds for this boy, this victim of such a tragic accident. I am sure it pains each and every one of you, as it does me. But let us assume for the sake of argument that such a crime were *not* an accident. I ask you: What kind of person would commit such an unspeakable crime? A despiser of all children? A depraved beast of prey? A bloodthirsty killer? A disciple of Satan himself? A vampire? A cultist? A racist? A drunk? A fool? What kind of human would stoop to such a heinous crime?"

With a sweep of the arm, he directed the eyes of the jury to Thorne in the expansive way a singer gestures to his accompanist. His client was by now a picture of humility and debilitating grief. At that moment Thorne reached into his breast pocket for his handkerchief and blew his nose loud and vigorously, then dabbed the corner of his eye. Was the court about to witness an exhibition of snivelling teary-eyed mockery?

"Ladies and gentlemen, I ask you, do you see any one of those characterizations of evil in that man? Or do you see a law-abiding citizen of this society, who every year welcomed the children of his estate into his home, who every year gives money to The Nightingale Home for Foster Children, who has welcomed into his family the son of his housekeeper and adopted him as his own, so generous a man that he gave his long-time servant, Mr. Benjamin Carson, who is sitting right here in this courtroom, a wall-house with electrics to live in for the rest of his days? Here is a man who would do anything in his power today to restore life to that boy. I ask you: Is this the kind of man who would, in cold blood, murder a defenceless little boy?"

The jury were eating out of his hands, six whites, four half-whites, and two blacks, all creatures of the twenties and thirties, mesmerized not necessarily by his oratory but by the irony of this tar-black Bajan lawyer, wrapping his arms around the shoulder of this pure-white Englishman, who not five minutes ago was being savaged by one of his own race for spilling the blood of a black boy. These jurors grew up in a time and place when a fault line lay deep and wide as a canyon between whites and blacks. Times were different now; the fracture was still there but now blurred by the rise of the highly educated like Barrister Cunningham, who could today cross the divide to defend a white man, if for no other reason than to proclaim himself a child of the new order in a society in the process of healing itself. The jurors were impressed.

He turned away from the jury and took a moment to look around the court, to survey all in attendance. He was surprised to find one last arrow in his quiver. He hadn't noticed it before the proceedings began. He would now use it to slay the dragon that had been breathing fire down the neck of his beleaguered client, accusing him of callous murder, debasing his good name.

Turning back to the jury, he asked: "Where is the plaintiff in this charge of murder? Where is the boy's mother? Where is the father of the boy? Why are they not sitting here in court next to Counsellor Husbands? I'll tell you why, ladies and gentlemen: it is because the boy's parents are decent fair-minded people. They know full well it was all an accident. They cannot in good conscience come to this court and drive this innocent man to his hanging for an ACCIDENT!" He shouted out the word, banging his fist on the wooden railing of the jury box. He ended softly with: "And for that I applaud their decency and good conscience." He turned to the judge. "M'Lawd, the Defence rests."

Thereupon, Thorne's fate was placed in the hands of the jury. They filed out of the courtroom with pained faces. A pessimistic Solicitor

Trotman stomped out of the building in disgust. A soft rain began to fall. He strolled along the streets of Bridgetown, from one end of James Street to the other, up and down Swan Street, down High Street, over to Broad Street and back again. He had greatly wanted Cissy and Harold to be present at the trial, to be exhibits in the courtroom as was the inanimate exhibit of a deadly shotgun entered into evidence; to look into the eyes of the judge and jurors and have them see a reflection of themselves as loving parents. He felt that all his counselling had been for naught; that the two had surrendered before the fight was fought, preconceiving a legal system rigged against them. After an hour and a half of perambulating, deep in thought, from one end of the city to the next and back, drenched with rain and sweat, he decided not to return to the courthouse and in the pouring rain he walked dejectedly all the way from St. Mary's Row through Emmerton and Chapman Lane and back to his home in New Orleans. He would put his legal practice aside and devote all his time and energies now to politics, knowing that only the political will of the masses would champion real change in his beloved Barbados.

Meanwhile, back in Thornville, Cissy had made up her mind to be nowhere near the courthouse that day, reasoning that the carriage or miscarriage of justice did not depend on her presence anymore than it depended on the handling of the truth, but that in the final analysis it rested on the skilfulness of lawyers. If true justice were served that day, she would not be overjoyed, and if it were denied, she would not let the betrayal plunder whatever faith she still had in the basic goodness of people. So she confined herself to the cane-backed chair where she had been sitting the day she heard the two claps of gunfire, and proceeded to pedal the old Singer machine with abandon, as the bobbin whirred soft music in her ears.

Harold had gone to the beach. The beach was his sanctuary. It offered him immunity from all wrongs. On the shore he climbed onto the upended hull of a fishing boat, one of many that were left abandoned under the casuarinas like beached whales. He sat for hours squinting into the glare of the morning sun as it sparkled silvery sequins on the deep-emerald horizon. He surrendered his senses to the smell of the sea, to the white-blue-green gradations from sand to skyline, and to the soothing, soft repetitive lapping of waves. They calmed his spirit and prepared his mind for whatever news would eventually reach him from Her Majesty's Court.

At home, Nathaniel immersed himself in his schoolwork and in the fantasy of his toys. He knew of the court date but had already made his own peace and was moving on. From the first day of the investigation he had not been required, gratefully, to appear as a witness, just to provide a signed deposition of what happened that day on the hill at the wall. The loss of his twin brother had been like the amputation of vital extremities but now he refused to look back and focused only on his own healing.

Back at Her Majesty's Court the crowd anxiously reassembled, waiting for His Lordship and the members of the jury to reappear. A wood-dove found her way in through an upstairs east window, circled the body of the court and then perched high on a rafter directly above the magistrate's bench, upon which she released a pellet of excrement before she flew out in a flurry of white feathers. A chuckle rippled through the public gallery at this whim of the gentlest of birds. Pastor Gittens bowed his head and visibly breathed a prayer. Standing close to the main exit, Jay-Jay Johnson, who was acting that day as Court Reporter for *The Chronicle*, poised with pad and pen in hand.

The jurors returned. The Court Clerk asked the foreman to step forward. The foreman advanced, a stout middle-aged man in dapper brown suit and tie, a person whom everyone recognized as Sonny Clarke, a civil servant. A half-white Bajan, he was perhaps in the context of the case the perfect choice as jury foreman.

"Have you arrived at your verdict?" asked the Clerk.

"We have, Sir."

"Do you find the accused, Theodore Augustus Thorne guilty or not guilty of the wilful murder of David Prince?"

The foreman paused for a breathless second as if to induce an air of drama into the final proceedings and to savour that brief, once-in-a-lifetime moment of command before having to return to his prior irrelevance. Bajans in the public gallery held their collective breath.

"We find the accused not guilty of murder," he answered.

"And that is the verdict of you all?"

"It is."

In the blink of an eye the gallery was empty. Bajans scuttled down the steps and out the door, past the unseeing Lady Justice in the lobby, scurrying in every direction like rats fleeing a burning cane field. The court reporter dashed out and ran down Coleridge Street, back to his typewriter. The Thornville people mingled outside around the courthouse under the watchful eyes of the constabulary. They were all dumbfounded, shell-shocked as if a cannon had gone off in their ears. Ben Carson went home, vindicated. Her Majesty's Court had spoken.

Next morning, Mickey Norris heard a sharp whistle outside his mother's house on Nelson Street, looked out the front window and saw his friend, Harold Prince. He was standing, bareheaded, dripping wet in an early morning drizzle.

"Boy, come in out o' the rain!" he called to him.

Harold climbed the three limestone bricks that served as a front step to this plain weather-beaten, two-roofed wooden house and approached his friend standing in the doorway wearing a smile that beamed the words, "I told you so." Without looking into the eyes of his friend, he plunked himself down in the only chair, a Morris chair with a broken armrest, while Mickey sat cross-legged in the middle of the front house on a large oak steamer trunk with metal clasps that accentuated the antiquity of the room. Next to the window was a settee that declared itself Mickey's bed, the pillows and sheets still ruffled and tangled from the night before; and draped across the back were his street clothes among which Harold spied the garish outfit Mickey wore the day they met on Broad Street. He was still in his purple satin pyjamas. Shards of sunlight fell on rotted floorboards from holes in the roof, evidence that Hurricane Janet had had no mercy on this dilapidated house. The partitions were adorned with wallpaper, a colourful collage of tropical flowers. The flowers, a fair attempt in better times to embellish the house, were now tearing away from the walls like loose scabs.

"Welcome to mah humble abode," Mickey drawled, half-apologetically. "Now you see why ah left mah good job in the States to come back here. To get mah mother out of this rat hole before she kick the bucket. Brother, ah was born in this house and ah'm goin' damn well see the ole lady don't croak in it." And with the same breath, perhaps sensing a tension in the immediate air surrounding his friend, he asked, "How 'bout a drink?"

He reached into the seaman's chest that stored his mother's shiny silverware and fine English bone china teapots and teacups and saucers that had never been used; that were saved for the important guests who never came. His hands reappeared with a fifth of Kentucky Tavern bourbon and two glasses. "No ice ... sorry."

But there was something else on Harold's mind, something he needed more imperatively than ice. "I need that gun!" he said abruptly.

A knowing smile dawned on Mickey's face. "Now you're talking, brother," he said. Without questioning, he felt between the two pillows on the settee, produced a snub-nosed silvery .22 Magnum Revolver and handed it to his friend.

"Be careful, it's loaded."

Harold stared at the handgun as if it were the key to right all wrongs and then shoved it in his pants pocket.

"Yesterday could've been a day for true justice but it wasn't to be," said Mickey. "Now justice must be served. The bible says it: 'a life for a life'. The Law is not on your side, brother."

Just then, a voice called from the next room, from behind a white sheet that hung from the top of the doorframe like a stage curtain. "Michael! Who dat?" The voice was strained and raspy.

"Ma, it's a friend o' mine."

"Yer friend got a name?"

"His name is Harold Prince. Would you like to meet 'im?"

"Yes, I know who Harold Prince is. He and his family in *The Chronicle*."

Harold followed Mickey into his mother's bedroom and there, propped up on a low ball-poster bed, under a retracted mosquito net, was a frail, fair-skinned woman with thin white hair swept back and tied youthfully with a pink ribbon. Two skeletal feet protruded below the bed sheet. A white enamel po peeped out from below the bed and a bamboo walking cane leaned in a corner. Her face looked as old as Harold had imagined it from the sound of her voice. The dark pouches under her eyes and the fleshy folds were like rings on an ancient oak tree that recorded the passage of time. Yet when she smiled, a gleam in her eyes spoke of happier times, of a youth of self-indulgence that, in spite of everything, was without regret. It spoke of the good fortune to be undeservedly alive and to have cheated death when an earlier demise might have seemed fitting for the hazardous life she had led. Her smile was the smile of one who only looks back as if to look forward would only hasten the end.

"Hello, young man, I am Queen Ramona," she greeted Harold with a toothless grin. "Whew! You's a good-looking chap!" Mickey pointed discreetly to the side of his own head and made a circular motion to suggest that she was "not all there."

A colourful assortment of Cancan skirts, pink crinoline petticoats, skimpy shorts, stringy tops and embroidered bloomers hung from a row of wire hangers on one side of the room. These seductive clothes, like the raiment of some outdated profession, were no longer worn or needed. Given their proximity to the old lady, they took upon themselves garments of historical interest, purposely saved to accompany the "queen" to a royal sepulchre.

Harold was drawn to the countless pictures of Mickey's mother, large and small, framed and unframed, on the partitions, on the shelf, on the dresser, on the nightstand, everywhere. It was obvious to him that she was once an uncommonly beautiful girl in her youth, prized for her good looks, slim and sensuous with eyes that must have bewitched many a sailor in her day. The pictures were of young glamorous Queen Ramona in her glory days, in the red-light district of Nelson Street, posing, dancing, hugging, kissing, drinking, smoking, holding hands with sex-starved sailor boys in their proud whites, wallowing in a life of debauchery. Judging from the galaxy of poses and portraits it occurred to Harold that she must have known the name of every Norwegian frigate and every American warship that landed in Carlisle Bay in the early 1900s. Now approaching her seventies, was it unkind to see her as an old retired battleship herself, full of war stories that were best kept to herself?

"Man, I wuz de queen o' Nelson Street in my day," she said to Harold, smacking her gums contentedly. "Men eyes used to pop when I walk in de club. Soon as they land they asking fer Queen Ramona. Where is Queen Ramona? Nobody else but de Queen. Dem Yankee sailor boys wuz hungry to be wid a real woman, a coloured woman. That wuz against de law back in Amurca, the land of the free. So as soon as they land in Bridgetown, they brekking down de door at de Zanzibar Club. Hmm! Ask my son 'bout Amurca. God bless his heart!"

"Yes, God bless his heart!" said Harold to himself; "but he was no prodigal son, he left home with nothing and returned to his mother's side with a pocket full of money and a good heart."

He said goodbye to the queen and returned to the front room where the two friends lifted their glasses in a toast to whatever justice remained in the world. Neither man would speak further about the trial nor dwell on the verdict, but Mickey seemed pleased; he had done his good deed.

As Harold stepped onto the street, the rain stopped and the sun broke through the clouds to turn a sombre morning into a sunny glorious day. Walking to the bus stop on Bay Street, he softly patted the pocket that held Mickey's gun as if it contained a living, breathing creature. A warm feeling came over him, the feeling that he was not alone, that he was walking with a friend, and he found himself assuming the same fearless gait that he had observed in the way that Mickey had walked away from him that day on Broad Street. Along the way he drew a few winks and whistles from the short-time girls in the Nelson Street bars. One girl, who said her name was Diana, dressed in a backless halter-top and shorts that clung to her hips like a coat of satin paint, called out to him, "Hey saga boy, what's de hurry?" She would have liked nothing more than to lead him down one of those squalid back alleys, into her workshop and onto her semen-stained mattress, whereupon, with the fire in her hips, she would send his mind soaring on a cloud of blissful indifference. But his state of mind was implacable, far removed from Nelson Street, and his heart was most definitely in a different place.

The only voice resounding in his head was the voice of a middle-aged, well-dressed stranger, who approached him on the beach the evening of the trial. He said his name was Moses and that he had come directly from the courthouse to the beach because he knew he would find him there. He said the words, "Dey say de white man not guilty!" then shook his head and walked away.

Chapter 19

Quest for the Truth

AFTER THE trial, the village of Thornville, ashamed of its name and besmirched by its notoriety, yearned to return to a state of innocence and calm. As sure as the hurricane had left its swath of ruin on the landscape, so did the trial leave an aftermath of steady, rumbling discontent and revulsion for the law. And although people knew that the law favoured the rich and powerful who owned the law, they knew the path to fairness demanded depolarization of colours and classes that had scarred this fair land for so many years; and they knew that it would not be a linear path but one beset by the occasional miscarriage of justice. Still, the face of David in death lingered raw and the court's verdict remained painful and, at least for the present, nothing would mollify that pain, not even the vision that his death would serve to pave the way forward towards a more just society.

In the days ahead, Harold pondered his next move. No one felt that pain more acutely and more relentlessly than Harold; it grew within him like a pressing tumour under the heart, swelling and tightening like a fist until nothing would relieve it. When it was told to him that Thorne had channelled the image of a monkey onto his son, he considered the analogy a gross and unconscionable assault on his dignity, his race and on his pride as an adoring father. He felt he might as well have been impaled on the sword of Lady Justice down at the courthouse. It was to him as if the Englishman had plunged a long serrated blade into a still bleeding wound and twisted it around and around to retard any possible process of healing. He decided the Englishman's monkey story was too simplistic, too transparent to conceal his racist murderous intent. He asked himself: What else on earth could motivate a man to commit such a profoundly horrific crime but deep-seated hate sprung from some evil, demented character?

The trial was over but in Harold's mind questions of motive still remained. They kept him awake at night; they roiled his spirit; they stole his appetite for nourishment, patience for idle conversation and even desire to make love to his woman. His favourite beaches were no longer the havens they used to be. On occasional nights in Piggott's rum shop he was able to numb his senses but only for a few hours and at the cost of monstrous hangovers. He was grateful that Cissy was more fortunate than he. Her fortress was the Church. Always close at hand was her timeworn bible; it was her defence against all evil. Sometimes, while he sat brooding in a corner like a wounded animal, he would hear her voice around the house, humming, singing, and whistling songs of praise. At night she bowed her head, knelt beside the bed and thanked her God more fervently than ever before. He often wondered: How could she? What was there to be thankful for? She seemed to have dug deep down into some unchartered well of her own faith and found a wellspring of goodness and forgiveness not yet discovered by mortals.

Then there was her good friend, Gittens. He was aware of a layer of jealousy between him and the pastor; yet somehow he wanted him to be there at her side. He was good for her. And so, on his way home from the beach, or from the city, or from Piggott's rum shop, he would sometimes see the black Austin parked outside his house, and he would turn around and retrace his steps because he knew that Gittens could give Cissy the spiritual support that he could not. He could not even help himself, much less his woman. Gittens could save her from the torment that engulfed his spirit and threatened to destroy him as surely as it would destroy her if she were left alone. His love for Cissy transcended jealousy. He trusted Gittens.

Now here she was, cuddling next to him in bed, peaceful as a newborn, breathing deeply with that slow, rhythmic heaving of the chest, oblivious of his being fully awake and keeping perfectly still so she would not be disturbed. He hadn't slept a wink. He had paced the floor all night, and now that daybreak was upon him, he saw no point in persisting on lying with his eyes closed and coaxing the reluctant mantle of sleep. So he slowly, carefully disengaged his embrace, kissed her on the cheek and got up. She mumbled something faintly and fell back to sleep.

It was Saturday morning. His body was wracked with sleeplessness. Once during the night he had awakened from a dream in a sweat. Thorne had massacred the entire village and he alone was left to suffer. He decided now, once and for all, he would not be an insomniac for the rest of his life; he would free himself; he would seek the real truth behind the killing of his son. He sat on the side of the bed and, for the first time, the sounds of the village awakening to a new day registered pleasantly in his ears; these were the early morning sounds in every village in every parish in this island paradise: neighbourhood fowl cocks crowing in tandem, wood-doves cooing mournfully to one another in the mile trees, yard dogs yapping back and forth, tired feet shuffling along the gravel on the way to the standpipe, water buckets jangling, cart wheels rumbling, fish people hawking their sea eggs and flying fish, old women babbling mindlessly to themselves, and singing sweetly in his ears were the percussions of the windblown shak-shaks in the flambeau trees. Yes, these were the sounds of home; at last he was home after a long tumultuous sojourn in a faraway jungle of despair. He felt a new inward peace.

He dressed, washed his face and hands, opened wide the windows in the front house, filled his lungs with clean fresh morning air and gazing up through the trees beyond the guard wall to the big white house on the hill, he found himself devilishly intrigued with the thought of paying the Englishman a visit. What better time could there be before the day's involvements to knock on his door and solicit the truth? The truth would still the torment that had been raging within him all night and bring closure to the deed of this cold-blooded killer. It would liberate the soul of David, the David he saw in his dream standing restless at the end of a long tunnel, so that his soul could finally rest in eternal peace. He would take with him Mickey's .22 Smith & Wesson Magnum but surely not to shoot the Englishman or even to intimidate him, only to defend his own life if he found himself cornered and in danger.

He flung open the front door and walked briskly to the edge of the village, to Gittens's wall-house and knocked on his door.

"Mornin', Gitts." They hadn't spoken since the day of the hurricane.

"Man, what you doing up so early on a Saturday morning?"

"I need a favour."

"Another favour?" the pastor joked. "Come in, sit down!"

"I need to speak to you about Cissy."

Gittens ceased to be jocular; his heart skipped a beat. Did Harold come to tell him he was no longer welcome in his house? To accuse him of amorous advances towards his woman? That he should stay away from his family?"

"Cuppa tea?" he asked, walking back to the kitchen for a moment or two to slow the pounding in his chest.

"No, I'm in a hurry, Gitts. Sit down fer a minute so we can talk!"

They sat around the kitchen table and Harold began to speak. His voice assumed a grave, portentous tone. "If anything ever happen to me, Gitts, I want you to stay close to Cissy and Nathaniel."

Gittens was relieved but puzzled.

"Well, yes, but why should anything happen to you, man?"

Harold ignored the question. "Man, listen! I know how much you and Cissy care for each other. I knew you were in love with her from that night at the Marine Hotel on Old Year's Night. I did you wrong then, Gitts. I stole her from you that night like a hound dog. But I loved her too and you should know that love is stronger than scruples. As long as I live on this earth I won't let another man take her from me. Not even you, Gitts. But, God forbid, if I should die for any reason, get struck down by lightening or get knocked down by a bus or a cane lorry, or some mad fool shoot me dead, you are the only man I would want to take my place …"

"Don't talk stupid, man!" said Gittens, raising a hand in the air to put a halt to Harold's crazy talk.

Harold finished his thought. "Because I know you love Cissy too and you will do right by her."

"But Harold, I'm her pastor. Cissy is my sister in Christ." He said these words unquestioningly as if the mere thought would be bordering on the abominable sin of incest.

But Harold knew otherwise. "I just know," he said, and got up to leave.

Gittens looked into his eyes and saw fear but also a steely determination he knew would not yield to more questions. He had last seen that look on his face the morning he picked him up and headed to Thornville in the hurricane. As he walked to the door, Gittens asked, "Something weighing on your mind, man? Anything to do with that rape you told me about? Still haunting you? Want to pray about it?"

"Nah. That's all in the past, Gitts," he answered and walked out the door.

He walked back to where his house stood but, instead of entering, he crossed the road and headed up the hill towards the mansion. He convinced himself that he had reached beyond the point of thirsting for revenge and girding for violence; all that rancour he had held for weeks and weeks had been tamed by some subliminal voice of reason and now all he had in store for Thorne were questions of motive. Under the left pocket of his white cotton shirt that clung to his body, clammy with sweat and anxiety, he could feel the pulsating in his chest, drumming faster and faster with each step, up the hill, through the trees, towards the Englishman's house. As he parted the stubborn underbrush and ducked under the low-lying branches that conspired to bar his way, he could feel his whole body increasingly tense and his muscles tighten like ropes drawn taut. He groped along the side of the wall to where it abutted the asphalted driveway leading to the gate. A fleeting image presented itself of a burglar, his own self, furtively looking to scale the forbidden guard wall in the shadows of foliage, but now that he was beyond the trees, the unobstructed morning light emboldened him and quickened his steps towards the front gate. Then the faintest cloud of uncertainty crossed his mind and threatened the will he had so steadfastly held, causing him to argue within himself: "Why shouldn't I confront my son's killer? Why shouldn't he confess to the real motive? No man can face the law twice for the same charge of murder, so why shouldn't Thorne come clean? Why should he remain sequestered and silent in his fortress? Why should he not be made to see that behind little inconsequential David there was a father that stood as tall as he but younger and likely stronger and as proudly black as he was himself proudly white?" He repurposed his will and continued on.

As he approached, the whole house appeared much more imposing than he had thought it to be as if the trees had been purposely masking its immensity. For the first time he saw the three levels of living space wrapped by their individual verandas with rich mahogany balustrades. Never before had he seen so many windows or various-sized roofs belonging to a single house. But not for long did any of these things hold his attention; he was focused on the big wooden arched gate with the lion-head knocker. When he reached for it he had no plan of action; he would follow wherever his heart and his judgment led.

There was a jangling of keys, the gate creaked open, and standing before him was a handsome middle-aged woman of average build and of light-brown complexion. Long black tresses protruded from her headscarf. She wore a flowered apron but wasn't dressed in the standard livery of a maid as he would have expected. On seeing him, she brought a hand to her mouth as if to stifle a gasp; it was clear she knew who he was. Two or three likely reasons for his standing there must have fleetingly crossed her mind, and from the look of petrifaction on her face, it was obvious that she had chosen to assume the most chilling of all probabilities. She recovered and yelled for someone to tie up the dog. A small boy of similar complexion, with curly hair and not much taller than Nathaniel, came running from a far corner of the courtyard. "Who is it, Ma?" he called, out of breath.

Harold broke the ice. "I come to see Mr. Thorne."

Before she could answer, a chirpy, high-pitched voice called down from one of the dozen upper windows, "Who is it, Marcella?" It occurred to him then that Marcella was Madame Montmartre, the one that village gossip said was Thorne's woman.

"A gentleman here to see Mr. Thorne."

The voice called down again with a tone of irritation, obviously directed now to the gentleman. "What is it about? It is eight o'clock in the morning."

"My name is Harold Prince," he shouted up from the gate.

Silence. Within seconds, a door on the first level opened and Penelope Thorne appeared in the doorway, barefoot, in an ankle-length night robe with one hand clutching the stem of a cocktail glass and the other cradling a white longhaired Persian cat.

"Oh, Mr. Prince, I'm sorry, my father is not at home. He already left fer town. Would you like to come in and wait fer him? He should be back soon." And in the same breath, with her eyes still fixed on Harold: "Marcella, ask one o' the girls to bring Mr. Prince a cuppa tea or something. My father doesn't usually leave fer the city this early, but he had an appointment this morning and had to make a few stops before then."

Marcella now eyed Harold suspiciously before walking away, the boy skipping along at her side. Thorne's daughter turned and walked back to the doorway with a slight swagger that he surmised was more alcohol-induced than sensual since a faint smell of cognac lingered in her wake. Then she wheeled around expecting Harold to follow, and then seeing that he hadn't budged an inch, she beckoned with a curl of her finger for him to come inside.

"My business is with your father," said Harold, still holding his ground.

"Well, as I said, he is not here. Would you like to come in and wait or not?"

He followed her hesitantly through the darkened doorway, down a marbled foyer and up a spiral stairway with richly polished mahogany balusters on both sides, then down a hall and into what seemed a sitting room. It was ornately furnished with French baroque furniture set around a plush Afghan oval rug on which she now released the feline.

It occurred to him that the Thornes must have gone to extraordinary lengths to impress any stranger who crossed that threshold as he just did. His whole house could be swallowed up with room to spare within these four wallpapered walls graced with what looked to be original Victorian art. The brightly polished mahogany floor reflected a massive glittery chandelier that hung low over the centre of the room and in the far corner stood what looked to be a grand piano partially shrouded under a velvet custom covering. He was not only awestruck but the whole ambience of exquisite luxury struck him as obscene in a place just a few steps away from lowly, sparsely furnished wooden houses.

Then, standing in the disarming splendour of this medieval setting, she turned to face him and said in a voice that was both alluring and playful, "Hello again Harold, you remember me?"

He returned her gaze with a stony expression. He wanted to say, "Yes, I remember you. You are the little wench that climbed into my bed fifteen years ago in the middle of the night and turned my whole world upside down and caused my family to move out o' this village and me to have to change schools and then to be accused of ... "

Instead, he replied dryly, "Yes, you are his daughter."

Then the tone of her voice changed abruptly from coquettish to sympathetic. "Look! I am really and truly sorry about what happened, and so is my Dad. If only we could turn the clock back. It was an awful, awful accident. I even went to the cemetery to give my condolences to Cissy in person." She then demonstrated the sincerity of her words with a sorrowful pursing of her thin lips. His stare was cold and hard; he was not impressed.

She became defensive. "Look, Harold! My father may be a son-of-a-bitch but he is still my father and no woman would want to see her father hang. He said it was an accident. Please try to understand! He would've willingly pleaded guilty to a lesser charge. But murder? How could they accuse him of murder?"

Harold stood impassively by the door with his arms folded as her blue eyes, amplified by thick lenses, searched his face for some trace of understanding.

He began, "Miss Thorne …"

She interrupted softly. "Penelope."

"I did not come here looking fer sympathy. I am not even here to seek justice; the court has already spoken. The court cannot try your father again fer the same offence of murder. So he is in the clear. The reason I am here is to find the truth. My boy is dead and I owe it to him and to myself to know the truth of why he was killed. I do not intend to discuss this matter with you or anybody else but your father. And I am not leaving here until I hear the truth."

His voice broke. She reached out a sympathetic hand to his shoulder and in that instant her robe slid open seductively. Her touch was cold and moist. He took a step backward out of her reach, his arms still folded.

"If I have my way Dad will have to pay restitution."

"A life fer a life is the only just restitution," he said, "but his life is not for me to take."

Now, at the sound of footsteps approaching, he unfolded his arms and turned towards the door fully expecting her father to appear in the doorway. But it was a young servant girl with tray, teapot, cups, milk and sugar. Her face was guileless and plain, her movements keyed to every command, her answers formal and compliant.

"Thanks, Coreen, place it there on the sideboard."

"Yes, Ma'am."

"Is the tea nice and hot?"

"Yes, Ma'am."

"My father's back yet?"

"No, Ma'am."

"When he pull in, let him know he's got a visitor."

"Yes, Ma'am. Will that be all?"

Coreen exited the room, quietly, robotically, and padded back down the corridor. She hadn't even glanced his way and he marvelled at this abject and formal display of obsequiousness.

As long as he was waiting, he thought, he might as well be comfortable and pulled up one of the blue curved-back upholstered chairs with fluted legs and sat with his back to the wall, facing the door. Thorne would soon be walking through that door, he figured, and he would be alert and ready for him. He had no interest in tea; neither did she. Instead she picked up the cat and waddled over to the far side of the room, motioning with her glass to a softly lit curio cabinet where a panoply of colourful liquor bottles peeped out from behind a glass pane.

"Can I get you a drink instead?"

He didn't answer but thought: Why not! She must have a wide choice of ready analgesics for his pain, an assortment of liquid anodynes to numb his grief, mind-altering drugs to divert his memory from the real reason and the only reason he was there, tranquilizers to down the savage beast now running amuck in the black jungle of his mind. She returned with two crystal glasses and an assortment of bottles, setting them down on a low, marble-topped game table among chess pieces suspended in the midst of battle.

He protested. "Look, girl! I am not here to be entertained. I am just waiting here til your father turn up so I can ask him a question or two."

He had fully expected Thorne to be home at that hour of the morning, more likely in his pyjamas than out and about in the city. He was not expecting a confrontation but was still prepared, knowing that once the man had overcome the shock of seeing his face, he could easily retreat to his gun rack. But then, why would he? After all, he hadn't scaled the guard wall or entered clandestinely through the trees, but had stepped up boldly to the front gate and was admitted by the purported mistress of the house and by his own daughter. But now, here he was, sitting in the white man's drawing room, ensconced in his Queen Anne chair, clutching a glass of his Courvoisier, sitting across from his daughter dressed in a diaphanous pink negligee under a gaping night robe. It was all wrong, awkward, ironic, not the way he imagined it would be. He felt like a careless actor in his first live act, failing to follow the script he had so assiduously rehearsed. Perhaps he should have turned around at the gate and left to come back another day.

"Well, at least we can make a lil conversation til my father get back." She had read his mind and knew he was uncomfortable. "Or I could entertain you with a lil music," she joked, pointing to the piano in the far corner.

It occurred to him he had never really seen her face before at close range; his room was pitch-black that rainy night and, in any case, she was much younger then. But he did remember her nose, thin, pointed, decidedly not Negroid. Her hair, then too, was long, soft and stringy. One thing that came back to him, now hearing her speak, was her habit of injecting Bajan slang into otherwise perfect diction, alternating back and forth, as if this might have been her way of fitting in. He had seen her since then, but at a distance. On his way to work on his bicycle, he would sometimes see her riding her filly up though Cave Hill and Fairfield and back around Seclusion. In addition, he had no opinion of whether she was good-looking or ugly; his frame of reference for female beauty did not extend to white women, unknowing of what might lay under the masks of mascara, flush and rouge of the few faces he knew. He was willing, however, to accept the naturalness of Bajan women, whether pleasing to the eye or not.

Sitting across from him on the padded arm of an antique settee, she poured herself a drink and began with a nostalgic lilt in her voice. "I will always remember that night as long as I live. I wuz a lil fifteen-year-old virgin." She spoke the word, "virgin," with an impish curl at the corner of her mouth. "It wuz raining cats and dogs that night and I standing outside yer mother's house like a wet rat. No hat, no shoes. Ponging on de house, waking up everybody. Yer mother—God bless her heart!—took pity on dis lil scallywag and took me in that night, otherwise I woulda dead o' pneumonia. I never got to thank Mrs. Prince. How is she?

"It all start that evening wid a lil bassa-bassa I had wid Ma over some lil stupidness like rudeness or cussing—I don' really remember. I wuz her lil princess, pure as snow, not supposed to be like de ordinary foul-mout' girls down in de village, according to her. She begin slapping me over my head wid a carioca slipper. Whap! Whap! That wuz de last straw. That night I run out on de road and end up outside yer mother's house in de rain. I swear, I didn't choose your house to beg fer shelter; it was bare chance.

"Ma wuz strict as a general, always cutting my tail, whenever she feel like it. 'Don't do this! don't do that! stop this! stop that!' What a bitch! God rest she in she grave! But, y'see, she wuz de one wid de money. She would always remind Dad that when they got married he wuz poor as a church mouse. Which wuz true. But he love de ground she walk on. Before she kick de bucket, de ole hag said she wuz goin' disinherit me and throw me out on de street. Seriously, would you believe dat? Imagine me, a poor bakra on de streets o' Buhbaydus today. All o' dis you see here, dis nice house, de estate, de orchard, de cane field, de horses; all o' dis property wuz de ole lady's money."

The drone of her voice impelled him to reach for the cognac and reluctantly refill his now empty glass. His eyes wandered to the ceiling, to the floor and around the room, just to escape her piercing stare. He was as inattentive as her Persian cat curled up in a ball on the floor licking her paws and wiping her face conceitedly.

"Mrs. Prince wuz a darling," she went on, "she dried me off good and put me in a bedroom wid five long-legged girls in one bed to sleep til de rain stop. Poor soul! She meant well. I tried sleeping on de floor but it wuz too cold and hard. So after a while I decide to go looking fer a different room in dis tiny house and that is how I end up in your bedroom in your bed, lover boy." She laughed at her own words and reached for the gimlet, emptying the glass and refilling it with one smooth and seemingly well-practised motion. "Well, Harold, I wouldn't mind telling you that I wuz grateful fer de lil warm space there beside you, whoever you were, and you made me comfortable enough to fall asleep. I even showed my appreciation wid a lil kiss. Remember? Well, as it turned out, you made me feel more comfy than I wanted to feel. Although, I do remember saying not to try anything. But after all, I wuz in *your* space. Still, I had no idea you wuz such a lil tiger. Christ, before long, you wuz inside o' me like a torpedo." She cocked her head back and laughed triumphantly as if she had set a trap for him and he had tripped it.

"That is not how I remember it," said Harold.

"Well, anyway, when it wuz over, after I wuz violated, I got up and run home like a bat out o' hell. Marcella—you already meet she outside—sneak me in through de back door in my borrowed oversize blue dress. But Ma wuz waiting fer me at de top o' de stairs wid a tambrin rod and she give it to me good, licks fer sleeping at somebody house in de village and licks fer running 'way from home in de first place. Dad had to pull her off o' me."

Harold sat listening to Penelope roll out her version of what happened those many years ago, in his house, in his bed, and thereafter. As her story unfolded between sips of vodka, he felt himself stuck at a railroad crossing, watching and hearing a hundred cars rumble by, each one laden with extraneous cargo that was none of his concern, that belonged to some distant irrelevant past, and that certainly had no relation to the mission that brought him to the Thorne residence that morning. He had seen those rumbling, boring, endless freight trains in Western movies and no one (well, except for the bad guys) ever cared about what was in those cars anymore than he cared for her one-sided version of that encounter fifteen years ago.

She topped off her glass and continued. "Everything woulda turned out fine and de whole thing woulda been swept under de rug, except that after a while, innocent as I wuz at de time, I didn't even realize I wuz in de first trimester o' pregnancy, little fifteen-year-old me. In other words, de dough wuz rising in the oven." She stared at him to gauge his reaction.

He sat up straight for the first time. As her story began to take a new turn, his jaw dropped unconsciously. But then again, he thought, she was just spicing up her monologue with one or two mischievous lies to stimulate his interest.

She continued to lambaste her mother. "And that is when de ole witch went down in de village to see yer mother to give her a tongue-lashing and threaten her to keep quiet so as not to ruin de Thorne name. But Ma never mentioned to yer mother that her little girl wuz wid child. That was a family secret and one she couldn't live wid." Yes, he did know about her mother's confrontation with his own several months later.

"Ma insisted that I pay a visit to de part-time abortionist in St. George, Dr. Warden, de only one on de island that would do a scraping right there in de office. That was after Dr. Donovan, a friend of de family, refused to do it. But bad luck fer we, de abortionist suddenly died of a heart attack in de middle o' one o' his infamous procedures. He went to Hell literally wid blood on his hands. You have to understand, Harold, that in spite of all de nagging and de beatings, I wuz still my mother's baby, her only child, de one she had big plans for before all o' dis happen. She had my whole life planned out like a book. After St. Winifred's, I wuz to enrol at Marlborough College in London. She already had me lined up and married off to some bloke back in Buckinghamshire, de son of a family friend, a baroness. Up to now Dad says it wuz me that kill Ma, that I might as well had been de one that dropped de ten diazepam pills in she wine glass de night she took she own life. That same night she look me straight in my face and call me a lil trollop. She always used a fancy word fer one o' her imprecations, figuring that whoever she wuz cussing wouldn't understand."

Harold was bored. Time was getting on and still there was no sight or sound of her father. "So, tell me, girl, what all o' this got to do with me?" he asked.

"What all o' dis got to do wid you?" she repeated his question with an indignant stare. "Follow me!"

She got up, stumbled and then quickly steadied herself. He followed her with mild curiosity to the far side of the room, to a window with a slatted shutter that hung over the sill like a long eyelash. Directly below, he could see the east end of the courtyard lined with guava trees and sugar apple trees all along the perimeter. They were all bare. The one that caught his eye in the farthest corner next to the pool was a giant casuarina tree with two massive branches that formed a fork in which a brown-skinned boy, likely a teenager, sat reading a book and dangling his feet in the air. She turned to Harold, now switching to proper English to lend some gravity to what she was about to tell him.

"Go say 'hello' to your son! His name is Pierre Prince. Dad wouldn't allow him any other name but Prince. And so what? He is yours."

Harold moved away from the window, crossed the room and slumped back into his chair. "What you telling me, girl?" Once a liar, always a liar, he thought. But there was a certain raw sincerity in her voice, a yearning to finally tell it all. The boy was the same one he had seen with Montmartre at the gate asking her who he was. People in the village said he was the Creole's son. There was no reason now for Penelope to claim he was hers and his, other than to tell the truth, to relieve herself of some long-held burden of a secret.

Before he could say another word, she explained calmly, "Pierre thinks that Marcella is his mother. That was Dad's idea, not mine. He calls me Aunt Penny out of respect. He's a good boy. As you see, he's a bookworm. Got his own private tutors. Wants to be a doctor. He's bright. Handsome too just like his father. Yep!"

Still standing at the window with her back turned to Harold, she said slowly with the firmness of finality in her voice, "Okay, I am going to come clean. You came here for the truth and I am going to give you the truth." She walked briskly over to the liquor cabinet and removed a bottle of vintage pink champagne, twisted the wire top, popped the cork, lifted the bottle to her lips and took an ample swig as if it were the secret serum that would at last educe the unadulterated truth and spew it out before him to the last bitter drop. Averting her eyes from where he sat and reverting to perfect English so there could be no room for either solecism or misunderstanding, she opened up to him in a tone that would underscore the naked truth. "After my parents found out their little girl was pregnant, I told them I was raped in the village that night, raped by you, Harold Prince."

Harold straightened up. "That was a blasted lie!" he snapped. "Don't forget, it was you who came into my world, into my house, and climbed into my bed half-naked. Girl, why're you accusing me o' rape?"

"Well, I didn't tell you to go crazy that night. Well okay, let's say it was mutual rape." She laughed at the absurd oxymoron. "Anyway, after that night you could live in *your* world, but in *my* world life was hell. I had a whole lot more to lose than you. And from that night my whole life was ruined."

At that moment there was a thud that echoed up from the courtyard like the muffled jarring of a car door slammed shut. Harold sprang from his chair like a cornered prey. "Relax, it's not him," she said matter-of-factly. "Is only the gardener making a racket."

With the same casualness, she explained: "After that night, before Pierre was born, my parents were very angry people, angry that you, Harold, a black Bajan from down in de village, defiled their virgin daughter. Then after he was born, life became a living hell. The day before Ma killed herself, she took me off her will, disowned both me and the baby. But Dad was more reasonable, he was torn because, as he said, the bastard bore some of the Thorne blood. He had to find a compromise and that is where Marcella came in."

"Let me get this straight! First of all, as I recall, you were the aggressor. Second, your mother chose to die rather than be a grandmother to your son. You turned your back on your own son to please your father. But what I don't get is why the hell your father killed my son who had nothing to do with anything."

His words must have jarred a nerve; she tried to blink back the tears but she was overcome and they streamed down her face. Her hand trembled as she reached for the champagne. She filled her glass and, like her tears, the pink wine fizzed helplessly over the rim. It dribbled onto the table and down onto the rug.

"I owe my father. Not fer him I would be out on the street today like a stray dog. So I had to stand by him and help to save him from the gallows. And I also love my son. I did the next best thing fer him; he is safe with Marcella. Now I need to save myself."

"And no one saved David. Why you didn't save him too?" he asked.

"Look at me!" she said, staring at her glass, "bloody lush that I am, trying to drown the past, everything that happened."

Harold was giddy with cognac and dizzy with the steady stream of revelations, but in a way he was grateful that finally all his self-doubt and self-incriminations were falling away in the light of her confessions.

After all, she confessed that the wild sex that night was consensual. Or did she? He still wasn't sure. "Mutual rape" made no sense.

That night long ago in his mother's house, when the two of them lay in his bed, listening to the rain thumping on the galvanized roof like a stampeding herd, the same rain that had conspired to bring them together that night, bundle them into one bed and then goad them into their first sex, they were two children from opposite worlds, their bodies primed and ready but their minds woefully unprepared. The darkness of night had blinded them both to colour; they were neither black nor white but mere mortals devoid of the concealment of prejudice and racial preference that would be inflicted upon them in their later years. His thinking that night was so fogged by the frenetic rush of blood and his first rush of rabid raging hormones that he could not be sure of who was the initiator; even the moment of penetration was in a haze. He was too intoxicated then with lust, almost as intoxicated as he was now beginning to feel from an hour of drinking the Englishman's cognac.

He got up to leave. He now had the answers he had been seeking: his beloved son, David, had been killed to avenge the primal sin of rape of which he felt wrongfully accused. But strangely, the walls were shifting and the floor was tilting slightly under his feet, sufficiently to warn that the brandy was encroaching on his faculties. He had never been much of a drinker. He set his empty glass down; it toppled and fell to the floor.

"Don't go!" she pleaded. "Don't go just yet!"

He slurred, "Woman, I got what I came for. I know everything I need to know. I know the truth. It was lies and hate and shame and colour and class. All o' that evil in this house is what killed my son. Why not me? Why David? He didn't have a damn thing to do with you people. He didn't know you. He didn't know your father. And on top o' all that, you people disguised him as a monkey to beat the law. But I know the truth now and so does David. Goodbye!"

He took two steps towards the exit and she sprang up from the settee and blocked his way. When she jumped to her feet, the night robe slid from her shoulders. Freeing her arms, she flung the robe onto a chair. She was undeniably drunk.

"Well, don't you want to meet yer son? Pierre is yours too, he got yer last name, your blood is in his veins and now that you are in this house he might as well know that you are his father, not some man in Martinique. Right? It is not too late."

Harold could detect the deception in her voice. She was toying with him again, playing a mind game, trying to manipulate his emotions, removing one pawn and sliding another in its place just as cleverly as if they were sitting at the marble-topped chess table in the corner. There had been only one David and there could not be another; there could be no substitute, no consolation prize. The little boy in the courtyard, even if he were conceived in a lowly straw bed in the village and the son of a working-class peon, was now living in a different world, a white world, and would never be asked to look back to where he began. Why should he? How long had he been immured, concealed in the Thorne closet of lies and secret shame, re-labelled like contraband and insidiously handed over to a Creole woman who had a percentage of black blood like this boy? And to think that his own mother had defied all maternal instincts and joined with her father in this contemptible scheme, all because the boy, by no fault of his own, was thought to be sired by a Bajan, not of their race and not in their class. These thoughts sickened him to his stomach.

He reached for the knob and she flung her back against the door, spanning the width with her outstretched hands. He would have to force his way out.

"Well then, wait fer my father, he'll be home any minute!"

"I don't need to see him. I know the reason he murdered my son, it was because of you and your damned lies. You and he can rot in hell!"

"Well, if it is revenge you want, imagine my father walking through this door and seeing you and me in this house, in this room like two reunited lovers. That would be your own sweet revenge."

"Girl, I didn't come here looking fer revenge, just the truth. Let me out!"

"He won't hurt you now, I swear. He already did his deed. Now it's your turn."

"Move from the door! I'm leaving!"

She was panting now with creative ideas to keep him from leaving "Better still he come home and find his beloved daughter once again butt-naked right here with you. Two white and two black legs intertwined in passionate sex right here on this floor on his white rug. Oh God! That would be something!" She laughed. It was more like a witch's chortle, mocking and wicked. The acrid fumes of alcohol floated from her mouth like a toxic mist. She drank the last drop but still clutched the glass.

Suddenly she reached to her waist and untied the braided belt that had kept her tenuously clothed and let the gown fall slowly, flirtatiously, from her shoulders, to her hips, to her feet. Then she stepped out of the tangle of cloth, reached out and wrapped her arms around his neck, pressing her naked skin to his body and pulling him down to the floor, to her father's white plush Afghan rug.

Before he could prise her arms away she aroused his curiosity with the intriguing words in her ear: "I have something else to tell you."

"What else can you say? You said it all."

"You came here fer the truth and I gave you most of the truth, except …"

"Except what, woman?"

"I am ready to tell you the rest of the story. And after you hear the whole truth of what happened, you can take yer pound of flesh right here and now. Make me pay fer my sin like David paid fer yours, the sins of the father. You can kill me now and put me out of my misery fer good. It was not my father that shot David, it was me." She blurted it out as if it were rotten meat that had been stuck in her craw for days.

He was speechless. She collapsed in a paroxysm of tears and fell back on the floor, naked, her arms outstretched. Alcohol had unmasked the truth. Her final confession pierced his drunkenness and exploded into his consciousness like a blast of dynamite. It was the final truth. She reached for him, but he was determined not to be entrapped again by the touch and sight of her nakedness. He was more startled than aroused by it, by her skin as white as paper. He wrestled her arms away while she continued to cry and then laugh wildly in her inebriated stupor. As he again reached for the doorknob, from her knees she held on to the fly of his trousers. In that moment he could not bring himself to hate her; his only regard for her was pity. Still in his own half-drunken state, he stared through her thick lenses, deep into the translucence of her bulging blue eyes and there he saw the faces of her father and mother. They were equally deserving of his hate as she. At that instant, she and her parents were one and the same. In the farthest depths of his blurred subconsciousness, voices rang out deep in his head. Clear as a bell, they called to him: "A life for a life." These were the exact words that had been ringing in his ears, night after night in his dreams, hour after hour in his inner torment, from the men in Piggott's rum shop, from friends like Mickey Norris, from strangers who stopped him on the street to share their condemnation of the verdict. The voices dared him to reach out and wrap his bare hands around her scrawny neck, the way hers were clutching that glass stem and squeeze it until the haunting ghost of David drifted away contented and forever back into the tunnel whence the voices came. In his mind's eye he saw himself as in a mirror, bending over her, clutching her throat while she gurgled and flailed at his feet on the floor. Her spectacles flew in the air and the champagne glass shattered against the wall, but none of it to him was real, just a figment of his imagination fuelled by too much drink. He imagined her gagging, her eyeballs bulging, her lips moving though they made no sound. Voices echoing from some dark chamber of his mind continued to repeat, "A life for a life! A life for a life!"

Suddenly the round-faced cat vaulted sprightly onto the serving table, then up to his chest, meowing, lamenting and baring a mouthful of tiny pointed teeth that dug deep into his arm. The pain jolted his drunken mind back to reality. Instinctively he flung the cat to the floor. The voices in his head were now silent; all was quiet again. It was then he realized he had not been imagining; she was indeed writhing and convulsing at his feet. He had strangled her with his bare hands. In an instant she was dead.

He took one last look at her lifeless body and bolted out the door, down the spiral stairway, through the foyer and out the door. Madame Montmartre and the boy were standing at the gate while she fumbled for the key to unlock the chain. "Goodbye, Mr. Prince!" she called out to him as she stared at his bloodied arm where Penelope's cat had left her mark. The boy also held him in a curious stare. He quickly discerned that the gate was not courteously opened for him but for a white Jaguar approaching up the driveway. It slowed to a stop. The uniformed chauffeur everyone knew as "Cuffie" but whose real name was Cuthbert slid from behind the wheel and began walking towards him. He was a tall, bony, tight-lipped man from another parish who never mingled with the local men, one who had never been seen without his official black-peak chauffeur's cap. He belonged to Thorne's inner circle of servants. He called out as if to impress his employer: "Wha' you doin' hey, boy?

Harold fearlessly and calmly replied, "Tell yer boss I now know the truth!"

The chauffeur turned around, a quizzical expression on his face, and was about to report to his boss in the back seat peering through the tinted porthole when Harold called out with another cryptic message. "And tell him it was an accident!" Cuffie slid back behind the wheel and the Jaguar continued on through the mansion gate.

From the moment he felt the sun on his face and breathed the fresh open air, the alcohol began to gradually release its grip, but in its aftermath there grew within him a crippling sense of fear, shame and remorse. His whole body was shaking. He, who had never physically harmed another living creature, had taken a human life. Was he no less a murderer than Penelope whose act, granted, was likely premeditated? Was his own sin, by comparison, a case of momentary primordial rage without forethought thus rendering it less despicable? Perhaps he had fooled himself into believing that the sole purpose of his visit was a quest for the truth when lurking beneath it was a deeper, darker hankering for vengeance and for the justice that had been denied him by the law of the land. The feel of Mickey's gun in his pocket only compounded the contradiction. And whereas Penelope in her drunken self-delusion had thought her own sensuous body could commandeer his emotions the way it did fifteen years ago, and in a single orgasmic release defuse the vengeance she knew was boiling inside of him; and whereas she envisioned her father's horror and revulsion on seeing the two of them sprawled naked on his floor in complicit intercourse would be ample payback; nothing less than a life in exchange for David's was enough for Harold. Yet amidst all the morbidity, the guilt and the senselessness of it all, he now felt a strange, inner peace. He had been shorn of a great burden.

THERE ONCE WAS A LITTLE ENGLAND

From the altitude of the mansion grounds, he stood with his hands on his hips and surveyed the whole breadth of the Thorne estate, and for the first time he grasped the immensity of the land that was theirs: the orchard, now brown and blighted; the rustic woodland beyond it; acres of burnt cane fields in the distance; the road that delineated the tenantry from their own private property; the demarcation of rented lots, one on which his own house stood; and then behind the lots, a wild expanse of prickly nettles, brambly dunk trees and thorny bushes, a waste of good land where no one ventured but which, no doubt, would soon be cleared for more lucrative lots. The village down below took on a different dimension: in the distance the houses were quaintly charming as in a picture postcard; none was decrepit, drab or even poor as he often saw them when he walked by. Even Joe Walrond's dilapidated house was a child's delightful drawing. His and Cissy's pink house was no more conspicuous than any of the rest, and people he was supposed to know going to and fro on the cart road were just forms. They were all bloodless, brainless automatons. He could not help but think: "So this is how they see my people down below from this lordly height."

He looked towards the west where he could see a stretch of the horizon and the ocean, blue and pure and peaceful. As he made his way down the slope, away from the scene of his crime, he could hear the angry barking of the lone Alsatian.

It was said that in Barbados there were three places where a man could go to cleanse his mind, if not his soul: the church, the rum shop and the sea. He chose the sea as he always did and jogged past his house—his family would likely be still in bed on a lazy Saturday morning—past the village houses still slumbering, through the cane piece, down to Seclusion Road and across Black Rock and finally down to Brandons Beach.

Like sheet lightning, which refrains from striking the earth but conserves its fury and flashes only behind the clouds, the news about Penelope remained for hours within the confines of the mansion. Perhaps it was the shock of discovery, the same incredulity that possessed Harold from the moment he released his murderous grip, that made Thorne unconsciously lock the door before collapsing on the floor beside his dead daughter. In that instant there was no mystery as to how she died, or at the hands of whom, or even less so, why. She was all he had of his own true blood and after being overcome by an avalanche of grief, he was filled with enormous guilt. Although deep down he had loved his daughter more than anyone alive, he knew he had made her life a virtual hell; had condemned her day after day, year after year, for bringing dishonour into his home; had accused her of killing the wife he dearly loved; had called her names like "slut" and "harlot" and "whore;" had labelled the son she bore a black bastard and had given him away to a near-stranger to hide his shame. His precious daughter had become damaged goods and her son not worthy of the Thorne heritage. He was convinced it was he who drove her to kill David Prince in order to spite his father for her life of misery. He felt as guilty as she. But not in a million years would he have wanted the boy killed; murder was not his intent.

After the shooting that morning in September, the least he could do was step up and shield her from the court and from the wrath of the people. He took her place. The weapon was his Remington two-inch-bore shotgun; he kept it leaning on the side of the house on the landing, next to the wooden stairway, surely not for monkeys that time of the year, but for target practice, shooting at blackbirds when he had time on his hands. The timing was eerily coincidental: the boy in the tree and his daughter's happening on the landing next to the gun. She had been drinking. Not even Marcella knew it was his daughter who pulled the trigger. Marcella was his confidante; he could trust her with his own life but he wasn't sure he could trust her with Penelope's. Neither would his lawyer, Cunningham, be allowed behind that wall of secrecy shared with his daughter. He left it up to the barrister to do what he could with the far-fetched imagery of an out-of-season mango tree, a monkey and an old man's delusional mind. Cunningham was such a skilled lawyer, he knew how to win with the flimsiest and most baseless of evidence. He was helped by the fireproof testimony of his unintended star witness, the Superintendent of Police. His only truthful admission to both of them was that he was incapable of murder; bigoted, ruthless, yes, but without a murderous fibre in his body.

But there were witnesses to the shooting. When the blasts reached his ears and he tumbled out of bed and ran downstairs to find his daughter collapsed on the landing drunk to the world, in the corner of his vision were Mr. Marshall and Sampson, their eyes wide with disbelief, their feet riveted to the ground with fright. They dropped the patio chairs they had been securing before the storm and scurried back to their quarters. When the constables turned up for their statement, the two loyal servants protected their master and gave nothing away. He resolved there and then to buy their continued silence. Next day he sent for the two men, presented them each with a furnished room in the mansion and, except for a seat at their master's table, they could have the run of the house.

It had been a while since he discovered the body. Madame Montmartre, seized with an awful premonition intensified by the sound of sobbing coming from the sitting room, knocked frantically on the door, then broke the lock with a mighty kick and burst in to find Thorne on the floor in tears and visibly distraught. She fell to her knees and began to retch at the horror of the scene. Penelope was on her back, naked, her legs splayed as if she had been violated, her eyes bulging more than usual with surprise. Montmartre, with a palm to her mouth, gasped at the sight. *"Mon Dieu! Mon Dieu!"* She still had the presence of mind to reach for the telephone next to the game table, but he motioned to her to wait until he could gather his wits. She went to his side and was struck by how quickly the fortitude and control he had always exhibited had melted away, and for the first time she saw him as a man who could feel, cry and was snivelling like a child. Before long, the snivelling turned into a torrent of tears. The sight awoke a measure of tenderness within her that she had never felt for him before; she cradled his head in her arms.

She had her own feelings of guilt; since her master was not at home, she should have sent Mr. Prince away; but then, it was Penelope who had invited him into the house and chose to entertain him privately. In due course she would explain that fact to her father in order to minimize her share of blame, though in her heart she believed the blame rested with him, that he was the one who shot the man's son, for which crime Penelope was made to pay the ultimate price. But now there were larger and more pressing questions weighing on her mind: How would she break the news to the boy she had mothered all these years: that the one he called Aunt Penny was gone? If not now, when would be the appropriate time for the boy to be told that the one he called Aunt Penny was really his mother? Would he hate her for having misplaced his love? Would he hate his mother in death for having in life denied that he was her son? For the first time she felt dirty and ashamed for having been corralled by Thorne and his daughter into their trio of scurrilous deception. She left the room in search of Pierre.

Thorne eventually rose from the floor and slumped onto the settee. His grief was slowly and inexorably giving way to an all-consuming rage while Penelope's cat cuddled beside her, asleep and indifferent.

It was not until six that evening when the servants scattered, that the news burst out of the mansion and flooded the village and beyond, and Bajans gathered on the road in little conspiratorial circles to add their own slants to the story, to append their own conclusions and pass new versions along to others who hadn't yet heard. It was the chauffeur who put two and two together and who divined the truth of what really happened upstairs at the mansion; he had seen Harold retreating from the gate and had weighed the meaning of his words meant for his master's ears. But the chauffeur was Thorne's trusted henchman, long ago sworn to secrecy of anything that took place within his walls. He had nothing to say.

Chapter 20

Flight

HAROLD STOOD atop a sand dune at Brandons Beach gazing across to the infinity of the horizon where his thoughts could be clear and unimpeded. His thoughts were of his family. He thought first of his father who had chosen to live all his life at sea, not wanting to be tethered to one place, not even to Barbados, a place he loved dearly, preferring the unpredictability of the wide open seas to the knowing everyday travails of living among his people under the heels of the colonial powers. He had distanced himself from even his own family. As Harold admitted many times, he didn't know his father well enough to love him but he loved the image he had created of his father, his own ideal of fatherhood. When his father died he resolved to love his own boys more profoundly than he himself was ever loved.

He thought of Cissy whom he could not now face, and who loved him much more than he deserved to be loved. He knew he could run to her even now with blood on his hands and she would love him no less. He thought of his mother, the one who taught him right from wrong but who, through that singular prism reserved for her only boy-child, could see only the good in him, never the bad. Even now, she could never bring herself to believe any of this; she would blame others. How he wished he had told Nathaniel more often how much he loved him! He deserved better than a killer for a father; he deserved a model like Gitts. And so, because he had such selfless love for his family, he would not now flee to their side to complicate their lives and to poison the air around them. Neither could he flee into the arms of the law; killing a white woman would be unpardonable in Her Majesty's Court and unfathomable even among his own people. He would stand a better chance for a measure of sympathy if she were of his own race. Even so, an expensive, effectual legal defence as that put forward by his wealthy adversaries would be beyond his reach. All he wanted now was the understanding of those who knew him that the revenge he had exacted, rightly or wrongly, was for David; that it was to ensure that the soul of his beloved son, robbed of his future on account of a rape of which his father had been unjustly accused, would now rest in eternal peace.

The shore was deserted except for boys on horseback in the distance grooming their horses; he had seen them before. He kicked off his shoes, strolled down to the edge of the sand and, fully clothed, waded out into the cool, tranquil, inviting water beyond where the deeper, greenish blue met the translucence of the sandy bottom and shoals of silvery frays swirled playfully around his feet. From there he swam farther out with brisk powerful strokes to where he could no longer stand and slowly lowered himself with his hands outstretched and leaving only his head above water bobbing like a rubber buoy. He filled his mouth with sea water and squirted it high into the air like a geyser, as if he were spitting, or pissing on the world he was about to leave behind. Then, with his arms tucked in, he slowly drifted downward below the surface until he could no longer hear waves crashing onto the shore or the whistling of earthly winds, just a playful gurgling around his ears; and to where he felt no longer himself but some other being suspended in a holographic bubble, untouchable and out of harm's way. He held his breath as long as he could and defied the nausea of drowning until his lungs protested and released their last ration of precious air. Only then did he kick and flap his way back to the surface, shuddering at the thought of having been at the threshold of unconsciousness. But at that brink of drowning he had felt an inner peace; at that one moment the ocean had dissolved his torment; and so, after a while he willed his spirit against the protestations of his vital organs to thrust his body back down into that nether weightless world where he would stay, thrashing, kicking and sputtering, until the natural struggle for life relented and his whole being finally surrendered into the embrace of the sea he had loved all his life.

Esmay came running in a frenzy, her hair half-combed and wild, her arms flailing, her skirt and petticoat billowing in the wind as she crossed the road to Cissy's house bursting with the news. Cissy was taking her morning bath in the privacy of her backyard, standing on a platform of flat rocks, ladling water from a barrel onto her shoulders with a calabash bowl. She heard the agitated pounding on the front door which had been locked for her bath time. Nathaniel was asleep. She hastened to cover herself and rushed to the door to see her neighbour, wide-eyed and spluttering with excitement.

"Girl, you ent hear? Thorne daughter got kill," she panted.

"Penelope?"

"And guess who they say kill she?"

"I don' know. Who?"

"Harold."

Cissy felt for the edge of the table to steady herself and then flopped down in a chair staring blankly at her neighbour's face and then into space. Not only was her man incapable of killing but equally implausible was a reason to kill the Englishman's daughter. And where was Harold? Was he being maliciously framed, running from his accusers? She knew instantly from experience where she would find him, where he always could be found in times of distress. She flung on a dress and headed out the door with Esmay in pursuit. Following the precise route that Harold had taken hours before, she ran towards the sea, intent on scouring every inch of sandy beach.

The two women walked the shoreline shading their eyes from the glare of the almost-midday sun beating down on their backs, from Batts Rock to Brightons to Brandons to where Pelican Island pierced the high tide just west of the Bay. Their soles and calves began to protest from slogging for miles in the wet sand. They started back and along the way they searched in the shade of every manchineel and casuarina tree, behind every cluster of sea grape trees and hibiscus hedge, between every sand dune, among the dozens of upturned fishing boats that lay on the shore like giant pods. They enquired of every fisherman tending his nets if they had seen the likes of him; they all knew him. Cissy scanned the sea dotted with dozens of black heads on the surface of the water. Saturday morning bathers were already populating the beaches. For one heart-stopping moment after another, every man's head and torso that popped out of the water looked to be Harold's. Her mind insisted that it would be the sea and no other place to which he would flee, knowing how much he loved the ocean. Then mindful of how able a swimmer he was, she came to the only logical conclusion: that the sea had claimed him as its own and he had gone willingly. She would listen for the news of a drowning or of a body washed ashore because she knew he would not surrender himself to his accusers. But, as it turned out, neither would the sea surrender Harold's body. He would not be found that day or on any other day.

Pastor Gittens's Austin Farina could be seen parked next to her front step when Cissy and her neighbour rounded the gap and parted ways. He had heard the news and was standing, expectant, waiting in the open doorway. As she approached, he scrutinized her face keenly as if to gauge the level of her despair, but instead he saw the vacant expressionless look of someone who had been lost for many days and then plucked unexpectedly from the depths of some unforgiving jungle. She threw herself wearily into his arms and they both huddled there in the middle of the room without a word between them. Her eyes were dry: she had no more tears to shed. She saw him as her only remaining tower of strength in a life once idyllic but now falling apart. The plaintive words now resounding in Gittens's ears were suddenly meaningful and poignant: "If anything should ever happen to me," Harold had told him, "I would wish you to stay close to her and to Nathaniel." Now it all made dreadful sense.

He stayed with Cissy and her distraught son until nightfall and then impulsively drove his car up the hill, up the tarmacked driveway and parked momentarily facing the mansion. Inside the mansion there seemed to be an eerie calm like the calm before Hurricane Janet blew in off the Atlantic months before and began her rampage. He remembered Harold telling him that day on the way home about the girl who barged into his bedroom and into his life with equal ferocity when he was at an innocent age, and had in one night turned his world around; and how he had to keep the name of the girl out of the cesspool of Bajan gossip for all those years, not even mentioning her name to him, a man of God, sworn to hold in confidence the confessions even of a purported rapist. Still, he would never have imagined that the girl in his bedroom that night was the Englishman's daughter.

He drove on to his church, entered, walked down the aisle and knelt at the altar. He would now pray for the soul of Harold as he had done weeks before for the soul of his son, except that now he would offer pleas to the Almighty for mercy and forgiveness. He believed then that his friend was guilty of killing, but innocent of rape.

THERE ONCE WAS A LITTLE ENGLAND

Across the street, the door to Piggott's rum shop was closed. It was late; all rum shops by law had to be out of service by eleven. But he still could hear the undulating rumble of men's voices, the occasional blasphemy and the continual clinking of glasses and bottles. The banja music that poured out at night and floated across the road to disrespect his church was muted. The thought came to him like an epiphany as he rose from the altar that the men in the rum shop might know the real Harold Prince better than he, and some aspects of his character even better than Cissy. He regretted not knowing him as well as he could have, not having tried as hard as he could have to draw him into the fellowship of his church. Had he done so, he was sure that Harold would have walked the path that Cissy had chosen and would today be safe in the arms of his church. He knew that Harold had frequented the rum shop since his son was killed and might have shared his intentions with Piggott's patrons leading up to that fateful visit to Thorne's house. He knew that liquor had a way of baring men's souls.

He dared himself to cross the road, climb the four or five steps to the shop, pull open the door and startle the men inside at the unlikely sight of a man of God entering their unholy den. As he appeared in the doorway, the dozen or so men around the barroom fell silent and still as a single frame in a movie reel. In the enclosed air his lungs were instantly assaulted by the smoke of a dozen cigarettes while the fumes of alcohol singed his nostrils. His pupils had not yet adjusted to the dark; each man was a shadow, except Piggott, who stood behind the bar in the glow of the illuminated liquor bottles with a pencil held snugly behind one ear lobe and a cigarette behind the other.

He greeted the pastor: "Good Evening, Brother Gittens. What brings you here?" There was a hint of disapproval in his voice as if he thought the pastor had come to rebuke the perversity of his surroundings.

Gittens promptly got to the point of his visit. "Harold Prince, you think he did it?"

Piggott's response was quick. "You asking me if he kill de girl? Well, de answer is no!"

"Well, who did it?"

The shopkeeper left his station behind the counter, walked around and came face to face with Gittens as if his proximity would lend weight to what he was about to say.

"De jurisprudence o' Buhbaydus is wha' kill de woman. If de Law did do what it wuz suppose to do in de first place and punish de guilty, we wunt to have a man running 'round looking fer justice fer his son. Barrister Cunningham and Thorne is de ones that got blood on dey hands. If de court didn't want to hang de white man, then fer Chrissake, charge him fer manslaughter and put 'im up in Glendairy fer a year or two, but to come back wid a sentence o' not guilty wuz enough to send de boy father stark staring mad. Many a night de man wuz here in dis rum shop pouring his heart out, drinkin' like a fish, drinkin' like he never drink before in his life and cryin' out fer de justice that he wuz denied by Her Majesty's Court o' Law. So now you know where de blame lies fer de death of Penelope Thorne." The shopkeeper was agitated; the tendons in his neck stood out and his eyes were on fire, his face rigid with conviction. "Harold wuz my good good friend," he added.

Gittens ventured another question: "Why did the girl have to die?"

A voice shot back at Gittens from the far end of the barroom where a man sat with his face hidden in the shadow of a broad-rimmed Panama hat and behind a cluster of empty beer bottles. "And thine eye shall not pity, but life shall go for life, eye for eye, tooth for tooth, hand for hand, foot for foot, Deuteronomy 19 verse 21." It was the Old Testament biblical law of retribution with which the pastor was quite familiar but the man did not address his question as it pertained to the girl. The voice came from the most unlikely of sources but from a man who obviously knew his Scriptures, and as the man emerged into the light, Gittens recognized him as Joe Walrond, the man people deemed the village drunk. As if to punctuate his contempt for the premise of the pastor's question, the old man punched his own chest with his fist and belched. There were mutterings of approval all around. The pastor thought of two or three passages from the New Testament that he could also quote verbatim to rebut the boozer, but which would serve no other purpose than to add fuel to a fire that might have already been raging in the rum shop before he walked in. Persistence in arguing in disfavour of the girl's "life for a life" would only raise the voices of Harold's friends to a new crescendo of righteous anger and force the old man to reach into his encyclopaedic memory to come up with another outdated quote, this one about the "sins of the fathers."

    It was clear to Gittens that in the eyes of the men, Harold had been wronged by Thorne and wronged by the Court and thus had taken the law rightfully into his own hands. He was satisfied nevertheless that they had no idea of the encounter many years ago between Harold and the girl, though he would not put it past the intuitiveness and creativity of Bajan gossip. In good conscience he would let that secret die with the two of them. Not even to Cissy would he mention it. But little did he himself know that the same encounter could be traced to the boy who now lived in the mansion and that his birth had sparked more than one instance of tragic senseless death. He turned to leave. Behind his back he could hear a chorus of indignation. He felt as though he had thrown kerosene on a smouldering fire and walked away.

    Within minutes, the news travelled like a flaming javelin across the miles that separated Thornville from The Ivy, through Fairfield and Eagle Hall and Bank Hall and Bush Hall and Carrington's Village and finally to a house in The Ivy to tear into the heart of Ma Prince and thereafter to plunge her whole family into a profound state of melancholy. Neighbours converged on the house offering whatever comforts they could, but to no avail, as the woman hugged her belly and bawled all day and all night. The house was once again enveloped in deep irremediable sorrow.

    In Thornville, a pall descended on the village. People looked towards the mansion on the hill, curtains drawn, lights dimmed, silent as a mausoleum. The only movements observed were the comings and goings of the coroner, the constables, the servants and Reverend Elliott, the Anglican vicar. In the village, people fully expected that any day the Englishman would burst forth in a paroxysm of insanity and rake all the houses with a sweeping barrage of gunfire, and seeing he had nothing to lose but his own life now that his whole family was dead, his parents, his wife and his only child, would climb out of his foxhole like an embattled infantryman with guns blazing and storm the village, and not just target

Harold's house but the whole village, since it was said that to every white man, one black man was all black men.

    It was the morning of yet another funeral. Gittens awoke to the doleful knell of church bells pealing a slow ominous rhythm throughout the village as they did the morning of the hurricane. As he lay in bed, he was struck with an idea; it was like a voice in his head; he would go to pay respects to the dead woman. He knew her only from afar as the Englishman's daughter, the young and vivacious white woman who turned up at the last minute to say goodbye to David and then to pass a note to his mother. Cissy never mentioned the contents to him and he never enquired.

    He got dressed, went out to his backyard, plucked a few pink geraniums, wild purple pansies and some pieces of fern, twisted them into a crude wreath and headed down to Black Rock to St. Stephen's Church. There was not a parking space to be had anywhere in the vicinity of the church, and so he parked on the cricket grounds, strolled to the church entrance and joined the procession down the aisle to where the casket lay just next to the chancel. He lay his wreath down among a pile of flowers just as she had laid her own wreath on David's coffin in Gittens's churchyard minutes before the interment. He wondered if his gesture was merely reciprocal or had he been moved by some moral compulsion to get dressed and come to the church for the funeral of a stranger. It entered his head that perhaps Harold's belated remorse and penitence were embodied in this impromptu wreath of wild flowers, and that Harold had somehow spoken to him and asked him to come to the funeral. He was convinced that Harold had killed the girl but in his heart he did not believe that he meant to, for what reason would he have had to do so.

    Seated in the front row was Thorne, next to the woman people called "the Creole," her face bowed and veiled. The alleged son of the Creole sat at the end of the pew next to the man Gittens recognized as Thorne's chauffeur. The entire front row was silent and grim. He scanned the packed congregation and concluded that, besides the servants, his might be the only black face among a sea of white faces that contrasted sharply with black suits, black dresses, black robes and black veils. That was until a crusty old voice, a familiar voice whispered in his ear as he paid his respects to the deceased. It was the voice of his friend, Ben Carson, the mortician.

"Bad job, Gitts," he whispered, "too much o' rouge. She look like tinted ceramic. I coulda did a better job fer my ole boss."

He moved on and left Ben hovering over the coffin, shaking his head and subjecting the corpse to his critical eye. But the ever-faithful servant of along ago had likely come with kind sentiments for his old boss and was likely still unable to reconcile the human dichotomy of a murderous heart and a generous spirit. Moreover, he would likely give the benefit of doubt to the Englishman; after all, the man had already been exonerated by the court.

Just ahead of Gittens, shuffling along in the viewing line, was a short, fat, bald-headed Irishman with a handlebar moustache the colour of mustard. They recognized each other instantly. He was the well-known Doctor Donovan from Peterkins, the one he surmised was their family physician. He was married to a Bajan, his second wife, a registered nurse who assisted him in his practice. Well aware of their anomalous marriage within a society not yet receptive to multiracial couples, he and his young black wife moved discreetly. He spoke imperfect Bajan with a distinct Irish brogue, a manner of speaking inculcated from long marriages to women of different cultures. Gittens remembered him as an old-fashioned physician based at the Barbados General Hospital in town. He was old now and modern medicine was quickly passing him by. He treated every conceivable ailment from centipede sting to consumption principally with one of two medicines, either penicillin or Jamaican white rum. Nevertheless, he had earned a stellar reputation among the upper class as an able gynaecologist and obstetrician, one who could be relied on to take care of their women, a fact that swung into focus when he turned to Gittens and asked, "Tha' ole lady, Sister Innis in de village, she still deliverin' babies?"

"Yes, and she is a very good midwife," answered Gittens.

"Aye, I am sure she is."

As if to answer a question that wasn't asked, he whispered in Gittens's ear: "De wife did want to come to de funeral. She always liked Penelope, but she say she father is a wuffless dog." Then he said,

"Excuse me," and turned to the sad-faced Englishman, whispering in his ear a long stream of consolations. Continuing to the end of the pew, he leaned over to greet the boy.

"Sorry about yer mom, sonny boy," he said softly.

"Thanks, Doc, but she's not my mom. I call her Aunt Penny," said the boy.

"Not yer mom? Well, I should very well know, don't ye think? I'm the one that brought ye into this world, me lad."

The boy gave the doctor a look that seemed to defer pitifully to his presumed senility, while the old man shook his head from side to side as if to acknowledge that the boy's reply was brought on by trauma and intense mourning to the point of denial.

He then turned to Gittens. "Boy denying he mother and de woman lying right there in front o' him plain as day. Now how in God's heaven ye mean to tell me he don' know he own mother from he aunt? Huh? And I am de very one that extract him from he mother's womb."

Gittens sided with the boy; he too believed the old Irish doctor was slipping; after all, the whole village said his mother was the Martiniquen.

He had not planned to stay for the service; he never cared for the overly structured Church of England liturgy that frowned on improvisation and spontaneity of spirit, but curiosity got the best of him and he lingered in the back. Sitting next to him was a stylishly dressed Englishwoman whom he did not recognize but who was revealed to him from the greetings of others as the wife of Barrister Cunningham. She smiled at him from under a black wide-brimmed hat decorated with plastic grapes and a gold hatpin. She was not accompanied.

"You must be the pastor from Thornville, aren't you?" she asked, leaning towards his ear so as not to be overheard above the muted buzz of the congregation.

"Yes, I am. And you must be the wife of the famous barrister."

"You're a long way from your own church, I'd say," she said ambiguously.

She had a fairly affable, innocent face that dispelled any suspicion of meanness; he had no reason to read any suggestion of mischief in her words. She was right; his Pilgrim Holiness Church was a long way figuratively from this Anglican Church with its pomp and grandeur, with its cavernous nave and high-backed padded pews and cushiony kneelers and gold-leaf pulpit, its treasury bursting with the profuse tithes of the rich and middle-class. Was this what she meant?

"Yes I am, in more ways than one," he answered matter-of-factly.

She paused as if to weigh the subtlety of his answer, then turned to more serious matters of the dead, saying: "It's never fair to say unkind things about the dead, they are no longer here to refute them, but if you ask me, this didn't have to happen. This girl could be alive and kicking today. She and I had a talk some time ago at a cocktail party at Government House about her father. As someone once said, 'the departed are always easy to misquote' but if my memory serves me right, she didn't want her father to spend one day in jail, much less to hang for shooting that child. Frankly, she didn't deserve to die for him, did she? But as sorry as I am about her, I still think the killing of a child is more egregious, don't you? I tell you, in the absence of justice, the old monster, vengeance, will sometimes try to balance the scale. That Harold 'whatever-his-name-was' wanted justice, he didn't get it so he settled for revenge."

"Revenge is such an ugly word," said Gittens.

"Yes, it *is* an ignoble word, isn't it? Frankly, I prefer to say that he was out to redress an injustice and teach the Court a lesson."

"But wasn't your husband Thorne's defence attorney? I was in the courthouse that day."

"My husband will tell you that his job is to defend all those who seek his defence."

"Even the indefensible?" asked Gittens combatively.

"His role is not to dispense justice," she replied. "That is the job of the judge based on the laws and on the verdict of a jury. It's the laws that needs to be just."

"The law may be just, but the application and interpretation of the law will always favour those who can afford a skilled defence, someone who knows how to manipulate it," said Gittens.

"Yes, a skilled defence does have its advantages," she countered.

Gittens felt at that moment compelled to pick up the sword of his fallen comrade. "But the law is supposed to intercede between the advantaged and the disadvantaged," he told her. "It shouldn't favour one side or the other and justice shouldn't be predicated on the ability to hire a skilled defence lawyer like your husband."

"Right. But if a man's life is at stake, you can't very well blame him for seeking the best defence he can afford."

"True," said Gittens, "and therein lies the problem with a society of classes where justice will always take the side of the rich. Do you think the man would have drowned himself if he had the wherewithal to hire a defence lawyer as skilled as your husband? Don't you think he would've hired someone like Barrister Cunningham to prove to the Court that he didn't intend to strangle her to death? That it was an accident like the accident that killed his son?" He went on: "And can I ask you why your husband is not here standing by his client?"

She raised her chin in the air, stared straight ahead and said, "Well, I can tell you he doesn't go to funerals, weddings or christenings. He is a man without sentimentality, a true defence lawyer."

Father Elliott emerged from the vestry, ready to commence the funeral service. Gittens excused himself. The booming pipe organ with its rich elegiac strains followed him to his car and he could not resist a surge of envy of these Anglican churches whose survival did not depend on pittances from the poor and the trickle of handouts from benevolent missionaries. He envied this titan of Western Christianity with its umbilical ties to the Mother Church and its tapping of tithes from the rich.

And then his thoughts turned to Doctor Donovan. Perhaps he was really the crazy one, confused with the identities of all the mothers of all the babies he had brought into this world over the years. He concluded that it was more likely that the doctor was confused than that the boy was denying his own mother when clearly everyone else knew his mother was the Creole sitting right there in the front row. "The man should really hang it up," he said to himself, "before he start giving babies to the wrong mothers."

Chapter 21

A Windstorm of Rumours

IN THE days and weeks that followed the death of Penelope Thorne, Cissy found herself living in the eye of a tornado: a windstorm of rumours, conjecture and even malicious inventions swirled around her every moment of every day. She yearned to escape even for a little while from the tentacles of the village: women reaching out to her to quench their unquenchable thirsts for sordid news, for confirmation of titillating rumours circulating around the island and of gruesome stories seeping out every day from the mansion. She grew weary of neighbours coming to her with sympathy in their eyes but begging for lurid details about "Harold and de white woman." Questions like "how long he did know she?" and "how he could kill de woman?" and "he rape she first?" pursued her like a nagging buzz in the ears wherever she went. Newsmen were banging on her door all hours of the day, seeking to fill in the blanks of their presumptuous editorials about Harold and, as they put it, his *femme fatale*. Even on the warmest days she kept her windows closed from peering, inquisitive eyes and seldom went out except to the standpipe, to Mrs. Piggott's food shop and to church. And even in church among the sisters, except for Sister Innis and Sister Ruth, she felt the chill of their virtuous rebuke as these holy pilgrims passed her in the aisles. Not long before then, there was no end to their outpouring of goodwill and sympathy for the loss of her boy-child. "Chile, God will never give you more than you can bear," they would say. Now, even in the house of Christian fellowship the air around her was abuzz with scorn. But on balance there was a growing generosity of understanding from the brothers in the church, rushing to defend her from the same sisters who accused her of foreknowledge of whatever took place between Harold and the woman. Or was it that now she was seen to be available, vulnerable and in need of a man's shoulder in her time of distress?

In the dozen or so years that she and Harold lived together, she never delved into his past, or he into hers. She knew with his looks he was likely irresistible to women before she knew him as he was to her when they met. To her it was preposterous that Penelope Thorne, her childhood friend, could have been the skeleton locked in his closet all those years. Moreover, the idea of her man, as gentle as he was, killing another being was as alien a notion as the man in the moon. It was more likely that he had confronted Thorne and somehow his daughter got in the way and was killed. Then chased by Thorne and the imbecilic police that kowtowed to white people, he had chosen death by drowning rather than to be cornered and to surrender to a system that would show no mercy to a black man with white blood on his hands. That was the picture in Cissy's mind. She remembered how he had been so consumed with the death of his son that the lack of sleep had starved his capacity to think straight. Throughout the night he paced the floor, to the front window and back, and then back again, pausing each time to stare out in the direction of the mansion on the hill shrouded in the black of night. She called to him to come back to bed and he lay awake, still as a log. At the break of dawn between sleep and wake, she sensed the rise of his half of the bed as he left her side. She was not alarmed; he often sneaked off early to the beach to beat the late morning sun. Not until Esmay came banging on her door that day did she know that he had gone to see his son's killer. Then combing the beachfronts with her good neighbour, scanning from shore to horizon for some sight of him, she could not help but recall his obsessive insistence that there was some morbid secret lying behind the walls of the Thorne mansion.

Now she herself was pursued. The police, though, left her alone. They had closed their books on the investigation; as far as they were concerned, the murderer was lying in a mossy grave somewhere off Brandons Beach or in the belly of some mammoth whale, "like Jonah" as one of the officers said. Two bare-backed stable hands from the Garrison Race Track were grooming their racehorses that morning and reported to the police seeing a man swimming out from the shore and disappearing "far, far, far out in de sea." Their description, "big able black man wid broad shoulders, sideburns, white shirt, brown short pants," matched perfectly the one who, according to Thorne's statement, was leaving the mansion when he drove up to the gate. He had refused to offer them any knowledge or speculation of what had brought the man to his house. He left them to their own assessment of motive.

Little did Cissy know that the one who knew the secret of Harold's murky past was none other than the one she trusted most. But Gittens had sworn to breathe not a single word about that nebulous rape that had tormented Harold throughout his youth. As much as it pained him to see the mystery of it all driving Cissy witless, he could not in good faith break that seal between him, Harold and his God. When Harold knocked on his door that morning he saw fear deep in his eyes; but he also saw an impenetrable fierceness that left no doubt he was about to place himself in harm's way and enter the lion's den. When he dashed out the door he had seemingly lost all powers of reason.

Now, his mind wandered back to that morning when he and Harold set out from the city in the midst of the wildest hurricane of their lives and found themselves stalled in rising floodwaters. They were trapped in the front seat of his car while the rain pounded the roof like on that stormy night of careless sex. And when the mood turned from tension to relaxed conversation, Harold decided it was time to shed the albatross he had carried all those years. But never in a million years would he, Gittens, have guessed that the girl in Harold's bed was the Englishman's daughter. In Barbados, this island of classes, they had been consigned by society to different orbits.

Still, unbeknownst to him and, for that matter, to everyone else was the rest of the story: Pierre Prince had been a closely held secret in the Thorne household.

Chapter 22

De Apple don' Fall Far From de Tree

ONE SATURDAY morning, bright and early, Thorne's immaculate white Jaguar was seen leaving the mansion. His chauffeur was at the wheel as usual but the Englishman's silvery head was not seen through the porthole. Instead, the head was that of a woman alone in the backseat, leading to speculation that Madame Montmartre was the sole passenger. They were heading to The Ivy.

The Ivy was a cluster of mostly wooden houses similar to the ones in Thornville, but this suburban village lacked any kind of distinguishing landmark or iconic edifice like the Thorne mansion, unless one considered as such, a blue-soap factory on the edge of the main road or the sprawling wall-house of a popular Bajan doctor at the junction of Howells & Ivy. But The Ivy could boast of entitlement: residents for the most part were proud owners of their homes and land, not at the mercy of an imperious landlord, for which reason Ma Prince had chosen to move there after being forced out of Thornville. Here too, she was close enough to her son and his remaining family for a leisurely stroll on a cool balmy afternoon from The Ivy through Carrington's Village, past the villages of Bush Hall, Bank Hall and Eagle Hall to Tudor Bridge and from there through Grazettes and finally to Thornville.

On Saturdays in Ma Prince's kitchen, as in most Bajan kitchens, cou-cou was the order of the day. Not surprisingly, she was already dicing her green okras and sifting her cornmeal, preparing to boil a big iron pot of seasoned water, when through her parted kitchen blinds she caught a glimpse of a slick white sedan pulling up to her front step trailed by a half dozen barefoot children, running, blown away by the rare sight of a motorcar in the gap. Wiping her hands, she hurried to the front door and came face to face with a light-skinned woman, smiling faintly, dressed in black down to her ankles. Except for one or two stray curls, her hair was hidden under a black bandanna that matched her black dress and black shoes, all of which declared that the woman was in mourning. She held forward a sparkling glass vase filled with freshly cut light-purple orchids. While Ma Prince did not recognize the woman, she had seen the motorcar before; it was the only one of its kind on the island. Since she was sure she knew the owner, she made the quick calculation that he had either sent the visitor on a mission or, at minimum, had loaned her his driver now leaning smartly against the bonnet keeping a wary eye on the wide-eyed children milling around.

"Good mornin', Mrs. Prince! You don' know me, but my name is Marcella Montmartre. I am Mr. Thorne's housekeeper but I am not your enemy, I come in peace."

Ma Prince found her words forthright but not entirely disarming since the mere mention of Thorne's name tended of late to raise her hackles as much as her blood pressure. Yet the visitor's soft nasal voice with its patois intonations conveyed a message of rapprochement that was at least pleasing to her ears. She accepted the flowers.

Marcella Montmartre began plaintively. "First, let me say that I very sorry about your loss, madam, first your grandson and then your son. Can I come in?"

"Lady, you can come in as long as you don' mention that man name in my house," warned Ma Prince sternly.

Ma's home stayed ready for guests. The house was always a congenial atmosphere of tastefully decorated rooms and comfortable furnishings. Colourful flowers leapt from the wallpaper in every room and family pictures hung from every available space of partition. The front house, bright and welcoming, had been amply furnished for herself and her daughters: a mahogany set of dining table with eight padded chairs, a Morris chair in each corner, a rocker and two straight-backed chairs.

Another visitor to this house on this warm Saturday morning would have been greeted with an embrace and a glass of cold coconut water. But the stranger sat across the room on the edge of an armless chair, her hands in her lap, her fingers nervously twiddling a beaded necklace that looped down to her waist. Ma sat in her favourite chair, a cane-backed rocking chair with gracefully curved armrests. She began to rock gently. Two women from different worlds, their faces strained, held each other's gaze with the intensity of two roosters in the moments before a lunge and a clashing of beaks. The events that brought them to this juncture hung in the air. Tension rose in the silence between them and begged for conversation.

Madame Montmartre broke the ice. "Mrs. Prince, I have to tell you things that you do not know, secrets that only two people know, me and the man that you don' want me to mention by name. You may not want to hear what I come here to tell you, but I have to tell you anyway and then I leave and you never see or hear from Marcella again. I leave Barbados tomorrow. I go back to my ex-husband, to my family in Fort-de-France."

Ma's eyes widened with curiosity, then she shrank back in her chair seized with slight trepidation, for what secrets could there be that would compel this woman to leave her home in Thorne's big comfortable mansion and trouble herself to travel all the way over to The Ivy, likely to ramble around these confusing roads, enquiring of neighbours where could she find the grandmother of the boy who had been shot by the Englishman, and being told as she turned off the main road leading to Two Mill Hill, before she reached Howells Cross Road, to make two left turns and a right and then another sharp right by the standpipe next to the coconut trees, and that the one she was looking for would be the second to the last house in the cul-de-sac.

The house was the biggest in the cul-de-sac, clearly with wall-house ambitions; the facade was all-brick and the rest wooden with three gabled frames and a shed-roof. Whereas in the old days in Thornville the girls had to share a single bedroom, they were now all adults living in a spacious house and able to spread out into separate quarters. Mahogany doors had replaced the beaded curtains and sponge beds had taken the place of the dry khus khus grass that harboured blood-sucking bedbugs which kept the children awake most nights. One thing that could be said of Ma's late seaman husband was that while he gave her six mouths to feed, he nevertheless supported them well, providing many comforts that many of the other working-class in the neighbourhood could not afford, like running water, electric lights and telephone. Now old and retired from the cane fields, she now lived comfortably with her daughters off his Harrison Line seaman's pension.

Madame Montmartre had been taking in the homely surroundings, clearly humbler than her own, but she was no doubt mindful of the fact that this house was theirs while she had been only a transient in the magnificent house of the Thornes. Now who knew what life awaited her on her return to Fort-de-France? But there were more pressing things on her mind than to dwell on her own circumstances; it was a mission of life itself that brought her to this woman's house and she needed all the courage she could muster to ensure that the mission did not fail.

    Her mind now struggled to find the right words in her faltering English with the right tone of sensitivity to tell this good woman, still in mourning, that her son had fathered a son with the woman he eventually killed. First, she would most certainly confront a wall of denial. Then there would be the question of why had she not come forward before. She would need to explain how she herself had been ensnared by the Thornes in exchange for money and a taste of the good life. She had to prepare herself for a reactive outburst of resentment and even hostility. But the truth had to be told this day even if it meant she would be thrown out of Mrs. Prince's house along with her freshly-cut orchids and accused of boldfaced malicious fabrications about her deceased boy-child. One thing she knew for sure was that the living should never malign the dead, though in the case of Penelope she may have no choice. Who knows if this mother had even come to grips with the fact that her beloved son had committed murder? So why would she now believe he had impregnated the Englishman's daughter? Still, not to be denied was her own wish to absolve herself from the guilt of being a party to the deception and lies that weighed even more heavily on her conscience now that Penelope, a protagonist in the scheme, was dead. And then the intimation that her master was a racist who despised black people would further befoul the atmosphere in this tension-filled house. She would explain that the man whose name she did not want mentioned in her presence was not in favour of having the boy continue to live in his house, declaring that his objection was not based solely on his mixed race with coloured blood in his veins, because she too was mixed; but that it was because there would be no nurturing maternal presence left in the mansion once she was gone. She herself was faced with the predicament of leaving the boy behind with the Englishman and all his eccentricities, but she too had an obligation to reunite with her own estranged family in

Martinique. It would be impossible to take him with her. She had to belabour these circumstances that now surrounded the boy through no fault of his own.

She would assure Mrs. Prince that Pierre was bright, ambitious, respectful, mannerly, lovable, and all the superlatives that he justly deserved; that he had been privately tutored at home by the best professors; that he was already accepted into prestigious Harrison College for next year; and that he was the legal beneficiary of his mother's sizeable savings at Barclays Bank in Bridgetown. All of this was to appeal to the motherly instincts of this good woman with the insinuation that the boy should be taken into her family as one of her own, indeed as her own precious grandson and raised as honourably as she had raised his father.

First, the memory of her son had to be re-embellished in case it had been even slightly tarnished; there was always that certain point of concession even for a mother who believed her child could do no wrong. He had to be exculpated from even the thinnest suspicion that he had raped the girl, for such malicious rumours were beginning to circulate among the people. Despite her own involvement, she needed to find a way to ingratiate herself with his mother. She needed her trust. She began forcing herself to speak in the same saucy manner as Ma Prince and adopting an exaggerated Bajan accent.

"Fust of all, your son did not rape Penelope. That girl wuz wuffless from day one, you hear? From de day she got pregnant, she parents didn't want de news to get out. When de mother find out it wuz fer a Bajan boy in de village, she kill sheself and dead of a broken heart. And that is why de father had yer son in his craw fer all dem years. He couldn't get to kill your son because he could never get close, and after he couldn't take it no more, he kill your grandson instead. De mornin' your son come up to de mansion, it wuz me that greet him at de gate. He tell me he wuz there to see she father. But she invite him inside. Although he say that he wuz not there to see her, she insist. De girl wuz drinkin' all mornin' as usual and I don' know what happen upstairs in de sittin' room but I just know that he did not intend to kill she. If he did want to kill Penelope, believe me, he coulda kill she right there in de courtyard."

THERE ONCE WAS A LITTLE ENGLAND

An hour went by as Madame Montmartre continued to unfold the sequence of events from her point of view and Ma Prince in her rocking chair listened and continued to rock, interrupting only once to reach for her snuffbox and to sneeze away the stifling stench of deceit and shame and death. To her, the Creole's story was more suspenseful and more morbid than any American soap opera she had ever listened to over *Rediffusion* when at the end of the day she relaxed in her rocking chair before retiring for the night. But when, in the end, Montmartre dared to suggest that she embrace the boy as her own, she stamped her feet on the hardwood floor and the rocking chair braked to a standstill. Leaning forward, she grabbed the armrests and her eyes held the Creole in a burning stare.

"Lady, if she wuz all that wuffless, how you know de boy belong to my son?"

But the Martiniquen had come well prepared for the element of doubt. She reached delicately into the cleavage under her low-cut neckline and fished out from the vault of her brassiere a small envelope. From it she removed a black and white portrait of a brown-skinned boy and held it forward to Ma Prince as if it were the winning card in a game of chance.

"Or I can take de boy wid me to Martinique," she bluffed.

Ma Prince leaned closer, squinting so her eyes would not deceive. For a silent minute or two she studied the Polaroid, the contours of the face, the chin, the telling nose, the prominent forehead, the slightly pouted lips, the fearless eyes. Then the faintest smile illuminated her face. Unswayed by his curly hair and light skin, she must have recognized an unmistakable resemblance between her son and the boy.

"No, dis boy goin' stay right hey in Buhbaydus," she said. "De apple don' fall far from de tree."

The frigidity between Ma Prince and her guest gradually thawed and light banter began to fill the space between the two women. Granted, the visitor had not crossed the threshold of suspicion and suddenly become her friend; after all, it was clear she was an accomplice in the conspiracy, but there was one person innocent of all the skulduggery that took place in that family and that was the boy, and now that she seemed to repent her role in the scheme and was representing the boy honestly, perhaps she had earned a measure of forgiveness. But questions remained. Had she been a perfectly willing participant all along? Was she now changing her mind due to pressing guilt or was it because of a change of fortunes? Or was she sent by her master to find a way to dispose of the boy as if he were a contaminated suitcase left in his closet? These were all questions superseded only by the welfare of the boy.

Then came the moment, a sure sign that all was well and that the air was now clear between the Creole and the Prince household: a time to break bread together. Molly appeared in the room holding an oval porcelain tureen by its ears and placed it in the centre of the long mahogany dining table. She passed around a set of white blue-rimmed enamel bowls and, before long, Ma Prince, the Creole and the five girls were each digging into a dimpled ball of steaming cou-cou brimming with gravy and topped with generous helpings of stewed flying fish. A bowl was first dispatched outside to the driver, still patiently keeping watch, unaware of the pact that had taken place inside the house.

But there was much work to be done; the boy had to be told who he was. Montmartre, in spite of not being the boy's maternal mother, had played the role well; so well in fact that, like the diva who morphs into the very soul of her stage character, she saw herself the mother she had been pretending to be. But she knew that all the years of caring, loving and protecting could not forever mask the lie. Now the time had come to throw off that cloak of deception and bare herself as one who had in the beginning perform a service, but had also provided a cover for their shame, the boy's illegitimacy, the improprieties of an underage mother and a racist grandmother driven to commit suicide. It would all come to light one day, why not now? But had she not also served the boy well? It was she who paid for his private tutelage, albeit with their money. Did she not shield him like a carapace from their insults and belittlements? Did she not fill in for their indifference which without her caring would have caused his young psyche irreparable harm? In the end was she not a good mother? But was it enough to merit redemption and forgiveness in the eyes of the boy when she confronted him with the truth? It was left to be seen.

She left the home of Ma Prince with the promise to return with the boy the next day, on her way to the wharf in Bridgetown to board the schooner that would take her back to Martinique, back home to pick up the pieces of her own life. On the way back to the mansion, she mentioned not a word to the chauffeur about her meeting with Mrs. Prince; they both worked for the same master but the driver was on a much lower plane and not privy to such confidences. For the rest of the day and all night her mind wrestled with various means of telling the boy who he was. In the end there was only one way and no matter how painful the truth, it had to be told and it had to be told face to face.

The next day came, but there was no sight of Madame Montmartre or the boy. Weeks went by and Ma Prince never saw the Martiniquen again.

Chapter 23

A Reincarnation

It was now several months since Madame Montmartre left the island to return to her home in Martinique. At first, Ma Prince wondered why she hadn't kept her word; the woman had sounded sincere. Then as days and weeks went by, hopes of seeing the boy slowly drifted to the back of her mind and eventually died, cast aside on her growing stack of broken promises and dreams unfulfilled. She lived alone now: her girls, now grown and independent, had gone their separate ways, Molly to live with her husband, the saxophonist, in Holetown, while the others had abandoned the nest to follow their various dreams in England and Canada.

One day at noon, the out-bound red and green General Bus that plied the route between town and The Ivy pulled into Ma Prince's cul-de-sac. Rain had fallen heavily all morning and the tarpaulins had been unstrapped and unwound all the way down to the runners where the conductress, a leather satchel hanging from her neck, had been skipping sideways from bench to bench, collecting the four-cents fare. The Bedford, now draped with canvas on both sides like an Arabic headdress, was chugging up the gap from house to house, depositing passengers and parcels along the way, foregoing the scheduled bus stops.

It was that time of day when Ma Prince would hand the driver a wicker basket with whichever meal he had ordered for his lunch, and he would proceed to the end of the turnaround, the end of his route, and sit and partake of it before returning the basket, then reversing the hand-painted wooden sign at the front of the bus and heading back to town. She was now in the food catering business. Lately, she had been forced to drop cou-cou from the lunch menu; at sixty-six, arthritis had begun to encroach on her right elbow, restricting that robust motion of the cou-cou stick required to effectively stir the cornmeal to its proper consistency. Nevertheless, her reputation as the bus drivers' favourite cook had not suffered.

That rainy day, the Ivy bus pulled up to her front step. The driver, a tall, skinny but a proud and elegant man, slid from behind the wheel and walked briskly to Ma's front window. Bus drivers rotated frequently and this one she did not readily recognize as one of her lunch customers. As he came closer, she recognized him as the chauffeur who had brought Madame Montmartre to her house that day and had waited patiently outside while the Creole disencumbered herself of her secrets. She burst out, "Hey! I didn't even know it wuz you at first. Look a' my crosses, you mus' be Cuffie that does drive fer de white man!"

"Cuthbert," he corrected, "and I don' work fer that man anymore. That man is a criminal. I work fer de General Bus Company now and I workin' dis route today fer a reason."

"I know," she said, "you come to order one o' Ma Prince delicious lunches."

"No, but I got somebody in de back o' my bus that come to see you."

Ma flung open her front door. A brown-skinned curly-haired lad, dressed in short khaki pants, green jersey shirt and white open-laced pumps, ducked under the tarpaulin with a valise in his hand and walked boldly towards her front door. As he climbed the steps, her jaw dropped. She gasped at the uncanny resemblance to her departed son. She saw a fairer and younger reincarnation.

"G'day," he said smartly. Then he stammered with some uncertainty: "I—I—I understand I can—can come and—and stay here—here for a while?"

Speechless, she backed away from the doorway staring at the boy's face, her mouth wide open. She reached for a chair and sat. He opened a valise, rummaged through it and removed a folded sheet of onionskin, which he handed to her as formally as if it were an official letter of recommendation. She didn't even glance at the name, Pierre Prince, on his birth certificate but instead opened her arms expansively like an eagle in flight and took him in, holding him fast for a few rapturous moments and then breaking into alternate fits of tears and laughter. Unaccustomed to such effusions of affection, he tensed and looked away, not returning her embrace, his head cushioned in the cleft of her bosom. Then releasing himself and anticipating her question about the whereabouts of Montmartre, he explained: "She stuck it in my book bag before she left, took it from Aunt Penny's dressing table…"

"You mean yer mother dressing table," said Ma Prince.

"No, I mean Aunt Penny's," he said, somewhat obdurately. "She will always be Aunt Penny to me. Mom wanted to bring me but I told her to go to her family and I would go to mine." He added, "When the time was right." There was a tinge of uncertainty in his voice but he was more comfortable now; the stammering had gone away.

Pierre had long ago made the retrospective calculation that he was born around 1940 and that his father was of French origin and was living somewhere in Martinique, perhaps estranged from his mother. This of course was never questioned; his surname was also French, pronounced praNHs with a nasal N. His surrogate mother made no attempt at the time to correct those assumptions; she told him his father was imprisoned in Fort-de-France and beyond her reach and his as well. He had been disciplined to address Penelope as Aunt Penny, only as an expression of respect for an elder.

With Montmartre now gone from the mansion, Thorne suddenly fell out of favour with his chauffeur who had served him unquestioningly for fifteen years. The fierce loyalty that had obscured Cuthbert's vision gave way the day he became aware of the depths of his master's depravity. That was the day he saw Pierre pacing from one end of the courtyard to the other, his head bowed, his eyes fixed on the ground as if searching for answers to a conundrum of which he happened to be at the centre. The boy confided in Cuthbert, told him what he had learned from his surrogate mother before she left. The chauffeur had had his suspicions from the day he saw Harold leave the mansion, his shirttail hanging halfway outside of his trousers, and with a look on his face as if he had seen a ghost. He had tried to make sense of the message he wanted him to convey to Thorne: "Tell yer boss I now know the truth!" It didn't take him long to figure out that the boy was at the centre of that truth and that he had been left motherless and fatherless in an unwelcome home. The ugliness surrounding that truth prompted him to toss the car keys in the bushes the same day and walk away from the mansion without warning, but not before offering to help the boy as soon as he himself was situated in a new job. Now, with Pierre deposited in his new home, he turned and walked back to his bus. Over his shoulder, he called to Ma Prince: "They had me fool too."

Everything Ma had learned about the boy, she thought to be a mingling of truths and lies told to her by Madame Montmartre. Yet she was grateful to her in a way. She believed now that Harold had given her a grandson because that singular truth, manifest in the face of the boy, needed no further corroboration, not even the official document that he now meticulously folded in half and replaced carefully in the bottom of his valise. That he was indeed her grandson was all she needed to forgive the Creole. Although she had deceived the boy, the custodial relationship between the two of them was nothing short of mother and son.

But Thorne she would not forgive, neither would she forgive his daughter, even in her grave, although she could not bring herself to condemn her own son, since in all likelihood he was not aware of having sired a child by this white woman. She told herself that in time she would let Cissy and the rest know about the belated addition to the family: a new son, brother and grandson. But the past was the past; she would not encumber Cissy with the shadowy details; it was a conception seeded long before she and Harold met. She was thankful that the boy was none the worse for the secretive road he had travelled and for all the sinister conniving that had been perpetrated around his young clandestine existence. She led him into Molly's now vacated bedroom and they sat on the bed, side-by-side, and talked.

"Son, dis is your room and dis is your house from now on. Ent no lies in dis house. No colour. No class. No shame. Only love. Everyt'ing in dis house is fer real. I am Ma Prince and just now you goin' meet yer stepmother and yer brother, and I goin' show you yer aunts. You have a big family. We goin' to Pastor Gittens bus outin' next bank holiday, and everybody goin' know everybody, and I don' give a hoot what nobody say."

With every few words her voice rose to a new crescendo as if to erase every last trace of shame that had shadowed him through the years. In its place she would instil the same pride that had sustained her own family in a society where discrimination of class and colour threatened everyday to strip them of their self-worth.

"Your name is Pierre Prince," she reminded him. "You is one o' de proud princes o' Buhbaydus. Your father wuz as black as coal but he had a heart o' gold and if he did know that you wuz his own blood he woulda own up. He woulda love you with all his heart even though he couldn't reach out and touch you through dem walls. Your mother wuz livin' in a house where pure white wuz everyt'ing in dis world and she had to choose between disownin' you and getting' put out on de street and losin' everyt'ing. To some mothers it woulda been a easy choice to make, but to she it was hard as nails. She did know how hard it is to be a poor bakra on the streets in Buhbaydus."

He listened attentively to every word, and then said softly, "Wasn't until she was dead that I knew who she was. Now it is too late to either love her or hate her so I will just have to forget her." He shrugged. He must have reasoned that feelings for the dead were emotions wasted unless those feelings existed when they had been alive. But he admitted his love for his surrogate mother, Montmartre, although his love for her was now tarnished and his memory of her forever corrupted.

"Welcome home, son!" said Ma Prince, reaching into her apron pocket for the ever-present snuffbox.

He got up and strolled from room to room as if to recalibrate his appreciation of home from the spaciousness of the mansion to this modest one-level wooden house with none of the nooks, niches, turns, upstairs, downstairs and fixtures of opulence to which he had grown accustomed. This was the first time he had set foot in a village house; all his life his family had kept him away from people outside of their social class for fear that he might be identified as the son of a Bajan of plebeian origin whose blood might be traced to the perceived purity of their own stock. One thing he now knew for sure was that his arrival on this earth, instead of conferring honour and pride, had instead rained disgrace and dishonour on his white family for all the time he was kept closeted within the mansion, quarantined like an infectious disease. He recalled one morning being beaten by his grandfather with a horsewhip for absentmindedly wandering out the gate and down the slope towards the village. The crack of the whip as it curled around his little torso summoned Montmartre running from the back porch to grab the thrashing arm and stop the onslaught. The woman he called Aunt Penny watched from the upstairs window, too numbed with alcohol or too uncaring to get involved. He still could remember the fire in the man's eyes as he backed away, his chest heaving with passion. But that was in the past now; this was his new home, among the working-class that he had been taught to shun.

Even the smells in Ma's house were new to him. The pungency of spices: curry, guinea peppers, ginger root, bay leaf and turmeric that had seeped into the wallpapered partitions over the years now oozed from the wood. Her various cook-ups for the bus drivers—salt pork, salt fish, ox tails, pig tails, fried this, fried that—all sent forth a spicy aroma, new to his senses. The only repulsive smell emanated from a corner of her bedroom where she kept her shrine and whence would come the biting scent of burning incense to fill his nostrils, evoking the stench of his grandfather's stale tobacco. But all in all, there was a warmth and an airiness about his new home that he had never felt in the mansion and he knew everything would eventually be fine.

He walked along the partition in the front room surveying the family pictures displayed as spectacularly as in an art gallery, while his grandmother strolled behind him in the proud possessive manner of a docent, pointing over his shoulder to this one and then the next. She singled out one portrait in an oval bamboo frame mounted in the centre of the wall distinctly from all the rest.

"And there's yer father," she said.

She paused to allow the face to register, to sink in, to begin to engender a fondness for the father he never knew. He saw the likeness of the man he had seen that fateful morning at the mansion gate, black, handsome, square-shouldered and confident. He had thought he might have come looking for servant work, perhaps gardening; no one had told him otherwise. He barely glanced his way though he did size him up fleetingly when he was leaving. He thought the man had grown tired of waiting for his grandfather. Afterwards, he heard the commotion upstairs and was later told what had happened, but the sequence that led up to it was kept from him. He had cried.

"And dat one over there is Molly, yer oldest aunt, married to a saxophone player, livin' in Holetown. And over yonder, yer other aunts, all livin' overseas, three in Inglund and de other one in Canada. So is just me and you now."

That first night, Pierre lay in his new bed in his new home and for half the night he stared at the ceiling and listened to the sounds of the village: the thumping of calypso floating from a party house way over in The Pineland, the house creaking in the night winds, neighbourhood dogs yapping back and forth, crickets stridulating in the bushes outside his window, the croaking of a bullfrog in the rain-soaked hedges. There was the occasional green lizard looking down curiously at him from the ceiling directly above his pillow and one or two snails under their coiled shells scrawling their slime on the window pane outside. It was his first night in a working-class neighbourhood; he felt strange but secure; warm wood surrounded him, not the cold, cemented prison-like walls that he knew all his life. He pictured himself washed up on unfamiliar shores, albeit surrounded by friendly faces.

He lay awake trying to unearth the mysteries of his past. The pieces of the puzzle had almost fallen into place, almost but not completely. There was the grandmother who preferred death to living with the defilement and ruination of her only daughter. Then there was the grandfather who blamed his daughter for his wife's suicide, for having shamed the family, for having introduced coloured blood into a long line of purebreds. There were other gaps in the puzzle, troubling uncertainties that could only now be met with conjecture; his parents had taken those truths to their respective graves. What demons had possessed his parents? What demons had driven them to their deaths?

He now resolved to disown them all, just as his grandfather and his mother had disowned him. They could all go to Hell. In his own mind he now fancied himself born from another womb other than that of Penelope Thorne. He considered himself henceforth a full-blooded black Bajan. He would now turn his back on the past and focus his thoughts on the road ahead: the College scholarship he had earned, the medical profession he longed to pursue and his long-held dream of becoming the best physician in all of Barbados. All that remained was to adjust to a less materialistic world, to learn to be contented with less, and thus to be happy. He closed his eyes and fell into a deep and restful sleep.

## 1965

Chapter 24

Vengeance of the Mighty

TEN YEARS had come and gone and the rise and fall of hopes and fears that these Caribbean islands would ever be federated were now resolved. The dream had fizzled in the end and the Mighty Sparrow sang about contentious politicians who had killed the dream.

Sorry, but no federation again, I think it's a big shame
After so much efforts and energy, is goodbye everybody.

And throughout the decade, every hurricane season without fail ushered in the ghost of Janet. She taunted the people of Barbados in the guise of every windstorm or flood or heavy downpour from July to November, evoking the memories of violence and death wrought by nature and by man. There had been a few minor storms from season to season. They were merely ambitious imposters: none could ever come close to Janet.

But to Cissy the loss of her son had been so profoundly heart-rending that the devastating storm of 1955 was little more than a metaphor for all the horror that had entered her life that day. And now, over a decade since her boy was killed, she could not help but return to the past and muse on what could have been, as she stood at her front window and looked across and up the slope to the spot where he fell. Then gazing towards the west over the rooftops in the lowlands and through the trees, she caught a glimpse of the sea, blue, sparkling and inviting, and in that instant the memory came flooding back of patrolling the beaches, she and Esmay, searching in vain for a sign of the man she loved who had fallen over the precipice of insanity. He had gone to be with the son he loved more than anyone or anything. Strangely, though the sea refused to offer up Harold's body, a fisherman had lately found a rusted revolver encrusted with black barnacles lying in the sand at low tide at the exact spot at Brandons where Harold had been spotted wading into the water. Mickey's gun was still fully loaded.

Just then a shrill voice pierced the morning air calling her name. Across the road Esmay had flung open her front window and Cissy knew right away she was about to receive the day's first morsel of gossip. But this time it would not be idle chatter but news that threatened to change the livelihood of every man, woman and child who lived in Thornville.

"Cissy girl, Thorne sellin' de land!" She blurted it out without a word or two of preamble to cushion the blow.

"You mean ...?"

"Yes, chile, we got to look fer someplace else to live. He want we off de land. He goin' punish all o' we fer he daughter."

Cissy was hoping for better news on this darkest of days; instead her mind was jolted from the depressing past to the dire present as Esmay belted out her message of doom from her window to Cissy's and all the way down the gap.

"He givin' we ninety days to move ... ninety days, that blasted scoundrel!" she bellowed.

Thorne had chosen this day, close to the ten-year memorial of the death of his daughter, to launch a new vendetta on the entire village. His daughter now dead, and his mistress having abandoned him, he was ready to make every man, woman and child pay for his lonesome misery. He made it official in bold, gothic letters on a painted signpost dated and planted at the entrance to the estate. As always, Thorne had retained the services of his old executor, Barrister Cunningham, to wreak vengeance on the people.

ORDER TO VACATE - Notice is hereby given to vacate all tenantry land in Ninety Days henceforth.
By order of The Cunningham & Thomas Law Office.

Cissy had grown impervious to bad news; it was just another bridge to cross, a hurdle no less surmountable than all the rest. Yet she thought it a wonder the village had survived the landlord's wrath until this day. The passing of time had not quenched his thirst for revenge.

She thought of how much Thornville had changed over the years. Behind the houses, the fruit trees—the ackee trees, the cashew trees, the mammy apple trees, the sugar apple trees, the guava trees, even the robust soursop trees—that had suffered broken limbs and had been stripped naked by indiscriminate winds were all again in full flower and giving forth their various gifts as they always had. But Janet had purged the village of many of its wretched, scarred and dilapidated houses. She had given fresh resurgence to others, now patched and restored; a new coat of paint here and there; upgraded and ready again for new storms. Now at the whim of this vindictive landlord each house would have to be dismantled and carted away to some other tenantry likely to be at the mercy of some other autocratic landlord. The only wall-house, the pastor's house, would likely be bought for a pittance and demolished.

Some who had lived through the hurricane were now dead, some had moved away, and some were new to the village. Joe Walrond was still beating the odds, still drinking, and no less. Ben Carson, the mortician, died in the past year at the ripe old age of ninety-one. No one came to his funeral except Cissy and Gittens, not even his old boss, Thorne, whom he believed to be innocent until the bitter end. But then again, Ben had no friends and no family; he had been a recluse all his life; he got close to people only after they were dead. Gittens entrusted his body to Codrington, the long-time undertaker in town, and thought the professional did as well a job as Ben could ever have done himself. "Ben would've been pleased," Gittens said. "But then, maybe not." He had been a slave to perfectionism, a quixotic goal in itself, impossible to attain in his profession, even at the hands of a masterful mortician like Ben.

Pierre Prince was now in England pursuing his medical career and almost at the end of his internment at King's College Hospital in London. He had spent a stint at Harrison College to augment his private schooling and to acquire his certificates. He was the youngest in the annals of the College to pass the Advanced Levels *cum laude* in chemistry, physics and biology. Blessed like his father with a mental quickness, he had whizzed past his peers and then, with the money from his own trust, he was off to England to pursue his ambitions.

Nathaniel was also away. Following in the footsteps of his seafaring grandfather, he took to the sea imbued with the same calling. One night when his mother was half-asleep and less resistant to aberrant ideas, he had whispered to her, "Ma, what you think about yer son goin' to sea and leavin' you here in Barbados?"

"Like how yer your grandfather left yer grandmother?" She pretended to appeal to his concern but knew well it was time to let go of him.

"Well, it won't be the same," he joked, "Pastor Gittens will move in."

It wasn't his answer—as insightful or as presumptive as it might have been—that she found intriguing but the notion that he believed the time had come for his mother to close the curtain on the past, a past consumed with the father he loved; and to open her heart and by extension make available her bed to another man. But Nathaniel was no fool. He had seen the pastor come and go without the usual bible in hand. He showed up at their doorstep promptly at suppertime, kicked off his shoes under the table and fell asleep with mild contented snoring after meals. He had seen him claim his favourite Morris chair in the front house where he would toss one leg over the armrest and talk for hours without a single reference to spiritual matters. It is true he had never seen him venture into his mother's bedroom where a metal-framed portrait of his father still leaned against the mirror of her dressing table flanked by two smaller mirrors that replicated the face of his father over and over. But he had no reason to believe the pastor would not cross that threshold the day he left home and set foot on the deck of the steam liner *SS Trafalgar* and head off to England to begin his new life. It was years later and he was now a midshipman in the Royal Navy Academy in London. He said in letters he had grown to love England and the English. His letters, frequent and cheerful, were addressed affectionately to both his Mom and Pastor Gittens.

Cissy had also seen changes in the way she looked. Her hair, once black, long and bouncy, had ceased to grow and now lay lifeless on her shoulders with a few renegade streaks of gray that exaggerated her years. Her face had not lost its beauty but her eyes were less playful except when Gittens was around. All in all, her looks had not suffered greatly, given all she had been through.

But the greatest change of all was yet to be revealed when Esmay dropped in that day. She had come to commiserate with Cissy over the thought of having to move out of Thornville and separate from her good friend. When she entered the shed, Cissy was bending over her wash tub full of blue soapsuds, kneading and thrashing some dirty laundry against the wooden ribs of her jucking board. When she stopped, dried her hands and turned to greet her neighbour, an almost imperceptible change in her appearance caught the keen eye of Esmay, who jumped back as if she had seen a tarantula crawling on her friend's midriff. Instead she had observed a slightly rounded protuberance on Cissy's waistline and a slight burgeoning of her breasts. Cissy already knew she had the makings of a belly but nothing that could have raised suspicion other than of a little fortyish fat around the middle.

"Girl, you wid chile?" Esmay burst out.

Cissy turned away with a childish giggle. "Girl, that is fer me to know and you to find out."

She had known almost from the moment the single-minded spermatozoon had accomplished its mission that she would be carrying the pastor's baby. She remembered the date. It was three months almost to the day. She had been busy with needle and thread, putting the finishing touches on a bodice when the pastor turned up at her door in blue, short-sleeved, open-necked shirt and stove-piped jeans, looking more like a spree boy than a clergyman. He called to her from the doorway: "Cissy, let's go fer a drive, girl, get away from all o' this persecution." She jumped to her feet, threw the fabric aside and in minutes was climbing into his motorcar. They whizzed past the neighbours' houses, indifferent to eyeballs staring and mouths gaping like baited fish. In her mind she could hear the neighbours saying: "But looka she doh! She man just dead and she tek up wid anudder man a'ready, and a pastor to boot." Harold had been gone for a whole decade.

But the day was theirs, a day when Mother Nature chose to put all her celestial magic on heightened display just for their pleasure: a resplendent sun, deep azure skies, a few low-hanging cottony clouds, fragrant breezes off the ocean that brushed their faces and tempered the morning heat as they drove by the houses flaunting their garden beds of local flora, lush and blazing with azaleas, croton, hibiscus, bougainvilleas, begonias, heliconia, ixora, desert rose; all sweeping by their windows in a moving kaleidoscope of nature's best. For a welcomed change, the day registered delightfully on these two long-time friends and slowly lifted their spirits with every minute of distancing themselves from a place that had seen so much sorrow, so much pain. It had been a long time in coming, a chance for the two to be alone, to escape from the scrutiny of neighbours, to get away from the whispers and the peering eyes. He was no longer wearied to his bones with the guilt that had haunted him for loving a woman who belonged to another, one whose memory still lingered in their presence though he had been long gone. He took her hand in his and could feel, as never before, a gentle acquiescence, a readiness to give him all of herself. She squeezed his fingers in return and in her eyes he saw gratitude and love.

"Where we goin'?" she asked.

"Surprise."

Without saying, she thought he might have in mind a day in the country. Perhaps in St. Joseph, to picturesque Bathsheba where they would sit alone on the hill and draw strength from that huge amorphous coral-rock formation that had been sitting in the shallow waters for a thousand years, and was inspirational, seeing that giant rock being eroded by the sea year after year and knowing that one day it would fall like mighty Goliath, like the mighty today who thought that their mightiness would have no end. Or maybe as far as St. Lucy, to the Animal Flower Cave, to be lost in the mystery and magic of the sea anemones, to be enthralled by this natural phenomenon in this farthest corner of the island. Or maybe just sit and unwind with a rum and coke in one of the beach bars the tourists loved to frequent at Foul Bay or at The Crane in St. Philip or at Bath in St. John. These were all her favourite places. But in truth it didn't matter as long as their backs were turned towards Thornville and all its misery was left far behind, at least for one day.

Gitts had other ideas. He would not let this glorious day and this opportunity go to waste; they were at last alone and away from the eyes and the ears of the village. Grinning like the Cheshire cat, he whispered close to her ear, "Cissy, girl, we have some unfinished business." At first she had not the slightest idea of what he meant until he turned down a deserted cart road that snaked through Thorne's dense cane field, so dense that they were sandwiched in between two walls of yellow-green cane stalks. He turned off the engine, turned to her and said: "Remember you and me and Duphus in this same cane piece donkey years ago?" A tingling memory rose from her teenage years. She remembered that hapless moonless night when Duphus Hinds happened upon them in the cane field with his fist full of matches to set afire the whole of Thorne's nine acres including the patch of matted earth they had chosen for their first night of sex. That night they scrambled out of the cane piece, back to the village, their young bodies aching, their juices yearning for release. But this day she felt pliant and relaxed, easy and submissive, ready to toss all inhibitions to the wind.

In many a Sunday sermon the pastor had held forth from his pulpit on the evils of lust, sex before marriage and weaknesses of the flesh; yet today the sin of fornication was to him the most forgivable of all sins. All the years of dreaming, longing, lusting, were now funnelled into this singular, glorious present that would neither be denied nor deferred. Now, inwardly panting like a hungry lion before the feast, he dispensed with all manner of foreplay. She climbed onto the back seat of his Austin Farina and surrendered to him on his virgin velour upholstery. His awkwardness was telling: it was clear to her he had never been intimate with a woman until this day. All the many years of celibacy, reaching back almost from his father's church, had stoked a volcano of torrid, untapped passion that erupted inside of her in one triumphant explosion. When it was over she felt his body against hers trembling like a fragile flower. Long tears of relief were streaming down his face. He had waited much too long for this moment.

Now here was Esmay, exultant with her new discovery, her new titbit for the day. "Cissy, you wid chile awright," she sang. "You cyant fool me, and you don' have to tell me who's de father."

Cissy had wanted to keep it a secret, even from her good friend, until one Sunday morning not too far into the future before the truth was beyond concealment, when Gittens would stand tall and proud in the pulpit and announce their wedding day and all would be well in the eyes of the church. But now that her eagle-eyed neighbour had uncovered her secret, it would likely spread rampantly from house to house like a cane fire. She made her neighbour swear she would not say a word to a single soul and to seal her promise Esmay brought a hand to her lips and kissed front and back, saying, "Cross my heart and hope to die!" The two women hugged and laughed and danced around and in the midst of their euphoria they both forgot about Thorne and his vengeful order to vacate the place they had grown to love.

Cissy could not have guessed that next morning, before the fowl cock in her yard crowed twice, the news that she was "mekking baby" would be all over Thornville.

It was mid-April that year when news leaked from the mansion that the Englishman was ailing. The sight of Doctor Donovan's Land Rover whizzing in and out of the mansion everyday gave some credence to the rumour. The talk, bouncing from house to house, presumed a broad range of afflictions, from whooping cough to consumption to a mysterious life-threatening malady inflicted by an old obeah woman who sold incense and candles on Roebuck Street. She was the grandmother of one of Thorne's servants and was said to work her necromancy with as little raw material as a single thread of human hair. People said he lived in his pyjamas all day and was thinner and weaker than he had ever been. They said his face was white as chalk. They relished the news; they had no sympathy, saying to one another, "Serve he right, he payin' fer he sins."

His house was always shuttered and looked abandoned. The walls were no longer white but streaky green. The verandas were now mouldy and discoloured. The doors and windows were in disrepair. Wild jasmine vines and bougainvilleas had snaked all the way up the east wall, skirting the windows and finding their way up to the eaves to spawn a blanket of leaves across the roof which, in earlier times, used to glitter white in the sun and was now a canopy of vines. The only sounds that emanated from behind the walls were the old man's continual asthmatic coughing and the occasional barking of the lone guard dog, a warning to those who would dare to trespass.

But no one cared to trespass: the mango trees that lined the infamous guard wall had not borne a single fruit in all those years; people said all the trees had been stunted from the day Thorne shot the boy on one of the branches. The only fruit trees left in the orchard that bore with any measure of fecundity were wild dunk trees. They hung over the wall temptingly but guarded their sweetest and reddest dunks with the sharpest needles that nature ever invented. So the village boys were no longer tempted to cross onto Thorne's property, plus the thought that he might shoot always lingered in their adventurous minds.

Still, with rumours swirling around the village that Thorne was on his dying bed, the order to vacate his estate remained in force. It was then that one of the older village men, Charlie Blackett, a retired cooper by trade, summoned a meeting. Every man and woman was urged to meet in Charlie's backyard on Friday evening to discuss the landlord's order to surrender his land. Charlie, a burly gray-haired man with a serious demeanour, had worked for the Mount Gay Distilleries Limited until recently when he was dismissed for surreptitiously attempting to unionize his co-workers. Sowing seeds of discord among the employees was the charge; in truth his efforts were focused on doing exactly the opposite. He had built his house with his own hands long before Thorne took possession of the land, and now that he and his family were suddenly facing expulsion with no other place in mind where they would rather live, he decided to put his organizational skills to work to mobilize the villagers as he knew how. Selling the estate, he agreed, was the landlord's prerogative, but the timeframe given to people to find new places to live he deemed grossly unfair. It angered him and spurred him to action. Every man and woman promised to attend the meeting

It was rumoured that the Thorne estate—land, mansion and all—was to be sold to Tory Reilly Enterprises, Island Developers of Westmoreland, St. James and, under the terms, all the land had to be cleared of houses before the sale could go forward. Charlie had mentioned the upcoming meeting half-threateningly to Tory Reilly, the American real estate man, on one of his exploratory walks through the village and was shocked when the developer called his bluff and promised he would be there. That Friday evening, Reilly did indeed make his appearance. A host of concerned homeowners convened in Charlie's paled-in backyard where they squatted on cinder blocks and perched high on empty rum barrels and half-built casks. Before the meeting, a bottle of Cockspur circulated among the men and people trickled in and out of the kitchen-shed where fish cakes and Eclipse biscuits were served along with Ju-c and ice-cold mauby for the non-drinkers. Much was expected of their leader, Charlie Blackett, a man known to be unafraid to lock horns with belligerent white men as he had proven in the past at Mount Gay Distilleries Limited.

"Ladies and gentlemen, y'all know why you are assembled here dis evenin'," he began with the gravity of a platoon leader calling his infantrymen to order to prepare their minds for the rigours of battle. In one hand he held a clipboard with several sheets of bound foolscap and in the other was a book entitled, *Rudimentary Principles of Property Law*. "Thorne want he land back to put up what they call in Amurca, condos, big apartment buildings like what they have in Sunset Crest and Silver Sands. He tired rentin' to poor people fer a few coppers every mont' when he could be mekkin' millions from ex-pats, diplomats, Yankees, limeys and all de other forners looking to stay in dis here paradise call Buhbaydus." His opening remarks were purposely phrased for the ears of the American, on whose face a smile was painted as fixed as a clown's mask. Charlie paused to elicit a few groans and vituperations from the crowd and then continued. "I really don' feel we should tek dis ninety-day ultimatum lyin' down; after all, some o' we born on dis land and been here fer ninety plus years from birth." With that remark he glanced over at bleary-eyed Joe Walrond, who, without evidence to the contrary, could easily have been thought to be close to a hundred.

Emboldened by the chorus of "Amen!" coming from the back row, he raised his voice to a fever pitch. "Where is dat blasted Trotman when we need legal advice? Like since he lost de election, all de wind dat wuz in he sails let out. He don' have de spine he used to have when he wuz lookin' fer votes. So I supposin' it left to me to show Thorne and Mr. Reilly here that we not goin' be pushed out by them and their barrister friend in no ninety days."

A voice grumbled from the shadows. "I did know that dis day wuz comin' from de time we show displeasure at how Thorne did treat Cissy Braffit and she family."

"Well, he got off so wha' more he want?" came another voice from the other end.

Another voice called out: "As long we been living on dis land, I t'ink we deserve first pick to buy we own lots, but on reason'ble terms. You don' t'ink so, Mr. Blackett?"

"Ninety days to move ent fair, maybe we could negotiate," Fitzroy Miller, the vulcanizer, complained in a more conciliatory tone. He would be hard-pressed to relocate his tyre patching and re-treading business. His shop was tucked like a cave into the front of his two-frame house.

Mrs. Mordecai, the milk woman, her corn rows tightly wrapped in a scarf, pouting and shaking her head from side to side, was less compromising. "Ninety days? Tell Thorne don' mek monkey sport!"

Charlie Blackett hastened to restore order. "Yes, ladies and gentlemen, dis is de end o' Thornville. We have no choice. De land is his to do whatever he please and we just have to find someplace else. There is no ifs or buts. But ..." Then came a pause suggesting that all was not lost. Raising his textbook of property laws in the air and turning to face Tory Reilly, he challenged the ruling. "Show me anywhere in de laws where a landlord can give a man only ninety days to pick up a house and mek arrangements fer a piece o' land. Show me!"

The smiling American, who had been sitting quietly on Charlie's retired toolbox with his back purposely against the wall, got to his feet with a hand in the air like a bright schoolboy about to shed light on some vexing algebraic theorem. He delicately removed a glob of chewing gum from his teeth, flicked it in a corner and took centre stage next to Charlie.

"First of all," he began, "Ah want y'all to know that ah'm on *your* side. Ah feel exactly the way y'all feel and if it were up to me, by golly, not a thing would change 'round here and you could live on this land, fer cryin' out loud, as long as you damn well please, and the same for your children and grandchildren and the whole of your posterity. But y'see, the problem is not Mr. Thorne, and it ain't Tory Reilly, and it sure as hell ain't you, the good people of Thornville. Time's achanging, mah friends, and Barbados is achanging along with the times. The village as we know it, mah friends, has become an anachronism."

"Wha' he mean by dah?" whispered Duphus Hinds.

Seymour Cutting interpreted. "He mean we belong in de past."

"The Barbadian village," the American explained, "especially desirable land like what we have here will no longer be known as a village. You see, every respectable piece of liveable space on this island will become 'So-and-so Heights' and 'So-and-so Terrace' and 'So-and-so Gardens' and 'Parks' and 'Rolling Hills'. Mah friends, there are people with big bucks from overseas as well as from the middle-class here on this island desiring to buy prime property like this—high altitude, gorgeous view, close to town, cooling breezes off the ocean, salubrious as heck, a clear view of the sea, ships coming and going, a short stroll to the beach. A man could relax on his veranda right here and enjoy what this blessed island has to offer. When the land is tired and fallow, mah friends, it has no value unless it is sold and better it be sold to the highest bidder. Can we blame this man, Mr. Thorne, for seeing the light? The writing is on the wall, mah friends, there is no future in sugarcane, the land is dying, you must give it new life and you will reap the benefits of tourism and people with big bucks coming to rejuvenate the land. Ah'm talking about a ton o' jobs, hotel jobs, service jobs, Yankee dollars, new roads, bright lights. Ah can see ..."

He halted in mid-sentence, for at that moment Charlie's galvanized gate creaked open and Cissy Brathwaite appeared, her hand in the air, requesting to be recognized. Every head turned. Wearing a loose-fitting black skirt that bounced and swirled as she strode to the front of the crowd, she turned to face them, and within earshot of even the children eavesdropping outside the paling, she lifted her voice.

"Excuse me, may I have a word?" Charlie Blackett and the American stepped back and ceded the stage. "A few things I would like to tell you about this Thornville girl, Cissy Brathwaite. My grandmother came to these shores as a little girl. She was a teenage indentured servant slaving on this land in fields of tobacco, cotton and canes. In her day, Thorne's mansion was known as 'The Great House' but it was really the House of the Devil then, as much as it is today. She lived long enough to see the Emancipation Act, even though she couldn't read a line. That was a long time before Thorne left England to lay claim to this piece o' land, long before Thornville was Thornville, when white people ruled this whole island with an iron fist, dictating to black people where to live, how to live, when to live, if to live. She gave birth to my mother prematurely in a field o' eddoes where she used to work behind where Thorne's riding stable is today. My mother worked as a seamstress right here in this village. She brought me into this world forty-odd years ago in the same house on the same lot where she was raised, the same house that my grandfather upgraded with his own two hands from an old slave chattel and the same house where I am living in today. That house survived many a storm down through the years, not to mention the natural ones like hurricanes.

With every sentence, her hand stabbed the air. "The same Thorne who owns this land today killed one of my two sons and caused his father to take his own life. I will tell you all something now that I was not prepared to tell you before today, that under this black skirt and inside this proud belly of mine is a new life waiting to be delivered into this world of racist, apathetic white rulers like Thorne, his money-grubbing cohorts and their Bajan lapdogs. But let me tell you this, whether boy or girl, I intend to have this baby months from now inside that same house, on that same lot, on the same bed in which I sleep every night."

There was a hush. The American's fatuous smile evaporated. She continued: "Moreover, if Thorne wants me to move, he will have to pay me a decent price fer that rickety house that had its origin in the hell days o' slavery. It is too old to move anyway. Otherwise, he can call in the police to tie me up, and carry me and this unborn child out of Thornville on a stretcher."

She stalked past the awe-stricken faces. They had never before seen this side of this Christian woman. Neither had she. Not a peep followed her as she strode out as quickly as she had entered. Then as she closed the gate and crossed the road, she heard the sound of boisterous applause resounding from Charlie's backyard, and at that moment she knew that the people were with her, and that her outpouring was neither too much nor too little, neither too sentimental nor too bombastic. She had a good feeling about herself.

Chapter 25

Return of a Native Son

WHEN IT was learned from his letters that Pierre Prince had completed his studies, first at the University of Glasgow and afterwards at the Royal College of Surgeons in Edinburgh, where he was accorded his Bachelor of Medicine, Bachelor of Surgery (BMBS), such splendid credentials were gibberish to simple folk like Ma Prince. All that mattered to her was that he had reached for a dream and it was now in the palm of his hand. Had she been able to comprehend the breadth and depth of knowledge he had acquired in England, she could not have been prouder. In fact, Pierre had been introduced to a realm of new pathologies and a range of surgical techniques that were currently beyond the scope of any practitioner in Barbados.

It seemed like just the other day when she had sent him off with a mixture of joy and sadness; later to stand at the picket fence that girded the Seawell airfield to wave at an imagined face; then to wait patiently until the BOAC turbo-propeller airliner lumbered down the tarmac, paused, and then took to the sky. And not a second before the aircraft dwindled to the size of a pencil point, did she turn her back and head home to wait for his return. Now the day was here.

A grand homecoming had been planned from the moment she read he would be returning that Thursday. The words that he was returning on a Pan Am Boeing Clipper from London, with a refuelling stop in Oslo, such flight details were over her head; she just wanted to know the day and the hour. Barely able to control her excitement, she set about organizing a welcome committee of friends and neighbours who could share the significance and pride of the occasion: a boy from The Ivy, her own boy, a native son had made good.

Everywhere Ma went, all around The Ivy, The Back Ivy, in town, even among strangers, the words purred sweetly from her lips that Doctor Pierre Prince was of her own blood and that "he got he own father brain" and she never failed to credit her side of the family for all he had turned out to be. She boasted that he had become someone important, a doctor no less. No mention was ever made of his mother and his mother's family; their names were unutterable in her presence.

His picture, taken in London, in scrubs, a stethoscope draped around his neck, was now hanging proudly on her partition with the rest of the family. Not only did Pierre share her own flesh and blood but in her mind he embodied wholly her only son, his father.

On that long-awaited day, Ma Prince, Cissy, and some chosen neighbours bundled into a hired chauffeur-driven Packard from Corbin Motors and headed to Seawell Airport in style. The terminal had the size and the modesty of a country farmhouse, with its tower like a silo jutting into the air; yet they were all dressed as for a garden tea party, for it was a Bajan custom to don the very best clothes for the rare trip to the airport. In the morning heat, the little terminal, brimming with travellers coming and going, was a swirl of three-piece suits, hats, gloves and full-bodied dresses, all suited to harsh North American winters and English inclement weather. In the midst of it all, Ma Prince and her people were zigzagging through the crowd, peering and craning for their first glimpse of Pierre. The hulking Pan American airplane that Pierre mentioned in his letter was already sitting, still throbbing, at the near end of the tarmac. He was nowhere in sight.

Earlier that morning she had laboured over a big pot of thick fish-head soup, replete with hand-rolled cornmeal dumplings and swimming with sweet potatoes, eddoes and yams freshly dug from her backyard. English cooking, she said, had deprived her boy of these healthy fattening ground foods, for "De Inglish don' know how to mek soup, is does be bare dish water." The sweet smells of coconut bread and cassava pone, Pierre's favourites, had been wafting in the air all night, as this kindly matriarch spared no effort to prepare a feast for the return of her grandson.

Every square-inch of her house had been scrubbed, every door and window festooned with blue ribbon. Balloons of his favourite colours, red and gold, hung from a branch of the Lady of the Night outside his bedroom window. Her dining table had been spread for this day when they would all sit around and gorge themselves on her delectable fish soup while bringing the young doctor up to date with story after story of how everything had changed in Buhbaydus. And how all the talk on the island was about Independence, striking fear in the hearts of those who feared they would be suddenly toppled from their pedestals of power.

Cissy had planned to wait until his appetite was sated and Ma's tough dumplings well digested to reveal the bad news: that Thornville was soon to be no more; that every homeowner would soon be driven off the land just as Ma Prince was expelled many years ago before he was born; that the landlord had joined with his Bajan barrister to punish the people, to even deny them a delay of the eviction. But, wait! This was meant to be a joyous occasion. So she would first lighten the air with less ponderous conversation, perhaps about her upcoming wedding and about his half-brother, Nathaniel, representing the Mother Country in the Royal Navy, and they would all join in to celebrate the return of this son of the soil. That was the plan.

Ma Prince saw him first, but from afar. She wasn't sure it was he. From the back, his hair was speckled with gray and his shoulders had that certain professorial hunch. He was flanked by two white men, one short and portly and the other, tall and lanky, both in dark business suits, now walking towards a long white chauffeured limousine that had been parked at the curb alongside the terminal entrance. It entered her mind that the two men could be politicians or salesmen or thieves, though to her the differences from one to the other were no less frightening. She had to get his attention. She took off, weaving through the crowd, running from the far end of the terminal, across the floor towards the men, perilously hampered by her stylish stiletto heels, waving and calling his name. "Pierre! Pierre!" She called out at the top of her voice. But the limousine doors were already closing and before she reached the sidewalk they were pulling away from the airport and heading away.

"Dog bite it!" she swore. Then turning to the rest of the party, she said, "No sweat, he goin' soon be home."

He hadn't seen her. Another welcome party had gotten there first. She had been upstaged. She chose to believe they were official men of business and protocol; that they had been waiting with open arms to swoop him up into the world of their own status. She blamed herself for not having written to say there would be a welcome committee with much fanfare. But then again, seeing the two white men taking her grandson away, she preferred to assume he had earned acceptance in a class that would otherwise have paid him little notice. Their eyes would not have seen beyond the colour of his skin, had he not proven he now had much to offer.

Much later he recounted to his family, with some amusement, the mistiming at Seawell Airport. They laughed and talked about the way he was unexpectedly but amiably greeted and then swept away by two men from the city. One of the men was Doctor Donovan, the Irish obstetrician and gynaecologist who knew him literally from the moment of his birth. The other man was the Chief Administrator of the Barbados General Hospital. On the advice of Donovan, the Hospital had been tracking his work at the Royal College of Surgeons in Edinburgh. Unbeknownst to him, the institution had followed his comings and goings, had been in contact with the College faculty for years, had reviewed his doctoral dissertation and was keenly aware of his thesis: *The Promise of Diagnostic Laparoscopy, a Minimally-Invasive Surgical Theory*. They were well aware of the Hospital's dire need for his services in the specialty of minimally-invasive surgery, which would of necessity curtail the time it took for patients to heal and, as a result, free up occupancy regularly for new patients in its limited space. That long-awaited day, as they drove away from Seawell, three men of the same cloth were in accord. He had armed himself with the skills that would prove of infinite worth to all colours and classes in Barbados. And so, in a society where a man's skin could be either his prison or his castle, his mixed blood would not matter at all.

Chapter 26

A Trilogy of Tragedies

THORNE'S VINDICTIVE ultimatum was coming to an end and the order to rid his land of these pesky mortals would not be met within the allotted ninety days. The eviction order was weighing upon Cissy in spite of the bravado she displayed at Charlie Blackett's meeting. Only the thoughts of her upcoming wedding would now and then lift her spirits and put a smile on her face.

Today, Friday, she was sitting on her front step looking out for Mr. Babu, the itinerant cloth vendor. He would stop by religiously on his biweekly rounds and ring the little dome-shaped bicycle bell. Then with the quaint head wobbles typical of East Indian expressions, he would extol the quality of his wares, a mountain of fabric samples strapped to the pillion. Her dressmaking business was flourishing; he kept her supplied with the latest fabrics from Thani Importers in town. She had already ordered a fresh supply of white bridal taffeta, chiffon and ivory satin, and in her mind rested the design of a perfect, exquisitely beautiful wedding dress with an exorbitant train and another equally stunning gown for Esmay, her maid of honour. She had planned to make flowing masterpieces that would be certain to enthral the guests and the gawkers at the doorway of the Pilgrim Holiness Church where she would stroll gracefully down the aisle to be proclaimed to the whole world as Mrs. Cissy Gittens.

Her thoughts turned to the man she was about to marry. In her mind there was nothing new about the love she shared with Gitts. For too long it had been restrained, purposely unexplored. Neither did it evolve or blossom like a flower in the way most love affairs do. To her it had always been extant and real, only obscured by another love that came between them and blinded her eyes even to the point of denial. Harold's departure and the passage of time had brought her love for Gitts into focus; it was all so clear now their union was ordained from the start. To them both, their love was a diamond that had been concealed under silt and hardened rock but was now unearthed and polished into a precious stone. In the front house, she would sit in the quiet of late evenings, sewing and knitting, her ears perked for the crunching of loose gravel outside in the alley next to the side door where his motorcar would pull in and sit until close to daybreak. No longer was he the shy pastor, the reticent lover who was more at ease with scripture than with bold romantic overtures. Now he would burst through the door with flowers or her favourite Bico ice cream or fresh turnovers for tomorrow's breakfast from the Purity Bakery man on the street with his bread cart and his lantern. How the pastor had changed!

But how about Harold, had she not loved him too? If anyone dared to ask, she would answer with an unqualified "Yes." Her whole conscious being had been so consumed with the greatest love for Harold in his time that not even Gitts could have displaced it. In her heart she was convinced that it was neither perfidious nor implausible to love two men, as long as one resided in the shadows of the subconscious and not acted upon as was her love for Gitts. Long before Harold came along, she knew Gitts, and she fondly recalled those first titillating, puppy-love romances when their first awkward attempts at sex were like a child's timorous steps to the shoreline of an enticing ocean. Somehow they never made it past the shoreline; almost but not quite, thanks to Duphus the arsonist, until recently in Thorne's cane piece. Perhaps it was Gitts who cloaked himself as just a good friend, giving way to Harold and taking on the role of a confidant and, later in life, her spiritual guide. Afterwards, her feelings for Gitts assumed the sentimentality she felt towards an adorable and precious possession, but one she could readily put aside without conflict of conscience.

Harold, on the other hand, was the torch that set on fire her latent sexuality and kept it aflame for all the years they lived together. Unlike the diffident Gitts, Harold had stormed into her life like a bold and dashing broncobuster, out to conquer and possess. Perhaps, if Gitts had zealously guarded the future that could have been theirs, it might have turned out to be a different story. Instead, she bore two beloved sons for Harold, further grounding a love that lasted until he was no more. Despite the normal ups and downs in the early years, she had no regrets for having shared the prime of her life with him. If only he had anchored himself in the Christian faith as she had, and had been able to weather their darkest storms as she did, he might still be alive today. Instead, revenge became his obsession and death his only escape. Still, he would not be forgotten; she saw him now, not hauntingly, but through the gauzy curtain she had closed on that other life.

She had written to Nathaniel in care of the Royal Navy Academy in London to tell him about the wedding and that his dream of his mother's future with his friend, the pastor, was about to become real. His reply was bursting with excitement; he always knew that day would come, he wrote. He swore he'd be home on leave just for the wedding. He told her in passing he was the only black sailor in his unit and already at the rank of First Lieutenant; he had just begun to serve on one of Her Majesty's destroyers deployed in the Middle East but should be back onshore in time for the big day. With a smile she tucked the envelope inside the rubber band that held his other letters on her dressing table, remembering his words the day he told her he was leaving home. "Pastor Gittens will move in," he had told her.

The day was the 12th of May, 1966. A soft, steady, misting drizzle that Bajans on a wedding day called "showers of blessing" was barely kissing the earth on a balmy Saturday morning when Cissy and Esmay, her married maid of honour, climbed the steps of Gittens's church under an impromptu canopy of umbrellas that lined the entrance from the road to the church door. Bajans came from near and far to gawk, applaud and offer their blessings; she had unwittingly become a celebrity. Even Mr. Babu made a surprise appearance outside the church dressed in a white silk kurta over his pyjama, his hands clasped at his forehead, his head bowing extravagantly at the sight of the bride. He had become Cissy's good friend, never forgetting her long-ago act of kindness.

The church was packed. The Christians came to see their pastor take his bride. The invited as well as the uninvited pressed together in the pews and spilled out onto the street. Reverend Flexon began with a homily on the moral rectitude of matrimony; some would say he was alluding admonishingly to the bride's former life of cohabitation. But there was too much pain in the past for her to revisit the path she chose, a path that, however contrary to the tenets of the church, had led her to this holy place in its own good time.

Their vows were exchanged and their hearts were joined. As they stepped down from the altar, her eyes raked the pews from front to back for the face of Nathaniel hiding in the crowd, perhaps behind Ma

Prince's wide crinoline hat or crouching below Pierre's broad shoulders. Her son was always the prankster who loved to surprise and she had no doubt he would wait to jump out of the congregation to her delight at the very moment she and Gitts floated down the aisle on their way to the exit. Even as they waded into the waiting crowd she fully expected him to be standing outside the church poised with a fistful of rice. He wasn't there.

A hired motorcar whisked them home in the rain and Gittens did his romantic bit, lifting his bride playfully over the threshold. Lying on the floor was an envelope with the striped red and blue airmail border; earlier that day the postman had slipped it through the louvers. In the ecstasy of the moment they set it aside, giggling like giddy teenagers, holding each other close for the first time as husband and wife, cherishing that interlude of privacy between church and reception after which they would be expected to share themselves with the crowd. Aching with longing for each other's naked touch, they hurried to close the windows and doors, she, the ones in the front house and he, the ones on the side; and on the way to their bedroom, began to undress, primed to make love for the first time as man and wife. Whereas fornication in the past always gnawed at their consciences as they lay naked in bed, from this day forward they could wallow in sex, for sex would now be blessed, even prescribed by the Holy Word. For over an hour they made love with a freedom and a joy they had never felt before; it lasted until they were both blissfully exhausted like two spent cannons.

Then they dressed, and on the way out the door to the reception, she glanced at the letter that had been set aside unopened. The envelope bore the official embossed address of the Royal Navy Academy in Portsmouth, United Kingdom. It dawned on her that Nathaniel had written with regrets. "Well, my son is in Her Majesty's Service now," she said proudly, "duty first." She read the first line, gasped and, clutching the letter, collapsed and fainted in her husband's arms. Nathaniel had been killed in action. He and two other sailors were caught by mortar fire in the Sinai Peninsula during a skirmish between the British Navy and the Egyptian military. Gittens grabbed the letter; it ended with the curious line that Lieutenant Prince had given his life in defence of the Mother Country. In that instant, the cold official words voraciously sucked all the oxygen from the room. With his wife in his arms, Gittens stared, stunned by the sudden transformation in the air from sheer rapture to utter gloom, like the sun blackened by a passing cloud that plunges every inch of its sphere into near darkness. He lay her down and rummaged through her chest drawers for the smelling salts. The second or third whiff of the ammonia awoke her to a realization of tragic irony: not only that her son had been taken away from her in the service of his Mother Country but that he had died in the most unlikely of places, the northern reaches of Africa, the birthplace of his forefathers. "Damn you England! Damn you! Damn you! Damn you!" The curse exploded from her lips over and over again to the point that Gittens now feared she would wilt and go mad under the enormous strain. But the vicissitudes of her past had toughened Cissy over the years; had cloaked her in armour of steel. Crestfallen but determined, she got up from the bed where her husband had laid her to rest. "If the Devil thinks he can beat me down, he got another thing coming," she muttered between clenched teeth. She combed her hair, washed her face from the ewer on the commode and then changed into a bright yellow floral dress and matching hat. Then she took her husband by the arm and walked out the door, her chin held high, and together they crossed the road to where family, friends, neighbours and freeloaders were already waiting to receive the newly wedded couple in Charlie Blackett's capacious backyard. Still, in the midst of hugs and congratulations and effusions of love and good fortune, her mind would not let go of that trilogy of tragedies: first David, then Harold, and now Nathaniel.

That evening towards the end of the day, Cissy, with the Royal Navy's letter in her purse, took the bus down to the city, to *The Chronicle*'s publishing house in Bridgetown. The numbness that had shielded her from utter madness in that first instant of reading the letter had worn away and in its place was neither anger nor despair but a sense of purpose. She pushed past the doorkeeper asleep at the punch-clock, climbed the steps to the news department and asked for Mr. Johnson, the courageous white reporter, whom she knew from eleven years ago. She wanted the story of Nathaniel, now weighing heavily on her mind, told to the newspaper's entire circulation and by the reporter she trusted most. She always read, in the Sundays Edition, the probing editorials entitled *The Travails of a Colonial People by Jay-Jay Johnson*. Who could better tell the story than he, the one who told the world of the tragedy that befell her other son and wrote about it fairly and fearlessly. His was the headline that drove Harold through that stormy night in September eleven years ago. He was the reporter who approached her at David's funeral with words of consolation beyond the calling of his profession, and later at a discrete moment, met with Nathaniel with comforting words not unlike those of a father towards a grieving son. Now she thought it fitting that he write the story of his life and death and close the chapter on her last boy.

As she walked towards his desk, he recognized her instantly though her head was draped with a black knitted shawl that fell loosely on both sides of her face as though her desire was not to be recognized in public. Her face was hard, her jaws clenched with some unstated determination. He was struck by the energy that seemed to flow from her innate strength, a strength that asked for neither praise nor pity.

"Please sit down, Mrs. Gittens." The news that she was now a married woman did not escape this reporter.

She removed her shawl, unfolded the letter, laid it on his desk and sat back with her arms folded.

He said, "I already know."

It had been a slow day for news. The island was at peace. He had spent all day scouring the chattering Reuters news feed for international news; on a slow day, world events could always be relied upon to feed the big hungry Heilderberg press in the basement. Coming across the wire service all day was a steady stream of unsettling news seemingly from every corner of the universe, item after item of civil unrest. Mankind was in turmoil. In the American South, blood flowed on the streets of Alabama as civil rights marchers pressed on from Selma to Montgomery, beset by angry white mobs, water cannons, tear gas and snarling dogs. Over in the American West, race riots set a whole California neighbourhood on fire as the people rose up in a place called Watts. Another story of a people halfway around the world told of a rebellion originating in a dusty field in a town called Soweto, where thousands of Africans were bloodied and beaten by the repressive forces of white apartheid. Their leader, Mandela, was in hiding. From England came a report of white "Teddy Boy" gangs armed with sticks and knives, out to attack and maim West Indians on the streets, in their homes, and wherever these children of the Commonwealth chanced to set foot in the land they called their Mother Country. These skin-head marauders were emboldened by Britain's Commonwealth Immigration Act that stanched the influx of Caribbean people. Yes, the world was in turmoil but Barbados was at peace.

Then from the printer emerged a headline that caught the eye of this young journalist. It was followed by a single paragraph that tapped out line-by-line until he ripped it from the platen and read it over and over, his heart thumping at the mention of Nathaniel Prince, a name he remembered well. It told of a Barbadian serving in Her Majesty's Navy in the Middle East. He was killed in the path of Egyptian gun fire.

"Yes," he said to her as she stared at him to gauge his reaction. "I got the news."

She leaned forward. "Mr. Johnson, I want you to tell the whole world that my son, a Barbadian, gave his life in defence of the English. He left his home here with his mother, crossed the seas and signed up to fight fer England. He gave his life fer England." Her voice was not loud but controlled. Yet the tone was strident.

"Yes, I understand," he said.

"But please don't stop there, Mr. Johnson! I ask you to go back eleven years and remind the people of how his brother died. Remind them of who took his life at the tender age of twelve. Tell them how our own court, Her Majesty's Court, let the white man who killed him in cold blood walk free. Saying how he took my son for a monkey. And now today, how his brother stepped up to defend England against Egypt, an African country, while not one Englishman stepped forward eleven years ago to speak out against their countryman. I read your columns, Mr. Johnson, you know how to make the blood of my two boys haunt the conscience of Thorne and his kind. Would you do that fer me?"

He took in her every word. Her request was not unreasonable. He was an articulate and incisive writer; he had at his fingertips the rhetoric to inflame, to anger, to arouse in his readers the best and the worst of passions. It would be a story of striking ironies: two young brothers, two lives, one taken, the other given, the barbarity of man towards man and the unfairness of life itself. He could write the story the way she wanted it; he had written a hundred gut-wrenching articles in his time, stepped on many toes and punctured many a callous conscience.

But he wasn't sure it would survive the publisher's redactions. Yes, he could recap the life of Nathaniel, heap posthumous praises on the young lieutenant and laud his meritorious service in the Royal Navy. But the killing of his brother, David, had been too combustible a topic in Barbados; and though, after all these years, a lethargic indifference had seemed to settle over the land, he knew the killing was still raw as the pus of an abscess. The publisher would likely warn: "Let sleeping dogs lie!" Publishers always had the last say on what the eye should read and what the people should remember. He wanted to explain why not to this disconsolate woman but she must have seen in his eyes the answer he hated to give. She quickly gathered up the letter, purse and shawl, waved goodbye and headed out the door.

It bothered him. She was right. Bajans had to be reminded of David, for only through the memory of his death could be seen the irony that marked his brother's dying. The stories of these twin boys had to be told, each in its own context, not just today but over and over until their blood seeped into the conscience of every white man on this island and stirred all black people to the awareness of their self-worth; that no man's blood is more precious or less precious than another's. He shot up from his chair, ran out into the hall, down the steps, out the door, and called after her on the street. "Mrs. Gittens! No problem. I am going to write it just the way you said." Although he was sure she had heard him, her head never turned and her feet never broke their stride. He decided he would make his case with the publisher, that truth must win out over fear.

He went to his typewriter. He was on fire. He felt in his fingers the same awesome power he felt on that day eleven years ago. He was ready to reopen old wounds, to grab the moribund minds of his readers and jolt them out of their lifeless apathy. In his gut he knew his column next day would give rise to a whole new groundswell of discontent by reminding them of David Prince, and today the end of his brother. The first line read: "In the absence of discontent a man's lot in life is destined to remain the same." But he knew well that in Barbados never would discontent rise to the riotous rage of the oppressed in those faraway places whence those other Reuter stories came. "And neither should it," he wrote with a dash of irony, "for apartheid, race wars and roving gangs of skin-head racists belong to those so-called 'civilized' countries."

Chapter 27

Intercessions

NEXT DAY the news rippled across the island and was magnified by the context of the boy's death. Although his death was knowingly in the service of Her Majesty's forces, it brought to fore the circumstances in which his brother had died. *The Chronicle* did not shy away from reviving the memory of David Prince and the stark contrasts of the two untimely deaths were striking. Yet another sorrowful cloud engulfed the entire village of Thornville and people walked by the pink house wondering what biblical curse had befallen this Christian woman to have lost her remaining son before his prime. Although no rancour or threat of vengeance was warranted—as was the case with his brother—the people bemoaned with equal fervour the loss of another son of the soil. That he had made something of himself, had gone abroad and had served a cause—albeit a cause they themselves would not have endorsed—gave him stature in their eyes. He was a treasured son.

Throughout Barbados, Sunday was the day for men's haircuts. In Thornville, the barbershop was a virtual barbershop, that is to say, a spot in the dappled shade of a thick-leafed breadfruit tree next to the house of the pastor and his wife. Curly King was the village barber. Short, fat and bald as an egg, Curly had an affinity for trimming hair, offering his services for whatever one could afford. The barber's chair was a hard upright mahogany chair with which the kindly Sister Gittens accommodated the men, passing it through her side window to Curly after church service. All she asked in return was that at the end of the day they gathered up the globs of hair that rolled and swirled in the wind like clouds of black cotton. She said they were likely to choke the ducks that wandered outside her gate. The men, mostly young and hip, had been lazing around with drink, smoke and small talk waiting for last week's haircut to be freshened, reshaped and parted on the left or the right or even down the middle, for in fact a ditch down the middle of the skull to the forehead was in vogue with the young boys that year. Squatting under the tree were Colin Bowen, Ossie Cobham, Owen Kirton, Breresford

Thompson, "Po Boy" Simpson, Knobby Phillips, "Bunny" Rogers, Gordon Brooks and others who kept coming and going.

An unusual malaise hovered over the barber shop, unexplained until one of the men introduced *The Sunday Chronicle*. It was passed from hand to hand and the obituary was read aloud. The passionate words that flowed from the mouth of each reader had earlier flowed from the heart of the reporter, Jay-Jay. He had taken to heart the words of a grieving mother and poured them into his column the next day. The words, just as he had predicted, flung the men into fits of anger and tantrums of swearing that befouled the air on that Sabbath day. While Curly clipped and clicked away with scissors and comb, the boys squatting on the tree roots took turns reading the heart-wrenching article that featured the lives and deaths of the two Brathwaite boys. At the end, some of the fellows were seen dabbing the corners of their eyes.

Curly asked the inevitable question: "But why de boy had to leave dis island dat so peaceful and nice and go all de way to Inglund to fight fer white people dat don' give one shite 'bout he or 'bout he own brother dat dey kill. Then on top o' dat, Thorne de Inglishmun dat kill he brother now want to throw we off de land dat rightfully belong to de people. Goddamn Inglund!"

There were mutterings of accord among the men, all except from the avuncular Henderson Cruthers, a retired wharf man, a person well respected for his occasional pronouncements of wisdom. He had been sitting quietly in the barber's chair while Curly scraped a straight-edged razor delicately along his chin. Although long retired from the wharf, he still wore his broad weightlifting belt loosely around his girth as if it were the belt of an undefeated world champion. Cruthers was a giant of a man with a thundering bass-baritone voice that commanded attention; he had earned the respect of the Thornville boys. He loved England and could recite from memory every British war and every battlefield from Cornwall to Hastings to the Suez and beyond. When the Marylebone Cricket Club toured the island, he rooted unabashedly for the English boys. So dedicated was he to the Mother Country, the boys called him "the Knight of the Round Table."

No longer able to hold his tongue, he flung aside the white sheet that had been tucked under his chin and jumped to his feet. He had enough of the men's ingratitude towards England and proceeded to lambaste them like a father would scold his insolent children.

"Listen, fellas!" he thundered, "Thorne is not Inglund and Inglund is not Thorne! We have much to thank Inglund for!" On his left cheek a bead of blood oozed from a nick suffered when he darted from under Curly's knife and a long vein stood out on the side of his temple like a welt. Mr. Cruthers was apoplectic with rage at what he had heard from the mouths of these young men. Pointing to the fingers of his left hand, he counted off, one by one, the blessings of living under the British umbrella.

"Inglund give us a first-class education," he told them. "She taught us parlimentry procedures. She hand we down de rule o' law. She save us from Hitluh. She save us from communism. She give us a hand in times o' drought. Besides, Buhbaydus come a long way from de time David Prince get kill. Men, y'all got to fergive and ferget and be grateful to Inglund fer all that we have. Where would we be today without Inglund? Today a black man like me can sit and have lunch at de Water Club or dance at the Drill Hall, no questions ask as long as yuh have on a necktie. Down at Barclays Bank in town, two or tree pritty dark-skin tellers now sitting at de front desk like all de rest. My next-door neighbour, Phyllis two teenage nieces goin' to the Convent Catholic school, if yuh please. Nowadays, long as yuh have money yuh can move into Belleville, Strathclyde, White Park, Fontabelle, Rock Dundo or Rockley regardless if yuh black, white or brown. A Bajan, blacker than me, now own a big able department store in Bridgetown, two floors complete wid escalator, de only escalator in town, excuse me! And today, a black man is skipper o' de West Indies cricket team, Sir Frank Mortimer Worrell—Sir Frank, compliments of Her Majesty de Queen of Inglund, thank you! I am tryin' to tell you young boys, t'ings different today. Wha' more y'all want?" His voice no longer scolded but appealed to reason.

But the boys were not impressed by this recitation of social advancements from an old black man who had lived through a catalogue of injustices and perhaps had been in his youth no less angry and no less impatient than them, but who, over the course of many years, had been tamed and seduced by increments of freedom and had arrived at a place where he never expected to be in his lifetime, and was now grateful to those who had so generously exceeded his expectations. These younger men squatting under the breadfruit tree could not have known the depths whence Mr. Cruthers had climbed compared to where he was today and had therefore set their own sights on broader and brighter horizons than the old man could ever had envisioned; and these young men gave no credit to Mr. Cruthers for having in his day greased the wheel of progress so that they themselves could now move forward with just a little more freedom than the old man could have experienced in his day. But the old man could not see beyond the present; and so, when one of Curly's customers, a big-bellied chap named "Slim," had the nerve to exclaim, "Is Independence we want, Mr. Cruthers," these words in the old man's ears were as preposterous and as obscene as a blaspheme against The Almighty. The old wharf man would not hear of it; he recoiled in disgust whether at the audacity or at the naiveté of these young upstarts.

"We all black people not ready fer independence. Tell me, what—what—what we goin' do wid independence?" he stammered in his rage. "Bajans don' know how to run t'ings. We need England to protect we from weselves."

At that moment, Charlie Blackett barged into their midst bearing another parcel of bad tidings: he had delivered the people's petitions and had been denied an extension. Every house had to move off the estate before the landlord razed the land. He had personally delivered the petitions to the office of the Governor in the Public Buildings in Bridgetown, to the ombudsman appointed to take care of such matters, and had left a carbon copy with Barrister Cunningham's secretary. Everyone man and woman in the village had signed, some more often than once. The official response was that the Government would not intercede in what the laws deemed a legitimate sale of private property. Charlie had done all he could.

Although boiling anger rose within each man, they now muffled their profanities among themselves, remembering they were within earshot of the respected pastor and his wife. These were grown men who had little power but possessed a rich arsenal of sweet-sounding and colourful obscenities that bounced from man to man, shot into the air and fizzled in the end like harmless bubbles. But cuss words gave vent to their frustrations and release to their impotent resentments. In the end they remained bitter but always within the precincts of the law.

But Cruthers considered the men's anger unfair and misdirected. "Don' be vex wid Inglund," he told them. "And don' be vex wid de Inglish. Be vex wid we own people. Be vex wid de snakes among us like that viper, Cunningham, that turn against he own, that don' even have de common decency to acknowledge de people petitions. Be vex wid we own people that vote fer Cunningham after he sell out David Prince down at de courthouse. Be vex wid a black man who would call he own people 'monkeys'. Is we own people we all should vex wid, not Inglund and not de Inglish."

The old man was trembling. He turned his back to the boys and stomped away with a dollop of shaving cream hanging from his chin. He had defended the Mother Country admirably and with honour and, though outnumbered, he had stood his ground with these cantankerous young men, these impatient men, these ungrateful men. He was pleased he had interceded on behalf of England.

Late into the evening and long after dark, the men were still sitting under the breadfruit tree, each man taking his turn to rail against those English "dogs," heaping scorn on their accents, their pallid faces, their mottled skin, their noses like bird-beaks, their flat asses, their stiff upper lips, their ill-fitting clothes, their food, their smell, their walk, their laugh, their talk, and at the end of the day they returned to their homes no more able to disavow the English than to repudiate their own mothers. In spite of the steady stream of invective hurled all day at the Englishman, there was likely not a trace of Anglophobia in the hearts of the men, for in truth they had been severed ages ago from the pride and the life-source of their original roots like a prolific plant ripped from the soil and then grafted for the enrichment of another. England had become their foster Motherland. They knew no other. They loved no other.

Barrister Cunningham had relocated his office from James Street to the bottom of High Street, closer to the heart of Bridgetown, and on the first floor of an office building noted for the animal gargoyles that clung to the façade. His office was more spacious and even more luxurious than the one before, befitting the stature of the most famous counsellor in Barbados. The gold-framed nameplate above the doorway was incised with the names, *Cunningham & Thomas, Esquires, Barristers-at-Law*, but in truth it was the senior partner who did the heavy lifting.

It was Monday morning and the barrister was sifting through documents needed to be signed by all parties for the transfer of Thornville Properties to Tory Reilly Enterprises, Island Developers of Westmoreland, St. James. The re-titling of land was one of those mundane matters that could easily be pushed off on Bernie Thomas, but Teddy Thorne was always a stickler for having Cunningham personally take care of all his affairs. Only one and a half weeks remained before the land would have to be cleared and there was no doubt that the full weight of the law would descend on any person who defied the order and refused to surrender the Englishman's land.

A memo had reached the barrister's desk that a petition had found its way to the Governor's attention threatening a delay of the eviction. He had only recently taken the initiative of getting in touch with the Governor's office to forestall any attempt to put off the sale, citing a legal clause that the sale of privately-owned property could not be politically barred without due course of extensive litigation. He recalled that only the other day there had been a man in the lobby of *Cunningham & Thomas* requesting a meeting about the said order. He said his name was one Blackett; he had come with a clipboard in hand. The barrister had pondered for a quick minute on whether he should see the man but then instructed his secretary to turn him away. "No appointment, no meeting," he said.

He was at that moment finalizing the paperwork when the secretary, a middle-aged white woman, poked her head in and announced, "Sir, there is a Dr. Prince here to see you."

"He got an appointment?"

"No sir."

The name, Prince, rang a faint, distant bell. His legal mind snapped to the likelihood the doctor had come for protection from a litigious member of the working-class.

"Show him in anyway" he told her.

The two men came face to face, the barrister still seated, his bulbous eyes peering curiously over his wire-framed glasses, and Pierre Prince, standing erect, unsmiling with hand reaching out to the barrister.

It had been a full decade since the barrister's infamous defence of Thorne and though he had been somewhat slowed by the years—his hair was now gray and receding—he had become one of the wealthiest black men in Barbados. One cursory glance around the office revealed a taste for opulence. The barrister sat behind an oversized cherry mahogany desk next to a matching credenza. Eight burgundy leather chairs surrounded a glass-topped conference table. Behind him, his wall-to-wall floor-to-ceiling library must have held every single law book from Plato's theory of law onwards. What looked like 18th century French Rococo art graced the wood-panelled walls and under the feet were brightly waxed checkerboard parquet tiles. At each side of the doorway a marble pedestal bore a sculptured alabaster bust, one of Shakespeare, the other of Socrates. The extravagance was all too familiar to Pierre; he had come from that rich, showy world.

"What brings you to *Cunningham & Thomas* this fine morning, doctor? I didn't get yer name," he asked jauntily.

"My name is Pierre Prince."

"What can I do fer you, Doc?"

"I am here, sir, to make a case on behalf of the people of Thornville. Your client, Mr. Thorne, is demanding through this office that the people vacate his land in a matter of days. I do not think that it is just."

"You asking fer a stay of execution?" asked the barrister.

"No sir, I am asking for an abandonment of the execution." His voice was cool but the words were terse.

Cunningham paused, rocked back in his chair, unbuttoned his waistcoat and removed his glasses as if he needed a relaxed moment of mental clarity to measure the seriousness of the request or even the sanity of the man standing before him. A mock smile was frozen on his face.

"My dear man, I happen to be Mr. Thorne's lawyer but I am damn well not his conscience. I have before me an application for the purchase of land and I have written consent from the landowner himself. I am only the lawyer entrusted with authenticating the sale. As an attorney in a non-criminal issue, I am neither for nor against the parties, the people of Thornville being one of those parties. There is nothing that you or I can do to stop this transaction. This is a done deal."

His tone was not combative but mellow with a faint trace of sarcasm. He rattled off these words without pausing to weigh their impact. The words neither betrayed compassion for the people, nor partiality towards his client. He motioned to one of two cushiony leather chairs on the other side of his desk.

"Please sit down, doctor. And, pray tell, what is your interest in Thornville?"

"I came from Thornville, Mr. Cunningham. Your client, Mr. Thorne, happens to be my grandfather."

Cunningham stared at his face for a second or two with his lips slightly parted, motionless in anticipation of a correction, a retraction, a slip of the tongue. Then his head reared back and his shoulders shook up and down, heaving with laughter as if he were quite willing to play along with some ridiculous charade. Failing to see amusement in the doctor's face, he turned to playful dialect to mock his absurd assertion.

"Man, impossible! Fust of all, Teddy Thorne is a white man. As far as I can see from where I sit, *you* not white. Before he wife dead, donkey years ago … and I happen to know de lady… she give 'im one daughter who wuz chileless, and de poor soul wuz murdered by some madmun that brek into de house one mornin', choke de poor woman to death. And then dis criminal climb pon top de dead woman and rape she right there on de floor. At least he had de decency to drown heself at Brandons Beach, just like dat. *De Chronicle* reported it different to spare de family shame, saying it wuz accidental asphyxiation, but I know de facts. So tell me, what de hell you expect de poor father to do but chase dese low-class people off he land!" Cunningham was now no longer the dispassionate lawyer "entrusted with authenticating the sale."

"I am telling you, sir, that your client is my grandfather," repeated Pierre. "His daughter was my mother. The man who killed her was my father whose son your client shot and killed on the 22nd day of September, 1955. That was a day that will go down in the annals of Barbadian history for two horrific acts, one of nature, and the other you should know very well because you had a hand in the outcome. You should remember the case the following year of the Crown versus Theodore Thorne. You defended him successfully. I know the whole premise of your defence. There were no monkeys in the mango tree that day, Mr. Cunningham. I was there." The words flowed from his lips as if he were reading from a prepared script. He had been briefed on the entire episode by his new family.

The barrister stared open-mouthed at the visitor whose finger was poised and pointed like a pistol at his face. Then he pushed back from his desk, stood up and walked over to the far corner of the office to where stood a walnut roll-top desk. He rolled back the top and produced a decanter of pale gold whisky and two lead-crystal glasses which he placed on his desk between himself and the doctor.

"Drink?" he asked.

"No thanks."

The barrister's brow was suddenly furrowed and shiny with sweat as his mind struggled to untangle this new web of befuddlement. He sat forward to grasp every word of the answers he would now seek to extract from this intriguing man who claimed to be the grandson of his client, Thorne.

"Now, let me get dis straight! Are you telling me you are the son of Harold Prince, de Bajan boy from down in de village?"

"Yes."

"And that he made a chile with Teddy Thorne's daughter, a white woman, all dem years ago?"

"Yes."

"Here in Buhbaydus?"

"Where else?"

"And you are *that* chile? But how ..."

"That's right!" said Pierre Prince. "I am also saying that unless this business of shoving poor people off the land is revoked forthwith, I am prepared to tell my story to the world, the truth of what really happened and why, in the case of the Crown versus Thorne. So, as you can see, it is in your interest to persuade my grandfather to change his mind and not persist in punishing these innocent people for something they played no part in."

The barrister was not about to yield. "The evidence, my dear doctor, is a matter of record. The jury hath rendered their verdict. The matter was settled in Her Majesty's Court of Law. Moreover, if de man wants to sell he own land, I cyan't stop 'im, de man is a stubborn man. Besides, right now all de elevated land in Buhbaydus, especially land close to Bridgetown in clear view of de sea, is in demand. Is all about economics, doc."

Although Pierre Prince could never have met David, the suspicion always lingered that his own birth had triggered a chain of hate, repugnance and revenge that led to the death of David. There was not a scintilla of doubt in his mind that his grandfather was the killer and all the talk of an accident seemed thin and contrived. Now sitting across from the barrister, he was ready to seize the opportunity to put an end to this harbouring of ill will. Now was the time to lay his trump card on the table to save the village and to right some wrongs at the same time.

He said to the barrister in a tone and with a cadence that was firm and final, "Mr. Cunningham, your client is an old man; he has little to lose when I expose him. But you, sir, stand to lose much more. It will bring an end to your illustrious career, sir, when it is known that you and your client perjured yourselves in a court of law. Your future in politics too will go up in smoke once I reveal the truth. Once the fair-minded people in this island know that you deceived the court, you will be an object of disgrace in Barbados for the rest of your days."

The barrister bristled. He drew himself up in his chair and glared at Pierre. He did not take kindly to threats. In the courtroom he never let them go unchallenged and often won, not with counter-threats but by the power of language and his knowledge of the laws to disarm and weaken his opponent. But this young impudent doctor had boxed him into a corner where the truth could not be circumvented. He knew his defence of Thorne ten years ago had been as fabricated as a sandcastle, and now this man sitting in his office had the wherewithal to unravel the tapestry of lies he had so carefully woven for judge and jury. He now believed that this man who called himself Thorne's grandson was not only the belated witness; he was also the belated evidence, the motive behind the murder. Cunningham reached for the canister, poured a straight shot of whisky halfway to the rim and gulped it down with a look of distaste on his face. "Let me see what I can do," he said.

"Very well, good day then!" said Pierre. And without a handshake he got up and left.

The barrister sat in pensive silence for several minutes before he reached for the telephone. He sat staring at the empty chair in which the doctor had been sitting and likely wondered if the proposition he had been handed could be cast as a flagrant case of blackmail. But he could not risk challenging the doctor, his reputation and future were at stake;

and so, he breathed a sigh of helplessness and vulnerability, the emotions that pervade the lobby of a bank whose vault has just been expertly and expeditiously robbed.

Chapter 28

Dawn of Independence

WHEN CISSY saw her neighbour come running, approaching at breakneck speed, mouthing words that were in her wild excitement utterly unintelligible, she knew she would be the recipient of news, news of seismic importance, news that had just reached her neighbour's finely tuned ears.

"Cissy, girl, Thorne change he mind … he not selling de land." The words breathlessly escaped her lips between snatches of air. Reaching the house, she collapsed in a chair like a rag doll, feigning relief, her feet outstretched, her arms falling loosely by her sides.

"How you know?" asked Cissy.

"De sign, dey tek 'way de sign, de sign gone!"

"You sure?"

"Yes, I tell yuh, he change he mind, thanks to good ole Charlie Blackett. He put de fear o' God in de ole wicked brute. We got to go 'cross de road and thank Mr. Blackett."

Long before Pierre's intercession with the barrister, the cool American speculator and land developer, Tory Reilly, had had no doubt that the transfer of Thornville Properties to his realty establishment would go forward unimpeded by all the protestations and signed petitions. Before a single house had moved, he had already set in motion a major transformation for the estate. His vision was that it would no longer be called the Village of Thornville but "Fair Hills." He was confident that the newly founded University of the West Indies campus in Cave Hill would presage a new vitality and prestige for these static and sterile environs. His business acumen told him the property's value would multiply tenfold and that the rich and middle-class from far and wide would flock to his real estate office for a piece of Fair Hills. Already the promotional wheels were turning: *Fair Hills, a Taste of the Good Life*. Amenities befitting a modern community were set to fall into place: electricity, running water, telephone, street lights, a wide tree-lined street from one end of Fair Hills to the other, as welcoming and as smoothly asphalted as the road that led to the seller's mansion. His dreams were dashed. Without further explanation, he was informed that Mr. Thorne, on the advice of his lawyer, had decided to abort the sale.

Esmay was partly right. After it was learned that the landlord had capitulated and ordered his servants to remove the dreaded sign at the top of the gap, Charlie Blackett became the hero of Thornville. He was even heralded throughout St. Michael as the only man who knew how to navigate the power base. People said he should enter politics, run for the House and bring their future grievances to the attention of those in power just as he had done for the Thornville people—this, despite having failed to do the same for his co-workers at the Mount Gay Distilleries Limited. Bajans came from all corners to thank Charlie for saving the village. They lined up at his door with gifts: ground provisions, black pudding, fried fish, sweet bread, great cake, all kinds of cooked meals: tokens of gratitude, humbly accepted. He became known as the saviour of Thornville. Pierre's intercession with Cunningham would remain forever a secret.

To this very day, no man would admit that he or any of his forebears ever lived in a village called Thornville. One would more likely say he was from Grazettes or Fairfield or Cave Hill or Black Rock than to mouth the word "Thorne" and feel the heart palpitate for the next hour over the wrong the Thornes wrought on an innocent family. No wonder the name receded into obscurity, and the shame it conjured up for years is today buried in the past and hardly mentioned until this writing. Yet almost from the day the eviction order was grudgingly rescinded, the place became the most liveable of any village within miles. How was that to be? Well, the modernization plans that were put in place for Fair Hills were already contracted out by Tory Reilly, bankrolled by Thorne and irreversibly set in motion in anticipation of the land sale. Now no longer would the middle-class need to move in to gentrify the village; the people would remain and in time become middle-class themselves.

Barbados Light & Power Company rolled in and began erecting lamp poles and stringing wires to the houses of a privileged few. Cissy's kerosene lamp with its soot-emitting chimney was retired from the centre table to the shelf next to the restored clay monkey. A naked light bulb now hung from a rafter in the front house and in the evenings white light poured out of her front windows and flooded the road beyond the hedges where her oil lamp never before could pierce the deep shadows. All along the gap Thornville came alive at night. She cast aside her four flat irons, coal pot and Dutch oven after Gittens bought her a brand new General Electric steam iron and electric stove from Barnes & Company. The old walnut larder now shared custody with a Frigidaire from Musson, Son & Company. The corning jar that had kept her salt-meat fresh for months at a time now sat abandoned in the yard with the broken clay pots, the icebox and the slop bucket. But though its wooden ribs were worn almost flat, her jucking board would not be discarded; it kept its place next to the oak tub in the yard: washing machines were not yet up to the task.

For many days, workers from the Barbados Water Authority were gouging the roadside, laying their pipes for the first gush of clean potable water from the island's natural coral aquifers. Gittens had a private standpipe mounted in the yard; there would be no more shuttling between house and communal standpipe now standing forlorn at the top of the gap like an old-fashioned derelict serving the poorest of the poor. But, alas, the indignity of the outhouse toilet would remain unchallenged: indoor plumbing was still a costly proposition, even for the Gittens' family.

People blessed the day the telephone came to Thornville. No longer would they need to make prior arrangement of time and place with some kindly proprietor in town to "beg fer a message" and be cautioned, "But don't talk long, this is a place of business." Cissy's newsy neighbour with the profuse gift of gab became the first subscriber. Morning, noon and night, Esmay could be seen through her front window, her right elbow cupped stylishly in her left hand, her new pink Princess handset pressed to her ear. While his wife prattled on for hours, Egbert sat proudly at his open window where he could be seen and envied by all, staring intently at the amber glow of his crackling, whistling German Grundig, honing his visual and aural senses for the coming hypnosis of television. In the meantime, Voice of America, Radio Caracas and The BBC took turns blasting from his window all night long, sounding a boastful message to the uninitiated: "Yes, we have shortwave in dis house." In other words, *Rediffusion* no longer held the ear captive. And from time to time the less privileged huddled like blackbirds under his window to catch the Joe Louis fights from America and cricket at

Lords; and at three o'clock on Sundays they gathered for "Songs of Praise" live and direct from Westminster Abbey.

In the village, as noted, not everyone enjoyed these material blessings. Sadly, some deluded themselves as being "higher up and better off" than the ones deprived; these emblems of class marked the haves from the have-nots; such possessions heralded a crossing over into the realm of middle-class. But thanks to a native son, the Thorne estate, handed down through the years and through layers of English landowners, would not be sold to Reilly Island Developers. These symbols of modernity—electricity, fancy appliances, running water, telephone—would no longer be exclusive to exclusive enclaves on the island. These emblems served as self-fulfilment; in their minds they had arrived. Meanwhile, Pierre Prince took no credit for coming to the aid of the people. Apart from vindictive Thorne and his traitorous lawyer, he alone knew he was the catalyst for the people's good fortunes.

In the months that followed his confrontation with the barrister, Pierre Prince gradually carved his own niche at the General Hospital, the sole hospital on the island, on the outskirts of town on Lower Bay Street. Serving the rich and the poor, it was a block-long sprawling building noted for its green-hooded windows, green awnings and gardens lush and green: the requisite illusion of total contentment and well-being within its walls. His personal office was in a coveted location on the upper floor with vibrant views of the careenage, fishing boats trolling and speedboats slapping the waters of Carlisle Bay. Most days he would likely be found on the first floor in the single operating room. His medical training in England had inculcated the basic fairness of serving equally the rich and the indigent without regard to their status and ability to pay. His mission to instil that same sense of egalitarianism was challenging in a society addicted to class. He proceeded to settle into his practice and in the span of a few months the name, Dr. Prince, the young surgeon, became known and respected in the community at large and even celebrated among his peers.

By some fortuitous and repeated crossing of paths, he found himself and old Dr. Donovan becoming good friends, even getting together for occasional dinners in Peterkins at the home of the Irishman and his beautiful black Bajan wife. He never tired of reminding Pierre of the one who held him upside down and slapped his bottom three times before he would take his first breath. At eighty-five, he was now retired but still hung around the hospital to counsel patients, some of whom, being infirmed and younger than he, allowed him to feel blessed with comparatively good health. It could be said that while the Irish doctor had climbed down from a long, illustrious career, Dr. Prince was now reaching towards the apogee of his.

Early one morning, opening the door of his office, Pierre was surprised to find him sitting, waiting for him, twisting one end of his moustache in the manner of an old man with something weighing on his mind. He had made himself comfortable in Pierre's swivel chair facing the door.

"How goes ye, young fella?" he greeted Pierre in his Irish brogue.

"Hi Doc!" Pierre sat on a corner of his desk poised for some earth-shattering revelation or some profound medical opinion he was dying to share, for why else would this aging retired doctor leave his bed at this early hour of the morning to come and ensconce himself in his office chair. He braced himself.

Donovan started: "I wuz wondering ... d'ye ever think about yer mother, Miss Penelope?"

"Not much," answered Pierre.

"D'ye hate her?"

"I don't have time to hate, Doc."

"Good answer, laddie, good answer. Well, y'know, yer mother wuz not a bad woman in de beginning. She wuz literally a rose among thorns. I mean literally. I happen to know that growing up she never had a racist bone in her body. Yer Aunt Cissy used to be her friend. Sometimes I used to think she wished to be coloured too, de way she used to laugh and swagger and carry on with real Bajan slang all through de house upsetting de ole fogies. She just happen to be born into a family that didn't care much fer coloured folks. Thorne would keep people like Cunningham and de Creole woman on a leash because he needed them both. But you? When you come along wid yer brown skin, you messed up de bloodline, man." He chuckled at his own joke.

"Well, I just couldn't help it," said Pierre with a straight face.

"Man, I remember how confused you wuz at de funeral when I had to tell you that de woman in de coffin was yer mother. Remember? I bet you thought I was off my rocker. Jeez!"

"Yeah, I thought you were crazy, man," said Pierre, recalling that day at St. Stephen's Church, sitting not far from his surrogate mother.

"But she coulda done worse," continued Donovan. "She coulda had an abortion. Abortions wuz easy fer a white woman in dem days. They offered me a good piece o' change to do de job. But I told them I bring babies into this world, I don' take them out. So they went lookin' fer some abortionist in de country, but he was already dead. Yer mother coulda had you adopted by a total stranger but she gave ye to that Creole lady instead, to keep ye close to her so she could see ye grow to be a man."

"Well then, I owe you one and Marcella too," said Pierre with a smile.

"Aye. But have ye ever been a lil bit curious about Mr. Prince, yer father? What kinda man? Where he come from? How he pass on?"

"My father was a mirage, Doc. Saw him for a quick minute, then he was gone."

"How 'bout yer half-brother, David?"

"Only when I see his picture on Ma's wall. I still wonder what reason my grandfather had for shooting David."

"He didn't."

"Then who did?"

"It was yer mother who shot 'im."

A wall of silence fell between the two men. Pierre by now had become used to Donovan's bizarre conclusions though he often attributed them to encroaching senility, but he had often been on mark like the day he told him the woman he called Aunt Penny was really his mother. But this time the facts were not on his side. His grandfather had sworn in a court of law that he was indeed the shooter, though he had lied distastefully about mistaking the boy for a monkey. The evidence was never disputed by the jury.

"Doc, what makes you think he didn't kill David?"

"I didn't say he didn't kill 'im. I said he didn't pull de trigger. If you ask me, they both killed David, he and his daughter. He willed it and she carried out de sentence. Just goes to show that hate alone can kill. She so loved her father she would kill fer him."

Outside of Madame Montmartre, Donovan had been the closest to Thorne. He was speaking as though he knew things about Thorne known only to them and God. As the family's long-time physician he had chosen this day and this moment to loosen the Hippocratic muzzle, for the time had come to share with Pierre, as doctor to doctor, the family secrets that were no longer deserving of privacy.

"Yer grandfather confessed to me and Father Elliott dis morning from his deathbed and when a man dying he ent got nuttin to lose but his damn soul and all his evil secrets will pour out like a bust pipe. Fer donkey years, I been telling yer grandfather to put away de goddamn pipe and stop swallowing that cigar juice, but de man would not listen. Bad news, my son, pulmonary pneumonia, last stage. Couldn't lick de ole streptococcus. It got the best of 'im. Methinks he's too far gone."

Donovan paused, waiting for a reaction. There was none. He got up, walked over to Pierre, rested a hand on his shoulder and looked directly into his eyes. "Yer grandfather asking to see ye, son. He told Father Elliott and me to send fer ye to come and see 'im."

Pierre shook his head. "I can't help him. You yourself say he's too far gone."

"I mean, he just wants to see ye, son," repeated Donovan. "No doctor can help de ole codger now. Not even a whippersnapper like yerself."

"But why on earth would he want to see me now?"

"I don' know but I swear on a stack o' bibles, son. Couldn't believe me own ears meself. Kept callin' yer name."

"Where is he?"

"Room 206, pay ward."

"Let's go," said Pierre.

They hurried down the corridor, down a stairway, across the expansive and congested public ward that reeked of antiseptic and poverty, past the vacant faces of the sick and dying, dodging the white-clad orderlies wheeling their gurneys in all directions. Then at the far end they climbed a flight of stairs to a quiet secluded section with gleaming ceramic-tiled floors and wallpapered halls and airy private rooms overlooking the Bay, and finally to room 206.

He was lying on his back, the bed sheet pulled up to his neck, next to a window with a panoramic view of the sea, a view he had cherished all his days living in the mansion. Instead, his eyes looked dimly at the ceiling and his mouth, now toothless, was wide open to capture every molecule of air that it could. The tubes that had been hanging from bottles of life-inducing fluids were no longer plugged into his arms, as if they had served as best they could and had decided they could do no more. He must have heard their footsteps; his lips moved to form words but they made no sound; his head would not even turn to acknowledge their presence. His ashen face and sunken cheeks were foreign to the brash giant of a man that Pierre once knew as a child, tramping around his house, cussing, bullying, barking orders, venting his racist rage on a bastard grandson.

The air in the room was heavy with death and despair. A single flower lay limp in a vase on the table beside his bed. His only friend left in the whole world was Donovan, who offered him more compassion than love, and even so, sparingly. All his other friends were either dead or their backs turned. The loyal Ben Carson had already departed and Barrister Cunningham, according to his own wife, was "devoid of sentimentality." All his family had gone on before him, except the one he had rebuffed.

Pierre stepped forward, glanced at the chart hanging at the foot of his bed, lowered the sheet and held his right wrist to monitor his pulse. These acts were more a force of habit than of necessity: the electrocardiograph screen across the room clearly showed a life slipping away by the seconds. The dying man's eyes slowly left the ceiling and turned to look dimly into Pierre's. He struggled to raise his left hand; it shook and fell back to his side. Again it trembled with the effort to reach out. His pale, anaemic fingers had been tightly clenching a sheet of paper that had been folded many times over so that it was now the size of a dainty napkin. He uncurled his fingers and released it into Pierre's hands, his lips quivering, too weak to enunciate the words that rose from a dying heart. Pierre leaned down and whispered in his grandfather's ear, "Peace!" before he unfolded the paper and realized it was the deed for the Thornville property, including the mansion, his entire wealth and the whole estate. The name, "Pierre Prince" was scribbled in a corner on the "Designated Assignee" line. Suddenly he realized the reason he had asked to see his disavowed grandson was to atone for all the hurt. He thought the old man had stopped at the gates of Hell and turned around for one last repentant look at the trail of ruin he had left behind. It was inconceivable to Pierre that a single gesture of generosity could efface all that devastation and make everything right in that instant before his descent into darkness. In a brief moment of repulsion, he considered refolding the deed and giving it back to his grandfather but then realized that nothing could ever be returned to the dead, for at that very moment the blue wave collapsed and traced a straight line across the screen. Donovan instinctively fingered the sign of a cross on his chest. Pierre pulled the sheet up over the old man's head, beckoned for the nurse and silently left the room.

In his gut he felt a tinge of pity for his grandfather; he was a member of the old guard, an anachronism who hung on too long to the old-fashioned colonialist mindset of white supremacy. He knew it was too much to expect, although he wished it, that the deep-seated consciousness of class and colour that still lay over the land of his birth, that crippled the minds of the people, black and white, would somehow accompany this old relic to his grave. But it was not to be. Unlike Donovan, Thorne and many others had failed to cross over into that newly enlightened space that was now Barbados.

Returning to his office, Pierre was impelled to pick up the telephone and tell Ma that the Thorne era had come to a close. There was no rancour in his voice, no hint of elation or even relief, just the words that the old man had died in his presence. Her voice came through the earpiece, loud, fearless and outspoken: "Son, all I have to say is, day does run til night catch it." It was clear to him that Thorne's death would not diminish his grandmother's bitterness; that it would likely stay with her until the end of her own days like an open wound that refused to heal. But he knew her wounds were deep, perhaps too deep for her forgiveness: a secular heart is not constrained to forgive. And although he knew he could never compensate her loss he would try anyway to make it up to her as best he could. He decided he would not say who did or who didn't pull the trigger that day. The question was moot: in the words of Doctor Donovan, "is de same difference."

Back in Thornville, later that day, when Esmay rushed out of her house and hurried across the road, bubbling over with the news so she could hardly speak, she had already been pre-empted by the immediacy of the telephone. Cissy and her husband had already breathed a prayer for the Englishman's soul. Later, all the lights in the houses in the village were burning well into the night. Against the backdrop of the mansion, now in complete darkness, they glowed brighter and whiter than ever.

The year 1966 was fast drawing to a close. It was November, months since Cissy announced her pregnancy in Charlie Blackett's backyard, weeks since the death of the English landlord. The Caribbean Federation that had been fearfully predicted many years ago by Penelope Thorne at the Governor's reception had been scuttled with much regional jealousy and infighting among black men in their separate corners of the Caribbean. But the dream of many was finally coming true: the pride of national statehood was at hand. Day after day, schoolchildren had been practising for the big parade, waving their Government-issued miniature Trident flags, their voices hoarse from rehearsing and rehearsing the new anthem:

We loyal sons and daughters all / Do hereby make it known
These fields and hills beyond recall / Are now our very own

Soon these sons and daughters of Independence would fondly bid the old Union Jack goodbye. The hoisting of the Broken Trident and all the other symbolisms would signal the unravelling of the political strings that had bound them like marionettes to the colonial powers. Some would pause to look back at the road that brought them to this milestone; others would not and would choose to close the door on history, fearing that the bad might overshadow the good and embitter their spirits at a time when their spirits should be free to dream big dreams.

Now, Gittens lay in bed next to the love of his life and his mind drifted back over the years to a time and place when his life had little meaning beyond the church. Since that bittersweet day of their wedding his life had begun afresh. He was today a contented man. Harold's face, ornately framed, smiled back at him as if to say he was pleased he had kept his promise and had taken his place. His picture was appropriately moved from her dresser to a sidewall, still in view but less central. He had barely gotten to know him before he stepped aside and sacrificed his own future to avenge the killing of his son. He prayed that God in his heavenly mercy had reunited him in death with his boys.

Then he thought of people he knew who had stamped their footprints in the long slog towards the new order. Some had moved on before its time. There was old Doctor Donovan who, with his Bajan wife at his side, died in his sleep in his house in Peterkins. Then there was the benevolent Professor Cartwright, Harold's teacher and mentor, now also dead and gone. He had read that Jay-Jay Johnson was no longer with *The Chronicle*; he had begun publishing his own community magazine, *The New Bajan*. The American evangelist and his missionaries were back in America now; new ones would be coming soon to take their place in the sun. Over the years these torch bearers had helped to blur the lines between colours and classes though—truth be told—the yielding of economic power would prove far more intransigent and those vital reins would remain firmly in the hands of a few white men to be handed down through the years only to their own progeny. But this too would change with the passing of time, he was sure.

He had heard that Virgil Cunningham had quit his law practice and was now devoting his time, his legal savvy and his skulduggery to politics. Trotman had failed as a politician. He had since then broadened his study of the Law and was now a full-time barrister in New Orleans, still working on behalf of the disaffected. Since the infamous trial in Her Majesty's Court, he had worked unceasingly on behalf of Bajan women still two steps behind their men in the workplace. Women with new equality now owned their own homes, drove their own motorcars, joined the constabulary and played cricket at the Oval. St. Winifred's, the Anglican School, had surrendered and flung wide open her doors.

The landscape was changing. Tory Reilly, the American speculator, was mistaken about Thornville but right about everything else; indeed the tourists were coming in droves to this fair land and the landscape was indeed "achanging" as he had said it would. The once bountiful fields of sugarcane were dwindling and their smoke-belching factories were fewer. But everywhere else the island was moving on.

Old Betsy had seen her last days, now sitting in the alley beside the Mission Hall, lame and leaky, rusty and run-down. She had served him well, carried him through the years, through the most violent hurricane in recent times.

Now here he was, lying next to his love in this lowly wooden house. When his father died he had offered to move them both into the wall-house he inherited but she begged him to stay; her modest pink house had become her sanctuary. Even nowadays they would find themselves gazing up through the trees to the mansion on the hill. The guard wall had been demolished, replaced with a wire fence; it was the first order of refurbishment after Pierre Prince, the new owner, took possession of the estate. The mansion gate with the lion-head knocker was often left unchained and some days the hens and goats would wander out the courtyard and find their way down to the village. And every Easter from the mansion heights, the children's self-made kites soared high above the houses like seraphs paying homage to Thornville's most famous kite flyer.

Now, as if to heighten these moments of nostalgia, a voice came floating on the night air, an old man's gravelly voice. He was singing an old familiar hymn but it was out of tune, the lyrics slurred and garbled.

There is a green hill far away outside a city wall

Ageless Joe Waldron was staggering home from Piggott's rum shop. Lately, his tired old house had collapsed like a pack of cards. Of its own volition: it happened on a windless day. He had lived all his life deadened to the cares of the world; now he made his home in Ben Carson's brick house, unfazed by his adjacency to Ben's former death room.

It had been a long night of tossing and turning for Cissy, here lying next to her husband, pregnant and fat. As the first rays of a new day began to peep through the jalousie slats, she felt the pangs coming and going, but now they were fiercer and relentless. Gittens ran down the gap to fetch Sister Innis and the venerable midwife, now old and weary, came hobbling with her obstetrical leather satchel in hand. At her side was her niece, Veronica, wide-eyed and eager for her first course in midwifery. Not far behind, Esmay came running, barefoot and still in her nightie. And soon the petulant crying of a newborn at being rudely expelled from the known into the unknown pierced the morning air in Thornville.

It was the dawn of Independence. The promise of a bright new post-colonial world crept above the morning horizon like the sun-kissed shore that welcomes an embattled ship after a long night of floundering and drifting in uncertain waters. Into this new land of promise, Cissy Gittens delivered her third baby boy.

THERE ONCE WAS A LITTLE ENGLAND

ABOUT THE AUTHOR

Enrico Downer was born in Barbados, schooled at various institutions of learning in Barbados, Puerto Rico and the United States. He first joined Value Line, a NYC publisher, and later was Correspondent with a Division of Airco International in New York and Wisconsin. He served with the US military in the Far East. He currently lives in Florida. This, his second novel spans the decade before the Independence of Barbados from Great Britain.

Printed in Great Britain
by Amazon